Divided Together

A Novel About
Political Intrigue, Church Anger,
a Little Romance & Passionate Politics

Mark Mirza

CTM
PUBLISHING INC.

CTM Publishing, Inc.
Atlanta, Georgia USA

For all the effort you do this on,

Cindra, thank you you do to pat

Mark
Col 4:2

**Do not put your trust in princes
(Psalm 146:3a).**

If your political passion, hinders your relationship with your Christian brother or sister, you are wrong — even if your reasoning is right.

Divided Together

Unless otherwise noted, all Scriptural quotes are from the NIV, as read in the second edition of "A Harmony of the Four Gospels, by Orville E. Daniel, Baker Books, 1996

-A brilliant way to study the gospels, by the way. (The Author)

Contents

Preface

Washington D.C., A Prayer Meeting

In my prayer ministry, God has opened up some pretty unique doors. One is the opportunity I have each month, to go to Washington D.C. and pray with our elected officials, and often their staff.

With this, God has somehow fixed my brain so that when I arrive in D.C., I arrive without an agenda. I'm not interested in fixing the way anyone thinks. I simply want to 'bear the burdens' of people from both sides of the aisle. It's truly amazing.

Through this attitude of mine, which, believe me, is from the Lord, I have learned something I never would have discovered if I arrived each month with my own agenda. I have learned that these men and women are regular people, and they need to be prayed for as such.

Too often our political passions make our prayer focus on one 'big political thing' after another. I'm not here to dissuade you from praying this way. On the contrary, if that is what God has called you to do, then by all means do it.

But that's not my calling. In fact, let me tell you what I hear when I ask for these men and women's prayer requests, in D.C.:

"Mark, I miss my family."

"Mark, why would God put me in a job I hate so much?"

"Mark, I'm so concerned for my children and my grandchildren."

"Mark, my mother is in hospice, and my wife has to take care of it all by herself."

"Mark, last Sunday at my church, an old friend of mine came to me and started yelling at me, simply because of a bill I supported."

I could go on. But let me tell you what else I hear from them, as I bear their burdens:

"Mark, thank you for praying for me."

"Mark, I'm so grateful God brought you into my life."

"Mark, you hit the nail on the head with that prayer."

Sometimes, they don't say anything. Sometimes there are just tears.

Leonard Ravenhill used to say, "A person who is intimate with God, will never be intimidated by man."

I tell congregations all the time, "You want your Senator or County Commissioner, or Mayor to stand up strong? Then start praying for the 'little' things in their life. In fact, email them, or text them once in a while and ask them how you can pray for them. And when you pray for them, watch how you will encourage these folks through the simple act of bearing their burdens in prayer."

When I am in Washington D.C., I usually stay two days. I try to attend a Bible Study or prayer meeting the evening I am staying over.

Recently, after a time of sharing, I was asked to speak. So, before we prayed, I spoke on what our political passion often looks like in the church.

One of the staffers, Amelda, whose office I walk into each month, had just shared with the group that when she goes back to her home church, she catches all kinds of grief from her friends, because of the party affiliation of her boss.

I know Amelda well. The first time I was in her office she told me, "Mark, I believe God has me here to be a light in the darkness."

I began to share, "One of the things I love about D.C. but the church doesn't see, is how many of you worship together and pray together, even though you work for diametrically opposed Congressmen and Senators."

A few embarrassed laughs came from different parts of the room.

I looked every one of them in the eye and then said, "I'm very proud of you, because of what I see in you. Unfortunately, I do not see this 'Unity in Christ,' in the church.

I suspect all of you experience what Amelda referred to. Am I right?"

Sobering "Yeses" and "Amens" were called out.

"I've been watching politics for forty years, but only recently have I seen its impact in the church. Has it always been there? I don't know, but most of you aren't old enough to have watched forty years of this, so let me share with you what I see. It'll dovetail with Amelda's concerns."

The vast majority of the staffers in these offices are young people, twenty-somethings, if I had to guess. I've decided that a huge part of the reason for this is the incredible stamina and energy needed on a daily basis.

Additionally, something else I have seen in these young staffers is their incredible efficiency. I suspect these young people make great hires when they leave D.C.

In one way it excites me to be around these energetic "kids," if you will. But in another sense, I wish our elected officials had more "grey-haired" counselors.

Anyway, I went on. "Over the last forty years, I have watched the evolution of our passion for politics influence our tolerance of opposing political views. It has gone from mild disagreement with one another to outright hostility. Allow me the freedom to say, this hostility has its roots in a 'Nuevo Tribalism.'"

A number of people nodded. They knew the word and so I asked, "Have you ever considered 'Tribalism' and what it looks like in our politics of today?"

I watched for a moment, as men and women waited expectantly, and then told of my friend who helped me see this issue more clearly than I could have ever seen it on my own.

"Let me tell you about a good friend of mine," I said, "from an African country, which need not be named. One day he frankly shared with me, 'Mark, if the leader of our nation is from a tribe other than mine, my responsibility, as a good member of my tribe, is to hate that leader,' which made me lurch backwards when he told me.

He didn't say this with pride or arrogance, but simply with the reality of his life. For days after he said this, his words lingered in my ears. Even on my way home, flying over the Atlantic Ocean, it bothered me."

I continued. "This friend of mine and I talk regularly, and I couldn't get his statement out of my mind. So, one day I tried an experiment with him. I asked him to pick two leaders, one from his tribe and one from another tribe who are both highly placed politicians."

"'That's a no-brainer,' he said, and he had the two leaders in mind."

"Make sure they both claim to be saved."

"'They do, and, I believe they are,' he answered."

And then I had him pray for the guy from his tribe with whom he agrees.

Some of the folks in the prayer meeting knew where I was going and started to nod.

"Then I asked him to pray for the leader who comes from the other tribe, 'But, I want you to pray the same way for him, that you prayed for the first one.' And that's when there was dead silence!"

"He couldn't do it." I told those assembled for the prayer meeting.

"And this is where we are, in our nation, and in the church today." I said.

"This is what Amelda was talking about."

"Note," I said, "I'm not talking about, 'In the world.' I expect the world to treat each other the way they do. They are not equipped with the Holy Spirit, like Christians are. The church, however, is equipped to handle our disagreements differently than the world, right?"

Strong "Amens," all around.

I told them, "Those of you here in D.C. live out Christian unity, and these prayer meetings reflect it."

I find a lot of my ministry is encouraging the saints, and believe me, these folks in D.C. are easy to encourage. They are like the Border Patrol Agents I recently spoke to in Laredo, Texas. I describe that experience as men and women who were "Dialed-in" to being encouraged. That's what these folks in D.C. are like. They want to be encouraged.

I went on, "But in the church we are not living out this Christian unity. Instead, we are judging others according to their voting habits. You are not, here in D.C., but we are, in the church, and it is loathsome to me. We in the church are acting just like the world and we do not see it."

I went back to my example, "Why couldn't my friend pray the same for both leaders? My friend is a Godly young man, as well as a solid Godly teacher and leader."

I paused to give them an opportunity to digest my words.

Then I continued, "The reason he couldn't is very simple, and it has to do with his identity. He has a greater identity, and therefore unity with his tribe, than he does with the Lord and therefore those associated with Christ. You see, his unity in Christ, is superseded by tribal unity."

Amelda sheepishly raised her hand, "Pastor Mirza," she said, "Isn't that a little harsh?"

I responded. "He never saw it until I asked him to pray for both party's politicians and in seeing it, he still couldn't pray for the other guy the same way. I do this experiment in churches now, and I see the same inability to pray."

I went on, "Let me simply remind you what Ephesians 6:12 says. Do you remember?" I asked her, as gently as I could.

"Pastor Mirza. . ."

"Mark," I corrected.

She hesitated, but said, "Umm, Mark, doesn't it say our struggle is not against flesh and blood?"

"Exactly," I replied, smiling large at Amelda.

"So, stay with me," I said to everyone. "When you see people in our churches, angry with those who hold differing political views, why are they so angry?"

"Because their identity is in their political party, rather than in Christ," a fifty-something, sharp dressed man called out from the back.

"Precisely," I paused to get his name.

"Jack," he said.

"Precisely, Jack. And that's why I'm so proud of what you are all doing here. You are living like the Body of Christ, regardless of party affiliation. The truth is, you are demonstrating the unity you have in Christ. You are not angry with one another, even though you hope their candidate loses at the next election."

Everyone laughed and we went to prayer.

When we were done praying Amelda asked me for any other insights. She said, "This division in my church is under the surface but it is obviously there, and it is really burdening me."

I told her, "Amelda, I understand; I call it the Judas Iscariot syndrome."

She looked at me uncomprehendingly and I explained, "In the church we claim to have our trust in the Lord, but listen to the way people talk about their elected officials, both the ones they agree with, and the ones they disagree with. So often, Amelda, I believe they are really communicating that they do not trust God."

Again, she flinched, questioningly. I went on, "On my YouTube channel[1] I have a video entitled, 'Calling God a Liar when We Pray' where I challenge our attitude and lack of hope when we're talking to God. Watch and listen to the way people pray about and talk about our political leaders, Amelda. Their attitude will tell you if they have put their hope in 'princes' or in God."

"Okay," she questioned, "But what does Judas have to do with that?"

I smiled, "Good question, Amelda. Judas wanted a political Messiah, didn't he?"

She nodded her head.

"He was so blinded, that rather than trusting in the God who spoke the Word at which the universe leapt into existence, rather than entrusting his life to the God who came to earth because of His great love for us, out of his arrogance, Judas held onto his desires and his goals, and his end was death."

I paused so she could take in my words and then ended with, "Amelda, Jesus made very clear what our friends are living out when they do not want to trust God. They are not submitting themselves to what His word clearly says about why all leaders are in power.[2] The bottom line is God puts people in power, or Paul made a mistake in the first two verses of Romans chapter thirteen.

When they refuse to submit to God, they begin to disagree with what God seems to be doing. I believe they are selfishly holding onto their ideology and that's the Judas-way."

"But Mark," she sounded like she was pleading. I felt bad for what I saw in her eyes. And she finished her thought, "They are so convinced they are right to be angry at this leader or another leader, and therefore, with everyone who agrees with the leader they despise."

"I know, and do you know what that shows you so clearly, Amelda?"

She shook her head. I gently touched her shoulder and said, "It shows you the incredible ability of sataN to deceive."

A tear trickled from her eye and she asked, "How do I help them?"

"You don't. Only God can fix them, and only if they want to be fixed. Remember, God has their address. You lift them up in prayer, entrust them to God, leaving them in His hands."

And then she said something incredibly profound. She said, "The evil one has a vested interest in us being divided in the church."

I looked at her sadly and she continued, "If we could just get together as a body, oh, what we could accomplish!"

"Good word, Amelda. I agree with you, but beware; there will be people who will use that very argument to justify their belief that everyone else should follow their political passion."

With a big smile, she understood what I was saying. "That's because they do not want to trust the Lord, especially when they don't like what He is doing."

I chuckled and said, "You were listening."

"Of course, I was. I was taught to listen to my elders."

We both laughed.

When I was getting ready to go, Cary McAdams, a friend of mine, who is a Congressional Chief of Staff, on the Hill, pulled me aside to tell me about a story he heard, which might be of interest to me. He knows I like to write historical Christian Fiction. He didn't have lots of details, but he got my mind twirling with ideas for a new book.

Thanks to Cary, I have now spent the last year investigating the facts he shared with me that night. And he was right. It's a very compelling story. I hope you enjoy it, even if challenged by it.

After the prayer meeting, Cary and I walked down First Street, past the Cannon House Office Building and the Capitol South Metro Station, to the Tortilla Coast, a Mexican restaurant I thoroughly love (except for the Fajita smell it leaves in my clothes).

While waiting for our meal, Cary laid out a story which I knew would be my next book.

He said I would like the story since irrational political anger and unreasonable judgment and rage, both inside and outside the church, were the hallmarks of what happened. "It's the point you were trying to make tonight, Mark."

He continued, "Mark, the names of the principals are Jude and Issy. They've been in D.C. forever and believe me, all of us who know them, love them. They are Religion Consultants."

"Great," I said, a little too quickly, "I'm up for a new challenge. Where are they and how do I reach them?"

"Well," Cary hedged, "Mark, if you will trust me, let me tell you about Jack. He is a high ranking agent at the FBI and he can tell you of the espionage and counterintelligence stuff that occurred, if he wants to, and if he is able to."

"Espionage and counterintelligence? Hmm, okay. I'll look into this." I said.

He sat back and went on. "Jack attends our prayer meetings, sitting in the back and is usually very quiet. I was surprised he even spoke up tonight."

"He usually attends with his protégé, Billy 'Something,'" said Cary. "But I didn't see him tonight. Anyway, Jack is who you want to talk to."

"Jack? Yeah, I think he answered a question of mine tonight. Sharp dresser, fifty-something?"

"Exactly, that's him."

I leaned back thinking about what he had shared with me thus far, when I was bumped by some young staffer whipping around the corner in this lively little restaurant.

Sitting up straighter and deep in thought, I asked, "What else do you know about this event, Cary?"

"Only that Homeland Security was involved, as well as some guy in the Warner Robins Counterintelligence department, cyber security people here in D.C. and some prayer-guy from Macon, Georgia."

This was getting more and more mysterious, and more and more exciting, the longer I listened.

As an afterthought he said, "And there was an Atlanta pastor involved, I think."

By the time we had finished eating and fellowshipping I had all the contact information Cary could give me, including the Religion Consultants, the FBI agent, Jack, and the Macon prayer-guy, Dr. Dale Riley,[3] whom I already knew.

I try to sleep on a book idea before I get engrossed in working out the details. I want to make sure my interest isn't a passing whim. But flying home to Atlanta the next day, my interest was still peaked, and I started to think about Judas Iscariot. I thought about how his passion for the political ideology he preferred pushed him to turn his back on God Incarnate.

"And we all know how his life ended," I said to no one in particular.

Over the next few weeks, I met with Cary's contacts, expanded those into other leads, including others in Macon and D.C. who became sources for what would become this novel.

Within a few months, I got to meet a lovely young couple (at least I think they're a couple), in another Prayer meeting. They seemed to know more about my story than I could have imagined. I enjoyed taking these two, Billy and Sammie, out for dinner at my favorite Mexican restaurant, the Tortilla Coast. (This time I put my clothes in the hotel's plastic dirty-clothes bag, so the rest of my things didn't smell like fajitas.)

"Good job," I told myself and decided my wife would appreciate the gesture.

All through the investigative process, I kept playing with the idea of weaving the historical account of the traitor, Judas Iscariot, with the information I uncovered of the husband and wife, Religion Consultants team.

"Yes," I decided. "It could work."

I was sold on the idea and started writing because there was a unique twist to this story. You see, the husband and wife, Jude and Issy, are both Religion Consultants, but they work for opposing Presidential candidates!

I wouldn't want to be in their home on election night!

----

[1] www.Youtube.com/ctmprayer

[2] Romans 13:1-2

[3] Dr. Dale Riley is a fictional person. His story can be found at www.ThePray-ers.com, in The Pray-ers series of novels

Ancient Introduction

2000 Years Ago, Jerusalem, The Last Supper

I sat at the table with men I now loathed. The last ten or eleven months, probably since the aftermath of the feeding of the five thousand, I had become less and less a part of this self-righteous clique.

We had all been together for the previous three years or so, and we knew each other well. I say we knew each other well, but the truth is, I knew them, but I don't think they have a clue what was going on in my head. And now, I didn't care.

I was just there to confirm the evenings plans,[1] get my things, and be on my way, albeit, with a little heavier money bag.

As I looked around, I saw Peter, such a big stupid child. He had just asked Jesus to wash his whole body,[2] not just his feet. Such a moron.

Didn't he know this foolish Rabbi was taking us down a path which would lead to an unnecessary martyrdom?

And John, that young, skinny little runt. He was on pins and needles of excitement, with Jesus' latest words about those who are leaders, those who are servants and those who are getting a kingdom.[3]

His whole family is in the "better-than-thou" crowd. Wasn't it his mother who just last week asked Jesus to allow her boys to sit at His left and right sides in heaven?[4] Such arrogance. John is a selfish, uppity, rich kid.

Every conversation of the recent days and weeks, it seems, has to do with heaven.

I was looking around thinking, "These foolish men. How can their focus be heaven when we are on earth and there's so much that can be accomplished here with the right political leadership? These men are missing the big picture."

This crazy Carpenter I've been following for the last three years is going to be a selfish, personal martyr, rather than a selfless, national Saviour. Numerous times recently He had the crowd behind him. All it would have taken was a step in the right direction from Him. And He refused.

He refused!

I was done following this charlatan. If these men wanted to follow Him, to who knows where, they could. But after tonight, I was getting out and taking as much with me as I could.

I was stewing over all these things when Jesus looked at me. We locked eyes for a moment, and I could tell He was troubled.[5]

17

Foolishly, I immediately wondered, what I could do to help Him. Stupid me. I know not to think that way, I know it, and so I scolded myself for that being my first reaction.

Then He looked away. But He was speaking now, and I watched the others hang on every word which came out of His mouth. They seemed entranced by His words. Well, I was not! And I never would be again.

As He talked and the others watched, mesmerized, I mentally counted what was in the money bag.[6] The night before I had met with some of the political and religious leaders of the various sects.[7] I knew how badly they wanted Jesus. And I knew I would squeeze a good number of silver coins out of them.

I smiled. "After all, they had agreed so quickly to pay me.[8] Thank goodness, they are such greedy men," I said to myself.

As I was thinking about my finances, I remembered an odd sensation, from last night. When I had headed to meet with the chief priests and officers of the temple guard, something tangible had come over me, or in me, or something.[9] I don't know what it was and right now, I didn't care.

I went back to calculating how much money I would have when I distanced myself from these fools. It was then I noticed the disciples around me. They were looking at one another, questioning themselves.[10]

I decided to reengage in their folly, so I too looked around as one bewildered. I remember thinking, "What puppets, these disciples are."

Then Peter motioned to the uppity runt, John, to ask Jesus something.[11]

Jesus looked at me briefly and responded to them. I couldn't hear His words, but I saw the entire picture in that instant. I now understood completely. Jesus was going to blame me for His failure to become a political leader.

I began listening more intently and I heard the men around me asking one another if they were going to betray their Rabbi.[12]

"What? What did I miss? Why is that even on the table?" My mind was a flurry of questions. "Does someone know I met with the religious leaders last night?"

And then I started to get angry. These guys were wondering about something only I had the foresight to see and do.

"You idiots," I wanted to say. I wanted to tell all of these fools the truth and just about did, until I thought of the money bag, which they might take away from me if I told too much. I also thought of the added sum I would be getting soon and decided I would remain silent. After all, I deserved this money.

I could bear a little while longer with these so-called friends.

Jesus then dipped a piece of bread and gave it to me.[13] Peter and John's eyes grew wide in surprise for some reason. Mine were still suspicious and now I was getting angrier. Somehow, they knew. Somehow.

But Jesus' eyes showed hurt. That caught me off guard. I now floundered. All I could do was play dumb.

I repeated what I had heard the others say. "Surely not I, Rabbi?"

And He responded softly, with pain in His voice, "Yes, it is you."[14]

We looked at each other for an eternity in those few seconds. I no longer saw Peter and John, only Jesus.

After a few moments I looked at the bread with anger and disgust. He was not offering me a peace offering but rather an affirmation to do my part in this sordid game He was playing.

I remember thinking, "What a fool He is." And so, I took the bread, shoved it into my mouth and immediately my senses were rocked, by what, I don't know.[15] But the feeling was the same as I experienced the evening before.[16]

I looked back at Jesus, into those hurt eyes as He spoke again, but somehow, I got the feeling His next words were not for me.

He said, "What you are about to do, do quickly."[17]

I slowly got up and backed away from the table. There was something inside me which wanted to sneer at Jesus, but I was too scared of having the money bag stolen from me by these traitorous "friends."

I also think I was scared of Jesus, maybe, I don't know for sure.

I just needed to get out of there and get on my way to the religious and political leaders of the Jews.

Would these foolish men know why I had left?[18]

"Did Jesus know where I was going? How could He? He seemed to know something, though. But, how could He?" My mind was again full of questions.

It was dark when I left,[19] which was fine with me, because I wanted to get this over quickly, and be on my way.

As I left the upper room, I couldn't help but think about the previous three years.

I found myself asking, "It wasn't always like this, was it? I used to enjoy these times, didn't I?"

I felt like something inside of me was mocking me. It was bizarre. And then as quickly as I reflected on my time with Jesus, I realized when my future with Him had changed.

As I stepped onto the street, I said, "That was it." I said it so sourly I could have spat the words out. I saw what had turned me from being excited about this political Messiah to understanding He was just a fake.

Now I was snarling. In fact, I seethed with anger. It was a loathsome, hateful anger. The feelings were worse than I think I have ever experienced. I didn't understand the depth of them or where they were from, but they were oozing out of me with every step.

Some nine or ten months ago Jesus fed the five thousand[20] and the crowd saw the miracle that it was. They knew Jesus was the Prophet, who was to come into the world, and they advanced on Him to make Him their king, but He withdrew.[21]

He withdrew!

It made me sick, just thinking about it again! "He is a pathetic coward," I snarled as I walked to the Pharisees who were at the Temple Guards' post. That event was when I knew I would stay with these fools only as long as I needed to.

Well, my time with them was over, and I was glad. I had a better offer (praise Jehovah).

---

[1] Luke 22:6

[2] John 13:9

[3] John 13:27-30

[4] Matthew 20:21

[5] John 13:21a

[6] John 12:6

[7] Luke 22:4

[8] Luke 22:5

[9] Luke 22:3

[10] John 13:22

[11] John 13:23-25

[12] Mark 14:19

[13] John 13:26

[14] Matthew 26:25

[15] John 13:27a

[16] Luke 22:3

[17] John 13:27b

[18] John 13:29

[19] John 13:30c

[20] John 6:1-13

[21] John 6:14-15

Modern Introduction

September 27th, Arlington VA, 40 Days Before the Presidential Election

I had been up for a couple hours, spending some time in prayer, and in the Word, before my day went crazy. Today was bound to be another twelve-hour day.

Actually, all of the days lately have been very intense. It is the last Thursday, in September, exactly forty days before our presidential election and I'm the Religion Consultant for one of the candidates.

And my wife? She is in politics too. In fact, she is also a Religion Consultant. But she works for "the other presidential candidate." Yep, we're on opposing teams.

Hi, my name is Jude. My wife is Issy, and this is our story.

Forgive me but I'm stressing a little because she got into the shower late today, and we're running out of time to read our devo before work.

Our morning devotional is a little unique. Monday through Saturday we read a particular passage, the same passage, each day, and then on Sunday, before we go to church, we study it together.

During the week, after our devo we usually ride into the city together, getting off at the Capitol South Metro Station, and then we each head off to our respective offices. People who know us sometimes joke that we each go to our respective corners.

I just laugh when they joke like that, because Issy and I have a great working relationship, which we are determined to maintain. And, thank the Lord, our employers trust us. As well they should!

I better explain. Issy and I often work for opposing candidates. Our political views are not the same, to say the least. But our work ethic has been bathed in prayer and has become the foundation of our lives and of our ministries, if you will.

When we share them with prospective employers, to my surprise and Issy's relief, they usually accept our work ethic and commitment, which means they hire us.

There are only two commitments we make, but they work for us, and our employers.

First, we promise to live out Colossians 3:23, making sure that in every single thing we do, every bit of work we engage in, we work at as if we were working for the Lord and not our employers, who are usually candidates. They don't always know how to respond to this, but they realize they can expect excellence from us, in everything we will do, or are charged with doing.

Second, we will not share any trade secrets with the other. Nor will we say anything which would give the slightest hint to the other person about our candidate's plans. In fact, if we are ever in doubt about something we want to say, or ask, our rule is that we default to shutting up.

We go so far as to not even go to one another's candidate's parties, which they often have for staff and spouses, or partners. We will never put the other in a position to hear something they ought not to know.

As such, the only parties we've attended together lately have been church soirées.

Issy and I are very active in our church. We have been involved in church work or ministries for nearly all of our twenty-nine years of marriage, which is why we do what we do now, and, thank the Lord, we have excellent reputations.

I should probably explain what we do as Religion Consultants. Our focus includes two areas, international and domestic.

Internationally, we help our candidate maneuver through the political minefields of International Religious Persecution, and the religious nuances of delegates which will be met by people on our teams, assuming we win the election.

Domestically, there is a plethora of Faith-Based things we get involved in, from Prison issues, Schools, Adoption, Outreach, Jewish relations, Child-care, Food banks, etc.

Most of this stuff was rarely discussed publicly, prior to the Bush 43 years. He opened up the government to Faith-Based Operations and it has become a huge goldmine, or minefield, depending upon your candidate. But that's why Issy and I have jobs.

Since we don't talk about our work, our home life is focused on our relationship with the Lord and with one another, and sometimes the Washington Redskins, who, did amazing this last season. Of course, with the "Nats," World Series winners, we are now Washington Nationals fans also.

We've never had children. Issy has never had the maternal itch.

Another work issue we both have to deal with is religious folk who want to have an influence, although I don't know the principals with whom she speaks. The closer we get to an election, the more they crawl out of the woodwork.

And they do crawl, like bugs.

Relationships in our business are a necessary evil and are often tough to navigate. After working with religious folks for so long, I can affirm the adage, "Church would be great, if we didn't have to deal with people."

A couple years ago I was speaking to a group of Southern Baptist leaders. The context of my comments had to do with Southern Baptist Deacons, but I accidentally said, Southern Baptist Demons. There was mild clapping, very little laughing, some cleared throats and a red-faced speaker (me).

That evening I told Issy, who quipped, "If the shoe fits."

Here comes my Issy now. "Baby, I started this short account of our…"

"Story?" she said with the playful sarcasm she has developed.

But it wasn't just the one word of sarcasm. Typical of my fun-loving wife, at the same time she spoke, she blew me a kiss, turned on her toes, and purposely dropped her towel, heading into our closet.

I stared in unbelief at this gorgeous woman I'm married to, knowing I have twenty pounds to lose while she looks, well, "exquisite," which I said a little too loudly.

"Thank you, baby," she responded.

I just shook my head.

"Hurry up, babe," I said, "Our devo is a little longer read today and I want to quickly go over it before we head to the Metro."

This week we are reading the portion of the last supper when Judas is sent out by Jesus. [1]

Issy turned slightly, just to tease me, and said, "Fascinating words. Jesus sending Judas out to engage the religious and political leaders of his day."

I looked longingly at her, both of us knowing we didn't have time for this. She added, "In this study you started us doing, dear, I'm seeing there is little difference in our political attitudes of today than those of Jesus' time."

"Yeah, I know baby. I have thought the same thing. People are as vocal and arrogant and selfish today, as they were two-thousand years ago."

This particular daily devo, for we both have a couple of them that we do, is something we started on the New Year's break.

For the last twenty-nine New Year's Eves together we have shared a tradition. We make two choices; one is which movie series we are going to watch that day, and the other is, what we will study in scripture together all year.

Don't ask me how, but a long time ago we learned to let one person make both decisions, and the next year the other person would choose. And in case you're wondering, yes, unequivocally, yes, I've watched a lot of chick flicks on New Year's Eve and Day.

This year was my year, so we watched the Mummy Series with Brendan Fraser. I still remember my thoughts that night, now nine months ago. Issy and I were in bed and I asked, "Did any line in the movies catch your ear, or stand out to you?"

"I can't think of any," she said sleepily.

I rolled onto my back and spoke, as much to myself as to her. "I can; 'what harm ever came from reading a book.'"

"Indeed, what harm?" I thought.

It's a foreboding line in both the first and second movies.

My idea for our devotions this year was to spend the next ten months of our lives, reading the last ten months of Jesus' life.

That day, New Year's Day, we had begun our reading with the feeding of the five thousand.

And now, today, some nine months later, we are exactly forty days before a presidential "ascension," and it just so happens what we are reading is exactly forty days before Christ's ascension.

"What harm has come from our reading?" I asked myself, still waiting for Issy to finish dressing.

I shuddered, thinking about that foreboding line, because this year had seen intense relationships, unforeseen challenges, cyber intrusions, new brilliant relationships as well as new difficult relationships and incredible peace.

And on top of all that, how much more has occurred from which the Lord has shielded us?

---

[1] Matthew 26:21-25, Mark 14:18-21, John 13:21-30

Chapter 1

This year's weekly devotional, which we will begin today, January first, is from a brilliant book I found years ago, <u>A Harmony of the Four Gospels</u> by Orville E. Daniel.

In the book, the author takes each incident, in each gospel, and lays them side by side. Then, he has made bold, the unique words, so you are reading a bit from Matthew, and then a bit from Mark, and so on, to get the full story, without redundant reading. It's really brilliant!

Issy and I both recognize the author had to take some creative license with a few of the dates and locations of stories in his narrative. There are some passages he put together that other theologians may not have put together.

But we agreed to over-look the small things with which we may disagree. This way we can enjoy this unique study of the gospels.

We are graduates of two prestigious seminaries, albeit, very different schools. One is known as very liberal and the other as very conservative. So, if we do not have boundaries, Bible studies done together can be a challenge.

January 1st was a Sunday this year and we began our reading, "Then, because so many people were coming and going. . ."[1]

August A.D. 29, Feeding the Five Thousand

I couldn't believe how many people were coming and going.[2] It was so bad; we didn't have a chance to eat. And I was hungry! Just when I thought Jesus was going to dismiss us to fill our bellies, He said we should go away with Him to rest.[3]

"To rest?" I thought to myself with anger seething out of me. Rest? I wanted to eat!

Sometimes this Nazarene Carpenter just doesn't have a clue. In fact, I wonder why I am still with Him. I mean, well, except for the fact they still trust me with the money bag, the fools.

Nevertheless, we got into one of the brother's boats (it belonged to either James and John or Peter and Andrew). I don't know, because I didn't look at the markings, I was just too hungry.

We immediately headed towards Bethsaida, which is a place I like, on the lake of Galilee. It's on the North East shore where there are lovely rolling hills and lots of solitary places. We were heading toward one,[4] but all I could think of was food, and holding out till the other disciples would fall asleep, when I could take the money bag, head to the closest town and get my fill of food.

I was hungry, and I realized I couldn't wait much longer. But of course, the moment we got there, the people noticed who we were, or who Jesus was. And they came to us. Didn't this supposed Messiah realize they were only coming around because of the miraculous signs he had performed on the sick?[5]

Even I could see that. But what did He do? Even though He took us up on a mountainside, and sat down with us, He still welcomed the crowd.[6]

I swear, He looked more like a Shepherd showing compassion[7] on His flock of dumb sheep than the Messiah who would one day rule the nations.

So, of course, with our stomachs protesting loudly, He began to teach them[8] and heal them.[9]

And He didn't just do this for a few minutes; He went on doing this until late in the day.[10]

Thankfully some of my "colleagues" started thinking right and went to Jesus asking Him to send the people away so they could eat[11] and then surely we could too!

When I heard Jesus respond to them, I immediately stood up, because I couldn't believe my ears. He told us to feed them![12]

What was He thinking? Didn't He know that would empty our purse? I was running His words over in my mind when He then said, "They do not need to go away. You disciples give them something to eat."[13]

And as if to make His point He asked Phillip where they could buy bread.[14] Phillip looked at me, wanting some support, and I held up eight fingers for him. He immediately said, something about eight months wages being needed,[15] or not enough, or something.

While I still couldn't figure out what Jesus was even thinking, He had already turned from Phillip and was asking of all of us how many loaves we had.[16]

And then Peter came and told Him, "Jesus, here is a boy here with five small barley loaves and two small fish. But, how far will these go with so many here with us?"[17]

And then Jesus did something He had never done in the previous two years I had been with Him. After He had us sit the people down in groups of hundreds and fifties, He took the loaves and fish, looked up to heaven, gave thanks and broke the food,[18] handing us the pieces to share with the crowd.

And He kept breaking.

And we kept giving.

And He kept breaking.

And we kept giving.

Everyone ate as much as they wanted.[19]

And then we gathered up the pieces not eaten. There were twelve baskets of food left over![20]

That's when I counted the groups and realized we had just fed about five thousand men, besides women and children.[21]

Jesus mingled with the crowds while my fellow disciples and I were speechless.

In all the time I had been with Jesus, I hadn't seen anything like this, nor conceived of him doing anything of this magnitude. And that was when my mind began to spin with all the opportunities here. They were so vast and I had never even conceived of them.

No more famines.

Unprecedented prosperity.

No need for hard work, praise Jehovah.

Possibly, no need to be concerned of the future at all.

What a goldmine this was!

I wasn't the only one who thought this way, for a number of men who had just eaten were heading to Jesus. But then He spoke the words which caused me to realize that this was the beginning of the end of my relationship with this shortsighted Messiah.

He told us to get into the boat and go ahead of Him to the other side of the lake.[22]

"But that's crazy," I complained to the other disciples. "Look at those men," I said.

"I heard them talking; they recognize Jesus is the Prophet and they want to make Him king. By force, if necessary!"[23]

I turned to face them. "Why doesn't He let us make Him king? It wouldn't have to be by force. Once the authorities see what He can do, they would make Him a part of their political strategy, and quickly!" I'm sure my eyes were bulging with excitement.

"And soon," I continued, "We would all have positions of authority and Jesus would be leading the Jewish nation, just like we've envisioned and just like our leaders have always told us would happen one day!"

I was ecstatic. But as I looked around at my colleagues, I could tell they didn't see it. What were they, tired or something? I was raring to go! This was exciting!

I thought for a moment and then realized what this potential Messiah had just done. This man Jesus had just rejected a political kingship. I began to lose enthusiasm myself.

"No, no, no," I yelled back to the shore. I lifted my fist in defiance and continued, "This isn't what I signed on for."

The men around me told me to shut up, and I sat back realizing something inside me had just died.

New Year's Day, Election Year, Arlington VA

I had Issy read the passage in the Harmony, by Daniel. I have a number of Harmonies, the most famous is A. T. Robertson's. But for ease of reading, we are using Daniel's because it keeps us from reading duplicate verses which may be in another gospel.

"So, what's your thought, baby?" I asked when she had finished reading aloud.

We use three strategic questions when we dig into a passage. A friend of mine, Chuck, who used to be with the Navigator's (he's now in heaven), gave me these questions a few decades ago. My wife and I have massaged them a bit, so when we study a passage, we ask ourselves, is there:

1. A Surprising Challenge

2. An Unusual Promise

3. A Job-Related Directive

For question three we turn away from one another and record our own answer as appropriate, without letting the other see. This is a part of our accountability to our competitive employers.

"Yes," Issy began. "I hate to admit I see myself likened to the disciples here, but I do."

I chuckled and she went on, "Just because I have a bead on what should happen, doesn't mean it will."

I sat there silently, and she continued, "The disciples were done for the day, but Jesus' compassion for those who were hungry overruled them. They wanted the crowd to go away, but it didn't happen."

I chuckled again and said, "Interesting Issy, I saw 'An Unusual Promise' in the same portion of this story. The promise was centered on Christ's desire to comfort."

She snorted playfully and then asked where I might have seen "A Surprising Challenge?"

"Surprisingly, pun intended," I said, "it was Jesus' lack of desire to be a political king. With you and me in the business we are, this is a hard one to swallow."

"I saw that too, darling," Issy said as she snuggled into me. Then she went on. "But the 'Unusual Promise' I saw was in the actions of the disciples. When Jesus said to sit the people down, they did, even though they only had five loaves and two fish."

"Hmm, good eyes, babe. I missed that."

We then both turned to our phones to make our own personal note of the "Job-Related Directive" from the passage.

I wrote two "Job-Related Directives." One was from the aftermath of the feeding of the five thousand. Jesus told the disciples to pick up what remained, so "nothing would be wasted."[24]

I noted that this is an important principle which I think most people want to live by. I need to help my candidate see this.

The other "Directive" I gleaned from Matthew 14:23 where Jesus goes up onto the mountainside, by Himself, to pray. I was briefly reminded of the different times He prayed. He prayed before choosing the Twelve.[25] Jesus prayed after important events, before important events, when He was tired at the end of a busy day and before the start of a busy day. He was disciplined to pray constantly.

I need to. . . No, I must encourage my candidate to have a similar form of disciplined time with the Lord. If Jesus needed to abide in His Father, my boss needs to abide in Him too. Perhaps I can encourage that, somehow.

We spent the rest of the day lazing around since there was no church today. And then we went out for a bike ride. The New Year's Day weather was not too cold and we have always enjoyed bike riding together.

When Issy turned forty I gave her a real treat. I took her out for a forty-mile bike ride. For weeks ahead of time I built up our miles (without her realizing why), so on her birthday, when we woke up early, I gave her a "gift" bag containing her riding clothes and surprised her with my gift of the ride!

She wasn't sure whether to hit me, or cry, but then I told her we were going to the theatre afterwards. Fortunately, we got home early enough for us both to take a nap.

I can't tell you what we saw at the theatre, but every day I enjoy looking at the pictures of us on the forty-mile ride. We have them mounted on our walls.

---

[1] Mark 6:31a

[2] Mark 6:31a

[3] Mark 6:31b

[4] Mark 6:32c

[5] John 6:2

[6] John 6:3, 5

[7] Mark 6:34a

[8] Mark 6:34b

[9] Luke 9:11b

[10] Mark 6:35a

[11] Luke 9:12

[12] Mark 6:37a

[13] Matthew 14:16

[14] John 6:5b

[15] John 6:7

[16] Mark 6:38

[17] John 6:9

[18] Luke 9:16

[19] Mark 6:42

[20] John 6:12-13

[21] Matthew 14:21

[22] Matthew 14:22

[23] John 6:14-15

[24] John 6:12

[25] Luke 6:12

Chapter 2

New Year's Day, FBI Headquarters

I was wrapping things up at my desk, a little early at the end of a relatively slow day at the Bureau. I like working New Year's Day, since my wife and I were divorced a number of years ago. Working on January 1st keeps me home on New Year's Eve. I don't need the trouble being out late can cause me. I'm too old.

My private phone rang just as I had locked my desk and turned off my computer. The caller ID glared at me, so when I answered the phone, I barked into the handset, "What do you want?"

"Jack, this is Pete at Homeland Security."

"I know it is. I don't want to speak to you Pete. You know that."

"I know, Jack."

He stopped abruptly and then asked, "Why don't you want to talk to me?"

"Because it's the first day of the year, Pete. It's a bad omen."

"Huh, Jack, I never supposed you for someone who is superstitious. Believe me, if I didn't have to talk to you I wouldn't. But I need to keep you in the loop on something."

I sat down and relaxed a bit. "Alright, Pete, what does the Director of Homeland Security have to tell me?" I then emphasized, "Me, the one who holds the second highest office in the FBI and was on his way home to watch the Redskins slip into the hunt for the Super Bowl?"

"Wow," Pete said, "You sure think highly of your loser football team, don't you? I'm from San Francisco, Jack. Your Redskins won't make it past my 49ers."

"What's up?" I asked.

"We had a cyber incident this weekend."

"Annnnd," I coaxed.

"It's aimed at our elections, Jack."

I sighed, took a breath and asked, "Do you want me to stay, so we can do this now, Pete?"

"No, Jack. Next week will be fine. Go home and see if your Redskins can make it past their wild-card game."

"Thanks," I said sarcastically and hung up the phone.

As I headed to my car, I was shaking my head thinking about Pete's call. "Just what I needed, another cyber issue in the midst of another contentious national election."

And then I thought of what he said, clearly in jest, but about superstition. Pete had always been hostile toward anything religious or superstitious.

"But why?" I wondered.

January 2nd, Election Year, Arlington VA

My day at work was pretty laid back today. The first day back from any holiday I always try to keep it as non-eventful as possible so I can focus on emails. When I am home with Issy, I rarely look at them.

So, I spent the whole day cranking out emails. Most of them are what you would expect. Since I am the religion liaison for my candidate, all of the religious folks who want an audience or want to have some influence with the candidate come through me. Plus, I work at engaging faith-based ministries, of all stripes as well as strengthening my relationships with other ministry people.

Most folks know to reach out to the candidate's scheduler, but we have a working agreement; unless the emailer is someone my candidate already has a relationship with, religious emails come through me, so I can make an assessment of sincerity.

I hate to admit it, but there are a lot of crazy people who dress themselves up as religious and may be for that matter. But, many do it for the sole purpose of "getting-in" with a person of power, especially a president. So, I spend a lot of time dealing with those.

Finally, I've got a lot of emails myself to walk through, having nearly thirty years in the business.

At the end of the day, I met Issy at the top of the Capitol South Metro station. That is where we always meet, to head home together. I love to get there early just to watch her walk. But when I saw her walking towards me today, I could tell something was wrong.

Instead of winking at her and giving her a quick hug, I lightly kissed her forehead, let her put her arm in mine and we walked silently down the escalators.

I know Issy well enough to know not to ask questions until she's ready to talk.

We live in a nice little multi-story condo just a few blocks off the Ballston Metro exit in downtown Arlington. The nice thing is that it is a short ride on either the Silver or Orange lines, from Capitol South. We really have an easy commute.

When we got home, Issy shared with me only what she was comfortable disclosing. I could tell two things immediately, first her boss had taken off the boxing gloves and wanted to go toe to toe, bare knuckled, over religion.

That didn't normally bother Issy or me. We both come from families where if you do not make your point clearly and strongly, you'd probably lose your role, or authority, or whatever it was you thought you had.

Playing hardball has never been a problem for us.

The second issue was the problem, which seriously bothered my bride. She was not sure what she could share with me, and so we invoked our rule we have, which says, when in doubt, we shut up.

All night long, the only hint I got about this issue was an off the wall statement she made.

Issy said to me, "Honey, I don't know why, but all day I have been a little paranoid, no, cautious, yes, cautious about the religious groups which are coming my way."

January 3rd, FBI Headquarters

My mom texts me once in a while. And I had just read her text when my secretary, Grace, told me Pete Beecham, the Homeland Security Director was here.

"Praying for wisdom for you." My mom always tries to give me something encouraging. I think she believes she is my own little Zig Ziglar motivator.

Pete entered my office without his usual entourage. And he had an unusually serious face, even angry. I've known Pete for years. We're about the same age and were at West Point together. We even did our first few years of service in the same units until personal interests took us in different directions.

Pete was always the guy who would find something to joke about. "Except when it comes to religion," I suddenly realized.

As I offered him a chair, he shook his head and asked, "Can we go into the Cage, Jack?"

I hesitated, but only for a moment. I trust Pete, and if he thinks we need extra security for this conversation, then so be it.

"It'll take a few minutes for me to secure the personnel, but sure. Sit down." He didn't.

So, I too remained standing and called my secretary. "Grace, I need the Cage. Secure it for me, please. I'm heading there now with Mr. Beecham."

Eighteen minutes later we were down in the Cage which is located in the bowels of the FBI building. The Cage is a room which was built to not allow any surveillance, so secrets do not leak out. It's a difficult room to describe. It sits in mid-air, secured by a non-wire substance. There are air pockets all around the Cage so the reverberation of words die before they reach a place where they can be picked up by cyber sniffing espionage experts.

Since cell phones are not allowed in the Cage, we both left ours in my office safe, usually a no-no, but such is the relationship Pete and I have.

When we sat down, he still held his cache of a few papers in his arm. He looked like a nutty professor. But when he lifted his eyes he said, "We have another problem with religious nuts, Jack."

I looked at him, nonplussed. In my mind I said, "Pete, various religious nuts have been a problem for over two decades."

He must have understood my look for he continued, "Jack, I fear these are the religious nuts who want to infiltrate every part of our government with their narrow ideology. When I see them on T.V. and watch them smile, they remind me of that old maxim which says, 'when they smile, butter won't melt in their mouth.'"

I didn't know if I should laugh or tell him to calm down or if I should pay close attention.

He still held his papers under his arm, which were becoming more and more disheveled as he spoke. I chose to not respond yet. I still had no idea what more was coming, which might be actionable, and how I might be required to respond. And why were we in the Cage for something this obvious, like religious nuts?

This too must have shown in my face, for he set his papers down on the table and pulled out one at a time.

They were marked with his own scribbles and notes, which he deciphered as he explained.

"Jack, we are looking at evidence which implies that a cyber-attack is imminent and it has something to do with the Presidential campaign."

"What kind of evidence, what kind of cyber-attack, Pete, and which candidate?" I asked.

"The evidence hasn't been released yet, and we are still too early in this investigation for me to tell you what kind of attack, but it appears to be pointed at one of the Religion Consultant's servers and that concerns me. Haven't I always told you we cannot let these religious nuts into government, or even have access to our government officials?"

"Pete," I spoke with a little more sarcasm than I meant to, "Are you trying to tell me you think an Iranian Mullah or a Billy Graham type wants to run this country?"

"You might be more correct than you think, Jack."

"But at this point, Pete, for all you know, it could be a Junior High kid trolling for fun. Is that right?"

He nodded and stood up. "This is my top priority, Jack. I'll keep you posted."

"I really wish you wouldn't," I wanted to say.

Chapter 3

Issy and I were up early on Sunday. We like to get up early and begin our study of the Word before we get ready for church. Sometimes when we're done, we'll go back to bed and cuddle, but we like to attend our church and we enjoy the fellowship, so we make sure we don't doze off.

Now on Saturdays, that's a different story. We take advantage of the time and eventually, about midmorning, make it out to our local café. But I digress.

Since Issy read last week, I read today. I love this story. It is the account of Jesus walking on the water. "By now it was dark, and[1] the boat was in the middle of the lake. . ."[2]

August A.D. 29, after Feeding the Five Thousand

We had left Jesus back with all the people, when He made us cross the Lake on our own. And even though we had the four professional fishermen with us (Andrew and Peter as well as James and John), we were still struggling to get across.

All of us were rowing.[3] And I don't mind complaining here, that is not my forte! I'm not a fisherman. I don't do hard labor. I shouldn't have been in this position!

Our oars were two-man oars which meant we each had a partner rowing with us. And, I'm happy to say, with Peter pulling my oar with me, there were times I could rest, without anyone knowing I was resting.

I think I'm a good actor, so I made it look like I was strenuously working when in fact I was resting in Peter's strength. "Hmm, I wonder if Peter noticed?"

Anyway, we had been at it nearly all night. With the winds so strong against us, we had worked hard but were still only halfway across Lake Galilee[4] and the morning light would soon be upon us.

All of us were exhausted when Jesus started to walk by us.[5] Did you hear me? He was just going to walk right by and not help us at all!

One of the superstitious fools near me cried out calling it His ghost, and then all of us saw Him more clearly, and, well, I guess we were all dim-witted and slow because then we all started to imagine it was His ghost.[6] Sometimes I'm so ashamed of myself.

Next thing we know, arrogant, macho Peter called out to Jesus. Well, in all fairness to Peter, Jesus had just called out to encourage us, reassuring us it was Him.[7]

So, Peter dropped his oar. And remember, I'm attached to that oar. I had to carry the weight of all of it! I wanted to scream at Peter, but he was already off our bench and heading to the side of the boat to join Jesus.

I couldn't manage the oar by myself, and the wind was still so strong I just stopped rowing and then I watched this idiot fisherman walk on the water. I don't mind telling you that I inwardly chuckled when he began to sink.

They walked back to the boat and Jesus helps the big fisherman get in and then something happened which completely shocked us. As Jesus got into the boat, the wind died down and ceased its bluster![8]

Our natural response was to worship Him,[9] which we did. And even though I didn't like Peter very much, one thing he said resonated with me and humbled me. "We were completely amazed," he said. "And the reason we were amazed was because of how slow we were to recognize the meaning of the loaves and fishes on the previous day,[10] namely, He has authority over everything!"

"Yeah," I screamed in my mind, "Jesus can solve the hunger problems of our nation, if He wants to!"

So, why, with all this power at His command, doesn't He let us make Him king? That's what I want to know!

January 8th, Sunday Morning, Arlington VA

"I always love that story," Issy began.

"Why is that, baby?" I asked her.

She looked a little sheepishly at me and then confessed, "Because it makes all my times of not trusting God appear more normal."

I chuckled and pulled her close to me.

"I agree, babe. I agree."

We were running a little short on time, probably because we cuddled a little too much earlier, and so I jumped right into our three Bible Study Questions;

1. A Surprising Challenge
2. An Unusual Promise
3. A Job-Related Directive

"That's actually the challenge to me, Issy, that I would recognize and then acknowledge when fears are in me and I am not trusting Christ."

"Hey, that's good, babe," she said. "The challenge for me is more subtle. And, I don't think I ever noticed this before. When Jesus got into the boat, He didn't command the waves to stop, they just did."

I looked back at the passage. She was right. I never noticed that before either.

Issy continued, although very humbly, "Jude, God is going to do what God wants to do. He will quiet what He wants to quiet and He will let roar what He wants to let roar."

She was looking down and I lifted her face gently with my fingers and said, "Including with this November's elections, my darling."

She had a tear in her eye which I gently kissed away and she smiled a humble, embarrassed smile.

I asked, "What's the matter?"

And then without missing a cue she said, "I was looking for a promise my candidate was going to beat yours badly."

We both smiled and then continued. She took a deep breath and said, "Jesus put these poor disciples through a ton of grief before they finally emerged as the bold leaders they became."

"And He was only with them for three years," I said, and realized her comment was one of those I simply needed to listen to and let her keep talking, which she did.

Ignoring me, she continued, "God is in control, and that is all I need to know, about challenges, fears, promises, my employment, etc."

"Good word, Issy," I kissed her gently and got up to get ready for church.

January 8th, Sunday Morning, Atlanta GA

"Clyde, get your tail moving, you were supposed to be online with me ninety-seconds ago. I've got a congregation to pacify and I want to know where we are in Operation Judas."

I like that name, Operation Judas, and I specifically chose it because his name represents, "traitor," and is made clear in John 6:70-71 where Jesus acknowledges He has a traitor among his disciples.

"The irony is so juicy," I thought to myself while I was still waiting on this nincompoop.

I intend to be the natural choice for the new Religion Consultant, when the current one is discredited, of course, after the presidential winner is identified.

We Christians finally have the ability to influence politics in a profound way, if the right "influencers" are in place. And I plan to be that influencer.

All this went thru my head as I got ready to yell at my slow-moving Lieutenant.

Finally, he said, "Pastor Mortenson, I have been testing the waters of both party's servers."

He put on a look of deviousness, childishness, something, I don't know, but then he said, "I now have access to both Religion Consultants."

"Why are you smiling like that you fool," I said sharply, but not as sharply as I wanted to.

"Umm, I, umm," he said, trembling a bit now.

"Good," I thought. The only way to get anything done is to crack a whip he knows I'll use if he is not careful.

Looking at my watch I said, "What else, man. I've got to preach in fifteen minutes, and you are invading my preparation time. Give me your latest update. Now that the two candidates are determined and are campaigning, it's time we start this project in earnest."

I had Skyped Clyde in, which is our standard procedure when he is out of town. But even then, we have strict rules about how we talk, what we say, and what we do not say.

He said, "As you know Pastor, both parties chose their candidates differently this year than in the past, so they'd have a longer campaign period. . ."

He hesitated and I immediately bit his head off with, "Don't be a fool. I know all that."

He sat there with his mouth agape and I said, "Speak!"

"Sorry, boss," he stammered, which I liked, and he continued. "I have inserted two cyber hacks. I don't want to overdo it and be noticed by their electronic watchdogs. My latest hack allows me to insert myself between the communication of each Religion Consultant and their servers.

From here I can reach out to contacts already on the server. I've reached out to a few already and they are getting interested in my emails. They are paying attention to them, which tells me we're moving in the right direction."

He looked down dutifully, as if he should bow, which he couldn't because he was sitting on a chair.

But I liked what I saw in him, so I said, sincerely, "That's the first intelligent thing you've said, Clyde. Keep it up. I need you to give me a progress report in ten days."

"On it," he responded, all smiles.

"Men, they are so easy to manipulate."

I turned off Skype, picked up my Bible and headed out of the corridor to my bodyguard who would lead me to the stage where I would preach today.

"Apostle, Pastor Mortenson," my bodyguard mumbled.

"What is it you moron?"

"Your dress is turned up in the front."

I looked down and fixed it. After a moment I said, "I'm sorry about the 'moron' thing, Anthony."

"Yes, ma'am, no problem," he responded, all smiles.

I like having a verbal whip.

---

1 John 6:17b

2 Mark 6:47a

3 Mark 6:48

4 John 6:19a

5 Mark 6:48e

6 Matthew 14:26

7 Matthew 14:27

8 Mark 6:51

9 Matthew 14:33

10 Mark 6:51e, 52

Chapter 4

January 12th, Thursday Evening, Arlington VA

Issy and I had been home long enough for us to exercise and do a couple loads of laundry. We decided, many years ago that if we didn't get the laundry done during the week, we'd have to do it on the weekend, and surely, God did not make the weekend for laundry.

We were folding laundry together when Issy said, "I'm sure you look at campaign schedules, like we do."

She paused but I didn't respond, or even look up. So, she continued, "Well, then you noticed today's schedule for this weekend's campaign stops means we are going to spend some time in churches."

"Yes, I noticed that, babe," I responded as I was folding one of my T-Shirts. I added, "Do you think it'll fix your boss?"

She tilted her head and said, sarcastically, "Ha ha, funny man, my husband."

And then she got serious, "But it does mean I'll be traveling some now."

"I figured that when I read it. Are you heading to Atlanta this Sunday with your candidate?"

She just nodded her head. We enjoy traveling with our jobs, even though we may not be traveling with one another. And we had been working "in-office" for so many months that this would be the first time in nearly six months one of us was traveling, so I was glad for her.

I asked her, "Do you think we ought to start cuddling now, to make up for this weekend?"

A while later we decided we should probably have some dinner.

January 12th, Late Evening, Atlanta Georgia

"What are you doing calling me at home?" I said angrily.

"Just listen. . ." Clyde went silent, wondering if he had reacted too strongly.

"Go on," I encouraged. I wished he'd be a bit more assertive, anyway. I kind of liked that. Kind-of.

"You know who's in town this weekend, don't you?"

"Of course, I do," I said getting frustrated again.

"Well, I've got an appointment with you know who."

I purred from somewhere deep inside of me. My eyes widened in shock. I had never experienced that sensation.

I could tell it shocked Clyde, too. He must have heard it, for he asked, "Boss, are you okay?"

Again, all I could do was purr a, "Yessss, Clyde, good boy."

Thinking quickly, I added, "Come to my office after church. Make up some stupid excuse for your wife and tell me how it went."

He hesitated and I said angrily into the phone, "What's the problem, you moron?"

"Umm," he began. "We are having dinner at the in-laws right after church. My wife's mom told us to not be late."

I tried to respond silently. "She would, the big. . ."

But I was too loud. Clyde asked, "Pardon me, Boss?"

Recovering I said, "I understand, Clyde. Tell your wife I am going to give her mother a special gift and that's why you need to come to my office. That should satisfy your wife and her mother, the big old. . ."

There was a long silence. Clyde knows not to get off the phone until I dismiss him or hang up on him.

Eventually he stupidly asked, "Are you still there?"

"Of course I am, you imbecile. I'm thinking."

After another long pause I said, "Come by my office tomorrow. Don't ask for me; just ask for a package from me. I'll give you a gift to hand over at your Saturday appointment."

"Good idea," I heard his screeching voice say as the phone was leaving my ear. I hung up on him.

"Gotta keep that control," I smiled to myself and entered the living room where I turned on my fifty-seven-inch plasma television.

I sat there contemplating what I would give as a gift. Two gifts actually. One for Clyde's stupid mother-in-law and one for Clyde's political meeting.

"What do I give this Religion Consultant?"

"What should I do, Lord?" I asked, walking to my home office.

For some reason I was reminded of the phrase in Scripture, an "angel of light"[1] which of course refers to the name Lucifer.

"Lord," I prayed, "Paul may want us to apply the term, an angel of light, to the evil one, but, I am convinced that Your angels are illuminated beautifully, and so I refuse to use that phrase only for the evil one, Lord."

I was just asking again, "What should I give. . ." when it came to me, my book on The Bread of Life, from John 6:22, to the end of the chapter.

As I smiled, I felt like I looked like a Cheshire cat, grinning wider than my face. Of course, I knew that was not possible. Then from deep down inside of my guts came a long low purr. It was masculine, but not scary. In fact, it was a bit intoxicating. I stopped and raised my hand to balance myself against the wall, and then again, I felt that wide-mouthed Cheshire grin and I knew why I needed to give her that book.

I quoted the last two verses, "Then Jesus replied, 'Have I not chosen you, the Twelve? Yet one of you is a devil!' (He meant Judas, the son of Simon Iscariot, who, though one of the Twelve, was later to betray Him.)"[2]

Yes, perfect for this Religion Consultant who might eventually be shown to be a traitor, assuming her candidate wins the presidency.

In what seemed like just a few moments, I was lying on my ultra-king sized bed. The dimensions are something like ten foot by twelve foot. I don't know, but, it's monstrous.

I couldn't remember how I got there though. The last thing I remembered, I was holding myself up in the hallway, thinking about the gift I'd have ready for tomorrow, the discrediting I was working these two Religion Consultants towards, and then what?

What? I couldn't remember.

Instead, I thought of the motivation for my plan. Power. I'm not afraid to admit it. I want the political power which should rightfully belong to Christians.

I laid there for a while. I have no idea how long, but then something inside me growled, "And our time of real influence begins this year." I smiled, "Well, my time of influence and power." That Cheshire cat grin was back, and I purred.

The next day when Clyde came to the office to pick up the special gift, I had left a note with the receptionist. He was to ask for me.

Making his way up to my office, he marveled at the view, as he always did, in fact, everyone did, which is why I chose this location.

Years earlier when my late husband and I purchased this land for our church we knew it was a depressed area, but in time it would grow. And it has.

My office is on the fourth floor, and the curving stairwell is opened to the landing below, so, we have full height windows (not inexpensive) which give a sweeping view of the skyline, from Buckhead to downtown Atlanta.

And, I'm glad to say, the monstrosity called the Coca-Cola building is just far enough out of the way that it doesn't hinder our view.

One of the reasons I like to have my door open is so I can hear people's exclamations when they walk up the stairs.

While Clyde is a bit of a buffoon, his army background and his current work in the Cyber Security departments of the US government, makes him perfect for my needs.

He came lumbering in, whistling in awe of the view into greater Atlanta on this cold but very clear day.

"That's always a beautiful site, Pastor," he said. He was not looking at me and for some reason that ticked me off.

"Stop being a simpleton, Clyde. I called you up here for a reason."

"Yes, ma'am," he said, straitening up, nearly to attention.

"At ease," I said sarcastically, and he immediately spread his legs, clasped his hands behind his back and looked above my head.

"I was joking, you moron. Sit down."

He did and then he said, "This is a really beautiful package. She's gonna like this."

"Shush," was my response.

"Listen carefully," I said very slowly, enunciating each word. "My message for her is simple. Don't get it wrong."

He leaned forward like a puppy dog. "Men are so predictable," I thought to myself.

"When you give her this gift from me, tell her, 'The Bread of Life which John records was a difficult message then. Following Christ can be just as difficult now. I'm here to serve you anyway I can.' Do you think you can remember that, Clyde?"

He nodded slowly, and I had my doubts, but he is all I had to work with.

"Now get out of here," I told him and turned back to my computer.

As he was leaving, he asked, "Why do you want to help her if you're going to submarine her later?"

"It's a ruse, Clyde." He looked at me stupidly. "A ploy. A trick." I bellowed.

"Oh, I get it, boss."

I turned back to my computer mumbling to myself. "If I don't keep a close watch on him, he's going to ruin my plan."

[1] 2 Corinthians 11:14

[2] John 6:70-71

Chapter 5

January 14th, Saturday Morning, Arlington VA and Greater Atlanta

"How was your flight, babe?" I asked, over the telephone.

We hadn't talked last night after she arrived, other than by text, because they had a late working dinner. Normally we would talk on the day of arrival. But this trip was put together at the last minute and some details needed to be worked out, hence their dinner.

So instead, we waited until her first morning in Atlanta.

"I do enjoy the way you and I fly. . ." she said with a smile in her voice.

"But. . . ?" I coaxed.

"Well, I like you and me using TSA PreCheck™, but it can't compete with having a private jet, like we did yesterday, baby."

We chuckled and then I asked. "How much time do you have?"

"I'm dressed, I just need to add a bit to my face and eat my yogurt, but I have plenty of time for us to go over the John passage."

"Good," I said, wanting to jump into my news. "You remember Congressman Applebee, babe?"

"Yes, from Nevada, right?"

"Exactly. He and I have been friends for quite a while and yesterday afternoon I was walking towards our Metro station, via Pennsylvania Avenue, and I saw him."

"On a Friday?" she asked.

"Yes, and late on Friday. Apparently, he had been at the White House for a closed door briefing on the ills of the world."

I continued, "But here's why I bring it up. I saw him from afar, because he was standing on the corner, with his hand in a perpetual handshake with some guy I had never seen before. And they both had their heads bowed."

Issy whistled and I said, "Yeah, imagine, Congressman Applebee and this guy, at the corner of Pennsylvania Avenue and Capitol Street."

She commented on the narrative, "The US Capitol on one side and the House Office Buildings on the other, and those two praying in between. Did you notice the passersby?"

"I sure did, some of them were rolling their eyeballs, as if to say, 'keep it in church, guys.' But many walked by nodding their heads, appearing to approve. It was awesome!" I said excitedly.

"Sounds like it," she agreed. "Who was it?" she asked, "If it's okay for you to tell me."

"Yeah, that was the best part. He's just a regular guy. When they were done praying, I said hello to the Congressman, and he introduced me. The guy is a former collegiate coach somewhere south of Atlanta. His name is Dr. Dale Riley."

"But now, let's get through our passage, and if we have time, I'll tell you more about him afterwards."

We had decided to do our study questions on Saturday, since Issy would be out of town until midday Sunday.

"Thanks, babe," my Issy said gratefully. "I appreciate you knowing how much time it takes for me to get myself ready for the world."

"Baby. . ." I started to say.

But she quickly cut me off with, "Down boy."

Which was too bad, as I had a brilliant, romantic comeback.

We read through John 6:22-71 and Issy started us off. "I'm glad I took the time on the plane to reread this passage because, it is a difficult one to get my mind around. Our author called it 'Christ's Discourse on the Bread of Life.'"

"I agree," I said and then I waited for her to share her further thoughts.

"Jesus seems to be doing a couple things here. First, He's slamming those who are looking for Him, not because of the miracles, but because they got their bellies filled. Verse twenty-six, I think."

"A surprising challenge, eh?" I asked.

"You bet, babe! It made me really stop and parse my motivations."

I smiled, listening to her, and she went on. "Am I grateful for my relationship with the Lord because I have a fire-insurance policy, or is there something deeper, motivating me?"

"Great question," I said.

She continued, "And secondly, the passage made me think about what I am doing in my employment and what my motivation is? Am I doing what I do because of the high of being with the 'super-powerful-people?' Oh, darling, I hope not."

She hesitated but I remained silent. "I don't think I am but I sure want to check my spirit."

"Do you mind if I pipe-in?" I asked.

"No," she said, "Go for it."

"This guy I met yesterday, Dr. Dale, said he is normally never here on a Friday, but one of the Senators invited him to a prayer breakfast, so he visited his other friends on the Hill."

"Anyway, I took him to dinner."

Issy interrupted, "You didn't!"

"What are you talking about, baby?"

"You know what I'm talking about, Jude! Did you take him to the Mexican Restaurant?"

"Yes," I answered sheepishly.

"I know not to put my clothes in the closet after I have been there, baby. They're in the bathroom downstairs and I'll take them to the dry cleaners later today. Our clothes will not need to be fumigated from the lovely Fajita aroma. Now let me get back to my story."

She was satisfied with that and I went on, making a mental note to get my suit out of our closet.

"So, let me tell you what this guy does, babe, because it leads straight into this passage. It's his motivation, if you will, and I think, ours too, even though one of us works for a loser and the other one is right."

She just tolerated me with silence and so I continued. "Dr. Dale comes to D.C. once a month, to do one thing. He prays with Congressmen and women, and Senators. And when they are busy, he prays with their staff. Baby, what he prays is what got me. He told me, when he comes to D.C. he doesn't give a rip about their politics. He prays with both sides of the aisle."

"Hmm," she said, "Then what does he pray?"

"He bears their burden. That's all he's in D.C. for. He said he's not here to fix the way people think."

I paused to take a drink of my coffee and then said, "We don't have time to talk about the various stories he told me, which are exciting by the way, but his motivation gets right to the heart of this passage of Christ's Discourse on the Bread of Life."

I took a deep breath and then asked, "Is it our motivation, Issy, to 'fix' the way people think or are we really committed to Jesus?"

"Hmm," I heard her say.

"Well, let me ask you a question," she said. "Jesus is obviously separating the wheat from the chaff, agree?"

49

"Absolutely," I concurred.

"Then look at the last two verses. They are sobering and they tell me to be careful from whom I take advice."

We read verse seventy, "Then Jesus replied, 'Have I not chosen you, the Twelve? Yet one of you is a devil!'"[1]

"I would agree, baby," I said. "I think we need to make our motivation and who we choose to listen to a regular part of our prayers. And since God honors humility, we need to pray for it continually."

"The disciples still had no clue Who Jesus really was," Issy said. "And there are too many voices today who want to deceive, because they too have no clue Who Jesus really is."

"I agree, love," and we prayed. Then she went her way, to return home tomorrow afternoon.

January 15th, Sunday, Arlington VA

The next day, Sunday, Issy arrived home just after I returned from church.

I met her at the door and hugged her. She gave an almost imperceptible lifting of her head as if to smell the air and I cringed because I had forgotten!

I was relieved when she began to speak. "I met an interesting individual while in Atlanta." She said, "I can't give you any of his contact information because I don't know where it will go, relative to my candidate, but he gave me a book written by his pastor, on, of all things, 'Christ's Discourse on the Bread of Life.' An interesting coincidence, don't you think?"

I raised my eyebrows. "Interesting," I said.

When she went into our bedroom to empty her suitcase, but I purposely hung back. And then I heard the words, "Jude!"

Okay, it was only one word. Just what I feared had occurred. I had become "nose blind."

I walked into the room with my best humble smile. I hoped I looked really pathetic. I was begging for some sympathy, and all she said was, "Fumigating my clothes is not coming out of our budget."

"Yes, baby," I said, knowing I had gotten away pretty easily.

I came over to her for a kiss but she just turned saucily and over her shoulder said, "Later, maybe."

January 15th, Sunday Evening, Washington D.C.

"Pete, your timing is lousy," I said, draining a glass of wine. "I'm here at home with a date. I'm grilling fish and I don't need the interruption."

"I get it, Jack. Just hear me. An odd contact was made with one of the candidate's Religion Consultants."

"I don't understand," I said.

"I'm not too sure I do either. But I think we need to talk about it, analyze the players, and have a game plan. Can you make the Cage available at 10 a.m. tomorrow?"

"See you there, Pete."

"See you there, Jack. And let me know how your date goes, too."

I heard some laughter coming out of my phone, as I hung up on him. He knew I was lying.

---

[1] John 6:70

Chapter 6

January 16th, Monday, FBI Headquarters, The Cage

Pete and I entered the Cage at exactly 10 a.m. the next morning.

"How was your date?" asked Pete.

"None of your business," was my reply.

"No, I'll tell you this, Pete. It was nice and boring, man. Nice and boring."

Pete smiled and I said, "I like getting older. All I'm interested in is some good companionship."

That seemed to satisfy him. He nodded and said, "Let's get started."

"Let me start off by telling you, Jack, this is all still very sketchy. Very few facts and very few conclusions. But that's not bad news; because it also appears we have caught the bad-guys very early into their plan."

I nodded, making notes and then I asked, "So, tell me what you know."

"At this point we know the Perp is someone in the Warner Robins Air Force Base Counterintelligence Unit."

This had my attention, so I asked for details.

"Patience, my boring old friend."

I have been in enough courtrooms to watch an attorney take the jury along a circuitous route and tie up the loose ends in his or her own way. So, I sat back and put my pen down on my tablet.

Pete continued, "Thank you. When I say he is in the CI-Unit, I mean, the documents we have seen are from Warner AFB, Counterintelligence."

"What documents?" I started to ask and then stopped.

"My team seems to think he is exploring, like the Junior High kid you referenced the other day, only it's not a kid."

"Why not?" I wanted to ask but I refrained.

"The documents are very innocuous and could have been written by any pastor or rabbi or mullah."

"Or Junior High kid?" I asked.

"The point is," he went on, ignoring me, "We believe the Perp is doing a trial-run, an experiment. Again, to what end, we don't know, but the fact is he has successfully uploaded documents, and not just to one candidate's office as we thought before, but to both candidate's Religion Consultant's servers."

He paused; I picked up my pen and made some more notes.

He went on, "Now that he's done this once, it paves the way for him to do it again."

"So, what do you want to do about it, Pete?"

He hesitated, which I did not like. But I can play this game too. I know the sales process; it's called the "silence close." He who speaks first loses. So, I waited.

Pete didn't say anything, he just looked at me. And I looked at him.

He started to grin, because he knew that I knew what he was doing, but I remained quiet.

Finally, he leaned forward and said, "Okay, you may not like this, but we've been at this for two weeks and we still have next to nothing. I think. . ." he paused, clearly questioning whether he should say the next words.

I looked intensely at him and I hoped I had conveyed my thoughts, but obviously I hadn't.

He sucked in a deep breath and said, "We need to start surveilling people in the candidates' offices so we can. . ."

"Are you out of your mind?" I snapped.

There was silence again.

I stood up now. "You are on a very short leash, Pete."

"These religious. . ." he started to say.

"You have no cause for anything you are thinking about the candidates' offices, Pete. The truth is, it could still be a Junior High kid, albeit a holy-roller, but you. . ."

"Alright, alright, alright! You made your point, Jack. What do you want us to do?"

I regained my calm and sat down again with my old friend. "Look, you've said it yourself. Your team, who's the best in the business, behind my team, has been on this for two weeks and you still have nothing. Monitor Warner Robins and stay on this. Be a bulldog, but do not get anywhere near the candidates' employees. If your team does, Pete, I'll be putting them in jail."

Pete sat back, "Mighty strong words, Jack."

"Pete, how bad is your memory? Do you really want to find yourself at the bottom of the elections fiascos we have had to deal with in the recent past?"

He joked, "Kinda makes you want to go back to 'hanging chads,' huh?"

"Have I made myself clear, Pete?"

"Crystal, Jack."

"Good," I said. Then to end on a better note, I added, "Hey, my Washington Redskins are still in it."

"Yeah, but they'll lose this Sunday to my 49ers."

As we were walking back to my office I told Pete to get me regular field reports, so I could see what his team is doing on this case.

He challenged me, "How regular?"

"Twice a week, Monday morning and Thursday night, until I'm comfortable with your operatives."

He drew back his lower lip, as if to say, "Eek."

Instead, Pete said, "Today's Monday. I'll have your first report on your desk by 5, Thursday afternoon."

I watched him go and then I said to myself, "I hate this. I really hate this."

When I got back to my desk there were fourteen messages, but one stood out. It came from one of the candidate's offices. It was their cyber manager. It read, "Experiencing some cyber anomalies with my religion consultant's server, can I come by?"

"Crap," I mumbled.

Chapter 7

I love making breakfast for my wife and when we get up early enough on a Sunday, I can make her breakfast before we read Scripture.

This morning I made my signature sausage casserole. Once in a while I take it to work, usually when I'm hosting a Bible study, and people love it.

I wouldn't say Issy loves it; she's not a "pepper" person, but with all the fluffy eggs and the thick sausage crumbles, the pickled Jalapeño peppers fit in great.

Wow, I'm such a good husband, I thought, virtually patting myself on the back.

This morning, after breakfast, Issy and I lay in bed reading the harmonization of Matthew 15:1-20 and Mark 7:1-23, entitled, "Conflict with the Pharisees."

"Then some Pharisees and some of the teachers of the law. . ."

September A.D. 29, Conflict with the Pharisees

I was listening to the religious and political leaders but watching Jesus' expressions. This wasn't going to be good.

Many of the men, who came all the way out to us from Jerusalem, were good men; men I trust. And frankly, they were giving some very sound and helpful advice to Jesus, but Jesus wasn't listening. I could tell.

I was sitting outside the group of us Twelve, eating, when Jesus stood up and started to quote Isaiah. I don't know for sure, but He may have misquoted the passage. At any rate, I'm sure Isaiah did not mean for it to be applied to our great religious leaders and politicians. What He said to the Pharisees was unmistakable though.

Jesus continued, "Isaiah was right when he prophesied about you hypocrites. . ."[1]

My jaw dropped and my eyes became the size of saucers. The leaders were simply asking Jesus about our traditional responsibilities as they relate to cleanliness. Why couldn't Jesus have responded nicely, or at least smiled?

Instead He went on and said, "These people honor me with their lips, but their hearts are far from me. They worship Me in vain; their teachings are but rules taught by men."[2]

I couldn't believe it. Didn't Jesus know He would need to cater to some of these men if He were going to unite the Jews?

"Where did Jesus learn His political savvy?" I was thinking to myself. I remember hoping He was done, but He wasn't.

Jesus then called them to account for their personal corruptness. At least I think that's what He was doing.

He seemed to sum it up by saying, "You nullify the Word of God by your traditions."[3]

And if that wasn't enough, Jesus called the crowds to him to explain the spat, which they had all seen and heard.

Looking them in the eyes and ignoring the Pharisees, Jesus said to the crowd, "Listen to me, everyone, and understand this. Nothing outside a man can make him 'unclean' by going into him. Rather, it is what comes out of a man that makes him 'unclean.'"[4]

I admit, the argument made sense but why couldn't He smile when he said it?

Then one of the Twelve said, "Do you know the Pharisees were offended when they heard this?"[5]

"You think?" I said sarcastically.

Then I heard Jesus say of the Pharisees, "They are blind guides!"[6]

January 22nd, Sunday Morning, Arlington VA

"Jude," Issy started the discussion of this week's passage, "Were the Pharisees and teachers of the law considered the political gurus?"

"If they were considered political gurus it would have only been in the minds of those who were expecting a political Messiah to come onto the scene and shake off the bonds of Rome on the Israelites."

I continued, "What I find fascinating in this passage, Issy, from our perspective as political consultants, was the passion they seemed to have for their way remaining the only way. They did not want any changes. They liked their traditions."

I paused and then went on, "Remember that at the trial of Jesus, we find they were so jealous of Christ that even Pilot knew it."[7]

"So, what's your point, husband?"

"My point, my dear wife, is my 'Surprising-Challenge.' I like things to move as they always have in the past. Change is not always good, but what Jesus is saying here, to me, is 'Jude, get over yourself. Maybe the same-old-way needs to change.' And frankly, Issy, change scares me."

She looked at me, nodding in understanding. "That might dovetail with what challenged me, namely, am I only honoring God with my lips?"

I grunted in understanding. "What about an 'Unusual-Promise?'" I asked.

Issy sat up tall and blurted out, "Clearly the confirmation that uncleanness in a person is defined by what comes out of their mouth."

She took a deep breath and then asked me, "What about you?"

I took a more sobered approach but used similar words, "Clearly the confirmation that blind guides lead people into a pit."[8]

There was silence and then I said, "Baby, let's not be blind guides to our bosses."

She leaned over and kissed me, but there was a smirk in her kiss and then she said, "Didn't the passage talk about the blind leading the blind? And then falling into a pit?"

I just looked at her, shaking my head because I knew there was a political comment behind her statement. She continued, "Maybe your leader is blind, my lover."

She immediately got out of bed and I tried to swat her, but she was already outside of my reach.

"Time for church," she said, running into the bathroom.

An hour and a half later, Issy and I were walking into church when Harold, our small group leader walked up to us.

Actually, he made a beeline for me and when I reached out to shake his hand, he neither proffered his, nor stopped walking. Instead, he pushed my hand aside and stood two inches from my nose.

"Jude, I can't keep silent anymore. I'm sick and tired of being polite to you. In my mind, you are. . . How can you work for who you do, attempting to put your candidate in the most powerful office in the world, and call yourself a Christian?"

He took a breath and went on. My wife stepped toward him, but without taking my eyes off him I put my hand on her arm and she stopped.

He continued, "I don't want you to come back to our small group. The things your candidate stands for, the things your candidate has said, the actions which will come about in this country if your candidate wins, sicken and disgust me. And by inference, Jude, you disgust me, too."

He walked off as quickly as he had arrived. I don't mind admitting, I was upset. In fact, while sitting in church I was actually shaking a bit.

"Do you want to leave?" Issy asked, and I shook my head no.

We sat through church and then walked home quietly. She could tell I was deep in thought.

"What are you going to do?" she asked, when we stepped into the front door.

"I'm not sure, baby. I'll have to pray on it."

The remainder of our day was pretty quiet; I couldn't even enjoy the Redskins' playoff game. Issy was honoring my need to process the morning's events.

As we went to bed, she caught me smirking. "What's so funny?" she asked.

"Oh, it's not funny, but I was just thinking of a famous line given some three decades ago."

She lifted her eyebrows asking to be let in on it. I said, "Rodney King, 1992, 'Why can't we all get along?'"

We both shook our heads and then I said, "Seriously, babe. I expect the world to act like this, but not a friend of mine, in my church."

We looked at each other, and then I added, "Our country is in the midst of great division, but our churches need not be. Isn't the church equipped to handle the ugliness of our day? If our unity is in Christ, how can we have disunity based on the way we vote?"

"I don't know, my darling," she answered.

I said, "We have got to seek the Lord. . ."

And my Issy kicked in, ". . .for unity."

We both went to bed and slept soundly, spooned together.

January 22nd, Sunday, Washington D.C.

Three days earlier, Pete was true to his word, and his report was on my desk at 5:00 p.m. I opened it, quickly perused it and then put it in my briefcase for home-reading. Fortunately, it was not Top-Secret yet.

I hadn't opened the file all weekend when the Washington Redskins playoff game started.

Surprise, surprise to everyone, including Pete, they were still in the hunt for the Super Bowl, but just barely. They came off a 4 and 12 losing season the year before, to be in the hunt, if the Cowboys would only have a few key losses. Well, they did, and then Washington upset them in the last regular season game, and somehow, Washington made it to the NFC Championship. Maybe they could get there again.

I picked up the files, expecting to turn off the Redskins quick loss to the Forty-Niners (which I would never confess to Pete), but it was a real game, and I never touched the files until late Sunday evening. What a game!

When I finally got to the file it was a boring read. Three weeks of investigation and still no specific Perps, still no awareness of intent, or even an understanding of the hacker's goal. Nothing of any significance had been fleshed out.

The only thing I knew for sure was that I would get to make Pete's day, while keeping him on a tight leash.

What I had to make sense of now, was my conversation with the Cyber Security Geek I had met with on Friday.

---

[1] Mark 7:6a

[2] Mark 7:6b-7

[3] Mark 7:13a

[4] Mark 7:14-16

[5] Matthew 15:12

[6] Matthew 15:14m

[7] Matthew 27:17

[8] Matthew 15:14

Chapter 8

January 20th, Two Days Earlier, FBI Headquarters

All afternoon was blocked off for this meeting. I didn't grow up with all of this cyber-stuff, so when I have a briefing which will focus on cyber action, I leave myself plenty of time to ask questions. I don't want to be rushed.

"Billy Marshall, sir," the pimply faced kid said, giving me a strong handshake, which shocked me.

He had just introduced himself to me and opened up a notebook on his computer when I jumped in and asked, "First, tell me in twenty words or less, why you're here?"

He balled up his hands into fists and then started talking, counting off the words as he spoke. I was impressed, for the second time, in my first meeting with this kid. He didn't stop to think what to say. He just started talking.

"Well, sir, I don't know if I'm dealing with a genius hacker or an idiot, and the directive says to report anything questionable."

"That was twenty-three words, sir," he said with a smirk.

"I like this kid," I said to myself, smiling back at him.

I then asked, "What was your first hint that there was a problem?"

He stopped and pursed his lips. He was contemplating something. He was acting like he shouldn't tell me something, so, I encouraged him saying, "Don't worry, son, share with me honestly, and tell me what you don't want in my report, and I'll accommodate you, as best I can."

He sucked in his breath through his teeth, and mumbled, "That wasn't a very good promise, sir."

I chuckled and asked further, "You're not doing something illegal, are you?"

With that, his eyes became like saucers and he said, "Oh, no, sir. Not at all."

"Then what's your hesitation?"

"Well," he mumbled, "I have a few homemade programs which I use only for. . ."

I laughed and said, "You're being proactive. I don't ever fault people for that, son. Billy, right?"

He nodded.

"Talk to me, Billy, you don't have to worry."

And with that, this young kid looked at me, as if he were sizing me up. I think he was deciding if he could trust me, so I remained silent giving him the freedom to make the choice he eventually would.

Finally, he said cautiously, "You remind me of my dad."

I just stared at him curiously, and he went on. "He died when I was thirteen years old."

We were both sitting, facing each other, and he continued, "He worked for Zig Ziglar enterprises and so when he would teach me, he would use philosophies based on the Bible and Zig."

The kid chuckled a bit and he said, "The last thing my dad ever said to me was, 'Billy, always work as if you're working unto the Lord,[1] so you do everything with excellence, and then,' then he would put on the drawl of Zig Ziglar and add one of his famous lines, 'if you're the hardest working person on the job, you'll be the last one to be fired and the first one to be hired.' I never forgot that."

"Are you telling me that's your work ethic, Billy?"

He shrugged and said, "Yes, sir, and I'm gonna trust you."

"You can, Billy. That you can."

Then he asked, "Do you know Zig Ziglar, sir? I mean, do you know of him? He's been dead for about a decade."

I grabbed a little desk plaque I keep in front of me and slid it across to him.

He picked it up and read it out loud, "I'm doing GREAT!" Under those words the plaque had the name of the one who used to say it, "Zig Ziglar."

Billy chuckled and looked at me.

I said, "I have it on my desk because it always reminds me that what someone says may not always be the truth."

And then Billy did something that solidified our friendship; he laughed at me. And it was obvious where his laughter was directed, but I wasn't offended or angered.

He said, "Sir, did you know that Zig was asked about that particular quote?"

I looked at him in surprise and he went on.

"Yeah, one day someone asked, 'Zig, aren't you lying when you say you're feeling great, when you really aren't?' And without missing a beat Zig responded, 'No, I'm not lying, I'm just telling the truth a little early, that's all.'"

I looked at this pimply-faced kid and immediately had a greater respect for him. He's sharp and unafraid. I like that.

"You can trust me with your personalization of your company computer, Billy. Now just tell me what you have done, before you tell me what you have found."

"Basically, I took the NSA computer monitoring system and simplified it."

"Why?" I asked.

"Imagine that you have a twenty-pound sledgehammer and you are trying to kill a bee. Every time you swing your sledgehammer the bee is moving before you get there."

"What's your point, Billy?"

"Well, the NSA system is great for listening to billions of words a day over millions of calls, specifically looking for trigger words or trigger signatures, but I work in an office with a limited number of people with a few specific computers and phones."

I like the way this kid thinks.

"So, I wrote a program which compares incoming email and text signatures and automatically builds unique algorithms for each person within my responsibility."

"My computer then tells me when texts and emails received are from a source outside of typical, or standard algorithms, for the particular person receiving them."

I cut in, "In other words, if a signature doesn't come from the same source each time, you are triggered?"

He nodded his head and I went on. "But what about when someone sends an email from their PC and then from their cell phone, or even a text from two different phones."

"Sir," he said with an air of confidence, not arrogance, "We are the US Government; it is easy to verify, electronically, if a signature is from the same person, even if it is from two different sources."

He further explained, "It's more like our credit card companies. They build algorithms based on our purchases so when a purchase is outside the ordinary algorithm it is flagged."

"Make sense?" he asked. Then he continued, "My way catches the little nuances whereas the NSA program misses them."

I leaned back in my chair looking up to the ceiling when I sensed him wanting to speak. I lifted my finger which silenced him.

A few moments later, I said, "So, the program you were given to monitor emails and texts was too big and bulky, so to speak, and you made one more economical?"

"Yes, sir, you see, I decided. . ."

I interrupted him. "I got it, Billy. You don't have to convince me. You had me at, 'I'm just telling the truth a little early.'"

We both laughed and I said, "Alright, get down to business, what are you seeing that brought you in here?"

He started to speak, and I interrupted him once more, "Give me the simplified version first, and if I need you to expand your explanation, I'll ask you specific questions."

He nodded and jumped right in, "Basically, I have noticed incoming emails and texts which have the same signatures but are coming from two different computers and phones which are so diverse they should not be linked."

"Any possibility these are just spams?"

"That's exactly what I decided they were at first, but then our employee started communicating with these spams."

"What do you mean? What kind of communication?"

"Well, sir, that's what makes me wonder if this is being carried on by a genius or an idiot."

He handed over a transcript:

Incoming Text: It was great to finally meet you the other day. I'm looking forward to our next meeting.

Outgoing Text: Thank you. Me too.

Incoming Text: BTW, I just talked to the boss. If you're ready, it's time to get you two together.

I looked up at Billy. I shrugged my shoulders, as if to say, "So what?"

And that's when he played his Ace.

"The incoming texts were from a throw-away phone registered to Counterintelligence in Warner Robins, Georgia."

I sat there stunned and spoke under my breath, "Warner Robins Air Force Base Counterintelligence."

He started to speak but I lifted a finger stopping him, which he dutifully obeyed.

After a while I asked, "Have you seen this incoming signature before?"

"Well, no, I hadn't, but knowing what to look for, I went back into incoming emails and documents and found two cyber-attacks from someone in the Warner Robins Air Force Base Counterintelligence unit."

"How serious were the attacks and what kind were they?" I asked.

"Well, in my mind, any attack is serious, but the odd part about these attacks is, I think the hacker was testing the water. As for what kind of attacks, they were a MitM Attack and an SQL Injection Attack."

"In old man words, Billy."

"Well, I suspect the hacker was just seeing how far he could get into the server and hard drive of our employee. As for the attacks, the MitM is short for 'Man in the Middle' which is what a hacker does when he wants to insert himself between a person and a server, which usually leads to gaining control of that server."

"In this case, the client is the religion consultant, right?"

"Yes."

"And the other attack you mentioned?"

"An SQL Injection Attack is used by a hacker so he can read sensitive information from the client's computer."

Again, I leaned back, and this time Billy knew to not say a word.

"Is there any other outgoing response, other than the innocuous text?"

"No, sir," he said immediately.

"And the two cyber-attacks came from the same place, Warner Robins Air Force Base, Counterintelligence?"

"Yes, sir."

After a moment I asked, "Who else knows about this?"

"Nobody, our instructions say. . ."

"I know what your instructions say, Billy. I wrote them."

I stood up and walked around the desk to my fifth-floor office window. I can look out my window and see Pennsylvania Avenue below me with a cross section of The Mall, beyond that.

I often look out at The Mall when I'm thinking. I looked to the right and saw all 555 feet of the marble obelisk, the Washington Monument, and then scanned towards the left to the US Capitol.

I had made up my mind, so I went to the chair next to Billy and sat down.

"How would you like to work for me?" I asked.

"But I already have a commitment to. . ."

I put up another finger. "But you haven't heard my offer."

"I'm honored, sir, but I gave my word to work for them through the election."

I smiled because he gave me a great answer. I didn't expect it but I'm glad he gave it.

"Is something funny, sir?" he asked with some hesitation in his voice.

"Nothing is funny at all, Billy. I think your dad would be very proud of your work ethic, son."

He gave a slight nod of thanks.

"When I said I wanted you to work for me, I meant clandestinely."

He hesitated and I said, "We will work out the details for the remuneration, but right now I have a job for you."

Again, the slight nod, and I continued. "I need absolute confirmation of who the perp, or perps, is/are at Counterintelligence in Warner Robins and I need to know who 'the boss' is. And let's hope it's not Bruce Springsteen."

I stopped and smiled at my own wit. But Billy just looked at me blankly. I wondered if he even knows who Bruce Springsteen is.

"Oh, yeah," he finally said. "Isn't he a part of the music genre your generation would call a classic?"

I just ignored him and asked him to meet me at 6:00 pm on Thursday evening.

He hesitated, but then he said, "I can."

"What's the matter, do you have a date for that night or something?" I asked sarcastically.

"Well," he stumbled, "My church meets on Thursday nights at 7:00 pm."

He hustled to add, "We are only a few blocks up the street though, so if I can get out by 6:45, that should be fine, sir."

"Hmm," I thought to myself, "The kid is also a holy-roller. Maybe I made an offer too soon."

I looked at him with, I'm sure, mixed signals in my eyes.

He assured me, "I'd be honored to serve you in any way I can, sir."

I slowly nodded my head and said, "This is temporary. Let's play it by ear."

He stood and almost saluted, and then he said, "I won't let you down."

I nodded to him that he could go and he headed toward the door.

"You can't leave a fingerprint anywhere, you know," I said to his back.

"Sir," he said, looking back over his shoulder, "I'm a computer geek, and I'm very good at 'geeking.' Don't worry."

After Billy left, I sent an encrypted email to Pete:

Your Warner Robins AFB CI Hacker is confirmed. Innocent text seen in my office from the Religion Consultant shows hacker refers to a 'boss.'
Jack.

---

[1] Colossians 3:23

Chapter 9

January 23rd, Monday, Arlington VA

Issy and I awoke to snow falling. It was beautiful, but it looked cold. Our coffee maker had started a few minutes before my alarm went off, so it was ready when I went to the kitchen. I poured myself a cup and sat in the living room with my Bible.

I had been reading through Romans and today I started the thirteenth chapter. I am finding that verses one and two are either viewed as famous or infamous, depending upon whether the candidate you voted for is in office or not.

I found myself returning to these first two verses over and over again.

Once, I made it down to verse five, before going back to the first two verses. But that verse just reminded me of Harold's verbal attack yesterday at church.

I didn't tell Issy this, but I suspect Harold's uncontrollable anger came from this very issue, his conscience, as lined out in verse five. I wrote in my Bible, "When disgust meets your Christian conscience, the result is either humility or anger."

I need to share that with Issy. I wonder if this is the problem in our church today.

I was back to verses one and two again, so I wrote them out in my notebook, from the HCSB Version:

"Everyone must submit to the governing authorities, for there is no authority except from God, and those that exist are instituted by God. So then, the one who resists the authority is opposing God's command, and those who oppose it will bring judgment on themselves."

As I wrote this, a recent news article popped into my mind. I couldn't remember the name of the actor, but he was complaining because he claimed he was being blackballed due to his political views.

As I sat back contemplating his claim and my experience yesterday, I was reminded of the words in one of Peter's epistles, where he says, "Why in the world are you surprised you are going through fiery ordeals?"[1]

I laughed at this actor, because, if I recall, he also claims to be a Christian. But, while I was judging this actor, it was as if the Lord hit me with a right cross and said, "Jude, why in the world are you surprised by what occurred yesterday?"

Immediately I got on my knees, I hope humbly, and confessed my self-righteousness to the Lord.

"Father," I started. I often pray out loud at home, even when it is just me and God. I find it helps me eliminate distractions. "Indeed, why in the world does yesterday's event with Harold surprise me? Forgive me Lord for my arrogance.

Somewhere Your word says we are to expect persecutions.[2] And didn't Your Son say those who are persecuted because of righteousness sake are blessed?"[3]

I immediately heard a high-pitched snort behind me. Issy was up.

"Did you think my praying was funny, darling?" I said with more sarcasm than anger.

"Oh no," she quipped, "That was God snorting at you." And then she winked.

"Pour yourself some coffee and come here." I said.

My Bible was still open and in front of my face, which it normally is when I am on my knees praying.

When Issy returned from the kitchen, I got off my knees and picked up my Bible off the sofa. I shared with her the last thirty minutes or so of my devotional.

"We need to look at these two verses, babe. I think they carry a tall order for us as Christians."

I read them to her in the HCSB: "Everyone must submit to the governing authorities, for there is no authority except from God, and those that exist are instituted by God. So then, the one who resists the authority is opposing God's command, and those who oppose it will bring judgment on themselves."

"So, are you saying you received judgment from God yesterday, because you have been rejecting God's chosen candidate, my boss?"

I tutted, "No, silly," I stopped and looked seriously at my bride.

"But I'll make you this promise, if God allows your boss to be made President, in just a little over nine months, I will acknowledge your boss was put in office by God, and your boss is who God wants in office."

I continued, "That doesn't mean I'll agree with your candidate's policies. But I won't resist or oppose their authority, either. I'll just work harder next time."

Looking her in the eyes, I could tell she was contemplating my words. She knew what my statement meant, and, I think, she was weighing whether or not she could say the same thing.

She leaned down and gently kissed me and said, "With this snow we may want to leave a little early."

"I agree," I said, getting up and pulling her close.

But she said, "No time, babe," and that ended that.

January 25th, Before Wednesday Prayer Mtg, Atlanta GA

Hearing the heavy steps of Clyde make their way closer to my office, I yelled, "Clyde, what's taking you so long?"

When he finally arrived, I told him to shut the door.

"Give me your update," I barked. "I want to know where we stand with both candidates' consultants."

He opened his briefcase and pulled out a manila file. The front was stenciled with three-inch-tall red letters on a white background, "TOP SECRET" and below that in smaller script, "Eyes Only."

"What?" I mocked, "You think you're James Bond now?"

"I'm just trying to bring a little operational prudence to this job."

"Just do what I tell you to, Clyde. I'll take care of the prudence."

He cowered a bit, which was where I wanted him.

He opened his envelope and withdrew a single page. It was neatly typed and he gave it to me.

To my surprise and relief, he gave it to me and was silent. There might be some hope for this clown yet.

And then I noticed that it was headed with "Operation Judas I." I just sighed and mumbled, "Idiot."

But what he had given me was in an orderly fashion and I didn't have to engage him. I just read.

OPERATION: JUDAS I.
Surveillance Report:

* Operational Objective:

> ** Take over winning candidate's Religion Consultant job.*

* Threefold Operational Sortie:

> *First, deeply plant traitorous files in both computers.*
>
> *Second, be helpful to both consultants (by being available), to both candidates (with finances), and both CoS, or Chiefs of Staff (offering fresh eyes to religious issues). Last point can be strengthened by the contacts fed to these campaigns who are aligned with Apostle, Pastor Mortenson.*

Third, when winner is obvious or announced, appear to be the whistle-blower which "outs" the "traitor," making Pastor Mortenson the natural replacement.

* *Current Operational Status:*

   Direct contact made with Consultant A.

   Indirect contact made with Consultant B.

I had made a few notes as I went thru the report and then looked up into his stupid grin.

"Have you got the files in their computers yet?"

"No ma'am," he muttered, "We talked about not doing that till later."

"Get started on the posts right away and then the uploads in the next few months. By the way, you still have access to their computers, right?" I pushed.

"Of course," he responded indignantly. "It's my job."

He looked at me with hard eyes, as if he wanted to say more, maybe even call me an unflattering name. But he knew his place and stopped talking with his mouth wide open. "Coward!" I wanted to say.

"Look, tell me about this indirect contact."

"I know of a prayer-guy in the Macon area. He goes to a big church, has lots of influential friends. . ."

"In Macon?" I said in disgust. "What good ever came out of Macon?"

But Clyde just kept talking, ". . .And from what I can tell, he's got some baggage which will cause him problems if and when it comes out."

I looked down and thought to myself, "Yeah, we all have that kind of baggage, Clyde."

"So, tell me about this baggage and why you are using him?"

"He recently got fired from Macon Poly Technic University, for something to do with terrorist tendencies."

"When did this happen? Why don't I know about it? Why don't I recall ever reading about it?"

"Well, this guy is a holy-roller who chose not to sue Macon Polytechnic University (MPTU). He believes that God is in control and so he intends to play the cards God dealt him."

"Another stupid male," I said out loud.

"I have also uncovered some quiet gossip which says the board of regents railroaded him out of the job, and no one wants it uncovered."

"So, with this goody-two-shoes attitude of not suing, the Board gets away with it." I said.

"Yes, ma'am, that's why I have. . ."

"It was a statement, not a question, Clyde."

And thankfully he shut up.

I sat back in my plush leather desk chair. I closed my eyes, lifting my face to the ceiling.

I don't know what Clyde was doing. He was probably watching me like an idiot. I put my hand to my stretched-out neck thinking, "I do have a beautiful, long, smooth neck."

Un-stretching and returning to my desk, I opened my eyes to see Clyde looking at me with a different look on his face, which I could not place. He wasn't looking at me admiringly, which he often does. And he wasn't looking like a cowed fool. Again, there was a hint of hardness in his eyes.

"What is your next step and when will it be accomplished?" I asked.

"Two next steps. First, to develop a tighter relationship with this Dr. Dale character, and then to reach out to more contacts which are already in the Religion Consultants' files."

"Timeline?" I asked sharply.

"Three to four weeks," he said looking dumb, again.

I opened my calendar and said, "Return here before church the last Wednesday of February."

He got up and I extended my hand, with my long fingernails, and sleek wrist. He too stood, but instead of taking my hand immediately he looked at it and then me and finally gave me a short handshake.

When he looked up at me, I saw those enflamed, possibly angry eyes again. "Stupid male," I thought to myself.

As he left, I could have sworn I heard him mumble like a young child does when they are angry at a parent.

Did he say, "Stupid woman, I've had about enough of her?"

"Oh, how rich that is." That clod. I looked at my watch and saw I still had ten full minutes before prayer meeting.

I stuck Clyde's report in my safe and then sat down at my desk. "What can I teach this congregation to pray for tonight?"

"Hmm," I thought, and then said, "I got it!"

I went to the worship center a few minutes early and was bombarded by people who wanted to talk. "This is why I have subordinate pastors." I was thinking this, but I actually think I said it to someone too, on my way to the rostrum.

At least a couple people remembered and referred to me as Apostle, Pastor Mortenson.

After the music minister led us in a few songs and then opened us in prayer, I stood up to announce our prayer focus tonight.

"This year will no doubt be a contentious one in politics."

"Amens," flooded the sanctuary, along with a few, "Lord, forgive us."

"I want us to prepare. I want us to know the Word of God. I want us to claim it."

I was in a groove, and had a cadence which the congregation responded to, we were a team. No wonder they like coming here, I make them think they are a part of this act.

As they calmed down, I said, "Turn in your Bibles to the thirteenth chapter of Paul's Epistle to the Romans."

I read the verses from the King James Version, "Let every soul be subject unto the higher powers. For there is no power but of God: the powers that be are ordained of God. Whosoever therefore resisteth the power, resisteth the ordinance of God: and they that resist shall receive to themselves damnation."

"You know I like to run a tight ship here." There were a few chuckles.

"It's okay, I know what some of you think of me, you can laugh. I'm not looking at you." And with that there were many a laugh, which made me angry. But I didn't show it and went on.

"While these verses clearly mean you are to be subject to me, here at our church, let me tell you what this also means. It means whoever gets voted into the office of President, in the elections later this year, will have been put there by God, and we will not resist them, even if we don't like them."

There was absolute and complete silence in the auditorium. "We will not resist the ordinance of God, my dear children."

We then spent the next thirty-five minutes in prayer, and the evening ended.

"Believe me," I said to myself on my way home, "Not only am I not going to resist them, I'm gonna support them."

January 26th, Thursday 6pm, FBI Headquarters

"Praying for wisdom on your behalf," came another text from my mom. I need to ask her if she thinks I'm getting dumber with age, because she seems to be praying for wisdom for me a lot lately. I'm not a religious man, but I figure if it'll help me do my job better, I'll take it.

Billy walked in and said, "Chief Master Sergeant, Clyde Smith, Warner Robins Counterintelligence unit."

I looked up from my desk, "Any news on the accomplices? Do we know who 'the boss' is yet?" I asked.

"Not that I can tell."

"Alright, Billy, keep looking for useful information."

I nodded for the door and he started towards it when I stopped him, "Oh, Billy, is the hacker still just testing?"

"Yes, sir."

"Thanks. Good job, son." He beamed and I looked down at my paperwork.

After Billy left, I sent another encrypted email to Pete:

Your Warner Robins AFB CI Hacker is Chief Master Sergeant, Clyde Smith; do you have his boss yet?
Jack

---

[1] Author's paraphrase of 1 Peter 4:12

[2] John 15:18

[3] Matthew 5:10

Chapter 10

I love the times we do our devo's together. I wish we had time to do this during the week, also.

Today we were reading about Peter's declaration from the harmonization of Matthew 16:13-20, Mark 8:27-30, and Luke 9:18-21. And this is where Daniel's book, <u>A Harmony of the Four Gospels</u>, is so brilliant. He takes us through the entire story, pulling a fragment of a verse from Mark and then Luke and then back to Mark before going to Matthew. I really love this way of studying the gospels. It just feels so full, so complete, so comprehensive.

I read, "Jesus and his disciples went on to the villages around Caesarea Philippi. . ."[1]

October A.D. 29, Peter's Declaration

"Why, oh why do we just walk around from town to town, making all kinds of friends, getting tons of people on our side, and still never talk about the coming political take-over of our God-given sovereign nation? After all, isn't that what the political Messiah was prophesied to accomplish?"

I kicked a few rocks with my sandaled feet.

I love walking behind all of the disciples. For one thing, I can pillage the money bag when I need to, and for another, I can complain.

"But seriously, God," Lately I have found myself praying about this, probably out of frustration. "God, why isn't this Prophet doing the sensible things He should? He has every opportunity and He is taking advantage of none of them."

We were outside Caesarea Philippi and I was hungry, but Jesus decided to stop and pray and he gathered all of us to pray with Him.

Frankly, I don't like that. I think prayer is a private thing and I shouldn't have to pray out loud in front of others.

As soon as I thought this in my brain Jesus said, "Judas," looking at me, not the other one. "Would you lead us in your favorite prayer of Moses?"

"Yes, Jesus," I answered respectfully. Everyone had turned to look at me and my hand was in the money bag. Fortunately, I put it behind me when Jesus turned to me.

"Did He see me?" I wondered.

"Noooo, He would have scolded me. Wouldn't He have? I sure would have." All this went through my mind as I closed the bag with one hand and left it in my belt, behind me, so no one knew what I was doing.

Then I lifted my arms to the heavens and quoted, a little harsher than I intended, "I don't get to go into the holy land. . ." Lowering my arms I pointed towards everyone, ending on Jesus, although not on purpose, I don't think. Anyway, I finished the passage, ". . .and it's your fault!"[2]

The disciples laughed and I added. "Well, that's the way I would have spoken to them too. A simple thing like hitting the rock instead of talking to the rock kept Moses out of the Holy Land.[3] That's just not fair."

Interestingly, while the other men were laughing, Jesus was not. He looked so somber. I wondered what was on His mind.

But I knew which prayer of Moses He meant,[4] and so I began. . .of course, I quoted it with my own nuances.[5] I don't think my stupid colleagues ever realized I took some liberty with my quotations. . .but Jesus may have, maybe. I began:

"Lord, You have been the dwelling place of our people and our great nation throughout all the generations. Before the mountains were born You brought forth this world from eternity and unto eternity, because You are God. When we die, You turn us back to dust. You even say, 'return to dust you mortals!' A thousand years according to You is no different than a day according to us. You sweep people away like the new grass of the morning gets swept away. In the morning the grass springs up but by the evening it has dried and withered like the nations of today."

With that statement, Jesus cocked an eyebrow, like He did when I started this nuanced quotation.

I don't think anybody else noticed it, but I sure did. Nevertheless, I continued.

"In the past we've been consumed by Your anger, Lord, and terrified by Your indignation. You set our iniquities in front of You, including our secret sins. They are opened up clearly in the light of Your presence."

I paused for a moment, and as the men looked at me as if I should keep going, something about those words caught me. I don't know what it was, but I stopped. 'Was it the comment about secret sins?' I couldn't say. After a few moments I continued.

"All of our days have passed away under Your wrath and we finish our years with a moan. Our days are a mere seventy years on this earth, eighty, if we have some additional strength. But even if we do, our best days are filled with trouble and sorrow. And Father, I don't claim to know the power of Your anger. But I believe there is a nation who will experience the great fear that is due You."

This time I didn't look at Jesus. I just continued:

"You have taught us to number our days and we know that with that has come great wisdom to us, often prophetic wisdom. So, we call upon You, Lord. We call upon You to relent. We trust You to have compassion on our nation very soon.

We expect You to satisfy us in the morning with Your unfailing love, so we can sing for joy and be glad all of our days, no longer in bondage."

I didn't look up, but I heard Jesus clear his throat, as if He was trying to say something to me. I was almost done so I wasn't going to let Him keep me from my glory, from my desire, from what I expect the God of Heaven to do in our nation very, very soon.

"You will make us as glad for as many days as You have afflicted us, You will even redeem the many years by which we have seen trouble. Instead, finally, we will see Joy. We look forward to Your deeds being shown to us, Your servants, with Your splendor to our children. May Your favor rest upon us and our nation Lord, our God. Establish the hard work of our hands. Yes, establish the hard work of the hands of us, Your people and Your nation."

Finally, I looked up at Jesus who motioned to me, asking me if I remembered what God said to Moses at the end of the passage that I like to joke about.

"I don't remember that, Jesus, no."

Then Jesus, again looking solemnly at me said, "When Moses complained to the Lord about not getting what he wanted, God said to him, 'enough of this Moses, quit speaking to me about this subject!'"[6]

It was obvious, and a little embarrassing, what Jesus was saying to me. But I didn't care. The other disciples were too stupid to know what Jesus was saying, and He was too foolish to understand this incredible moment in history, when the Romans could be overthrown.

Eventually He would listen to me. He had to. Oh, why do I keep hoping in this man, only to have my hopes dashed?

At that moment he turned to the other disciples and then asked them the most bizarre question. He asked, "Who do people say I am?"

My idiot colleagues answered all kinds of stupid remarks like, 'John the Baptist come back to life', or 'Elijah or Jeremiah' or some of the other prophets of so long ago.[7]

And then Peter stood up, cleaned off his robe and he soberly addressed Jesus. I was actually kind of impressed with Peter. That is, until he opened his mouth.

He said, "You are the Christ, the Son of the Living God!"

Immediately I thought, "What stupidity!"

And then Jesus surprised all of us by saying, "Blessed are you Simon, son of Jonah, for this was not revealed to you by man but by My Father in heaven."[8]

"What?!?!" I wanted to scream. But Jesus kept going.

"And I tell you that your new name is Peter, and on this rock, I will build my church and the Gates of Hell will not overcome it."[9]

He went on to mention some more accolades on behalf of Peter, but I was getting sick to my stomach listening to this nonsense.

And then Jesus warned us. He said not to tell anyone He was the Christ.[10]

"I guess not!" I wanted to scream. "I don't want You to be a religious head. I want You to be our political head."

February 5th, Sunday Morning, Arlington VA

The last two weeks for Issy and I have been very busy. The campaigns are cranking up. Since this incredibly unique year had no challengers to either party, they both started their campaigning early.

We're off to the races, so to speak. Both Issy's candidate and mine are traveling nearly every weekend, and often during the week, making campaign stops, which we periodically participate in, depending upon the contacts our respective teams expect us to make.

This time I was out of town when I read our passage. After I read, I said, "Honey, I've got to go. We have an early morning, but as I read this passage, I couldn't help wondering what it must have been like for Jesus with such diverse people around Him. He had the loving John, the doubting Thomas, the ever-faithful Peter, the traitor Judas. What a group."

"I wonder that too, darling," Issy answered as we said goodbye.

---

[1] Mark 8:27a

[2] Deuteronomy 3:26a

[3] Numbers 20:10-12

[4] Psalm 90

[5] Remember, the quote of Psalm 90 is according to Judas, not strictly according to Scripture.

[6] Deuteronomy 3:26b

[7] Matthew 16:14

[8] Matthew 16:17

[9] Matthew 16:18

[10] Matthew 16:20

Chapter 11

February 9th, Thursday Afternoon, FBI Headquarters

Pete was in my office, and he was steaming. "I don't want to go into the Cage, Jack."

I nodded, "Fire away."

"First, how did you find out about Clyde Smith being the hacker?" he demanded.

"Pete," I said, stretching out my hands. "Need to know, baby. Need to know."

"Well, I've got 'the boss' and three other perps, Jack. So, give me the freedom I need to properly investigate this."

"What are you talking about, Pete?"

"All of these perps are religious fruitcakes, Jack. They are probably all dirty and I intend to go deep and figure out what they are up to. You need to let me get to the bottom of it."

I was still nodding, but only to placate him as I continued to listen.

"I want to surveil the Presidential candidate's employee who communicated with our hacker," he said.

I'm afraid he noticed me wince.

"You're not going to tie my hands anymore, Jack. You'll keep getting your reports, but something funny is going on here, and it needs to stop before it is out of control."

"Before what is out of control, Pete?" I asked with as much patience as I could. But I knew what was coming. He had already told me. His prejudice against religious people was dominating his judgment.

"Jack, in our business, coincidences don't just happen."

I nodded in agreement.

He went on, "The only reason I am huffing and puffing at this, is because too many paths have crossed that in the course of normal events should not have."

"So, what are you guesstimating is the level of infiltration, Pete? Who are our perps, what are their crimes and what do they want?"

Pete withdrew his notepad and gave me the lowdown. I took some notes.

"Did you know, Jack, that the Religion Consultant of each of the two candidates. . ."

"Are husband and wife?" I finished his question. "Yeah, I know. It caused quite a ruckus up here when we vetted them over a year ago. They have impeccable records and both candidates are aware of the potential conflict of interest and they trust them. I wouldn't, but they do."

"I'll come back to those two, Jack, because they cross paths with Perps #1 and #2."

"You've started numbering them?" I wanted to laugh.

"Yes, and as of now, I count at least five."

"At least five perps? How did we go from one hacker to five perps, Pete?" I was incredulous. "Is there anything inherent in their activities which make any of them suspect of criminal charges? Anything?"

"No," Pete said a little disappointed. "I mean, besides the hacker, no."

"I'm just reading between the lines here, Pete, but you sound like you are saying, 'There is nothing in their activities which make them suspect, but because their tracks touch, I am bothered and I think they are dirty.'"

Pete nodded his head. "Once we learned about the wife meeting the hacker on a recent campaign trip, we looked into the husband. And guess who he's just met with?"

"Surprise me, Pete." I said.

"A Christian looney-tune from Macon, just outside of Warner Robins, near the hacker."

"I know where Macon is, Pete. So, you are going to charge this other person, with what? Guilt by proximity?"

He ignored me and continued. "I am calling him Perp #3. We briefly looked into this guy. On the surface he seems to be a mild-mannered regular guy, but he was fired by MPTU under suspicious circumstances. In addition, Jack, he is a 'Christian' guy who comes to D.C. once a month to pray with Congressmen (and women), Senators, and their staff. He is, apparently, very well liked, has lots of open doors, and is making inroads on both sides of the aisle."

"So, what?! Maybe he's lobbying for something. And what do you mean, Pete, 'both sides of the aisle?' How does he get away with that? Does he lie to one side or the other or both?"

Pete cocked an eyebrow and said, "No, Jack. We've checked his website and his social media. He claims to, 'not care about their politics,' if you can believe that."

I sat up now, scribbling furiously and mumbled. "Who comes to D.C. and doesn't care about politics?"

Pete said, "Here's a quote from one of his posts, 'I don't give a rip about their politics, I'm merely there to pray for them, bear their burdens, then they cast them on God, Who gives them peace.' Some mumbo jumbo and lies like that."

I sat back, thinking about my old mom. Pete started to speak again, but I needed to think. I held up a hand.

I wrote down my mom's initials and then the question, "What do you pray?" I remembered her telling me she prays for people by burdening, no, bearing. . .peace. . .casting. I don't recall, but some things like that.

I looked at Pete and said, "Clearly the guy is a loon, Pete. But we have a lot of loons on the Hill, so what?"

Pete continued, "Well, it appears he met with Perp #5, this last Friday night for dinner."

"If by #5 you mean the husband, Jude, who works for the other candidate, why is this an issue? They're both in the Holy-Roller business." I said. "As of right now, I can tell you, I completely disagree with you assigning Perp's #3, #4, and #5. I think you've flipped, my old friend."

We were both steaming mad. I needed to reel this in so we could, as a team, get to the bottom of the hacking. So I asked, "Tell me about the Counterintelligence (CI) guy you are calling Perp #2. Is he who led you to Perp #1?"

"Yes, and as you know, he made direct contact, a few weeks ago with Perp #4 and has been in periodic text/email contact since then."

"Wait, wait, wait, Pete. Quit calling the wife and the husband Perps #4 and #5. I can't believe you, man."

I stopped and shook my head. The more Pete talked, the more this sounded like the Keystone Cops. "Tell me about Perp #1. Have you decided who he is?"

He just nodded his head and showed me the photo of a very beautiful middle-aged woman.

"He is a she?" I asked, impressed. I gave a long low whistle, and said, "We don't haul them in just because their gorgeous, old buddy."

That's when Pete pulled out a Criminal Rap Sheet as long as my arm, with what looked like Supplemental Complaint Reports, for each entry.

"Who is this woman?" I asked.

"She is a pastor of what is today called a mega church, and I believe, Jack, she is trying to insert herself into both parties so that by this November she can sell her influence for personal financial gain."

"Can't she just be a good looking. . ." I didn't even finish the sentence.

He pushed over the Criminal Rap Sheet, which read:

- Husband's Death, Suspicious
- Business Partner's Death, Suspicious
- Mother-in-law's Death, Suspicious
- 3 Ministry Partner's Deaths, Suspicious
  - These last three left her in sole ownership of her T.V. stations, her radio stations and as a result, her offshore holdings quadrupled.
  - There is a fourth ministry partner, but he is in hiding, so now all of the moneys from his hundreds of foreign churches go directly to her. Apparently, this also gives her some approval to change her title from 'Pastor' to 'Apostle, Pastor.'

"I don't know, Jack, I don't get it."

I looked over the list again and then asked, "Pete, what connects her with the other Perps?"

"Perp #2 is the connection. He seems to be in most, if not all the locations, when somebody mysteriously dies. Plus, he attends her church, an hour and a half away from his home. And this is Georgia. There are tons of other churches he can go to. Anyway, he is in contact with her much more than a typical parishioner would be. He lives a lifestyle way above his monthly income, and as you know, he works with hi-tech computers at Warner Robins Air Force Base, in the Counterintelligence unit."

I shook my head back and forth trying to take it all in.

"He's the centerpiece, Jack."

We sat there not saying anything for a few minutes. And then I asked, "Okay, Pete, say you're right. What do you want to do?"

He started to open his mouth and I said, "And don't tell me surveil. We are not going to get ourselves embroiled in surveilling anyone's campaign."

"So," I went on, "Where do we go from here?"

I could tell I had just taken the wind out of his sails, but I didn't care.

"Well," he said, "Since you nixed surveilling, let us begin by asking discreet questions about our perps."

"And who are you calling your perps?"

He started to hold up five fingers and I stopped him. "No, your Perps #3, #4, and #5 are not perps. Get that out of your head, unless you find something concrete."

"I've gotta ask questions, Jack. Or I can't discover anything."

"Discreet questions?" I asked.

Pete sat there and didn't move for a long time. Then he let out a long sigh. That was his tell, his body language which told me he'd agreed to my request.

"Discreet," he promised.

I lifted my finger slightly and he took a breath.

"Pete," I said, "besides the CI guy from Warner Robins, what makes you think any of them are dirty?"

"A hunch," he nearly spit the words out. And he repeated them, "A hunch."

I shook my head.

I don't know what else Pete said; I was busy thinking about my meeting earlier in the day with my latest clandestine recruit, pimple-faced Billy, whom I was growing to trust, more and more.

Finally, Pete left, and I picked up the file Billy and I had walked through.

Same Day, Earlier, FBI Headquarters

It was just after lunch when Billy entered my office and sat down.

"First let me ask you Billy, did you get your first two paychecks?"

"Holy smokes, yes, sir! You doubled my tithe."

I have no idea what that meant, but he was happy and that was what I wanted.

He went on, "But how did you know my bank account information?"

"Is that a serious question, Billy?" I asked. "We're the FBI, for crying out loud."

"So where are we at with our do-nothing hacker?"

"And influencer," Billy added.

That got my attention. This was new. "And influencer?" I queried.

"Yes, but may I ask something?"

"Sure."

"The last time I was here, I brought you the Warner Robins Air Force Base Counterintelligence worker, Clyde Smith's head on a platter. I expected the gig to be up and for you to take him into custody."

"You were surprised he stayed on the job, Billy?"

"Yeah. I mean, yes, sir."

"Why do you think I left him on the job?

"The only thing I could imagine was there is a bigger fish out there that you are hoping he leads us to."

"We're gonna make an agent out of you yet, son. So, tell me why you are calling this guy an influencer now, and can you tell me on whose behalf he is trying to influence? His own or someone else's?"

Billy looked at me trying to be as serious as he could, "You know boss, sir, each time we've talked about this operation, I get the feeling you know a lot more than you're telling me. May I ask, why?"

I smiled big at him. "Billy, you can call me Sir, you can call me Boss, you can even call me Dude, like a lot of your age likes to say. And do you know why?"

He just shook his head, and I went on, "Because I trust you to do the absolute best job for me, so long as you are not distracted."

He smiled broadly, and I felt bad having to put him in his place, but he needed to learn this lesson in a way he would never forget it.

I put on my hard sounding, first sergeant voice, "But listen to me clearly, you snot-nosed geek. If I'm not telling you something, there is a reason behind it. Now I need your exceptional work ethic and I need your very precise capabilities. But I need your focus on the things I direct you to, and nothing else. You are to trust me that when you need to know something, I will tell you."

His mouth tightened then quivered slightly, and then tightened again. I let him struggle for another moment, and then added.

"I'm very proud of you, son. I'm very proud of you, Billy, and I need you. So, keep busting your tail for me, okay?"

"Yes, sir," he said solemnly.

"Now tell me why you are also calling him an influencer."

"I noticed he tried a new cyberattack. He has started to do what is called an Eavesdropping Attack."

"Is that as obvious as it sounds? Is he trying to figure out what your religion consultant is doing?"

Billy nodded.

"And then what does he do when he grasps what the consultant is thinking or saying."

"Well," Billy scratched his head.

"Don't think, just speak." I said, a little more roughly than I wanted to.

Billy began speaking immediately. "He's not listening to everything on the Religion Consultant's computer. He is only focusing on religious contacts who are in her database, which seem to have advice for her, but I don't see where she

83

has ever asked for advice from them and in addition, I don't see where she added them into her database. I think he put them all in there, not her. And now he's striking up conversations with these friendlies."

"Friendlies?" I asked.

"I've been watching some spy movies," Billy confessed with an embarrassed grin.

I tried not to smile and asked him to tell me about the emails.

"Nothing to tell. He's talking a lot of holy-roller God-talk, as if he is trying to convince Issy of the various contact's credibility by saying things like, 'I've been praying and God has told me. . .' a couple of them even added, 'praying all night long.'"

I lifted my finger and he quieted down. "So, let me get this right, Billy, our Perp, Clyde, is sending emails to Issy, as if he is this or that particular contact in her database?

"Yes, sir."

"Can you tell if she's buying it?"

"Hard to say, sir. I get the feeling these emails are meant to intimidate her into believing their might be something mutually beneficial in a business or campaign relationship with them."

"Fat chance of that happening," I said. "I have read her work history. The woman is tough as nails."

And then I sat back and wondered if Pete's concerns weren't so far out of bounds. He may not have the right perps, but the wacko attitude of these religious contacts is real enough.

It was all making my head spin, so I asked, "Billy, do people actually believe stuff like that?"

"Yes, sir." he said.

"But, Billy, isn't that a little silly. I mean, how does God speak? In an audible voice?"

Billy looked like he wasn't sure how to answer and I just realized I may have insulted him. So, I added, "Billy, my mom says she talks to God, and she obviously talks audibly but I've never asked her how God answers her."

He looked as if he were weighing his words. "First let me tell you; I read the tone of this guy's words and knowing what we do about him, I'd say he is lying, which means he hasn't heard from God."

"Safe answer," I said, "Now, I really am curious, so tell me, how does God answer when you pray to Him?"

He took a deep breath and said, "I have heard from God often, boss. . ."

This sent up a gargantuan red flag in my head.

Billy continued, "But I have never heard God speak audibly. . ."

"Whew, I'm glad for that detail." I thought.

"Usually when God speaks it is by Him prompting my spirit, my guts, or my conscience about a particular subject. But I know me, sir, and I want to verify, if you will, that what I 'heard' is really from God, so I check Scripture, the Bible, and see if what's in His Word confirms or contradicts what I think I'm sensing is from the Lord."

"I confess, Billy, a lot of that went over my head."

"Sir, if a person has a relationship with Christ, it begins to make sense."

And then he stopped.

"Sir, a bad-guy is trying to pull the wool over the eyes of a very decent staffer in my office. That's the bottom line."

"Alright, Billy, I'll accept that answer, for now."

"Thank you, sir."

Chapter 12

February 14th, Tuesday, Atlanta GA

"Why are you calling me at this time of day?!" That was what I wanted to scream into the phone, but was not able to because Sister Woodard was taking me to my seat in her salon.

Instead I clicked on the button which sent an automatic message, and I typed in 7pm.

Hopefully that idiot Clyde can wait till then.

"I hope that wasn't nothin' serious, Sister Mortenson?"

I gave a little correction through my throat, which she picked up on immediately, "I mean, Apostle, Pastor Mortenson."

Ever since my unfortunate business partner went missing and left all his churches to me, we have changed my title, so it is consistent with my position, namely, leading hundreds of churches.

Everyone still calls me pastor, but I am trying, one at a time, to get the lowlier, simpler people to correct themselves, but many of them are just so slow.

I've decided that this woman is such a loudmouth, if I can get her to call me Apostle, Pastor Mortenson, I can then introduce it to the church, and they will follow suit.

Old Lady Woodard is slow on the uptake. She kept talking. "I shore do love our church, Mrs. . .Apost. . .Past. . .Ma'am."

I smiled at her, somewhat condescendingly, which she probably didn't notice anyway.

"Are you getting plenty of business from us?" I changed the subject.

"Oh, I surely am. I've had to hire three new full-time associates, ever since you announced it from your pulpit you were comin' to see me."

"Great," I said. I'll just look and see if her giving has improved also.

I smiled. I didn't want to talk, so I just shut her up by saying, "If you don't mind, I'm going to just rest my eyes while you do. . .umm, what you do so well."

"I surely will, and if you falls asleep I'll let you snore, like you did last time."

At that she laughed and inwardly I snarled but said nothing.

An hour and a half later I left Sister Woodard, two hundred and fifty dollars lighter, but with beautiful nails on hands and feet, and with some fresh quaffing of the hair. I loved it.

At seven o'clock on the button I called Clyde, who had made some excuse to his wife to extricate himself from her.

"What do you want, Clyde?"

"I had lunch with Dr. Dale today. He is the one who goes to D.C. once a month and has made contact with one of our friends."

"Keep going," I said, reading my emails.

"I decided you need to know more about him, since I dropped your name, talked finances with him and began the process of drawing him in."

"How does he get his financing now?" I demanded.

"He trusts God," said Clyde.

To which I guffawed.

"I'm serious, I asked him the same thing and at first he replied, 'I don't know how I live,' And then he got embarrassed and said, 'Of course I know. God places it upon men's hearts to donate, and they do.' Which I'll admit, sounded like a holy-roller line. So, I went a different route."

"I asked him, 'How many people give to your ministry, monthly?'"

"He looked a little suspiciously at me, so I said, 'I represent a ministry which likes to help other ministries.' And that seemed to appease him."

"So, what do you want from me, Clyde. Do you want me to give him five or ten thousand dollars? Or should it be more?"

"No, no, no, ma'am. That would be way too much. I looked his ministry finances up online, and the government department I hacked says his annual donations are under fifty-thousand dollars per year."

"Wait, Clyde. Are you saying this man is in our governmental halls, with our elected officials, praying with them, sharing his brand of Christianity, encouraging them, and he brings in less in one year than we pay in utilities, in the same timeframe?

"Yes, ma'am," said Clyde with an air of superiority.

"Did he tell you how many people give to his ministry monthly?"

"Yes, ma'am. And that's the good news."

Clyde paused as if to build up a crescendo. "Speak, Clyde, speak!"

"Nine people," he said.

I gave him a low whistle, because I kept hearing more and more for our potential with this man. Besides his funding, I liked what I heard about his dismissal from the university. Depending upon the circumstances, this could make him very vulnerable in our hands. After all, he won't want this information out in the public.

"Tell me about lunch," I snapped.

Clyde is so slow. I wondered if it were possible for him to talk any slower.

"Let me tell you what I learned," he said.

I was getting frustrated with this conversation because it wasn't moving fast enough. I wonder if I could teach him to speak faster. I decided Clyde had ninety-seconds before I hung up on him.

"He meets with people from both sides of the aisle and has relationships with both the elected officials as well as their staffs."

Clyde dutifully paused, so I could think through what this meant.

After a long fifteen seconds I made sure he was still on the phone, and then told him to keep going.

"I started asking him about specific people and he clammed up, but I think he was just being a tease, not wanting to give away too much, too soon, especially if we might be a source of income for him. I think he was just showing me enough of his hand to keep me interested."

"So, what makes you think he has influence, Clyde?"

"Well, of course, I had to put my interrogation hat on, without tipping my hand to him."

I never know how much of this stuff to believe, coming from Clyde. While I think he's an oaf, he might actually have some brains. So, I let him keep talking without interrupting.

"The first thing I did, boss, was to analyze the breadth of his contacts, which seems to reach into every facet of elected officialdom."

"Next, I squeezed out of him anecdotal stories I could analyze for authenticity. And it was the stories he told about the congressmen and senators which made me think he is everything we want and would give us all of it, for the right price."

Clyde paused as if I was to congratulate him, but I simply said. "Okay, super spy, do you mind sharing the anecdotes with me?"

"Oh, uhm, yes," he struggled to say.

"The first story I can relate is about a Congressman he went to visit. Apparently, the Congressman was in another appointment, but when Dr. Dale left his office, out a side door the Congressman came running, calling his name, just to meet with him."

"Really?" I asked doubtfully.

"Yes, ma'am."

"And he just told you this freely?"

"Well, I may have had to use a few counter-espionage information gathering techniques, but, yes. He told me freely. Let me tell you another."

"Dr. Dale told me about a Congressman who wanted to meet with him so badly, he excused himself from a Committee meeting he was in, to come and talk with him."

"And on the heels of that, he told me about a Senator who passed up a closed-door meeting at the White House to spend time with him."

Clyde started to speak again, and I told him to "Shush." Which, of course, he did.

This was good stuff and if Clyde was as good at ferreting out information as he seemed to be, we could have a goldmine here.

I started to think this contact may be the way into these Religion Consultants' lives. I chuckled to my devious self, tapping a sharpened nail on my recently capped front teeth and re-engaged listening to Clyde.

"Well, he didn't tell me exactly, of course, because it was our first real meeting, and I think he was checking out the monetary considerations we would be open to giving him. . ."

"Yes?" I had to spur him on again.

"But I think he was hinting to me about Congressmen and women with family relations problems."

"Like what, Clyde, like what?" I wanted to shout at him but was forcing myself to be patient.

"Well," he said slowly.

If Clyde was near me, I would have kicked him or punched him.

"He hinted towards families who must have drinking problems or something else real bad, because the Congressman often sleeps in his office."

"Shut up!" I cried out. I wanted to think.

But he kept going, completely oblivious. ". . .One of our consultants is wanting to have regular contact with him again, and it sounded to me like they are working out an exchange of information sortie."

"A what?" I asked, irritably.

"Oh, I'm sorry, boss. That's military speak for determining how they would clandestinely pass information back and forth to each other."

He paused and then asked, "Do you know what clandestine means, ma'am?"

"Shut up, you fool," I said as harshly as I could.

After a few moments I said, "Clyde, are you embellishing any of this?"

There was a long pause as if he didn't know what embellished meant, so instead of insulting him, which I really wanted to do, I rephrased the question.

"Are you making any of this up?"

"Of course not!" He almost tripped over the words. "I couldn't make this stuff up."

"That I believe, Clyde. That I believe."

"Thank you, ma'am," he said.

What a moron; thanking me for insulting him.

"One more thing, ma'am."

"Yes," I said as patiently as I could.

"He's back in D.C. next week and already has plans to meet with our. . ."

"Our, you-know-who, right?"

"Umm, yes, ma'am." He couldn't help himself, so he went on. "Umm, you and I are still meeting at your office in less than two weeks, so I'll try to have an Operation Judas status report by then."

I shook my head and spoke. "Got it," I said, and then hung up.

Same Day, FBI Headquarters

I was working late and was ready to head home when the eyes-only communique from a Homeland Security Listening Post came across my secured comms line.

OPERATION: JUDAS I.

Surveillance Report:

14, February 7:01 pm till 7:37 pm

Transcript:

      Attached

Summary:

Since we are surveilling Perp #2, we recorded his telephone conversation in evening with Perp #1. And we were on hand when he had lunch with Dr. Dale Riley (Perp #3), but there was too much noise for our team to hear all details. What they did hear, though, seemed to correspond with the telephone conversation.

Distribution:

Classified, Director Pete Beecham

Copy, FBI, Eyes Only: Jack Jones

I skimmed the transcript and sat by my phone, jacket in hand and waited for the call.

Sixty seconds later it came.

But there was no welcome, no hello, no nothin' just, "I told you they were dirty, Jack. Just a little more grunt work on our part, and we'll have enough information to nail those two Religion Consultants, also. With a little luck, they'll all do some serious jail time."

I didn't say anything.

And he continued. "In fact, I suspect the consultants will be going to jail, along with the prayer-guy and the two controllers, Clyde and the Pastor, whom we surveilled tonight."

"May I make one request, Pete?"

"Ask it, Jack. But I can't promise to give it to you."

"Fair enough. I only ask that you not haul in those you are calling Perps #3, #4, or #5, Dr. Dale, Issy or her husband Jude, not for questioning, or anything, until you have something solid on them. And. . ."

He gave a sharp intake of breath, loud enough for me to hear over the phone, and I knew what he was thinking.

"Okay, I have a second request." I just kept talking so he wouldn't interrupt me.

"I merely want to be in the loop, so I know what it is you have on them, before you haul them in as criminals."

He was silent for a long time. Finally I heard his sigh which told me he had acquiesced to my request.

"Also, Pete, I'm sure you plan to, but make your next report on Dr. Dale. I'm not comfortable calling him a Perp, but I agree with you that having lunch with the CI-Guy warrants some investigation."

"Finally," I asked very calmly, "Did you attach any significance to the name, 'Operation Judas' that your Perp supplied us?"

"No, why?" he asked.

"I don't know, Pete, but I think we need to find out." And I hung up.

Chapter 13

Something has changed in the narratives Issy and I are reading. The gospel truths as seen through this harmonized view, has caused something to pop out like lightning, especially in Matthew's account.

In the Bible study aid I have been using, R. A. Torrey, while referring to Peter, asks us to consider, "Do we think we know better than He [God], what He ought to do?"

We read, "From that time on Jesus began to explain. . ."[1]

October A.D. 29, Christ's Predictions & Peter Rebuked

Something around us had changed and it is obvious with the words we started hearing from Jesus.

I didn't like His tone. It was too eerie, even scary. But he started to speak very frankly to us about events which He seemed to have no control over. It sounded like these events would overtake Him, and, I supposed, us too.

No, I didn't like this at all. "This is not what I signed on for," I kept thinking.

These people are such morons. Finally I said, "If this is going to take place in Jerusalem,[2] then why don't we just stay away from Jerusalem?"

A few of the men agreed with me, especially Thomas.[3] He didn't want to die with Jesus either.

I was still confused about something. How did Jesus know all these things will happen to Him?

There was something He said that did make sense, though. He said, "I will be rejected by the elders, chief priests and teachers of the law."[4]

To me that made sense because of how he had recently insulted them. But then the next thing He said made me think He was just being melodramatic.

He said, "They will make me suffer many things and they will kill me."[5]

Really, this was about all I could handle, until He made his next prediction, and then I knew He was a loon. He said, "On the third day after my death, I will be raised to life."[6]

I looked at Peter and raised my eyebrows, which I hope communicated, "Peter, this guy just isn't right."

I think it did, because Peter immediately took Jesus aside and lowering his booming voice began to rebuke Jesus, saying, "Never Lord, never will this happen to You!"[7]

And then Jesus, always ready to say the wrong thing at the wrong time, rebuked Peter right back, but Jesus' words were brutal.

He said to Peter, "Get behind me, sataN, you are a stumbling block to me; you do not have in mind the things of God, but the things of men."[8]

We all heard it and we were all stunned. Peter was one of Jesus' favorites. But for Him to talk to Peter like that, something was wrong. Something was changing in this little band of ours. Perhaps something had already changed.

Andrew pulled Peter aside and sat him down.

But Jesus wasn't done. I mean, He was done rebuking Peter. And, thank goodness, because I don't think Peter could endure that again, not that I cared. I was caring less and less for these men.

There was another crowd with us. There was always a crowd. Anyway, Jesus pulled the crowd together and maneuvered them alongside us. He was within arm's length of Peter and lovingly put a hand on Peter's big shoulders and said to all of us, "If you are going to follow me, you must deny yourself."[9]

He then squeezed Peter's shoulder. It was a very tender moment, even for the big stupid fisherman, for he looked up into Jesus' eyes and Jesus said to him, but also to all of us, "If you want to save your life, be careful, for you will lose it, but if you are willing to lose your life, for My sake, you will save it."[10]

I stood in the back of the crowd and pulled a bread roll out of my bag. "This is crazy-talk," I said to no one in particular. "This is crazy."

But Jesus kept talking. He was talking about getting rich, losing one's soul, and being ashamed of Him (which I often was lately). He called us a sinful and adulterous generation. I decided to stop listening. I couldn't handle anymore.

And then I heard Him say one last thing. He said that some of us there with Him, "would not taste death before we see the kingdom of God come with power."[11]

I just looked down in disgust and said, "Sure Jesus. I'll believe it when I see it. You've had plenty of opportunities to show the power of God by taking control of our nation. And You've refused."

February 19th, Sunday Morning, Arlington VA

"What must this have been like for these followers of Jesus, babe?"

"How do you mean, Jude?"

"Well, every time I read this account I can't help but think these men were just walking the streets of ancient Israel, and without them knowing, their circumstances were changing and Jesus was trying to prepare them for things that would happen in the near future."

"Are you're saying these guys had no clue?"

"Exactly, Issy. Tons of things were going on around them and they couldn't see it."

I paused because it was obvious Issy was contemplating something. And then she said, "So, a surprising challenge might be, asking God to make me aware of what is going on around me."

She was still thinking and then went on. "And an unusual promise would be that even though I do not see what is going on, I can trust the Lord to prepare me."

"Wow," she continued, more to herself than to me. "The job-related directive can be very challenging too, without telling you what is on my mind, of course."

I chuckled and kissed her gently for always being protective of our employment commitments.

And then I said, "I am also fascinated about how life must have been changing around these first century men and women without them realizing it."

I looked at Issy and then said, "Baby, things could be swirling around you and me and we might not be seeing it. Let me pray my promise and challenge."

Issy and I bowed and clasped hands. "Father," I started, "I am so grateful for Your Son's example here on earth with His disciples. What a wonderful promise to know that no matter what is spinning towards Issy and me, or away from us, You are in control. And Lord, I'm challenged to trust You, for whatever You have up Your sleeve for me and Issy, whether we see it or not. In the Name of Your Son we pray, Amen."

I looked at my watch and then at Issy who seductively raised her eyebrows at me.

We got to church a few minutes late and I didn't see Harold anywhere. I hate to admit it, but it was sure a relief to not see him.

As we left church it was still bitter cold, so we put thick gloves on, which kept us from holding hands the way we like to. Instead, Issy grabbed my arm and leaned her bundled-up head into my shoulder.

As we trudged on, I told Issy I think I need to keep our pastor in the loop about the little flair-up with Harold.

She agreed, and added, "But not in a tattling way, just in a, 'Pastor, I want to keep you in the loop,' sort of a way."

I agreed and shot off an email to him as soon as we reached home. I wanted to send it while we were walking, but I needed to keep my gloves on.

Shortly after arriving home, a text came through. It read, "Jude, this is Dale. I forgot to tell you, I'm going to be in D.C. this Tuesday and Wednesday. Are you up for some Mexican food again?"

I told Issy about the text and she asked me to remind her who this guy is. I told her, "He's the guy who comes to D.C. each month to pray with elected officials, and often the staffers."

I invited her to come along which she was interested in doing, "If we do not do Mexican." I knew what she was thinking, "If we do Mexican food, you'll do the fumigating of my clothes."

---

[1] Matthew 16:21a

[2] Matthew 16:21m

[3] John 11:16

[4] Mark 8:31m

[5] Luke 19:22a

[6] Matthew 16:21e

[7] Matthew 16:22

[8] Matthew 16:23

[9] Luke 9:23a

[10] Luke 9:24, partially paraphrased

[11] Mark 9:1

Chapter 14

February 20th, Monday Morning, FBI Headquarters

I was livid at Pete and he knew it. "I don't know how you came up with this. But I told you to keep me in the loop before you made operational decisions."

I was just getting started and I continued, "Listen to me clearly, Pete, you do not get to surveil the two candidates' employees. Do you understand?"

I paused and he didn't respond fast enough so I said, more loudly, "Do you?"

He nodded his head, a tiny bit embarrassed.

I decided to give in and said, "Because of the Presidential campaign, I don't want any names used in your reporting. Go to Perps #1 through #5 on all correspondence. Got it?"

He nodded.

And I continued. "Again, I don't know how you came up with this information, and I don't want to know, but what are your plans when your Perps #3, #4 and #5 have dinner together?"

"Look," he said, getting angry at me now, "If you are not going to let me surveil them, I have no way of getting on the record exactly what they are plotting."

I shook my head at my friend.

"Observe, that's all, Pete. Observe."

I got up to indicate the meeting was over, but he remained in his seat. After a moment he got up, and without a handshake left my office.

I called my receptionist, "Grace, I want to see Billy as soon as possible."

February 21st, Tuesday Evening, Arlington VA

I introduced Issy and Dr. Dale and we sat in a booth at the P. F. Chang's restaurant a few blocks from our home in Arlington. They initially sat us down by a window, looking out onto Glebe Road, but it was too cold there, so I asked if we could be reseated.

As they reseated us, I chuckled and told Issy and Dale, "Look at all those others moving to different tables. I guess it took us to be courageous enough to move so others could ask for different seats, too."

We all looked but Issy's eyes picked up something I had missed.

We immediately ordered appetizers. Issy and I got the Lettuce Wraps with their great homemade sauce and Dale asked for the Edamame which I normally don't get because they are salty. However I was glad we got them. They weren't as salty as I remembered. Actually, they were excellent.

We had a sweet time of fellowship, which is what I was hoping. I knew that during dinner we'd be able to talk shop, ministry and otherwise. Right now, I was just interested in getting to know this man, this servant.

The main courses came and Issy's was the Kung Pao Chicken, with chili sauce and peanuts, but no onions and peppers. We both eat that way, no peppers and no onions, unless it's Mexican food (which we don't do too often because of the Fajita-Fear-Factor). I had the Fried Rice, always a favorite of mine and Dale had something new on the menu. It was called Korean Bulgogi Steak and it looked wonderful. The Mongolian glaze looked like something we could have had for dessert. I think I'll get it the next time.

As we started to talk about our ministries, Dale reached into his pocket and pulled out a small card which he slid across the table. It was postcard weight and about four inches by five inches.

Immediately behind us a skinny customer pushed back his chair, knocking into mine. He seemed to stand up rather quickly and turn around, so I maneuvered as best I could to get out of his way. I had to lean over my table and that caused me to drag my arm through my Hot and Sour Soup. I can't say I got grumpy, but for a moment it was an awkward situation.

Come to think of it, he never came back to his seat.

After the interruption, Dale simply said with a smile, "This is my version of P.C. which is a prayer card, as you can tell. I bring these to everyone when I am in the city."

Issy and I leaned in together reading it.

Dale continued, "These men and women may be brilliant doctors or lawyers, but they're not theologians, so I always make sure I leave them a card which shows them how I am praying for them."

Issy nodded and asked, "What kind of responses do you get from these folks."

"Oh, Issy," he said, with genuine pain in his eyes, "My heart goes out to these men and women, and their staff."

"How so?" she encouraged.

And then Dale sat back, clearly thinking about what he could say. We waited patiently until he leaned into us and spoke.

"Of course, like you two, I'm careful to protect sources and descriptive information, so let me just share a few generic stories."

He now smiled humbly and said, "The pictures in my mind of these folks are all so precious. These are regular people on Capitol Hill. You know that as well as anyone."

He went on, "A famous old guy who is now in heaven, Leonard Ravenhill, used to say, 'A person who is intimate with God. . .'"

"Will never be intimidated by man," I finished.

"Exactly," said Dale, with a smile.

And then he went on. "My job, and the reason I can get into all these offices, is not because I want to fix the way some of them think. When I get to D.C. I truly do not care about their politics."

"My job is to help them bear their burdens by[1] teaching them to cast the burden on Him who cares for them,[2] and then I watch them receive some peace, which completely transcends their understanding,[3] and transcends mine for that matter."

He was speaking slowly, but we remained silent. We didn't want to interrupt.

He confessed, "It is amazing to me, Issy and Jude, how God uses me, in spite of me. I sum up what I do like this, I encourage folk through the simple act of bearing their burdens in prayer."

"Hmm," I said.

"Let me tell you of the things I pray for."

We nodded and he began, "I always stop into these offices, even if I do not have an appointment with the Congressman or Senator, because I want to leave them a new Prayer Card."

"Well, I have a very good relationship this particular Congressman and when I stopped he was in a meeting with someone, so, like always, I dropped the card with his scheduler and left, heading down the hallway to another office."

"And then all of a sudden, this man came charging out of his office calling my name. This guy just wanted to spend a few minutes in prayer, which we did, right there in the hallway. It was so sweet."

"Sounds like it," Issy said.

"A few months ago," Dale went on. "I had an appointment with a Congressman who got tied up in a committee meeting, so the staff who are always busting their tails to help, escorted me to his committee hearing, since a break was coming up.

Dale sat there and chuckled a bit to himself. He was obviously remembering something and then he shared it with us.

"This Congressman came into the room, during his Committee meeting break and said, 'Dale, I am so concerned for my family as I see the ways things are going in our nation.' To which I replied, 'Congressman, it's only going to get worse.' He looked at me like I had just punched him, and then I explained, 'Paul said things would be worse before the coming of the Lord.' But then, clearly by the grace of God, I added, 'And that's why God has you here, Congressman. God knows you will fervently pray for this country in ways very few can.' I was able to encourage him, in a back-door sort of way."

Issy and I sat there listening and contemplating what Dale was saying and the precious ministry this sweet man has.

He went on, "I don't always get to meet with the Congressmen and women or Senators. Recently I was on my way to a Senator's office, whom I have tried to meet with for months, but just before I got there he got a call from the Capitol and had to attend a closed door briefing of some kind."

"So what do you do in those cases, Dale?" Issy asked.

"I pray with the staff," he said. "When they let me," he added.

He then told us about staff he has prayed for, including families of staff with major dysfunctions.

I said, more in passing than as a question, "It must take a while before people can trust you."

He smiled real big and said, "Yep, and they often give a genuine sigh when they realize I don't want anything from them."

"I also pray for and with people I meet in the halls. I'm thinking of the guy who cleans the men's restrooms in the Dirksen Senate Office Building, or the cook in one of the cafés. Or the group of loud people I heard walking down the halls talking about Jesus. I stopped them, told them what I do, and it was a blessing to them, and me, because we all prayed together."

"There are so many examples. I saw a Congressman running up the stairs and I stopped him, gave him a prayer card and he went on, or the one who was coming out of the elevator and he looked really beat-up. But I gave him a prayer card and a few months later we started praying together."

"I see the time soon when I will need to come to D.C. for three days, instead of just two."

"I was in one Congressman's office, and when he realized he could trust me, he sighed audibly and said, 'Dale, why would God put me in a job I hate so much?' Tough question. But these guys have no one to talk to about these things."

Dinner was over and no one was interested in dessert, so we paid the bill and headed for the door. I gave Dale a man-hug and he gently hugged Issy and headed north to Fairfax Drive. He was staying at the Holiday Inn just a block up the road.

As Issy and I headed towards home, just a few blocks away, there was a lot of commotion around the restaurant, which seemed odd, for the time of night. Cars were whipping in and out of parking spots heading in the same direction Dale was walking.

As we arrived on our street, a van came towards us slowly and then sped by us. Just before it sped off, I caught a glimpse of the guy in the passenger seat. I could have sworn he was the same skinny guy who sat behind me at dinner.

When we got inside our condo, Issy said, "Did you notice when we moved tables in the restaurant how many others who also moved were wearing earpieces?"

---

[1] Galatians 6:2

[2] 1 Peter 5:7

[3] Philippians 4:7

Chapter 15

February 23rd, Thursday Noon, FBI Headquarters

"Billy," I was exasperated. "Tell me you have more than this."

Based on the way Pete was talking, the two religion consultants were ready to disavow their nation and turn to God knows what.

"Sir," Billy said, "I've looked into all the ways we have of connecting cyber-attacks to individuals. I have exhausted subscriber information, IP addresses, geolocation history, and open sources."

I decided to change direction.

"When you were here last time, you said the Warner Robins Counterintelligence guy was developing a broad base of friendlies, of contacts which you said he was encouraging onto the Religion Consultant."

"Yes, sir."

"Did you find out who the friendlies have in common, if anyone?"

Billy gave a long whistle and said, "I'm not sure it's going to be helpful, sir."

I was immediately short with him and exclaimed, "Why don't you tell me what you have, and I'll tell you if it's helpful."

"Well, sir," he said, "These friendlies are all outgoing and therefore comfortable with all sorts of ministries and ministry leaders."

"What do you mean?" I coaxed.

"These people all have connections which go back and forth from social media to automated emails to personal texts and periodically breaking bread together, when in the same towns. It's almost impossible to say if there are unique relationships."

I had to decide how much to give this kid and how much to hide. He could probably tell I was weighing something, so he remained silent.

After a while, he finally spoke, "There is something new which I haven't shared with you yet though. And it might help you."

He continued, "I found something from the Warner Robins character which bothers me. It is an encrypted file which was entered deep into my colleague's computer, but not so it could be accessed easily."

"What did it say?"

"Well, that's what is so bizarre. It is a document which simply states the name and contact information of various ministries and how they can help the other candidate."

"The other candidate?" I asked.

"Yeah, each paragraph, for each contact, seems to be written by completely different people (based on the tone and choice of words), and they are explaining the strategic ways they will be helping the opposing candidate. This is not something which should be within Issy's grasp, if it's not being given to our boss."

I was nodding my head slowly when he went on, but I was busy thinking this investigation has just taken an ominous turn. And I had no idea where it was going.

I stood up and walked over to the plate glass window which overlooks Pennsylvania Avenue. I was staring at nothing in particular, and as a million thoughts ran through my mind I decided on a course of action.

I turned and asked, "Billy, what is your relationship with your counterpart in the other campaign?"

"Sammie? Great! She and I have been buds since we joined the US Government Cyber Crew (USGCC). As you know, after the previous Presidential election's fiascos, the USGCC was established to be a non-partisan Cyber Crew."

"How's that working out?"

"What, our ability to be non-partisan?"

"Yeah."

"I think really well, boss."

I turned back to the window.

"Does the USGCC still meet weekly?"

"Of course, sir. I seem to recall you made it part of the requirement."

I remained facing the window and he went on. "The mission is to boldly go where no one has gone before, by meeting weekly to maintain non-partisan accountability."

"And?" I asked still looking out.

"And what, sir?"

"And are you crew members remaining non-partisan?"

"Actually, we are, surprisingly."

Now I turned and walked towards Billy, eyeing the chair next to him.

"What do you know about Sammie, Billy?"

When I said that, he blushed, so I shut up just to see where this went.

"Umm," he stumbled. "Umm, she's about my age. She's very pretty, and I think she's single. Umm."

"Billy, that wasn't what I meant."

"Oh," he said and then really blushed.

"How good is Sammie, Billy? How do her skills compare with yours?"

He looked up at me with a smirk and asked, "May I cut to the chase, sir?"

I nodded.

"She'd notice if I were trawling around in her server."

I had made my decision. "Alright Billy, I want you to put all of this information together, in your 'cyber-geek' way, so it can be easily explained to another cyber-geek."

The kid blushed again.

"And Billy, the information needs to be in a format an old guy could figure out and use."

"Oh," he said, disappointed.

"Do I get to. . ." he started.

I lifted a finger. "Need to know, Billy, need to know."

"Yes, sir. When do you want it?"

"Have it couriered to me this afternoon."

"Done," he said, nodding his head, and I in turn nodded my head towards the door.

He headed for the door and I headed for my desk.

I had what was bound to be a real scrappy meeting in about forty-five minutes with the head of Homeland Security, and he wasn't going to like my directives.

"Grace," I called through my intercom.

"Yes, Mr. Jones?"

"I need Sammie Prescott in my office tonight."

"Yes, sir. By the way, Mr. Beecham is here."

"Already? He's early."

"I said that, sir."

"Tell him he'll have to wait."

"I did."

"Did he and my previous appointment see each other?"

"By the 'splittest' of seconds, no, sir."

Later Grace told me she watched Billy get onto the elevator, which she does for every visitor of mine. And just as the elevator closed, the one next to it opened and out stepped Mr. Beecham with one of his associates.

Grace has access to a loaded pistol in a specially outfitted pencil drawer. The drawer has to be a little deeper than normal to hold her Glock 21. She's a very good shot and has large hands, hence the larger pistol, for a woman. But she needs the bigger gun. Her job is to stop those wanting to reenter my office to do me harm. She is authorized to use deadly force, if necessary, which means she needs to shoot accurately, even through a plate glass window.

It is her responsibility to make sure everyone leaving my office gets into the elevator. Once they are heading down the elevator, they are building security's problem.

Fifteen minutes later I was ushering in a fuming Pete Beecham.

"I'm delivering today's recon file to you directly because I want to talk about what is happening under your nose, and why you are not allowing the gloves to be pulled off."

Leaning up against my desk when he walked in, I held out my hand which he briefly shook before he sat down.

I opened the file he handed me and went to sit down myself, pulling out the single page.

OPERATION: JUDAS I.

Surveillance Report:

21, February 8:01 pm till 9:42 pm

Transcript:

>   *N/A*

Summary:

>   *Perps #3, #4, & #5 met privately for dinner. Perp #3 handed over document at beginning of their meet, which was successfully shielded by Perp #5. Their body language suggests they talked strategy before heading out.*

Distribution:

>   *Classified, Director Pete Beecham*

I made a show of turning it over, and then looking in the file again.

"Kind of a small report today, Pete." I said, trying to hold back a grin.

I couldn't hold my sarcasm back, so I asked, "Three teams of four?"

He got up and headed for my door, sneering. I had to give it to him, he knew when he had a weak argument. And knew to not challenge me, simply based on a hunch.

But I stopped him before he got to the door. "What can you tell me about Perp #3?"

"The prayer-guy?" he spat.

"Yeah, the prayer guy who gets into offices and had the word 'terrorism' assigned to his name?"

"Nothing yet, Jack." He took a deep breath and said, "I don't like what I'm seeing. It doesn't hold consistent with a terrorism label, but the words are still there when we talk to some of his colleagues."

I nodded and he walked towards my door before he turned back to me.

"You may find this hard to believe, but I don't want to write anything permanent that may be inaccurate, even if I don't like these players. And I don't like them. And in my opinion, they are the real criminals here."

"What? Pete have you lost your mind? Perp #2 is cyber hacking, probably under the guidance of Perp #1 and these three holy-rollers are having a meal."

"Yeah, whatever," he growled and started to turn the door handle, but stopped.

"Wait a minute," he continued, realizing his people had been followed, "How many teams did you have there, Jack?"

I smiled and asked, "At the restaurant or at the innocent-until-proven-guilty-party's house?"

He opened the door and left.

He may be ticked, but he's a straight shooter and that's why I let him have a little rope.

Chapter 16

February 29th, Wednesday Evening, Atlanta GA

Clyde entered my office before church with his four-year-old daughter, Sofie, so while I wanted to bite his head off, I found myself complimenting the lovely little urchin, even though Clyde and his wife spelled her name wrong. Poor girl is going to be corrected every year in school and only learn how stupid her parents were.

She was on his lap and he mouthed, "I'm sorry."

But not as sorry as I was.

"I've started uploading files." That was all he said, and for tonight, that would be enough.

I said, "Thank you," nodded my head towards the door and he and the little brat left.

I had to be strategic about my next steps. Having ministry leaders beholden to me was one thing, but I needed to begin to make physical contact with some of the principals.

"But how often?" I wondered.

I sat there thinking about how I dreaded flying to Washington D.C. every few weeks.

And then I thought of this prayer guy. "Hmm."

I texted Clyde, "Did we make the donation to the prayer-guy?"

"Yes," was the reply.

Same Evening, Washington D.C.

Even though we have small groups during the week, we also have a Wednesday night prayer service. Issy was out of town on the campaign trail but I left work early to attend.

I like our prayer services. A full one third of the church shows up which is a big deal. Our pastor combines short explanations of verses with a chorus or verse by a small praise team and then we in the congregation pray, based on what was just read or sung.

It happens so smoothly that we run through a one-and-a-half-hour prayer service in what seems like a few minutes. It's really a sweet time. And tonight was no different.

As I was walking out of the church Harold tapped my shoulder from behind. I turned and I think my smile faded a bit. Nevertheless, I held out my hand, which he grabbed briefly.

He mumbled, "Pastor wants us to work out our differences or he said he would step in."

His wife was behind him, looking down, not wanting to meet my eyes, so I gave her the courtesy and didn't say hello to her. I focused on Harold.

I asked, "Do you want to go into the worship center and talk?"

But the strangest thing happened. He just looked at me. We stood there for an entire minute before his wife prodded him.

I don't know for sure what was going through his mind, but I was thinking about the can of Chicken Noodle soup that awaited me at home. And then, as if I was watching Wile E. Coyote, Harold's face started to turn color. He was fuming, and I was trying to not laugh.

I think his wife noticed me holding back because she said, "Harold, why don't you two. . ."

"No! No, I can't yet." And he walked out the door with his wife in tow.

She turned back and mouthed the words, "I'm sorry," and they were off.

Later that night when Issy and I talked, we prayed for Harold, asking the Lord to soften his heart and to give me the presence of mind to be sensitive to his anger, while being obedient to the Lord. Among other things, I prayed that my words would be full of grace, seasoned with salt,[1] rather than salty and seasoned with grace.

Issy said she'd be home the next afternoon and we said goodnight.

Same Evening, FBI Headquarters

I sat down with these two computer geeks, Sammie and Billy. They had made their hello's in my waiting room, where I purposely let them sit, unsupervised for a good fifteen minutes.

Grace, who is accustomed to working late, kept her eyes and ears on their conversation. It was not recorded, but it was listened to.

When she showed them into my office, she gave the slightest shake of her head. They had passed my test. They did not bring up why they were here, even though both knew, and they both knew the other one knew too.

"I'm getting too old to keep managing clandestine activity," I was thinking as they walked in.

"I thank you for seeing me this late. For obvious reasons, I don't want you two seen by others, at least not together."

They both nodded and I continued, "There's a reason why the US Government Cyber Crew (USGCC) was initiated. And there's a reason it is non-partisan. And this, what we're doing tonight, is the reason."

Again, they both acknowledged the fact.

"Last week, Sammie, when you and I met, I didn't show you any of the files Billy had for me, because they were not redacted. It is critical that in these meetings, every single public name and private message is completely redacted. The only way you two can work together is if your principles can trust your counterpart."

I paused and drank nearly a full glass of water. "With that being said, I recognize the hypocrisy of redacting names but not redacting electronic addresses, or signatures. We will have to live with that because the electronic signatures are our concern and you both need to have access to them."

I let my words seep in and Sammie clarified, "So, when Billy and I exchange documents, we redact principles names, but allow electronic signatures and addresses to remain, right?"

"Correct," I said and then nodded to Billy and he gave a number of pages to Sammie, all of which had major redactions.

A few minutes later she put the pages down and spoke. "After our meeting last week, I started looking for spam emails which looked suspicious."

She speaks with a southern drawl that is more Billy Graham, than Bill Clinton, which tells me she did her growing up years in the area of North Carolina. And it reminded me of the vast number of dialects in the south alone.

She continued, "In all honesty, I didn't find any which caught my eye, but with these IP addresses, I will start looking for specific bad guys."

"You two need to find a clandestine way to meet because I don't want you in my office every couple weeks, unless we have appointments."

"Can we go out to dinner, and talk?" Billy asked a bit too eagerly. I saw Sammie blush.

I cocked my head towards Billy, which made him blush, and then the two kids looked at each other, saw the other blushing and then blushed all the more.

Nothing was said for a few moments. I couldn't believe it. They liked each other. I was afraid I would need to hold their hands if I didn't dump them.

"Look," I said with my 'dad voice,' "Are you two going to be able to work together?"

The both sat up straight and tall, "Yes, sir," they said in unison; I wanted to believe them.

I then went on. "I have a safe house in D.C. which you two can use. It is in the condos behind the News Museum on Pennsylvania Ave."

They were both trying to picture the location. "It's on the other side of the Archives Metro Station, from here."

That seemed to help so I continued, "The condo's address is 565 Pennsylvania and our condo is on the third floor. Sammie, when you two meet, you go in and out through the front doors and use the elevator. Billy, you go through the back entrance on C Street and take the stairs."

I looked at both of them and they nodded. I then handed them two cheap phones. "These are not agency issue phones and they will not be tracked, especially if you keep your texting limited."

I paused and decided I wanted to see them blush again. "I want you to use these phones as if you are flirting with one another."

I paused and smiled watching them react. I think I even chuckled at them.

To my surprise, Billy recovered first and started suggesting signals, times and meanings of certain phrases they'd use to text to each other.

I sent them over to a table on the other side of my office so they could work out their tradecraft and I read reports. Fifteen minutes later they returned and began telling me their plans.

"Stop," I said, "I don't need to know. I trust you to figure it out, work with each other, and put a clear noose around our bad guy, or bad guys."

"I have an additional directive for you two. There may be friendlies from another agency looking at your servers from their offsite location. If you see them, record it but do not let them know you are watching them."

"Yes, sir," they said in unison, again. It would have been cute if I wasn't so fatigued by this problem about which we seem to know so little.

"Goodbye, kids," I said, nodding towards the door.

"One more thing," I said as they got to the door. "Do not speak of these things outside this office or the condo. Which reminds me. You're not dating, right?" And they blushed again. "So, outside this office you go in different directions. If you find yourself in my elevator together, you ignore each other completely."

They nodded and left.

March 1st, Thursday Morning, Atlanta GA

"Who in the world does he think he is?" I was fuming when I got into my black Model S. It does zero to sixty in under three seconds and if I were not careful, I would test that right now. I hadn't been this angry in. . . I don't know when.

The so called "Prayer-Guy" had just turned down my request. What kind of an ignoramus is he? Didn't he know that my donation of a thousand dollars required him to figure out how to accede to my request?

"But that idiot dismissed me out of hand," I fumed while purposely backing my foot off the accelerator. "So, his precious little congressmen and senators need their privacy, do they?"

I yelled towards the closed window, "You'll pay for this insult, you moron!" I wanted to yell it to the passing world. I started to lower my window so others could hear my anger. But the wind would mess up my hair and I immediately changed my mind, after all I paid good money for this "do."

---

[1] Colossians 4:6

Chapter 17

I have been looking forward to this passage in our book, <u>A Harmony of the Four Gospels</u>. It is on childlikeness, tolerance and forgiveness.

Since Harold and I still can't get together, I'm hoping this passage can help me. When he and I are in front of each other lately, he just goes silent, but he is silent with rage. It would be scary if I didn't want to laugh at him, which I confess I tend to want to do.

Earlier in the week, our pastor called me for an update. He said, "I don't need any specifics, I just want a general update."

I thought for a moment and responded, "We're moving forward, Pastor, but it's a process."

"Has he invited you back to your small group yet, Jude?"

"No, but Issy and I are so busy that we. . ." I didn't finish the sentence because he interrupted me.

"But that isn't the point, Jude."

"I know, Pastor." I tried to sound soothing. "But this is going to take a while. If you don't mind, trust me and give us some more room."

We were both silent and then he responded, "Alright. I will give you the room you want."

"But why is he acting like this, Jude? I've never known Harold to be this out of control."

There was a long pause and I knew he expected me to answer, but I didn't want to. The more silent I was, the more silent he was.

So eventually I said, "Pastor, the problem is a simple one. Harold has allowed his identity in his politics to be more important than his identity in Christ. He would never admit that but that is what he's living out."

"How can a Godly man become so. . ."

I didn't let him finish. "Pastor, before you throw stones at Harold, think of the news outlets you listen to. When they start talking about political issues that wind you up, what do you do?"

He paused and said, "I look for something to throw at the T.V."

I laughed and said, "May I suggest there is something else you should do?"

"Of course. Speak, Jude."

"I believe you should turn the T.V. off and should have even turned it off *before* you got angry at those wicked, wacko people you disagree with so strongly."

"And guess what? Because we react the way we do at times, you and I and Harold are just alike."

"How so?"

"Oh, Pastor, I don't want to go there."

"Jude, I trust you and I love you and I know Scripture does not say Q-Tips sharpen Q-Tips. It says iron sharpens iron,[1] so, speak!"

I took a deep breath. "Sir, when you and I and Harold get aggravated at another human being, we are ignoring Paul's very clear statement that. . ."

"Our struggle is not with flesh and blood.[2] Is that what you were going to say, Jude?"

"Yes, sir."

"Good word, Jude. I needed to hear that. Keep me posted, okay?"

"I will, sir. Thank you for the call," I said and he prayed for me.

"Father, I praise You because You are a God of relationship, and as such, You encourage relationships among us, the Body of Christ. I trust You to restore unity between Harold and Jude, and Lord, let those in our church who are observing this clash, see You instead of this noise. Amen."

That was earlier this week. And now Issy and I would be talking about this passage.

She read, "An argument started among the disciples. . ."[3]

October A.D. 29, Childlikeness, Tolerance & Forgiveness

We were sitting down eating in a friend's home. "Finally," I said in a hushed voice as my colleagues continued a discussion which started on the road outside Capernaum. They were finally interested in who the greatest in the kingdom of heaven would be.

I said to the one closest to me, "It's about time we have this discussion. If Jesus is going to reorder our nation and restore our leadership in the world, those who are leaders in this kingdom will need to know it."

Matthew just looked at me and shook his head.

"Idiot," I said to myself. "How would he know anyway? His only understanding of leaders is looking at them as a nasty-old tax collector. No wonder he joined this band; to get away from his disgusting career."

When Jesus entered the house, the talking stopped instantaneously causing an unnatural silence.

Jesus asked nonchalantly, "What were you guys arguing about on the road?"[4]

He always seems to ask in a way that makes me suspicious. I think He knows more than He is letting on.

We were silent, except for me munching on my sandwich. I've learned, with this group, you eat when you can. And so I make no apologies; I just eat!

Our silence didn't last very long though, because Jesus said, "If anyone wants to be first, he must be the very last, and the servant of all."[5]

This kind of talk from Jesus frustrates me so!

His incredible brilliance is evidenced by the fact He really did know what we were arguing about. And then equally incredibly foolish words come dribbling out of his mouth.

"How will this man ever lead?" I wondered.

And then I answered my own question, "Of course, with us, the Twelve, as His real leaders."

I hated this back and forth unstable thinking in my brain. One day I see Him as a leader and the next, I am ready to go away, taking the money bag with me.

I was reveling in the thought of being a leader over some portion of the world when I looked up and Jesus had a child stand among us, He hugged the kid[6] and then said the silliest thing I have ever heard. He said that only children can enter His kingdom.[7]

He then talked about humility[8] which I thought I understood, until He referenced children again.

I try to listen closely to what Jesus is saying, but sometimes His words are just beyond me. I listened so closely I even stopped eating for a few minutes and then He said that when we welcome children, we are welcoming Him![9]

At that I stopped trying to figure it out and just concentrated on eating.

That's when the uppity John told Jesus, "We tried to stop a guy we saw yesterday trying to drive demons out of someone. He was invoking Your name even though he wasn't even a part of our group.[10]

But Jesus scolded us! "I can't believe my ears," I said to Matthew. "Why is He scolding us?

But Matthew just shrugged his shoulders.

Then I heard Jesus comment that those who give out water will get rewarded.[11] "Well, it's about time," I whispered to no one in particular.

Jesus started talking about judgment, which I dismissed out of hand because I don't judge others. "I am careful with my actions and attitudes," I thought. "I don't need to worry about that. I can't speak for my esteemed colleagues, however," and I chuckled at my own wittiness.

Jesus really laid it on us. He kept talking about children, but He also talked to us about those who wander off. I disagreed with Him, reverently, of course. But then He said, "If a man owns a hundred sheep, and one of them wanders away, will he not leave the ninety-nine on the hills and go to look for the one that wandered off?"[12]

"I'm sorry, Jesus," I said. "Why would I leave the ninety-nine to possibly be ravished by wolves?" A number of the disciples agreed with me, which emboldened me, so I went on.

"I see that as bad stewardship, Jesus."

He just smiled at all of us and talked about how happy the owner would be when he found the one. I didn't get it. And I still don't.

Shortly thereafter, Peter asked one of his few, very good questions, "How many times shall I forgive my brother?"[13]

But Jesus' answer was again so contrary to common sense that I couldn't take Him seriously. Frankly, it was disappointing to listen to Him, especially the parable He used, and then the interpretation He gave to His own story, which included throwing the more aggressive guy into jail.[14]

I probably would've handled the debt owed to me the same way as that guy. If it's my money, I'll handle it the way I want. But to jail some guy who's simply trying to get his money back? I don't think so.

March 18th, Sunday Morning, Arlington VA

"Wow," was all I could say. "Brutal passage in light of my situation with Harold."

"Yeah, I thought about that too, sweetie," Issy said thoughtfully.

"I think the surprising challenge," wanting to change the subject, "was the humility all over this passage. I have always seen the children portion separate from the forgiveness portion and separated further from the unforgiving debtor. But I never put them all together and certainly not with the foundation of forgiveness."

Issy picked up on where my mind was going. "Good word, hubby. The unusual promise, for me, is right at the beginning, and I have to admit, that when I started reading it, your words from a few weeks ago flooded into my mind."

"Was I that wonderful?"

She just ignored me and continued, "It's about when you brought out Romans 13:1-2 and the implication that you would be supportive of whichever candidate won. Clearly, I wasn't willing to agree with you. But after today's passage, I'm softening."

"Which part of the passage, babe?" I asked, humbly I hope.

"Right at the beginning, when Jesus puts down the disciples for arguing about something as crude as who will be the greatest. And then when He brought out the child, what immediately went through my mind was your Romans 13 passage. God is the one in control. You and I are to do what we do with excellence, and if that means arguing strongly for our candidate, I'm okay with that. I don't mind playing hardball, even with you."

I nodded my agreement.

She continued, "But what we cannot do is let our passion cause us to think, 'Our way is the right way, and what God does, or allows is wrong.'"

I laughed and Issy looked up at me.

"I'm sorry, babe," I said. "I just had a picture of your candidate losing and you telling God He was wrong and I started looking for lightning bolts headed for you."

Serious again, I said to her, "This Prayer-Guy, Dr. Dale, has a video on his YouTube channel that addresses this issue. He calls it "Politics and Arrogance."[15]

"I asked him about this YouTube video the last time he and I talked. And I asked him about our passion, yours and mine."

Issy gasped and looked at me scared to death.

"No, no, no, baby, not that kind of passion."

She relaxed and started to breathe again and I went on, "I told him that you and I have great passion for our candidates. I then asked for his opinion, 'When is our passion taken too far?'"

His answer was simple, "When our passion causes us to break fellowship with believers, our passion is wrong, even when we're right."

"Ouch," Issy said.

After a long silence I said, "It goes back to the simplicity, and the reality, that the Holy Spirit lives inside us, so we as Christians are without excuse."

She picked up the refrain which I say so often, "I expect the world to act like the world, but we in the church should not, and cannot."

"Good word, babe. Very good word." I added.

"Hey," Issy began tentatively. "I know we are committed to not sharing our job-related directive, but perhaps this one I can share with you."

I nodded and she continued.

"I'm not being funny and I am not throwing stones at your boss, mine is just as bad in this area, but we need to encourage these two, to be committed to humility."

She was being very sincere and I just listened. "Jude, look at the various ways Jesus talks about humility. He talks about it with regards to children, with regards to the ones we argue with and also in our areas of forgiveness. I know this passage is about, what did the author call it, 'Childlikeness, Tolerance, and Forgiveness,' but what Jesus really taught was humility."

"You know," I said to my bride, "Your boss is lucky to have you."

She just smiled, humbly.

That morning in church, Harold came up to me, biting his lower lip as he spoke and said, "I want you to come back to our home group, but only on the proviso you do not talk politics."

I hesitated which Harold obviously noticed.

"Harold," I said, "I would like to agree with you. In fact, I'm absolutely content not talking politics, but that isn't fair to the group. You need to give them the opportunity to talk about this, if they want to."

"You're impossible!" he growled and strode off.

---

[1] Proverbs 27:17

[2] Ephesians 6:12a

[3] Luke 9:46a

[4] Mark 9:33b

[5] Mark 9:35

[6] Mark 9:36

[7] Matthew 18:3 (Remember, Judas is interpreting Jesus' words from his perspective, which is not always the perspective of truth)

[8] Matthew 18:4a

[9] Mark 9:37a

[10] Luke 9:49

[11] Mark 9:41

[12] Matthew 18:12

[13] Matthew 18:21

[14] Matthew 18:34

[15] https://MarkMirza.com/politics-arrogance/

Chapter 18

March 19th, Monday Afternoon, FBI Headquarters

I came in from a late lunch and pulled the envelope out of my safe.

Fifteen minutes after it arrived I had received a call from Pete who'd asked if I'd read it yet.

"No, Pete, I'm out to lunch. When it arrived, I put it in my safe. I'll call you when I get back." And I hung up the phone.

That was an hour ago.

So now I extracted the envelope. It said, Top Secret, Eyes Only. Inside was a single sheet:

OPERATION: JUDAS I.

Field Report:

12th-17th, March, All Day each Day

Transcript:

>   *Available Upon Request*

Summary:

>   *Tailed Perp #3 all week, sat next to him at lunch on Thursday where he seemed to have a working lunch with a former MPTU colleague. They talked openly about his action plans in D.C. He appears to be working on a highly sensitive guide to influence voters. His words were, "What and when are we willing to submit to?" My conclusion was that the ultimate goal is regular, ongoing, manipulation. Voters were going to be manipulated somehow.*

Distribution:

>   *Classified, Director Pete Beecham*
>
>   *Copy, FBI, Eyes Only: Jack Jones*

I called Pete in Homeland Security. "I read your report. I would like to see the transcripts of the lunch. What are you wanting to do here?"

"I want to go deep into his background. I want to know all the details around his being fired from the university and what part terrorism played in this. I also want to know how serious he is about manipulating people's voting. Is that code for something? I don't know, Jack, and that's what bothers me. I've always thought this guy was dirty and I think we're getting closer to his real intent."

"Pete, you have been going deep for the last three months on Perp #3 and you have yet to find anything significant."

"Jack, I think if we haul Perps #4 and #5 in immediately, we can get some dirt on Perp #3."

"Pete," I was so angry I stood. "Don't be an idiot! Unless you find out they are stuffing ballot boxes, you stay away from the Religion Consultants. Do you hear me?"

There was silence on the other end.

I changed subjects, "Pete, I need to ask you about Perps #1 and #2. Have you lost interest in them?"

"No, Jack, not at all."

"Well then what is your 'gut' telling you about them?" I asked with as much sarcasm as I felt safe exuding.

I heard him take a long slow breath before he finally said, "I think Dr. Dale is the dangerous one."

"What?" I was still standing. "How can you say that with the rap sheet of Perp #1 being what it is?"

"Her issues are circumstantial while his were specific and not refuted. How many people do you know, Jack, who would not argue the loss of their job and reputation?"

"What if you are reading this all wrong, Pete?"

He continued, "There's another reason I am not putting much stock in her."

He paused and I waited for him to speak. "She's too rich."

"Huh?" I croaked.

"She's got too much to lose and our psycho analysts don't think she has what it takes to jeopardize everything she's built up for herself in this precarious way."

"Seriously?"

"Yeah, I'm being told that the religious mind is screwed up into a direction which makes them less dangerous when they have a lot to lose."

I was incredulous but remained silent.

"When the Taliban/ISIS controllers send out a suicide bomber, whom do they send? Answer: They send out the poor kids. Why? Because the rich ones don't want to go meet Allah while they still have their toys on earth to play with."

After a long time of silence, I said, "Pete, do whatever you want to do to the Prayer-Guy, short of arresting him, but stay away from the candidates and their staff. Do nothing to them."

"Got it." Pete said.

I could hear the grin on his face.

"Keep your reports coming," I said and I hung up.

Same Day, Washington D.C. Metro Station

We walked up the Capitol South escalators together. It was a brisk morning, a little more chilly than normal. But we kissed gently and then I took a step in the direction of my office. But I felt a double tap on my gloved hand which Issy was still holding.

Double tapping one another is a code we have for, "Pray for me."

I turned back and reassured her I would. That morning she said she was going to try and address humility, from a Christian perspective; just in general, as something her candidate could practice in campaigning.

I prayed for my Issy, that she would have wisdom to write it with a scriptural foundation, in case there was any push-back.

When I got to my office, the place was buzzing and there was a big bright note which said, "The boss wants to see you."

I immediately called the scheduler.

"See you here at 10:00 A.M. Jude," she said.

At five minutes before the hour I was standing in my boss's outer chamber. I have learned that these folks' schedules are so busy you never show up more than five minutes early.

Right as the second hand stood straight up, the door opened and I was ushered in. My candidate was there on the phone, while three top aides shuffled papers and looked at me. These were people who would surely have a cabinet position if we were elected in seven and a half months.

The chief of staff, Garrett Hali, pointed me to a chair and spoke on behalf of the candidate who was still tied up and seemed unable to shake the caller on the other end.

"Jude," Garrett started, and the other two execs sat next to me, "In every election cycle there are the typical 'Voter's Guides,' right?"

I simply nodded as it was more of a statement than a question. He continued.

"We would like to come up with our own voter's guide but with a few caveats."

I just kept listening.

He looked around at the other two and the candidate who all nodded for him to keep speaking.

"Jude, we don't want the guide to have its roots in anybody who is in the public's eye. There is too much potential dirty laundry on everyone today."

I nodded and before I could speak, he went on.

"The second caveat, Jude, is that it needs to be for religious people, since our stats tell us eight out of ten people claim some sort of religious affiliation."

I smiled at them and asked, "What about a guide from a seventeenth century English pastor, of whom very little is known?"

All four of them looked at each other, then at me. Their mouths were agape.

"Did you know I was going to ask you about this?" Garrett asked slowly.

"Of course not. But I am in the religion business so. . ."

"So, when can you give me a first draft?"

"As soon as I get back to my desk?"

The boss, still on the phone, looked excited but the others in the room looked dumbfounded.

One of them said, "Jude, you know I've never been of fan of your working for us with your wife working for the opposition, but, can you explain why you already have what we didn't even know were going to ask you about until this morning?"

"Sure, I understand your hesitancy. I have a friend in the prayer business who collects old Christian books. He has a seventeenth century, thirteen-hundred-page religious book, just like mine. One thing led to another and we started talking about a voter's guide written in 1656 by the same author. He said it was brilliant back then, but is a must read for today."

I paused and then added, "I have rewritten it into modern English since the Olde English was too hard to follow."

Our candidate, listening to both the caller and me, gestured for me to keep going, which I did.

"It's a sermon, at a time in the history of England when they were very severely divided. Much like the USA today. The pastor takes the first half of the booklet and talks about how he sees his nation, England, in a particular passage in Isaiah. But in the second half of the sermon this seventeenth century preacher tells folks how to vote, scripturally, while making a big deal about not telling them who to vote for."

They immediately looked at the candidate who nodded vigorously.

Garrett took over, "Two things, Jude. First, send me the document and then call me thirty minutes later. I'll be at my desk waiting for both."[1]

As I was walking out the door, he asked me, "Why did you take the time to rewrite it into modern English?" He said it almost suspiciously.

"I don't know," I said honestly. "It didn't take too long to do and it's a better document now for it."

Still suspicious, he asked, "You weren't planning on using it elsewhere, were you?"

"Of course not, Garrett." I noticed the others were steeped in their own conversations and the candidate was still on the phone.

---

[1] This is actually a real booklet which is in the appendix at the back of this book, and is also found at www.MarkMirza.com/Politics

Chapter 19

March 19th-20th, Monday & Tuesday, Washington D.C. Capitol Hill

I arrived into Ronald Reagan International Airport on Delta flight number 2638 at 9am. Clyde suggested I book this flight for myself, him and my bodyguard, Anthony. He said congressmen and women often take this flight at this time.

I bought a first-class ticket for myself and comfort plus tickets for them. Sitting in first class certainly has its benefits, but not on this flight. I sat next to some businessman who was overly full of himself and all he wanted to do was talk to me.

Thankfully the flight was only an hour and a half. I waited outside the jetway for my slow-moving companions. "What took so long, you two? I've been waiting here with all these 'regular' people for nearly an hour."

I always insist we rent a big black SUV, which we did, but then we sat in traffic as the Metro train went by us at least a dozen times. I fumed, just sitting there, but I've been on the MARTA trains in Atlanta, and there was no way I was going to do that here.

I had appointments this morning with our two state Senators, which we were nearly late for, and then afternoon appointments with five of our fifteen Georgia Congressmen, two of whom are women.

As I walked into each office, meeting lowly receptionists, I was amazed by a couple things. First, they were eager to make sure we were comfortable. They almost fell over themselves to make sure we had water, soda, etc.

I decided it was a little over the top and they can't possibly treat everyone like they were treating me. It had to be they were just catering to me because they know who I am.

The next thing that surprised me was how busy the staff were. I bet they don't get paid as much as I pay my lazy personnel. I'm going to have to do something about that when I get back to Atlanta.

At the end of the day we went to the elegant Willard Intercontinental Hotel, where I had booked a $700.00 suite. But I purposely booked Clyde and Anthony in the Holiday Inn, down the road, away from me. No way would I pay what it costs to have them stay here. Plus, I like to have a break from them.

We sat down for a drink in the bar, but I told them they were on their own for dinner. "Did they smirk when I told them that?" I wondered.

Clyde said our two candidates' meetings for the next day were on the schedule in my portfolio. One is before lunch and one is right after lunch. I told these two morons to be at my hotel no later than 10 a.m. and we parted company.

I was glad to be rid of them for now. However, they can be useful. Because of their size I introduce them as my bodyguards and that seems to suffice, as well as make my station in life plain to everyone.

When I got to my room, I pulled off my $600 Jimmy Choo Romy 60 pumps, beautiful in black suede. As much as I love them I did wish women would just wear flats! Then I closed the curtains tightly and raised the heat in my room. All that walking had tired me out and my feet were hurting. Oh, what I wouldn't give for a foot massage.

The next day, our two appointments seemed too rushed to me. I didn't like feeling as if I were merely a part of the cattle being moved in and out of both candidates' private offices. I suspect that will change when they see the contents of their "gift."

As I left, I gave them each an envelope with a copy of a generous check which I had made out and mailed to their respective advertising agencies. I suspect they called their ad agencies to confirm receipt of my checks. The checks were for the same amount and they were both received with grace. But I'll bet their jaws dropped when they opened the envelopes.

I also made sure to look each candidate in the eye and tell them, "I'm here to serve you anyway I can." To which they seemed to respond gratefully.

There was a point in each visit when I had to delicately dance around a question and it came from the candidates' Chief of Staff each time. I was asked if I would attend their gathering when they next visited Atlanta.

"Of course, I'd be honored." The words were more of a stammer, at first, fearing they would probably want me on stage and I was supporting both candidates. But then I saw my out and energetically agreed. "The only thing we'll need to do is double check my schedule. I am very busy, you know."

Later in the day while I was in the Delta Sky Club Lounge, I received a personal call from each candidate, thanking me for my "generous" donation. Each of them asked if I would host a group of very high-end donors at my home. Again, I enthusiastically told them I'd love to, "if my schedule allowed."

After we hung up, I smiled to myself and chuckled a little more loudly than I had planned. "Million-dollar checks go a long way."

Clyde who was sitting opposite me asked if everything was okay.

"Perfectly," I murmured. "Perfectly." And up from my belly came a low purr.

March 20th, House and Senate Office Buildings

I got a call from Dr. Dale. He was back in town. We weren't able to get together, but we spent a few minutes talking about the 1656 voter guide which he sent me when we first met.

I told him that this brilliant sermon from 1656 England had been passed up the ladder to my boss.

I told him how I took the sermon and rewrote it into modern day English, just for ease of reading.

"Great idea," he said. "I'd love to see it in a modern English wording. The Olde English was pretty tough to follow at times."

I chuckled without telling Dale that in the Presidential Consultant business we always tried to dumb-things-down so there would never be any miscommunication. I sent him a copy from my phone while we were talking.

We had a great conversation and when we parted he added, "If you change your mind and can meet, I'm staying in the Holiday Inn, down the street from the Willard, InterContinental."

We hung up and I opened the document I had sent to my boss and the Chief of Staff.[1]

I had simply written a highlight of the first half, but I sent the entire second half, the voter's guide (as I was now calling it).

The document read:

Author:

The pastor who gave this sermon in 1656 was William Gurnall. There is very little known about him, except that back in the mid seventeenth century he wrote a thirteen-hundred-page book on Spiritual Warfare. I happen to have that book and I can affirm that his attention to detail is microscopic.

The Sermon:

In the first half of the sermon the writer gives a message based on the first chapter of Isaiah and how, by application, he sees his own country. He indicated that what God said to the Jews of Isaiah's time, he could see God saying to his nation, 1656 England.

As I went through his sermon, I admit that I too saw our nation, modern-day USA, and I could see God saying to us the same things He said to the Jews in Isaiah's time. I did not include the entire sermon for you, but I can send it if you would like.

The Voter's Guide:

I looked at my watch and saw that I was running out of time. I needed to get to the Metro station soon, so I just perused the section titles of the document.

Why We Vote

- Because We Steward for God
- Because We Speak for God
- Because We Stand for God

Who Should Get Your Vote

- First. Look for the fear of God in those you choose
- Second. Look for wisdom and proper gifts
- Third. Enquire whether they are Christians
- Fourth. Look for courage and resoluteness
- Fifth. Find purposeful focus on the nation's public affairs
- Sixth. Choose those who have healing spirits
- Seventh. Look for a desire to serve
- Finally. Find those faithful to the ministers and the ministry of the Gospel

What Occurs After We Vote

I was again amazed at this incredible document. What a great find. Dale was right. He had told me the document was, "Brilliant back in its day, but a must-read for today's troubled times."

March 22nd, Thursday Evening, FBI Headquarters

Pete's file arrived from a Homeland Security courier, as usual, and on time. I sat down, opened the "Eyes Only" copy and was aghast at what I read.

"I can't believe Pete is right, but maybe, just maybe he has a point." I sat the report down and wondered what my next steps should be.

The report read:

OPERATION: JUDAS I.

Field Report:

19th-20th, March, All Day each Day

Transcript:

N/A, Observed only

Summary:

Tailed Perp #3 and recorded each Senator, Congressman and Congresswoman he spoke to. (In some cases he spoke to staff only, unknown which staff. Also do not know if Perp made a significant staff engagement, as he has at times, or if he merely dropped off paperwork of some kind). His hotel was the same as Perp #2. Perp #3 checked in the day Perp #2 checked out. After review with Senior Chief Pete Beecham, we have three questions to nail down. First, did Perp #3 go to a preassigned drop location since Perp #2 was in the same hotel, just the day before; Second, why didn't Perp #2 and Perp #1 stay in same hotel; and Third, why does Perp #3 come to D.C. on the same days, Tuesday and Wednesday. What is significant about these days?

Distribution:

Classified, Director Pete Beecham

Copy, FBI, Eyes Only: Jack Jones

"Crap," I said to myself. And then I called Pete's direct number.

"Finish going deep on Perp #3 and get a very deep file on Perp #2," I ordered.

As I was hanging up on Pete, I heard him say, "Perp #3 is the real bad guy, not Perps #1 or #2."

I brought the phone back to my ear. "Humor me, would you, Pete? Do them both."

I remained silent and after a few moments he let out a long sigh. That was his tell, his body language which told me he'd agreed.

I said, "Thanks," and hung up.

---

[1] Again, the entire document, rewritten into modern English can be found at www.MarkMirza.com/Politics

Chapter 20

The weeks seem to be slipping by us, so we chose to do the next two stories in the life of Jesus at the same time. They seemed to fit and they were both short.

It was extremely cold this morning and neither of us wanted to get out of bed to get our coffee.

I complained, "Baby, I made it last night, preparing it for us for today, surely that means you should get up and get it, don't you think?"

I was proud of myself; I thought I sounded very pathetic. Issy slowly sat up, letting the covers drop just enough and then gave me her own pathetic look.

When I returned with the coffee, she had propped herself on her pillow. She had her Bible sitting in front of her and a triumphant grin on her face. I got back into bed and murmured, "Not fair, Issy, not fair." And then I put my cold feet directly onto her warm legs.

She yelped and I grinned.

"I'll read, babe," I said with a satisfied smile.

And so I began, "As the time approached for Him to be taken up to heaven. . ."[1]

October, A.D. 29, Mistaken Zeal and Wanna-Be Followers of Jesus

I still couldn't figure Jesus out. He seemed bound and determined to go to Jerusalem,[2] even though He said he would face much suffering and even die. As of late, this seemed to be His mantra and yet I saw a confidence in Him.

And I realized He was not the only one who was exhibiting some zeal. Was He getting my hopes up? Was He getting ready to be that political Messiah I always knew He could be?

Jesus was, rightfully, being very careful about His approach into Jerusalem. It was no secret to us that the religious leaders had it out for Him. Still, He chose to go to Jerusalem, but covertly.[3]

He sent a number of us to the Feast of Tabernacles, through a Samaritan village, ahead of Him.[4] But the crazy Samaritans got angry when they realized Jesus wasn't going to stay there. A few of us stayed while the rest went ahead to the feast at the Festival of Tabernacles.

I was so hungry I wanted to go, but James and John, the bossy brothers, were organizing and directing us, and I was asked to stay.

When Jesus arrived at this Samaritan village, the people there didn't welcome Him at all. James and John indignantly asked the Lord if they could call fire down and destroy them.[5]

I've gotta be honest with you. You probably know what I think of James' little brother, John, but with that argument, he showed he could muster up some fight if he needed to, which I liked.

I looked up into the sky, waiting to see fire come down and wipe out the Samaritans. I admit I feared the God of Heaven might accidentally throw it at us, so I wanted to watch to be able to get out of the way, if necessary.

But once again I heard Jesus' words which confirmed my realization that He was less and less of the so-called-Messiah who would help our nation.

Jesus rebuked James and John![6] Can you believe it! He rebuked His own men for wanting to protect Him!

And then, to make matters worse, we just moved on. I was hoping to eat. We walked on to another village[7] and I had to wait that much longer for some much desired nourishment.

While we were on the road to the next village, a teacher of the law sidled up alongside us. He gave his flamboyant welcome, so we all knew he was a big deal, at least in his own mind, and then he leaned into Jesus to speak privately to Him, so I thought.

The truth is this teacher of the law wanted to join us. Immediately a couple thoughts ran through my mind, sarcastic of course; "Believe me, buddy, you don't want to join us. You never know when you're going to eat, the people don't like us, and Jesus refuses to accept the mantle of authority which should be rightfully His and ours.

Jesus simply responded with some crazy talk about not having a home.

A little further down the road we came across another man, friendly to our ministry and Jesus proactively asked him to join us, to follow us, well, to follow Him.

The guy was enthusiastic. Personally I liked him, but he told Jesus he needed to hang at home for a while. I didn't hear all the details as I was calculating in my mind what another mouth would cost us.

Then I saw Jesus look at me, briefly, and He said, "Follow me and let the dead bury their own dead."[8] I thought His words odd, because the dead can't bury the dead. But I also thought it odd the way He looked at me when He said that.

But Jesus still wanted the guy to follow Him, or at least Jesus wanted him to proclaim the kingdom of God.[9]

As I thought about it, I realized these two men turned out to be pretty indifferent to Jesus' ministry, but Jesus, instead of casting them aside, sounded like He had compassion on them.

It didn't make any sense to me, especially in light of Jesus rebuking James and John because they were the opposite of indifferent. They were zealous, high-spirited, ready to jump, which is a good thing, isn't it?

I was still scratching my head when another who had been following the last guy, came up to us. We were all still walking (thank the Lord, because I'm very hungry by now). This potential follower had to have heard the previous guy's excuses.

Nevertheless, he came up to Jesus and says, "I will follow You, Lord; but first let me go back and say good-by to my family."

I thought that was a pretty fair and reasonable request. I mean, I didn't like the reality that we were going to have to feed another mouth, but my experience showed these new guys often come with some money in their pocket which I would soon get into the money bag.

I also like the idea of this guy being one of us, because if we had any real trouble with the Temple guards; I could hide behind him. He was as wide as two men.

But sadly, Jesus just kept walking.

I was lagging behind contrasting the actions of Jesus during the previous few hours. By now I realized I was going to have to wait till we got to the feast before I could eat. Maybe that made me grumpy. I don't know.

But here is what I did know; Jesus rebuked James and John, for being good followers. But when it came to these non-followers, Jesus seemed to have compassion on them. "It just doesn't make sense," I thought. "Why rebuke your own guys and then feel sorry for those who are unwilling to do what it takes?"

March 25th, Sunday Morning, Arlington VA

"Wow," Issy exclaimed. "I'm glad we studied these two stories together."

I chuckled, "Really, why? I only did it because we are running short on weeks, and. . ."

"Look at the contrast in both accounts and then observe Jesus' reaction to them," she said excitedly.

I turned back to my Bible and the Harmony book.

"James and John showed great, albeit misguided, zeal while the wanna-be-followers of Jesus had more important concerns elsewhere."

I nodded in agreement and she continued, "Now look at Jesus' response. To the disciples, He rebuked them. But to the not-yet-followers, he showed compassion."

I shook my head, questioningly. "Issy, I see the zeal, and Christ's rebuke. I see the indifference, but as I read Jesus' response, I don't think I'd call it compassion."

"That's because you are not seeing Jesus' heart when He talked about foxes, and the dead, and plowing."

"You're right," I confessed to her. "I don't see it."

"Baby," she reminded me, "What do you always tell me about the world versus the church, relative to the way we act?"

"I always say the same thing," I answered, "The world is not equipped to handle things the way the church can, because the Holy Spirit lives in us, 'the church', but not in them."

The wheels were turning in my head now. "You're saying Jesus' compassion came out because He was sad for these wanna-be-followers, knowing they weren't equipped to follow Him?"

"Yes, Jesus had compassion on the unsaved, and by contrast, He had high expectations of His followers."

"That's good, baby. That's really good." I said, inching closer and closer to her face.

We kissed, long and slow.

We never did get to our questions, but I resolved to have extra patience, maybe even compassion, on those who think differently than me.

---

[1] Luke 9:51a

[2] Luke 9:51b

[3] John 7:10b

[4] Luke 9:52

[5] Luke 9"53-54

[6] Luke 9:55a

[7] Luke 9:55b

[8] Matthew 18:22

[9] Luke 9:60b

Chapter 21

April 4th, Wednesday Night, Washington D.C.

Issy had an extra skip in her step when she walked towards me as I was waiting at the South Capitol Metro Station.

"What are you excited about?" I asked.

"Why, you of course, baby," she quipped, with a twinkle in her eye.

We started to walk down the escalators but could only walk a few stairs since people were on both the right and left side of the escalators' steps.

"Don't people know you're supposed to allow people to walk down these escalators?" I whispered to her.

When we got onto the lower platform and awaited our train, she said, "Let's go to dinner at P. F. Chang's. It'll be on my expense account."

I looked at her warily and she added, smiling, "My boss authorized me to work on a project with my husband who is working for and promoting the wrong candidate."

I raised my eyebrows and sitting next to her on the silver line train for the next twelve or thirteen stops, I listened to her story.

Priscilla Ellsworth, the Chief of Staff, called Issy into her office and said, "Issy, I've been contemplating an interesting statistic. These stats are impressive, and maybe even scary, if we are not prepared for them."

After a moment, Priscilla had continued, "Did you know that when we add Protestants and Catholics together, they are roughly sixty-seven percent of the nation?"

Issy knew it was a rhetorical question, so she waited and her CoS went on. "There are some other religious groups in the USA, rounding up the religious peoples in the USA to approximately seventy-six percent. That means, Issy, only twenty-three percent of the people in the USA claim no religious affiliation at all!"

She looked up at Issy and asked, "Did you know that?"

"Yes, Ma'am," Issy responded, and then in typical Issy fashion, she added, "I don't agree with those numbers, but they're close enough."

The CoS apparently didn't care about the exact numbers, so she prepared to continue.

Just then their candidate walked into the office of the Chief of Staff. Issy said she started to stand but the CoS went on, nodding to their boss. "Issy, we have been talking about these numbers and would like you to jump on a project for us."

"Yes, ma'am. What would you like me to do?"

"This project would normally be overseen by our advertising department, but with you on staff we thought you could bring us a unique and specific perspective."

Issy waited for the directive. "Issy, what does seventy-six percent of the nation think about our news media outlets? Is the religious community buying what they are saying?"

Issy said the Chief of Staff looked at the candidate for approval and then said, "Issy, can you put together a non-partisan view of John and Jane Q. Public's views on our media outlets? We think it could make a significant impact on our advertising direction, since seventy-six percent of the nation claims a religious affiliation."

Issy said she sat back and then respond. "As you know," looking at both her CoS and the candidate, "My husband and I have a very stringent work ethic, which we are diligent to maintain, but I am thinking, if you want this to be non-partisan, it might not be a bad idea for us to both work on this, because there are sure to be things he will see that I will not."

Immediately, the CoS objected and said, "Can't you get someone from our own team?"

"Of course, I can ma'am, but it'll be partisan and you two want non-partisan."

"I don't know," she said, looking at their boss.

"You know," Issy went on, "My husband won't expect his name to be anywhere on this report. He doesn't care about the publicity."

It was a tense few minutes of silence when everyone was thinking it through. Issy was looking from the candidate to the CoS when she got the nod from the candidate, who immediately left the office.

Shaking her head uncomfortably, Priscilla said, "Okay, Issy, do this with your husband. But this better not come back and bite us!"

"I promise it won't, Ma'am. By the way, what's the timeline on this?"

So that night, at the P. F. Chang's on Glebe Road in Arlington, we started on what amounted to a white paper on religious people's views of the media outlets.

Same Night, FBI Headquarters

Sammie and Billy were in my office exactly on time, as expected. From what I'd observed, I liked their commitment to their work.

"How well do you two know your respective Religion Consultants?" I asked.

Billy looked at Sammie and I said, "Is your answer contingent upon Sammie, Billy?"

He blushed so deeply I couldn't tell where his pimples were.

"No, sir," he said, a little harshly, "I was looking at her to see if she wanted to go first."

"Oh," I said, surprised, and I was rarely surprised. "Both a scholar and a gentleman. Billy, I'm impressed."

I was actually embarrassed. Quickly I looked at Sammie, nodding for her to speak.

"Well," she said, "Until this project, I just viewed Jude as one of the staff. I really had no idea of his importance to the team, and I confess I still don't, but I am amazed at his work ethic."

"How so?" I asked.

"Because, sir, he is a bulldog when he is on a project. Now that I am looking into the management of his emails and texts, I'm seeing a man who methodically works an email till it is brought to conclusion. Even his filing method is pedantic."

Again, I asked for clarification.

"Sir, he doesn't keep emails in files; he is so methodical, that when he brings an email thread to a conclusion, he deletes all the previous emails except the last one, which has the entire thread. And then he puts it in the trash."

"Every one of his emails is in the trash, making all of his emails accessible by date, by person or by subject, and there is no confusion of duplicates, because he has deleted all of them."

I thought she was done, but she wasn't. "One more thing he does is to constantly update the subject line on emails; I suspect, so he can find them easier."

I heard Billy chuckling and I turned to him. "What's so funny?" I asked.

"Well sir, the couple are completely opposite in their email management."

Again, I asked for clarification.

"Sir, my colleague makes email files for everything. I suspect she has so many email files she probably forgets where some things are."

They both laughed now. Clearly geeks. And then I asked, "Do the two collaborate in any way at work?"

"Jude and Issy?" Billy asked. "They are so squeaky clean, there is no way they would ever do anything like that."

"They would never jeopardize their employment, or their reputations," added Sammie.

"I agree with you two. I just wanted to get your thoughts," I said and then nodded to the door for them to go.

Same Night, Arlington VA, Jude & Issy's Home

"I'd like to give her an overview of where we're going and then I'll do the research and let you read it. I think the Chief of Staff will feel better knowing I did the bulk of the work."

"Good idea, baby. I've been thinking about your task and want to maintain a clear and obvious separation between you and me, so make sure anything you upload to your computer does not have an email trail back to me."

"I had already thought about that and decided I would use a thumb-drive to transport any documents."

"Perfect, baby. This will be fun working with you, collaborating on a project."

Chapter 22

April 5th, Thursday Afternoon, FBI Headquarters

The envelope I got from Pete this afternoon was thick. I knew it was going to be an all-night read, so I ordered in and began to eat when I got a rare call on my private cell phone.

"Mom, what a surprise," I said, truly shocked. She knows how busy I am and has mastered social media, including texting. She always texts ahead of time, to see if she can call me. But this time she didn't.

"I hope I'm not bothering you, Son."

"No, not at all. I'm still at the office. It's going to be a long night and so I ordered dinner and just started working on it."

"Oh, good. Are you eating healthy?"

"Funny, Mom. Very funny, but I am eating a salad tonight, which someone keeps telling me is healthy."

"She's a wise mother who says that, listen to her once in a while, okay?"

"Of course, Mom. What's on your mind?"

"Well, Jacky. . ."

My mom has called me Jacky ever since I can remember. Even when I am around my colleagues she will call me Jacky. It's embarrassing, but what am I going to do? She's my mom. I guess she has some rights.

"Are you there, Jacky?"

"Sorry Mom, yeah, what's up?"

"I honestly don't know. Son. I just wanted you to know I was praying for you."

I never know how to respond to those kinds of statements from her. Do I humor her and tell her "I'm feeling the vibe?" No, she'd punch me out, even through the phone.

I respond as I always do, "Thanks, Mom, I'm sure I need it."

We chit-chatted for a few more minutes and then I said I needed to go.

"I understand, Jacky. Let me just lift you up before I hang up."

I don't even speak, because I know she'll keep going, so I just stay quiet and let her pray.

"Lord, God of heaven and earth, You have the address to my Jacky. I ask You to keep him safe and out of harm's way, but more than anything else, I trust you to give him wisdom. In Jesus Name, Amen."

"Thanks, Mom," I was saying when I remembered a note of mine.

"Mom, hey, Mom; before you go. I seem to remember you telling me. . . I don't know, some years back, that you were going into hospital rooms and praying with old people. Do you remember that?"

She laughed at me and said, "Yes, I remember that, Jacky, because I remember you saying, 'My mom, an old person taking care of old people.' Do you remember that, Son?"

"I'm pleading the fifth, Mom."

"Wise choice, Jacky. Anyway, yes, I do remember that; I still do, why?"

"Well, I seem to remember you saying something about 'burdens' and about 'casting.' I remember the casting comment because I immediately thought of fishing while you were talking about praying. For a reason I can't explain to you, I'm interested in what you did, or do, or both. Will you explain that to me again?"

"Oh, honey, I would love to."

I fear she thought she was going to get me converted. Nevertheless, her explanation was fascinating.

"When I go into a hospital room, Jacky, my job is very simple; I am there to bear the person's burden. Galatians 6:2 tells us to do that. Would you like me to tell you what the verse says?"

"No, Mom. I'm kind of busy. If you say the verse has to do with bearing another's burdens, I trust you."

"Okay, but I can if you want me to."

"Thanks, Mom, no."

And she continued, "Every time I pray like that for someone, it amazes me to watch them cast that burden onto the Lord."

"Is there a passage which goes with that, too?"

"Of course, Jacky, it is 1 Peter 5:7."

"Thanks, Mom, that's what I needed."

"But that's not all, Jacky."

"What, Mom?" I asked, getting impatient.

"The next thing that happens when I pray is what God promises in Philippians 4:7. He gives them a peace which transcends their understanding."

I sat there amazed at my mom. That was it! I exclaimed, "Mom, you are the bomb!"

"What does that mean, Jacky?"

I laughed and said, "Never mind."

And then I added, "Hey, Mom, doesn't the Bible say something about correctly parsing truth?"

And of course, she responded with a verse.

"Yes, Son, 2 Timothy 2:15 says we are to rightly divide the word of truth."

"So, if I check out these verses I can determine if you have correctly explained them?" I said with a laugh.

"Be careful, Son," she said with some clear caution in her voice. "The Word of God does not return void."[1]

We said goodbye, and I took my empty dinner plate out into my reception area, where the garbage would be picked up. I have always had an aversion to meals being dumped into an office trash can.

No matter how big the office, and mine is among the largest in the FBI building, the smells of food will linger. So, I always take my food out into Grace's space.

Walking back into my office, my mom's last words rang in my ears. What did she mean by that, "God's Word doesn't return void?"

I opened Pete's "Eyes Only" file. It was a DED. Or Deep Examination Dossier.

OPERATION: JUDAS I.

DED:

5, April

Transcripts:

> *Attached*

Summary:

> *Interviews at Previous Employment: At Macon Poly Technic University, where Perp #3 was just short of tenure, we interviewed all available regents. Three of the university's regents said the perp's actions looked suspiciously like those of radical right-wingers who cause discord, perhaps even violence, possibly on the scale of terrorism. They could not say what actions, in particular, which we conclude is*

139

because the Perp had concealed or disguised his true intentions so well. A fourth regent is dead (of natural causes), and the fifth regent said the charges were fabricated. This fifth regent also admitted to being a close friend of the Perp, so his credibility is suspect. We interviewed a close friend of the Perp's wife who also said the firing of Perp #3 was a hoax. When asked for clarification, the interviewee said the one who brought the charges was an old boyfriend of hers and wanted revenge on her new friends, Dr. Dale and his wife. She refused additional clarification.

Document Review: Looking into the Perp's private files, both online and in his home, we found a number of suspicious items: A) something called 'prayer cards' which he hands out each time he is in an elected official's office. We believe they have an obscure meaning but at this time are unable to determine the significance. B) We found a suspicious document marked as a 1656 English Sermon which Perp #3 often emails to others (including Perp #5 and a number of staffers and several Congressmen). Its significance is currently beyond our comprehension. C) There are three words which we hear often from him, "Bear, Cast, and Peace." The way in which these words are used is clearly suspicious and must have a meaning which we are still trying to run down.

Washington D.C. Surveillance: As stated above, every time Perp #3 visits elected officials and/or their staff, he claims he is there to pray. Then these same three words show up in his notes, "Bear, Cast, and Peace." These also seem to be used in his social media posts as well as his speeches given in front of other like-minded religious ~~nuts~~.

Perp's Timeline: We were already aware of his crossing paths with Perps #4 and #5, including a dinner where he deliberately hid a document from our oversight team. We have also noted his attendance in a hotel, the same one as Perp #2 (odd that Perp #2 stayed in a different hotel than Perp #1, although they were traveling together. BTW, we checked and there were plenty of rooms available in Perp #1's hotel). Conclusion, Perp #3 is not afraid to meet with Perp #2 in public but is keeping a buffer between him and Perp #1. Very professional. We were just setting up a tap on Perp #3's phone when we found he had a direct contact with Perp #1. The audio of the call was never recorded. Again, very professional. They must have known which words to stay away from so our automatic triggering devices would not engage. Nevertheless a few short weeks after the call, Perp #1 through two businesses, with hidden ownership, gave $1,000,000 to each candidate's advertising agencies, apparently, without candidates knowing about the other's agency receipt of same amount. Final item under, "Timeline" is the question, why does the Perp go to Washington D.C. on Tuesday and Wednesday, and never varies those days? Why not Wednesday and Thursday? We have investigated, to our satisfaction, that the Legislators schedules are wide-open all three days, while Mondays and Fridays are usually travel days. Why doesn't the Perp ever deviate from his itinerary? With whom is he coordinating? We don't know yet.

Distribution:

Classified, Director Pete Beecham

Three hours after I got off the phone with my mom, I closed the file, locked it away in my safe and wasn't sure whether I should laugh or cry.

I don't ever pray, but this once I ushered up some words, which really were more along the lines of a verbal sigh; nevertheless, I said, "God, my mom prayed for wisdom for me. And I need it. Are we looking like bumbling fools as badly as I think we are?"

I looked around not knowing what to expect. I did look intently at the walls in my office, though. I seem to remember something about God writing on a wall in front of some government officials.[2] After staring at my walls for a few seconds, I shook my head and got up.

"You're acting foolish, Jack," I said to myself and then cut the lights and headed for home.

---

[1] Isaiah 55:11

[2] Daniel 5

Chapter 23

April 7th, Saturday, The Indian Ocean

Clyde's report of Dale's speaking engagements went with me in my suitcase. I was taking my annual holiday, this year to the Noonu Atoll in the Republic of Maldives. It is an Indian Ocean resort which caters to the very rich. I will usually escape to Noonu, but sometimes I head to La Maltese on Santorini Island in the Greek Islands, or the Hotel Metropole in Monte Carlo.

Whichever I choose, they know me well and take care of my needs; even my bodyguard, Anthony, is well cared for, but of course, I always book him at a different hotel. When I am on Holiday, I have very little need for him and I want to see him even less.

I enjoyed the soft sand of the Sun Siyam Iru Fushi. It is a resort surrounded by cerulean waters. I spent the first two days quietly walking along portions of the fifty-two-acre resort, which are surrounded by groves of palm trees and a beautiful turquoise lagoon.

However, I prefer the water villas to the beach villas. After all, anyone can stay on the beach 'in' a villa; I prefer to stay 'on' the water, because the Plexiglas floors in the water villas allow me to 'walk on water.' How positively purr-fect!

The sky was fantastic on my third day and I decided to pull out Clyde's report while enjoying the weather and the water and the quiet.

"Oh," I thought to myself, "Why would anybody waste this beauty, by having to share it with some selfish partner or spouse. I couldn't imagine a worse way to ruin a trip. Yuk."

I breathed in the beautiful salt air and looked at the report. "Stupid, Clyde," I said to myself immediately. "His file still says, 'Top Secret, Eyes Only' like the moron he is."

I just rolled my eyes at the title at the top of the page, "Operation Judas."

I do like the simple outline and his abbreviated explanations though. I'm sure I couldn't handle it if I were forced to listen to his drivel.

OPERATION: JUDAS I.

DED:

Operational Objective:

Strengthen bond by attending Dr. Dale's speaking engagements, assuring him of our support, and continue to uncover vulnerabilities which should make him do what we need him to do, when we need him to do it.

Current Operational Status:

Attended three meetings, my notes are attached. Gave him another thousand-dollar donation, from us. After church I asked about his statement, "When he meets Legislators in D.C. he 'does not care' about their politics." Potentially a vulnerable spot for us to exploit, as these men and women he prays with must expect him to be very supportive of them.

I made a number of notes.

The first one was, "Quit speaking in the third person, you idiot."

But my second was, "It is time to move forward, Clyde. Let's review the incriminating documents which will be placed into the two religion consultants' files, and I want it done a.s.a.p. When I open up the documents to the candidates, my accusations need to be taken seriously so my knowledge of the documents must be unambiguous."

I looked up the verses Clyde had said Dr. Dale used, beginning with the "peace and joy" verse which says, "Now may the God of hope fill you with all joy and peace as you believe in Him so that you may overflow with hope by the power of the Holy Spirit."[1]

And then I found myself praying, "Lord, I trust You to lead me as to how I might have an influence in the life of this foolish prayer-guy and correct his theology. His influence on churches. . . Well, I really don't care about the churches he speaks in, but his influence in the halls of Congress should really come from a more knowledgeable person, like me, Lord, since I know how to claim joy and peace and declare it into existence in our elected official's lives."

I think I embarrassed myself by my large smile. No one is here in my bungalow over the water, nevertheless, my enthusiasm for what God wants me to do, is exciting, and, in a sense, about time.

I continued praying. Actually, I was praying and purring at the same time. "Knowing how to get joy and peace which leads to hope is my forte, Lord. So, I'm trusting You to put me in places of authority, instead of this Dr. Dale character, just like I believe You want me in the place of power for whichever presidential candidate is voted in."

I then looked up the stupid passage, used by many, many people incorrectly. Paul didn't even write this, as modern criticism has proved. Romans 13:1-2 reads,

"Everyone must submit to the governing authorities, for there is no authority except from God, and those that exist are instituted by God. So then, the one who resist the authority is opposing God's command, in those who oppose it will bring judgment on themselves."[2]

I was in my zone, having what must be God's nearly total concentration on my words, I continued in prayer, "Lord, I claim a foothold into the powers of the presidential winner, though a number of months off yet. I am faithfully trusting You, Lord, to honor my activities in preparation, knowing that nothing formed against me will stand. Amen, and Amen."

"Now that is real power," I said to myself. And then I laughed and I continued to laugh when from deep inside me a guttural sound escaped which, I confess, scared me at first. But then I recognized it for what it was; that 'angel of light' was making groans inside me, which cannot be uttered and which only the Father knows.

I growled and laughed. I purred and laughed. I smiled and laughed. I was euphoric and something was exciting my insides.

It was marvelous!

Just then I had another thought. It had to do with the eavesdropping cyber-attack Clyde had mentioned to me.

He suggested that we need to move from passive eavesdropping to active eavesdropping so we can hide the electronic signature of our emails.

I don't know exactly what Clyde's talking about, but I'm sure it will work; after all, it must be God's will.

I now realized it was time to have Clyde cyber hack the prayer-guy, Dr. Dale.

Just then I received a call on my cell phone. It was my private number so I immediately picked up. Very, very few people have this number.

"Good morning, Pastor," came the friendly voice from the other end. I nearly hung up thinking it was an overly enthusiastic telemarketer and then she introduced herself.

"I hope it's not too early," she half-apologized.

"No, Priscilla," I answered. "I'm actually on Holiday so I am five hours ahead of you in the Indian Ocean."

"Oh, well, I don't want to bother. . ."

"It is no bother at all," I said with all the charm I could. What I thought in my mind was, "You are a lying politician who steals candy from babies, while at the same time makes promises you do not intend keep."

Instead, I simply said, "It's my honor to serve you and the Candidate. How might I help?"

"Well, I think it's a theological issue and as such I am way out of my expertise."

"Hmm," I wondered while she was talking. "Why isn't she getting her Religion Consultant involved?"

I decided to probe, just a bit. "Is everything okay with Issy?" I asked in mock concern.

"Oh, yes," she hesitated.

I remained silent, knowing my prey was coming to me. It's the power of the silence close. She who is quiet the longest wins! Priscilla was an idiot, so I just waited.

We must have been on the phone for a solid minute with me not speaking, and then she asked, "Are you still there, Pastor?"

"Yes, Priscilla. I'm just here to serve you."

Again, a silence that seemed to stretch into eternity, but afterwards she said softly, "I have seen the outline of a document Issy is giving me in a few days and, well, I don't know why, but I am uncomfortable with something in it, and I think I would like fresh eyes on it."

"How exciting," I thought. "The beginning of the 'crash and burn' of a good for nothing employee."

"Will you be able to email it to me so I can review it and then report to you?"

"Forgive me for asking this, Pastor, but can you come here, to D.C.? It is an internal memo, so we'll need it reviewed here, onsite."

"I'm sure I'll be able to do that, Priscilla. I'll be arriving home in a week and a half. Will you have it by then? If so, why don't I plan to be there the middle of the following week?"

"Oh, thank you." She was truly relieved. "I told the boss we could count on you."

"My pleasure," I said with my silkiest voice and a hint of purring. "May I ask though, what is the subject?"

"Umm," she hesitated, so I just remained silent. "It has to do with religious people's views of news outlets."

"Well, I look forward to seeing you soon."

She immediately jumped in, "Umm, Pastor?"

By this time, I was done listening to her and wanted to go back to the sun and the heat. But I was my usual patient self.

"Yes, Priscilla?"

"Well, I just looked at Issy's schedule and she is not going to be in the office on Tuesday, the 24th, so if you can be here then, I'd sure feel better."

"Consider it done, Priscilla." And I hung up on her.

I actually felt bad about doing that. A little bit bad, anyway.

April 13th, Friday, Arlington VA

Issy and I had worked hard on this project for her boss each night. Now on the morning of Friday the 13th, she was ready to give it to her Chief of Staff. I'm in the religion business, not the superstition business, but I would be less than honest if I didn't admit that for a few moments I wondered if she should hand it in on Monday.

Nevertheless, the document was looking good and it was clearly non-partisan. It was just what her bosses wanted.

The document discussed various news outlets of choice; why we leave them, and why we stay, even when we've been lied to. The document also discussed the drug of "rage" which is used by news outlets to keep us returning to them. And then Issy brilliantly weaved in Dr. Dale's drug of "encouragement" which he gives congregations and made the argument that "rage" promotes anger while "encouragement" promotes security. I think she did great.

---

[1] Romans 15:13 (HCSB)

[2] From the HCSB version

Chapter 24

Yesterday, Issy and I grabbed a mid-afternoon movie at the local Regal Ballston Cinema and then went two blocks to P. F. Chang's.

Every couple months we like to go to the cinemas. And at the restaurant, the host sat us three tables away from Harold and his wife, G.W. I tried to not look over there, but more than once we caught one another's eyes.

Seven or eight minutes into our main course, Harold and his wife came over to our table. The two ladies went to the restroom and Harold sat down.

We were silent. There was nothing to say.

"How do we get beyond this, Jude?" Harold eventually asked.

I hung my head in humility and asked, "Why are you so angry at me, Harold? You are personally angry at me, with a vitriol that is, scary." I didn't meet his eyes until he started to speak.

"I honestly don't know, Jude," he said soberly. I could tell he wanted to keep speaking and I just waited for him to gather his thoughts.

"Jude, my politics are so important to me, that your choice of a candidate is hugely repulsive to me. Frankly, your decision to follow this candidate makes me want to throw-up."

I raised my head and my eyebrows.

He quickly added, "I'm sorry. I've finished eating and you haven't. Forgive me. But saying those words just helped me realize something, Jude. I'm not angry at you. . ."

He smiled humbly and said, "Even though I yelled at you."

I gently shook my head, slightly confused and then suggested, "Harold, our unity is in Christ. You and I are brothers in Christ. Our unity is not to be determined by our politics. Our unity is based on what we both have in Christ."

"The evil one is doing his best in our nation, to deceive us into focusing on the part of our politics we 'know' is right, when the real issue, which he doesn't want us to focus on, is unity in Christ."

I looked at him for a moment and saw him calculating in his mind. And so, I said, "Harold, I'm watching your eyes and I can tell you what you are thinking. You are saying to yourself, 'but I Am right.' Isn't that what's going through your mind right now?"

He nodded and I went on. "The devil has a vested interest in us not being united. He knows we get little or nothing done, if we do not have unity. And my friend, our unity will always be in Christ, regardless of my stupidity, in your eyes, when I am at the ballot box."

He chuckled, but he was thinking. He was digesting my words. "The girls are coming," I said, "So let me just leave you with this to ponder. If Paul didn't make a mistake, and if the first two verses of Romans chapter thirteen are true, then when God puts into office whom He wants, we have a responsibility to respond to that President differently than the world will, even if it's not who we voted for. But brother, if we are not careful, we can act just like the world, and why? Because we can let our 'rightness' in our minds supersede our unity in Christ. And that's just crazy, Harold."

He agreed somewhat. Just then the girls walked toward us arm in arm, which I was glad to see. They were both wiping tears from their eyes when they got to us.

Harold and I stood, and he hesitantly reached his hand out to me, which I gladly shook. He smiled but didn't say anything and we gave a brief man-hug to one another. Then they walked away.

Before Issy could speak, I said, "We're not back yet, but we have made a good step forward."

The next day, Issy and I were lying in bed, getting ready to study our passage for the week.

She chuckled and said, "You know what I was thinking when I saw Harold and G.W. last night?"

I looked expectantly for her to continue and she said, "Our study on the hostile religionists."

"Exactly," I said.

And then she read, "Now at the Feast the Jews were watching. . ."[1]

November, A.D. 29, Hostility and Compassion

I am so tired of all this traveling. Why can't we just go and rest for an entire week? Not only am I tired but we are running into hostility everywhere we go.

I'm over it! And, I don't understand it. He knew there was going to be trouble at the festival. It was so obvious that He waited until the Feast of Tabernacles was half over before attending.[2]

And then what did He do when He got there? He went straight to the temple steps and started teaching![3]

I was surprised when the temple guards came to us, presumably to arrest Jesus.[4] But instead of arresting Him, they stood there with their mouths open, listening to His great wisdom.

People were asking question after question, trying to trip Him up, and the poor guards didn't know what to do. But they did say something interesting. They said, "No one ever spoke the way this man does."[5] I'll bet that if they said that to the Pharisees, they would have been chewed out.

I actually felt sorry for them.

But there was another event of which I am in awe. The Pharisees brought in a woman caught in adultery,[6] which made me wonder why they didn't bring the man too.

Anyway, the compassion Jesus showed her touched me in a way I did not remember since the beginning of our nearly three-year trek. And His ability to silence these men who were out to trap Him;[7] I don't mind saying, that impressed me.

When He bent down and started writing in the sand, we all backed away, but I wanted to see what He was writing. The arrogant Pharisees came up to Him, looked at His writing, and then, surprisingly, they left, one by one, starting with the older men and working their way down to the youngest.[8]

Even more fascinating, was the comfort He showed her. Amazing!

April 15th, Sunday Morning, Arlington VA

Before yesterday, I hadn't applied this passage to Harold, but Issy was right. The application was glaringly right-on.

The personal rage Harold has had for me is like the rage the Pharisees had for Jesus. And it was all centered in the Pharisees' identity within their sect, rather than in the God of the Bible.

I was busy in thought when I heard Issy say, "What a great reality, a promise, if you will, that He is always going to be compassionate even in the midst of the most terrible of my sins."

"Great insight, babe," I said, and added, "I also noticed that His judgment on those who are guilty of judging is not necessarily flashy or crude, is it?"

"And before a long day, what did He do?" Issy asked.

"He prayed," I said.

"Yes, the first verse of John chapter eight."

She was on a roll and she continued, "And then in verse two He gets to the temple and starts to teach those around Him. I can't imagine what a comfort that must have been to the crowds."

I sat back to think and Issy stopped to allow me to process. I was thinking about all the Bible studies and prayer meetings on the Hill, which elected officials and staffers attend, weekly and even daily, both sides of the aisle, together, undivided.

I said, "If the public only knew that here in D.C. there are a number of Bible studies and prayer meetings happening and who are attending them, they'd be so encouraged."

"And surprised," she quipped.

"That's why what Dale shares in churches is so important, babe," I said.

"Let me end with verse three," Issy said. "Look at the incredible schemes the Pharisees went through, just to trap Jesus. How did they come up with this woman? What about the missing man? Look at their willingness to publicly humiliate one person, to get to another. Sounds like our modern-day politics."

We were getting out of bed when I said, before she could, "Sounds like your boss."

While I was proud of my quick wit, she just turned away and said, "Too bad, for you, mister; we HAD plenty of time this morning. . . ."

"Idiot," I said to myself.

Church was a blessing to me again. It always is, but today my pastor was brilliant. I pulled him aside afterwards and I said, "I'm not your dad, but if I were, I'd be very proud of you today. Great message."

He thanked me and then said, "A little birdie told me you and Issy were at P. F. Chang's last night with Harold and his G.W.?"

He said it as a question and I responded, "I wouldn't say, 'with them,' but we did talk for a few minutes."

"So?" he asked.

I simply said, "We're making progress."

But there was something else on his mind.

"When we talked the other day, why did you lump yourself and me into the mix with Harold's anger?"

"Pastor, he's just angry, just like you and I get at times."

He remained quiet. His eyes boring into me which made me understand he expected more.

"Pastor," I finally said, "I think our problem is as simple as what I see on the Hill."

"Which is?"

"So many men and women on the Hill get their identity from their politics."

I paused to allow him to digest my words and then continued. "We do the same thing in the church; instead of our identity being in Christ, our identity is in other things."

"But that doesn't explain our anger, Jude."

"No, you're right, but this does. As I told Issy the other day, 'When disgust meets your Christian conscience, the result is either humility or anger.' Harold's disgust came out as anger."

"Look," I said, "Politics is important, but if it keeps us from unity in the body, something is wrong. Personally, Pastor, to me it is a trust issue, or maybe a 'lack of trust' issue."

"Yeah, we had that discussion the other day, Jude. You are saying it's a trust in God issue, aren't you?"

"Bingo," I said.

"I got it," he said.

"Let me add, Pastor, that how we respond to those we disagree with demonstrates whether or not we trust God."

He just raised one eyebrow, questioningly.

"Look at our passion for politics in the church. I think a lot of it comes from a feeling of hopelessness if we don't get the "right" person in office . . . This kind of thinking is crazy."

"Actually," he said, rubbing his slight stubble, "this kind of thinking is actually putting our trust in princes."[9]

"You're right," I said.

"Harold's identity has been in his politics," said my pastor, "And it has been so strong that he didn't realize he was not trusting Jesus."

I nodded.

"Hmm, so trust in the Lord is the real issue. Is that what you're saying, Jude?"

Before I could answer, he stopped and looked startled. "Yikes, what you are also saying is that my anger on a particular subject, any subject, is communicating my lack of trust in God, relative to that subject!"

"Exactly, Pastor."

"And if I have righteous anger, Jude?"

"Pastor, if your anger or passion leads you to disunity with a brother in Christ, because they hold a different view from you, then you are wrong, even if you're right."

"Ouch," he said.

We man-hugged and parted company with him rubbing his stubbled chin. These young guys who preach without a shaven face, I don't understand that.

I walked up to Issy chuckling and when we walked outside towards home, I told her about my conversation with our pastor.

"But why were you laughing?" she asked.

"Because I realized as I walked away from him I was judging him, simply because of his stubble on his chin!"

She rammed an elbow into my side. "Just like Harold was doing to you?"

"Yes, but worse than that. I did to our pastor what the Pharisees did to Jesus in our reading this morning."

---

[1] John 7:11a

[2] John 7:14a

[3] John 7:14b

[4] John 7:32b

[5] John 7:46

[6] John 8:3

[7] John 8:6a

[8] John 8:9

[9] Psalm 146:3a

Chapter 25

April 23ʳᵈ, Monday, FBI Headquarters

Billy and Sammie got off two different elevators and came into my office foyer trying to act like they didn't know each other. I was at Grace's desk talking to her and I noticed their actions. So, a few minutes later, when they entered my office I said to both of them, "I appreciate the fact you are trying to keep your knowledge of each other hidden, but when you're in my office area it's ok to talk."

They both looked relieved which I thought was kind of cute and wondered how they entered the safe house for their bi-weekly meetings. But it did make me think about another issue, so I ask them.

"Do you two see each other at any other venues?"

They were silent and looked down at their feet, which I didn't like. I remained silent, knowing I needed to let them speak.

It is amazing to me how much people will say, that they normally would not, if one is just quiet. It's interesting. When there is silence, people want to fill it with words.

Billy spoke, "Boss we didn't plan this, but we both find ourselves attending the same church."

I looked at them warily, thought of religious rights arguments, and decided to ignore it, for the time being.

Getting started with our meeting, I asked Billy, "A couple months ago we talked about contacts in your colleague's files. I trust you have been following them. Is there anything new on that front?

"I looked deeper and found that these friendlies stay in touch with one another, and actually, fairly often. It's like they are one great big group or clique. And in lots of cases, various members of their staff stay in touch with one another. It is really odd. It's like they are all one extended family."

"Did you do any additional follow up?" I asked.

He responded with a red face and I said, "What? You're not getting in trouble, I like your proactiveness. What'd you find?"

"Well, I kind of, felt like I had a little authority from you. So I decided to look at periodic emails to and from this group of people. My examination was by no means exhaustive, but I did find one interesting and regular refrain. It had to do with the words, 'God has given favor to,' and they all referenced an apostle, whom they also call a pastor, who apparently has some political connections."

"Who is it?" I asked, knowing what the answer would be.

"Apostle, Pastor Mortenson from. . ."

"Atlanta. Yes, I know of her, Billy. Good work."

Billy and Sammie looked at each other in surprise, "How did you know that, boss?" Sammie asked.

"I've been working this case from a number of directions," was all I answered.

I was trying to think through the facts they were giving me when I noticed they were both looking at each other and I could tell there was something else which needed to be shared.

"So," I asked, "What else?"

Sammie took the lead. "We found something interesting. Not a problem, because we know them, and trust them, but it is a bit odd."

"What is it," I asked, already thinking about my calendar for tomorrow.

Billy now spoke. "I noticed a document in Issy's files which had her husband's signature stamp."

Sammie noticed my, "I don't get it," look on my face.

"It means the document came from Jude's computer," she explained.

"Why would he be giving her a document?" I said in a whisper, loud enough to be heard.

"That concerned me too, boss," added Billy, "especially when her notes on the document said, 'eyes only' and then the candidate's name as well as the Chief of Staff."

He continued, "I started tracking the document and made a note to tell you about it if it ever becomes a white-paper the candidate uses to make policy decisions."

"That's when Billy got me involved," Sammie picked up the narrative, "And I started looking for the origin of the document but determined its origin was not on Jude's work computer."

She looked at Billy who said, "Remember when we first met, sir? I told you I am pretty good at 'geeking.' Well, I put on my geeking hat and started looking for the origin of this document."

He stopped and looked over at Sammie who seemed to encourage him. It's actually kind of sweet to watch these two work together.

"Boss, the origin of this document was their home and the hours on which the document was worked, was late evening, every time."

"Collaboration?" I whispered, more to myself than to them. I stood up slowly and didn't realize it at first, but I was shaking my head, "Not Jude and Issy."

Billy and Sammie remained completely quiet as I strode over to my window.

I wasn't looking at anything in particular. "What was the subject of the document?" I asked.

"News Outlets and Religious People," one of them said.

As if not hearing, I continued, "Collaboration is contrary their work agreement."

After a few more moments I asked, "Just curious. How did the document get to Issy's computer? Was there an email trail?"

"No, sir, why?" asked Sammie.

I was getting angry now, not at Billy and Sammie, but at Jude and Issy. I have spent the last few months shielding them from Pete, who may have been right all along.

I hate having to eat-crow when there has been an inter-departmental blunder. I thought about it some more and realized, "No, that isn't my concern." For some reason my mom popped into my head.

"That's it!" I said, gritting my teeth. I turned to the two kids. My face was red, I could feel it. I spit out the words, "I can just see the newspapers now, 'Christian Couple at Heart of Political Espionage.' Another cyber challenged presidential election, and this one, on my watch."

My suspicions were now through the roof. "Are they doing what they promised to never do, namely, work together?"

Sammie's eyes welled up with tears. She now understood the critical situation I saw Jude and Issy in. She wasn't looking at me, but her concern was obvious. She asked, "You're not going to arrest them or haul them in, are you?"

I saw the fright in Billy's face too, but Sammie continued, "Sir, the moment their bosses' ability to trust them is questioned, these two people will be broken and kicked out of the business."

"There's got to be something we are missing, sir." Billy responded, anxiety in his voice. "Boss, we're talking about two very respected people's lives. You can't do this to them, sir, boss. You can't."

Because I was only partially listening to them, I ignored their direct challenge to my authority. I was still thinking of the implications of their revelation. I dismissed them asking, "Is there anything else you need to tell me?"

"No," they both said, looking at each other.

"Alright," I told them, "Then I need you to go. I have a lot of work to do now."

I looked at these two frightened kids with a little sympathy. "I know my reaction is causing you unease, but I have to think of the bigger picture. I have a lot of decisions to make and directional changes. But of course, keep looking for information you think I'll need."

Leaving FBI Headquarters

I couldn't believe what had just happened. Billy and I merely shared information about one document and now the lives of two people could be severely damaged or even ruined.

We had to do something about this. We couldn't let it remain in this state. "But what?" I thought to myself, "What?"

Since we started working together on this project, we had developed some cues which we'd use to communicate in ways that kept our friendship clandestine. Over the last few weeks our relationship had become one of deep personal friendship. Who knows, maybe even love? I blushed deeply thinking about falling in love with Billy.

One of the cues we had was passing by the other and giving a little cough. This meant "call me immediately."

I thought of Jude and Issy. I did think it odd that they had collaborated when their employment agreement is so clear. But knowing them, I couldn't see them violating their employer's trust. And how do we know they collaborated, maybe Issy just used Jude's computer for some reason?

There were too many things we still didn't know. And we needed to fix this.

In the elevator on the way down, I nonchalantly covered my mouth and gave a small cough. Billy raised his head a little but never looked at me.

Chapter 26

April 24th, Tuesday Morning, Homeland Security

Homeland Security has their office building on the other side of the Mall from the FBI building. I can leave my office, head down to the 9th street exit and walk straight through the Mall to Homeland Security.

It was a cold, brisk morning and a rare, late April snowstorm had been dropping snow for the last few hours. It was still coming down and was expected to continue till noon. Nevertheless, I was up for a walk and I needed one.

I had spent the night in my office, going back over all of the evidence Pete had sent me. While I had thought his department was acting more like Keystone cops than professional agents, by the end of the night I decided I may have been the Keystone Cop and they the dependable agents.

When I arrived, Pete's agents all looked warily at me. Interdepartmentally, we have good relations, but personally, our relationships were judged on a one-to-one basis, and, I admit, I often looked down my nose at these men and women, even periodically saying so, on the record.

"Frankly," I thought to myself, "they could have sneered more, and I would have owned it."

Pete started the meeting with, "As you can see, we are graced by the presence of our FBI friend."

He paused and there was complete silence. The stone-cold looks were more frigid than the snow which had gotten into my shoes when I walked over.

I stood up slowly and tried to keep the grin off my face, but I couldn't. I said, "I expected you to throw stones."

"They're outside," someone said and most of them snickered.

"I'll ask for an escort going back then," I jested.

"Not from us," someone else quipped, less of a jest than mine.

I saw a slight movement on Pete's part, but didn't want him to butt in. I needed to own this and deal with it, if I was going to get reliable interdepartmental cooperation from his team.

I made a calculated decision and arrogantly said, "I'm not here to offer you an olive branch."

I immediately saw Pete sit back. I knew he was thinking, "Jack, if you're gonna talk to them this way, you're on your own."

"And you don't have to like me; that's okay," I said, a little less arrogantly.

"No problem with that, Sir," said a wiry kid, respectfully, and a number of them laughed.

"But I'm also big enough to tell you I may have been wrong about this case. I have been holding you back and that may have been an error. That's why I'm here, on your territory."

I couldn't help myself, I added, "I hope you consider it an honor that I'm here."

By the last words I was purposely grinning. I'm good at keeping a straight face, but chose to not do so this morning, and sure enough, they loosened up for our meeting.

"You're not really funny, Sir," said the wiry kid.

"Oh yes I am," I said, as slyly as I could.

And then he got me. I didn't even see it coming.

"It's the way you comb your hair, Sir," he said.

To which even I laughed. I turned to Pete. "I like this kid."

Pete smiled and nodded to me, as if to say, "Tell them why you're here."

So I did. "I came to your sit-rep today because of some information I got last night. Pete has accused me of not telling him everything and he's right. I've been investigating this from another direction and then comparing my results with yours. Well, last night my team shared with me something very disturbing and I decided to humble myself and come over here to tell you about it."

"Eating a little humble-pie?" asked Wiry.

I went on. "I have been most concerned with Perps #1 and #2, thinking they are the real bad guys and Perps #3, #4 and #5 are innocents."

Wiry raised his hand and I nodded for him to speak. "Are we talking the same people when you state Perp numbers?"

"Valid point," agreed Pete.

"Jack, with what you have uncovered, I don't think we need to be secretive anymore on our internal documents. Do you agree?"

I stood there looking into space for a few moments and then agreed. "Perp #1 is the Preacher, Perp #2 is the Counterintelligence, CI-Guy, Perp #3 is the Prayer-Guy, Perp #4 is Issy, the female Religion Consultant and wife of Perp #5, whose name is Jude."

I looked at Pete's team and asked, "Are we on the same page so far?" I knew we were but a good working relationship demanded I ask the question.

They all nodded in agreement and I went on. Watching their faces I knew they were itching for the new information from my team which so radically changed my mind last night.

"I'll admit, I have been unimpressed with your operational name, 'Judas I.,' but after last night's revelation it's more appropriate than you realize."

I saw a number of people sit up straighter and listen more intently.

"Here's our situation. For the last few years our street credibility has been drug through the mud, based on foolish actions on the part of a few people in our agencies and elected officials who have gotten away with obvious misdeeds."

"I don't have to explain this to you. You've seen it and lived it. Many of you have kids who have tried to hide from teachers and friends what their parents do for a living because they run the risk of being humiliated."

Everyone solemnly agreed and I paused to take a drink from a cup of coffee which I had let cool down.

"We have rightfully been super-conscientious of doing anything which makes us look like we are a law unto ourselves. And, I want to thank you."

I locked eyes with each agent before I continued. "I want to thank you for allowing me to hold you back, but now I think we have clear evidence on two folks, who I believed were completely above board. But it's possible that they may be the masterminds, and maybe better said, the manipulators of the events we've been watching unfold."

My coffee was now the right temperature. It was warm but not hot. I took another drink.

"Now, I'm not completely sold on this but I'm persuaded enough to come here and eat some crow.

I continued, "I have been looking at this CI-Guy, Clyde, wondering if he could think this up. But I can't get there. He's a buffoon. And then there's the Preacher; her arrogance warns me of her strong motivation, meaning she may think she deserves to be in a place of influence, but my reason leads me to think she doesn't have the brains to carry this off either."

"As for the Prayer-Guy, he's clearly no dummy, and he has connections in D.C.; but I'm still wondering if he's being manipulated or doing the manipulating? Is he innocent? I'd like to think he is but his firing from the university keeps me from being convinced."

I slowed down to be sure everyone was tracking with me.

"And then there's Perps #4 and #5, Issy and Jude. To my mind, they were once considered pure as the wind driven snow. Now my curiosity makes me ask, 'How far have they traveled down the dark side?'"

159

"Could they be unelected civil servants who are taking advantage of a long-awaited opportunity? Have they set themselves up to win, whichever Presidential candidate is elected? What were their political leanings back in school and are their current decision-making, policy-advisement, etc. consistent with who they are and who they claim to be? Also I am now wondering if Issy's relationship with Perp #2 is really this recent, or if they have been preparing this for a long time."

"What added up yesterday, no longer adds up today," offered Wiry.

"Exactly, and now that I have allowed myself to think in these terms, I realize there is a lot I do not know about them." I acknowledged Pete and proceeded, "The bottom line is, do we have a couple who have worked the system for a long time, in the hopes of seeing their long-awaited plan come to fruition?"

I paused, not really looking at anyone.

My discomfort over what I had just suggested about Jude and Issy was interrupted by Wiry. "What do you think they want? Money, power, what?"

"If we are right about Jude and Issy, which I am afraid we may be, then I think the 'why' is as simple and as dangerous as their own self-righteousness. They want to advance their perspective, no matter how it is done."

"The end justifies the means," Wiry said, as much to me as to the others in the room.

"Precisely," said Pete. "And that's the incredible gravity, troops. If this holds true, they do not care what the voting public says. They won't let their ideology be hindered by something like, who wins, which is why they've worked so hard to be on both sides of the fight."

Slowly and with the strongest emphasis, I said, "If that's true, these two people are a clear and present danger to the sovereignty of our elections. The gloves come off as soon as we tie them to a crime."

"Tell them what you found and how you found it," said Pete.

"I can't give you the details on how I found it, but I have two operatives, one in each camp, running recon for me."

"What I can tell you," I went on, "Is that Jude and Issy clearly conspired to work together on a policy paper for Issy's candidate. The reason this is a big deal, is first, a condition of their employment agreement is to never coordinate with their spouse, and secondly, it appears they uploaded the document to Issy's computer in such a way that it could only have been done for the purpose of hiding an email trail."

"They have purposed to deceive," Wiry said.

"Affirmative," replied Pete.

"That's the way I now see it, too," I replied.

Pete then asked, "Jack, do we know what their ultimate end game is?"

I shook my head, "No." Then he continued.

"What you found last night can easily get them fired, and that would be the end of it, as far as those two are concerned; but it wouldn't deal with the other three. So, what do you suggest?"

"Simple," I said, "These five Perps didn't just come together. This has been a long time in the making. We need to get to the bottom of it and then connect all the dots. I don't care what their motivation is. I'm concerned about determining if this is home-grown or if there are foreign powers involved. Then we need to determine how big this is. Are there other players?"

On my way back to the office I got a text from my mom. "Hello Jacky, love you, Son. No need to call me back. Two things: First, I'm praying for wisdom for you and secondly, last night I heard a podcast from a pastor who is from D.C. or goes to D.C. or something. But he who talks about prayer like I do. I really liked him. Let me know if you're interested."

"Hmm," I croaked, "No, Mom, I'm up to my ears in prayer people and I'm thinking their prayers are bunk!"

Of course, I only thought it and didn't text it. Instead I responded, "Thanks, Mom. I think your God is giving me wisdom. Regarding the other, I'm kind of busy. Love you."

Same Day, Afternoon, FBI Headquarters

"Jack," Grace rang me, "Mr. Beecham is on, said it's urgent."

"Yeah, Pete."

"Guess who just 'accidentally' met today? The Prayer-Guy and the Preacher."

"Hmm," was all I said.

"She had just come out of Issy's boss' office."

"How do you know it was chance, Pete?"

"I don't think it was chance, Jack."

"Then why did you say it was?"

"Because that is what the Perps said to one another, loud enough for my guys to hear."

"These Perps' tradecraft is good, Jack, very good."

"Hmm, so, Prayer-Guy has contact with Preacher, who was just in Issy's boss' office."

I sat for a moment scratching my chin. I needed to go home tonight to get a good night's sleep. And then I got excited and asked, "Was Issy there, too?"

"No," Pete said, disappointed. "She was out on the campaign trail."

"Got it. Keep me posted," I said and hung up.

Chapter 27

Issy and I have worked for a lot of candidates in the past, but we have found that the heightened security on a Presidential campaign is both fascinating and a pain.

The flying part is great; we avoid airport waits by flying directly into the nearest Air Force Base. Last week I was on the campaign trail with my boss, our Chief of Staff, local Congressmen and Senators when we flew into Warner Robins Air Force Base.

We had an event in the Macon area, so I tried to meet with a couple of my new Macon area friends, Dr. Dale Riley, whom Issy and I have named, 'The Prayer-Guy,' and Clyde Smith who is the liaison for a very influential female preacher, who I hope to meet one day soon.

But security. The moment I wanted to leave our group after our event, I was followed by two new suits whom, I was told, were just there for my safety.

But it didn't feel right. It still doesn't.

Issy brought us some coffee and we opened our Harmony devotional.

I tasted the coffee and made a face. "There's no sugar, baby."

"What did Dr. Joseph tell you this week after your annual cardio appointment?"

I ignored her and started to read because he said I needed to lose the extra twenty pounds I was carrying.

She wasn't done though. "And your sodium intake, that needs to be reduced, too."

I rolled my eyes.

"Don't you roll your eyes at me, honey-bun. I just threw away the Morton Salt 'Umbrella Girl.'"

"Baby, we ought to hold onto it, just because it is such a classic."

"Nice try, buster, but no more salt."

I just started reading. "When Jesus spoke again to the people. . ."[1]

November A.D. 29, Hostile Religious Leaders

Lately, my mind is often scrambled with the accusations levied at Jesus and His answers which usually have a ring of truth in them. I'll admit, I do marvel at how He handles them; whether His answers are true or not, or wise or not, is another story.

This constant argument with the Pharisees and religious leaders is a case in point. Jesus is at the temple, telling the people who He is, when the Pharisees challenge Him.

In all honesty, I think they are so jealous of Jesus' success that they are making up arguments and parsing every single word to get Him off His game, in hopes the people will stop listening to Him.

A couple of the Pharisees, teachers of the law, interrupted Jesus with a challenge. Basically they were saying that since Jesus was telling about Himself, His testimony could not be trusted,[2] as it was circular reasoning.

If I were Jesus, I would have said, "A person tells a lot more about himself than he realizes when he accuses others, like you do when you accuse me." But of course, Jesus was more patient than me.

Later I stood back and watched this "dance," of the Temple Guard and the Pharisees whispering. Clearly, the Pharisees wanted Jesus stopped but He was not seized, almost as if His time had not yet come.[3]

And then the Pharisees said something that really outraged me. When Jesus said, 'Where I'm going you cannot come,'[4] they wondered, out loud, if Jesus was going to commit suicide.[5] And while Jesus remained patient, I wanted to yell and scream about how no honorable Jew ever commits suicide.

The more I thought about it, the angrier I got. Accusing Jesus of contemplating suicide was the lowest.

I myself have had a number of unflattering things to say about Him, but that He would commit suicide? That was a new low to which even I would never stoop.

And then, just when I think Jesus is being courageous, and intelligent, making wise arguments, He said something which was just foolish. He told the Pharisees they would die in their sins.[6]

I couldn't believe my ears. I started to walk away because now I was embarrassed of this so-called Rabbi of mine.

But then I noticed something very odd; even as He spoke, the people were putting their faith in Him.[7] It was amazing, this power He has over the crowds.

"Oh, Jesus," I thought to myself, "Don't You realize the power You hold?"

And then He said a few things in succession which made me nearly run away. He accused the Pharisees of wanting to kill Him.[8] I was seriously wondering if He were getting delusional.

Next, He told them they were like their father the devil.[9] And if that weren't enough, He said He didn't plan to be a liar like them.[10] He spoke so self-righteously, I thought.

Surely we were done. But no; He said something which made me angrier with Him.

Jesus had the temerity to say, of Himself, that He is the I Am.[11] Well, as you can imagine, these already frustrated Pharisees, who had been blocked with every accusation by the defense Jesus made, picked up stones to stone Him! But somehow Jesus hid and slipped away from the temple grounds.[12]

Sunday, May 13th, Arlington VA

Issy and I lay resting in bed. And then looking at the clock I disentangled myself from the sheets and said, "We need to go through this while we have time, baby."

She rubbed her eyes. She was still tired, but sat up, fluffed her pillows and said, "Okay, I'm ready. Where's our coffee?"

"Coming right up," I said and then went to the kitchen where the coffee maker was right on time, as usual.

When I climbed back in bed, she was already in her copy of our Harmony Devo.

"You sure spoil me, Darling. Thank you," she said to me.

It's the little things like that which make me want to serve her as often as I can. She was still talking so I needed to focus on the Word, rather than myself, and her, and me, and us. . .

She said, "Jesus was a master at dealing with lying accusations with truth. He always knew how to handle people, whether they spoke truths or lies."

She looked at me and then added, "Why do you think that was, Jude?"

"Babe, I think there was one reason and He tells us in this passage. I think He says it a few times. Look at John, chapter eight at the end of verse twenty-six, Jesus says, 'What I have heard from Him, meaning His Father, I tell the world.' Which tells you and me we need to be prayed up, read up, and in as close a relationship with the Lord, as we can be, Baby, especially as our respective bosses rely upon us."

I then added, "That is my not-so-surprising challenge."

"That was one of mine too, Jude, but I got it from the sixteenth verse, where Jesus talks of His standing with the Father."

"Look," Issy continued, "Look at verses twenty-three and twenty-four where Jesus gave me today's 'unusual promise,' which really is a negative promise. It says so clearly there are consequences which will impact time and eternity, namely, dying in one's sins."

She then looked over at me, with all seriousness. "Baby, we each have colleagues who will not spend eternity with us, if they died today. And I for one have not been the witness I could be."

"I have just one more thought, Jude. What if Harold is right?"

"Where'd that come from, Issy?" I asked.

"Look at verse thirty-two, it says, 'You will know the truth, and the truth will set you free.' Baby, maybe Harold is right and one of us is deadly wrong, in our politics. This verse says that if we know the truth, then the truth would make us free. Doesn't that imply that one of us is right, having the truth, and the other is wrong?"

This conversation creeps up every few years between us and I try to handle it the same way each time.

I said, "Baby, I think the Word is clear. First, it says, whatever we do, we are to do with excellence and do it as if we were doing it unto the Lord, rather than man.[13] Second, you and I both know we can be and are 'a light shining on a hill[14]' in our offices where people are unsaved. Third, God has given us a passion and fervency for what we do and until we hear from Him, we need to keep on doing it fervently. Finally, God is not a god of confusion; rather, He is a God of peace,[15] and as long as I have peace about what I am doing, I'm going to keep doing it. Just as you should, too. Keep working for your loser candidate, as long as you have peace, baby."

After she hit me and we lovingly tussled for a few minutes she asked, seriously, "I also marked verse forty-four, Jude. Look at the reference to 'your father the devil.' Is it possible one of us is working for the devil?"

I could tell it was an honest question, so I didn't joke. I just reminded her God called wicked Nebuchadnezzar, his servant, more than once.[16] "In fact, even Daniel tells us the same thing Romans 13:1-2 tells us, that God gave the leader his greatness, glory and splendor.[17] And lest we forget, baby, wicked Cyrus was called God's anointed.[18] I am convinced, Issy, God has us where He wants us and He is working out all things for the better."[19]

I paused and looked tenderly at her and said, "If there is any fault you have, Issy, it's that you want to always figure out the 'whys' behind what God is doing. But baby, 'Why' belongs to Him. It always does. Once in a while He shares with us the 'why,' but more times than not, He holds it close to the vest."

"There is a last promise; truly an unusual promise I need to remember, Issy, and it comes from the forty-fifth verse. Jesus makes clear that just because we share the truth, it does not mean we will be believed. Especially if the one we share the truth with is an unbeliever."

"That is really something to remember," she said.

"Right," I responded.

We needed to get ready for church.

---

[1] John 8:12

[2] John 8:13

[3] John 8:20

[4] John 8:21

[5] John 8:22

[6] John 8:24

[7] John 8:30

[8] John 8:37

[9] John 8:44a

[10] John 8:55m

[11] John 8:58

[12] John 8:59

[13] Colossians 3:23

[14] Matthew 5:14

[15] 1 Corinthians 14:33

[16] Jeremiah 27:6; 43:10

[17] Daniel 5:18

[18] Isaiah 45:1

[19] Romans 8:28

Chapter 28

Wednesday, May 16th, Washington D.C.

These last few weeks, we had been sailing through campaign issues furiously, but normally. This was our life and we were used to it. But when I met Issy at the Metro station after work, she was nearly crying.

"What's going on, baby?" I asked as I put my arm around her. We walked briskly over to the down escalators at the South Capitol Metro entrance and instead of walking down them, as we always do; Issy buried her head in my shoulder and started to weep.

My wife never weeps. In twenty-nine years of marriage, I've only seen her cry like this a dozen times, and half of those times were for a dog we used to have.

We boarded the metro and she sat quietly next to me. Just before the Ballston station, Issy said, "I get the distinct impression my boss doesn't trust me, anymore."

I looked at her seriously and asked, trying to get her to smile, "What basis does your loser candidate have to make you feel that way?"

It worked, Issy smiled and said, "Not the candidate, Silly, but Priscilla, our Chief of Staff."

We stepped outside Ballston station where the weather was a balmy seventy-two degrees. I crossed behind Issy, so I could walk beside the street, as always. My grandfather taught me to be a gentleman. I held her hand and we strolled along like kids out on a date. We walked on home and I started dinner while Issy sat at our kitchen bar and told me about her day.

When she was done, I knew why she felt the way she did.

"It started the moment I walked in the door. Apparently yesterday, when I took the day off, Priscilla started asking around about me, in such a way that it caused suspicion from others, which I felt all day today."

She started to tear up again. Clearly not like her. But I remained silent. There was nothing I could do; besides, I was kneading our 99% lean ground turkey, which we now eat thanks to my cardiologist. I was making patties and working in my secret ingredients so they will not taste like cardboard.

Another tear rolled down her cheek. This time she resolutely sat up taller, wiped it away with the back of her hand and went on.

"She disagreed with something in the joint report we did on news outlets."

"What?" I asked.

Not the right time though. Issy needed to keep venting.

"Apparently, three weeks ago Priscilla had a visiting pastor in to give her comments on my report. It appears this pastor is a shaker and mover in her community and a huge donor, too."

I nodded as if I understood, but I still didn't have a clue.

"When Priscilla sat me down late this morning, she asked me why I pigeon-holed people into watchers of one kind of news and not the other."

"What a weird question," I thought to myself. My eyes must have conveyed this to Issy, because she said, "I thought it was a weird question, too."

I merely nodded and she went on, "I'm glad Priscilla has this new pastor friend. I want her to bounce things off as many people as she has time for. So, I don't mind people questioning my work, Jude."

"I know, baby," I said, meaning it. "I know you believe there is wisdom in a multitude of counselors."[1]

Quick as a whip she came back, "There is a version of that text which says there is 'victory' in a multitude of counselors."

"Not this year, Issy," I retorted.

She smiled and went on, "It seems this pastor led Priscilla to believe my comments were somehow grounded in racism. This pastor said, 'Priscilla, those are the words I hear from my colleagues, fellow pastors, who refuse to expand their tribe.'"

My eyes went wide. Hers got narrow and angry.

"I don't know who this pastor is, but I. . ."

At this I forcefully interrupted. The patties were on the stove sizzling and my hands were nice and clean, so I leaned down, our eyes level. I am only a few inches taller than Issy, but with her sitting on our counter-height stool I needed to lean way down to be nose to nose with her. Then I stretched to her and gently rubbed noses.

"Baby," I said, "Slow down. Our struggles are not with flesh and blood,[2] right?"

She nodded and I went on, "In fact, God wants us to thank Him for everything,[3] right?"

This time she rolled her eyes, but I kept on. "So, lover, thank the Lord for this difficult day and this idiot pastor, and tell me how you responded to Priscilla."

My wife is no dummy. She has always recognized that Scripture is more important than her feelings, and, thank the Lord, she put her anger behind her and picked up her story.

"I was hurt that Priscilla would think anything like that of me and I told her so in no uncertain terms. She sat back and pondered before she responded to me, but her response was equally disconcerting. She said, 'I thought so too, Issy, but some of your colleagues here wonder if your religious grid of thinking keeps you from seeing social issues in their proper and modern light.' My mouth went wide when she said that, Jude. There was nothing for me to say."

"I wanted to ask, 'My colleagues? Which colleagues?'"

I put my arms around her for a few moments and then heard a crackle on the stove which meant I needed to turn over the patties.

Issy continued, "The rest of the day, every time someone looked at me, I wondered if they were the one stabbing me in the back."

After a pause she went on, "The next thing I wondered was, 'What does the candidate think of me?'"

I returned my attention back to her in time to hear her say, "I was hurt, and I was ticked."

Our T.V. isn't hooked up to any cable stations, so we like to watch movies we've purchased. And yes, I pulled out a chick-flick for us to enjoy during dinner tonight.

Thinking over what Issy had endured today, I was reminded of the persecution Jesus says is coming to those who follow Him. I made a commitment to get up early in the morning and reread that portion of Scripture.[4] But not because of the persecution caused by me having to watch a chick-flick tonight, you understand.

Same Day, FBI Safe House

Billy and I arrived at the same time. I don't know why I like him; he's not the most attractive guy I've ever dated and we're not even really dating, but I do really like him.

Anyway, we got there at the same time, sat down and Billy shared with me what he'd found on the server from Issy's Chief of Staff.

"Sammie, this is getting worse. I saw Issy when she left our CoS, Priscilla Ellsworth's office today and she looked like she was ready to cry."

I was shaking my head. This wasn't a surprise but what he said next was.

"Sammie, I then found a file note that Priscilla asked our candidate if she should invite the FBI or Homeland Security to investigate Issy."

"For what?" I asked.

"A racist ideology which would reflect on the candidate, if not dealt with quickly and decisively."

My eyes got wide and I asked, "What did the candidate say?"

Billy replied with a smile, "Thankfully, the candidate reaffirmed the party's trust in Issy. The exact words were, 'I have come to trust Issy greatly. I don't know this Atlanta pastor yet. You'll need some strong evidence, not just opinion. Sorry Pricilla. PS. I don't want your suspicions in her file, either.'"

Changing subjects, I asked Billy, "Have you seen Homeland Security's tracks looking through Issy's hard drive?"

"Yes, I'm seeing it from numerous departments and they are not covering their tracks as well as they used to."

He paused and then continued, "It's as if they are so convinced Issy. . ."

"And Jude," I added.

"You've been seeing their tracks in Jude's hard drive too?"

I simply nodded my head.

Billy continued, "I get the sense they are so confident these two are dirty and will be confronted soon that they do not think they need to cover any tracks. They just aren't concerned."

"I sense the same thing, Billy. I liken it to arrogance."

"And Jack, at FBI? What do you think is going on with him?"

"I don't know, Sammie. He's gone kind of quiet. But he hasn't given me any directives, so I'm going to keep looking for information which will help me connect the dots."

I was tired and Billy could tell.

"Come on, it's time to go," he said. "But before we do, let's pray."

Same Day, Atlanta GA

"This better be good, Clyde. I don't like Skyping you into my home. What do you want?"

His face, which was beginning to look chubby, was beaming. "You look like the cat which swallowed the chicken, Clyde."

For a moment his dumb face looked at me from my cell phone. I had heard this stupid quote last month on Holiday. If he looked this stupidly at me, I probably won't use it in a sermon. But I do like it. I like the cat's bravado. I imagine her strutting around.

Clyde was speaking.

"What?" I asked. "Repeat that."

"Operation Judas has begun in earnest. I just downloaded a file, deep into both hard drives, into which I will start adding the documents you gave me, making the principals appear disloyal."

I sat back and smiled my Cheshire grin, which I was becoming more and more comfortable with and certainly proud of.

After a long moment I came back to Clyde. "Nice job, Clyde." I decided I'd throw him a compliment-bone.

He was saying thank you or something. I don't know, because I disconnected the call.

Late, Same Day, Arlington VA

"Who was that?" Issy said, waking up.

It was 10:00 pm and Issy and I were asleep. But I had just taken a call from Harold.

"I hope I'm not calling too late?" he said.

"No, no." I assured him, coming awake and leaving our bedroom in hopes of not awakening Issy. "Glad to hear from you. What's up?"

There was a long stretch of silence, so I said nothing and just waited.

My phone dinged and a text came in from him.

It said: www.MarkMirza.com/Politics

"I recently found this website and I've been looking into his various posts. I don't know that I agree with everything he says, because a number of times he says he, 'doesn't focus on the politician's voting record.' Anyway, Jude, I thought you might find it interesting. Maybe we can talk about it."

"I'd like that. I got your text. I'll look into it starting tomorrow."

"Alright, goodnight," he said.

"Good night, Harold, and thanks for the call."

When I got back into bed I told Issy, "I think I just got an olive branch from Harold."

And then I heard her snore.

---

[1] Proverbs 11:14

[2] Ephesians 6:12

[3] Ephesians 5:20

[4] John 15:20

Chapter 29

Thursday May 17th, FBI Headquarters

Pete was sitting in my office, report in hand.

It was the end of the day, but I decided I needed another coffee. I offered Pete one, who said he didn't drink coffee after noon anymore. I wish I could stop drinking coffee after noon.

"I thought I'd bring it to you in person," he said with a grin.

He uncrossed his legs and leaned forward, handing me the file. We were sitting on the chairs in front of my desk, which I think is more comfortable and less confining.

I read his report which contained nothing new. In the back of my mind I had this niggling thought, "Am I listening too much to my mom?"

She had called earlier this afternoon and I took the call since I was between appointments.

"Hey, Mom. How is everything?"

"Oh, good Jacky. Real good." After a moment's hesitation she continued on, "How about with you?"

"Good, good. Just working hard, trying to keep you and all your Bridge playing friends safe from villains."

She normally chuckles at those kinds of statements, but this time she didn't and I waited till she spoke.

"Jacky, I just want you to know I've been praying for wisdom for you."

"Again?" I said, a little too flippantly. Quickly correcting my words, I added, "I mean, thank you, Mom." I couldn't help myself so I also said, "With all the prayers for wisdom, lately, I should be pretty smart."

She just chuckled and said, "One would think so."

And then she let out a real snort. I could tell it embarrassed her, but I asked, "Where did that come from?"

"Oh, I just thought of something your dad used to say."

My dad was former military, a retired Lieutenant Colonel who had worked with some sort of a church ministry in Iraq after Operation Iraqi Freedom. He was killed by a roadside bomb.

Mom was telling me what made her snort. "Your dad used to say, 'Grey hair is a sign of wisdom'. . ."

I picked up the refrain, because I remembered the rest of it, ". . .Or it's a sign you keep making the same mistakes over and over again."

"What does that have to do with me, Mom?"

"I don't know, son. I didn't say it did."

"I have to go," I said.

"Okay, but thinking of your dad just now made me wonder. . ."

"Yeeeees," I said, dragging it out, because I knew what she was going to ask. I hadn't been down to her place in Florida since Christmas.

"When are you going to visit me?"

"Soon, Mom. I mean it. Soon." And I did mean it.

So why was I thinking about that call, now, with Pete in my office?

"Tell me what we have on the two Religion Consultants, if there's anything new."

Pete leaned forward and asked, "Are you getting cold feet about this 'watching and listening' job?"

The way he asked the question made me curious and worried. "You're still not surveilling, are you?"

"Not exactly," he said.

"Look, Pete, what we found is against their employment contract, but not against the law."

I decided to circle back around to my question on surveilling, so I broached a different subject and asked, "You're not recording anyone's conversations, right?"

"Not exactly," again, from Pete.

"Pete," I was now concerned, "They have given us reasonable suspicion, but only in the slightest way. I told your group we should watch more closely. What did you do, Pete?"

"We have a watcher in each candidate's office."

I let out a huge sigh, "Pete, you are going to get us. . ."

But he cut me off and said, "They are there to only watch and listen to the Perps. Any conversations they hear they are merely reporting, not recording, and they are doing nothing regarding the candidates or any other staff, unless it directly relates to our Perps."

"Alright," I said, still a bit hesitant. "What isn't in the report?"

"How do you know the report is missing some information?" asked a surprised Pete Beecham.

"Because I know you, Pete."

He smiled, "Yeah, it'll be in Monday's report."

I nodded for him to continue.

"Two things. First, Issy's boss. . ."

"The candidate?" I asked.

"No, the Chief of Staff. She believes Issy to be leading the candidate astray. And second, Jude is passing on information to his candidate which he is getting from some obscure seventeenth century Christian pastor. And this information, this document, came from Perp #3."

I buried my head in my hands. "Tell me there's more, Pete."

His eyes lit up and he said. "We found an encrypted file in both of their servers, obviously deeply hidden."

"Have you cracked the encryption, yet?"

"No, not yet."

But he smiled.

"What else?" I asked.

The documents are completely encrypted, except the file name, which is Operation Judas."

I was still nonplussed.

"Do you know who Judas is in the Bible, Jack?"

I nodded but Pete went on as if he needed to explain it to me. I just let him. "Judas is the most outrageous of all of the traitors. These two know they can't name the file as to what they are doing, like "Our Traitor File" so I think, actually, we, my team thinks, they are using this code name to be clever.

After a moment I asked, "These are two religious freaks, how would they know about encrypting documents? A big day for them is when they see something exciting in Scripture."

"I don't know," Pete stammered. "I'm working on that. But there's one more thing."

I leaned back, nodding my head, as if saying, "Alright, what else?"

"We still haven't figured out why Perp #3, the Prayer-Guy comes out here every Tuesday and Wednesday, and never varies the days."

"Pete, I'm still thinking you may have a case here, but just barely, which means I am trusting your guys to remain super careful, keeping everything as close to the vest as they can."

He nodded in understanding, which I realized was the best I would get from him.

"I don't see any comments on the Warner Robins counterintelligence character though and his pastor. Why not?"

"We're following up on them, Jack, but in all honesty, all we're seeing is an arrogant pastor, gorgeous, but arrogant, and a trail from the counterintelligence unit which looks like curiosity-seeking Junior High kids. If we brought it to his superior's attention it would get him in trouble, probably demoted, but unless it's something serious, do you really want to bring that upon one of our own?"

"Pete, while your team keeps an eye on all five of the Perps, I still think the best you've got on the Religion Consultants is that they are colluding, which would be a violation of their work agreement."

"I hear you, Jack, but I intend to keep looking, because I think there's more going on than just that."

As Pete got into the elevator, Grace entered my office with two FBI reports. One read, "Safe House-3 Sit-Rep" and the other read, "Analysis, 1656 Voter's Guide."

Pulling out the cover page for each I jumped to the overview.

OVERVIEW: Analysis, 1656 Voter's Guide

Subversive Statements: None

Questionable Statements:

1. *Implied Voter Booth Tampering*

2. *Explicit Manipulation of National Direction*

OVERVIEW: Safe House-3 Sit-Rep

   Transcript of Billy Marshall and Sammie Prescott

Sometimes I think being in the spook business makes us paranoid. We end up believing everyone is out to tamper with or manipulate someone or something.

Maybe my mom is right; I need to start attending a venue where regular people go.

I had just read the basis of my team's analysis on the 1656 Voter's Guide and rubbed my eyes.

They took the wording which says, "God can and will, change people's minds behind the voting curtain, so they vote for the person He wants them to," and from that they extrapolated this might have something to do with voter booth fraud or tampering?

And then, where the document says, "To know the direction God is leading a country, look at the leaders He gives them," they decided this clearly must mean they intend to manipulate our country's direction.

I think my analysts need a break.

I read the transcripts of Billy and Sammie's meeting. These poor kids have no idea they're being recorded. "Why wouldn't they recognize that?" I thought to myself. "I'm a little disappointed in them."

At first, I was angry at them taking this rogue direction of looking for evidence to clear Jude and Issy. It is bad form and rarely ever makes for a good investigation when you begin with a commitment to the outcome you want to see. "Let the clues direct the investigation" is the mantra we're taught at the school. But these two kids have determined the end result and are now looking for clues to substantiate it.

I should just close them down. But the more I thought about it, the more I decided it could be good to have a team looking at similar facts, from a different perspective.

After all, if they keep meeting in Safe House-3, I'll not be surprised by their findings.

Chapter 30

Tuesday Night May 29th, Safe House-3

We met again, in the FBI safe-house. It has now been just over four weeks since Billy shared the findings which caused Jack's suspicion of Jude and Issy.

Billy opened us in prayer for wisdom. It was really sweet. He grabbed my hand, not in a romantic sense, but to pray. Although, it was a bit romantic to me.

I like Billy. Have I mentioned that? And I think I'm liking him more and more.

We found ourselves sitting nearer and nearer each other during our midweek prayer meetings and Bible Studies we attended, together, but not really together.

Anyway, behind the scenes, we had been working on finding the evidence against Jude and Issy, with the plan of figuring out if there was another explanation for it. We both know the FBI and Homeland Security folks may be brilliant at their jobs, but none of them are theologians, not that Billy and I are, but I do believe our thought patterns are more attuned to deal with religious documents than they.

"The first thing we need though, Sammie, are the documents Jack is basing his suspicions upon."

My jaw dropped open, "Are you talking about breaking into Jack's computer?"

Billy was silent, but I did notice a little mischievous grin. He just said, "I don't want to." And left it at that.

We sat there in silence for a few minutes.

"Billy, that's very dangerous, and illegal. Oh, I don't know."

He leaned towards me and gently held my two hands in his. "He has really soft hands," I thought to myself.

"Sammie, I read this verse today, Proverbs 29:7. I always read the chapter in Proverbs, of the day of the month it is."

"So today you read Proverbs chapter twenty-nine?" I said smiling. "I do the same thing."

"You do?" he asked, surprised. And then he went on, it says 'The righteous care about justice for the poor, but the wicked have no such concern.'"

"And in a sense, that's the way I view Jude and Issy. They are poor, in their situation, because they have no idea how close they are to being thrown into jail."

I interrupted him, "So, are you saying Jack is wicked?"

"No, not at all," he laughed. "I really like and respect Jack, he reminds me of my dad. But, evil or wicked advice? Yes, I think he's been given some."

He let my hands go and for a short moment I was flustered and a tad upset, but I quickly put those thoughts away.

He continued, "I did some cross referencing this morning and found verse eight of chapter thirty-one. It says, 'you must defend those who are helpless and have no hope.'" (CEV)

"That's a verse we use for pro-life issues, isn't it?" I commented.

"Exactly. The idea is that Jude and Issy's situation is helpless, as far as they are concerned. In fact, they don't even know they need help. But they do."

Billy stopped abruptly and then said, "Sammie, I admit that I'm a little scared of getting into Jack's computer, but I think I must help them any way I can."

He sat back, thoughtfully, and I could tell our relationship had gone to another level. To his surprise, and to mine, I kissed his forehead as I got up.

"Let's go to the table," I said. "And we'll figure out a plan of action."

"We need to connect all the dots," I said when we got to the table.

"But we don't yet know all the dots," Billy complained.

"Do you have any idea how Jack organizes his files? Does he keep them in a safe, online, on his phone or a tablet, or what?"

"I have no clue," Billy confessed.

"Then where do we start?" I asked.

And Billy did it again. He grabbed my hands gently, which I admit, sent a little jolt of electricity through me. He bowed his head and said, "Lord, we still have the same problem. We do not know where to start. Your word says that when we need wisdom, You will give it to us generously.[1] Father, we trust You for wisdom, for direction, for clarity, and for success as we try and help our friends."

I added, "But Father, if we are wrong, make it clear to us so we can let the natural course of events take place."

We remained quiet for a few moments and it was precious. It reminded me of my father who always says during those times of silence, "Be still and know that I am God."[2]

After a few more moments we looked up, but we didn't stop holding hands, which was kind of nice. I said, "I think I need to start looking much more closely at every file in Jude's name. If there are bad-guys afoot and they are in Jude's files, we will need to find out who they are and what their plan is."

"Good idea, Sammie. I need to determine what the various puzzle pieces are and then how do they fit together. Those are our immediate goals. Do you agree?"

"I do," I said and then blushed so strongly and quickly I could feel it.

Billy chuckled, "In the non-marriage sense of the phrase, of course."

I was too embarrassed to respond.

As Billy and I readied to leave Safe House-3 he grabbed my hand and gave it a squeeze, then we left, via different exits.

Same Night, FBI Headquarters

I was just getting ready to go home. It was another late night, but I got an urgent call from the transcript writer assigned to Safe House-3.

She said, "Sir, there is an imminent threat to your computer system. We expect it to happen soon."

Immediately my mind started to whir and I was thinking about recent cases and whose toes I had stepped on. While I was thinking, I asked, "Do we know the source of the hack?"

"Yes, sir. I just checked the transcription for accuracy."

I chuckled and realized what was going on. "You are talking about Safe House-3 and that would be the transcripts for Billy Marshall and Sammie Prescott, correct?"

"Yes, sir," she said. "May I ask. . . Is there anything romantic going on between them?"

This time I laughed out loud. "Yes, there is, but they don't know it yet. It's actually kind of cute."

"Anyway," I went on, "what's the scoop?"

"Well, sir, the male suggested breaking into your computer to figure out what documents they do not have, in order that they would be able to connect the dots and determine the innocence of two friends of theirs."

"That sounds right," I said.

And then I thought about it. My files are incredibly well hidden, and I have wanted to test this pimply-faced kid.

"Hmm," I said into the phone. And then, after a few seconds, I continued, "I just texted you my authorization to send this transcript over in the normal channels. Do not FastTrack-it, okay?"

From the other end of the phone I heard a hesitant, "Yes, sir. Are you sure, sir?"

"Thank you for your help," I said, and then hung up.

"Hmmm, I like Billy. Let's see what he can do." I sat down with a proud-of-him smile on my face. And then realized, "But you better not get caught, son."

Same Night, Atlanta GA

Clyde and I had a long appointment tonight. I had to make sure the hidden documents were what I had envisioned.

Nearly two years ago, I was on my winter Holiday in the southern hemisphere. I think I was at a luxury resort in Brasilia, I don't recall. Anyway, that was when I devised this plan to donate sufficiently to be known by both candidates, whoever they might be, discredit their existing Religion Consultant, and then be perfectly situated to join the team of the new President.

I believe this is the next step in God's plan for my life.

With the right culpable documents, in two hidden files, I will be able to quicken the demise of the Religion Consultant I choose to pull the trigger on. And now at the beginning of the summer, it was time to upload the rest of the papers while I increased my visibility to both candidates.

Clyde has turned out to be a pretty good Lieutenant. Today I had him bring me a printout of each document which I went through minutely, again.

Next, we talked about the logic of downloading everything at once or over time.

There were also new dynamics which needed review since this Prayer-Guy was on the scene who would, without knowing it, make himself a buffer between me and Clyde and the Candidates, as well as the husband and wife team, which was a huge coup for us.

All of the documents heading for the Religion Consultants' servers Clyde was routing through the Prayer-Guy's computer.

Life is sweet. By the time we were done I was purring. I was becoming less and less embarrassed about this and the sound was becoming more and more deep. It was almost scary. I say 'almost' because it was still very intoxicating

But I saw victory for Operation Judas, just a few short months away. My two year plan was about to come to fulfillment.

Same Night, Washington D.C.

I was examining Jude's server and trusting that Billy was carefully doing what he needed to do when my heart stopped.

I was making my way through dead files when I found a recent file, made to look like it had been there for months and months.

The signature stamp was something Billy had told me to look for. But I hadn't seen one in Jude's server until now. And it seemed to have an additional address stamp which I was not expecting.

It was from the Warner Robins Counterintelligence unit, but routed through a private, personal computer in Macon, Georgia, a small town near Warner Robins Air Force Base. The PC was registered to some guy named, Dr. Dale Riley.

The file was named "Operation Judas."

---

[1] James 1:5

[2] Psalm 46:10a

Chapter 31

These last few weeks have been difficult, especially for Issy. The level of pressure she feels at work has become more severe. And this is already a difficult time because we are nearing the end of the Presidential campaign.

My stresses have a broader genesis, though. In addition to the campaign, I see the challenges Issy is facing. I see the deception the evil one is perpetrating on my bride, and I have to gauge when and where to speak up.

The evil one's deception is so persistent and all-influencing. No wonder Paul makes it clear in the scriptures that the location of Spiritual Warfare is in our mind.[1]

"Baby," I said to Issy, "It's time to wake up."

By the time she was awake, our coffee was made; I got up and brought her a cup. I tell you, I'm such a good husband. I didn't realize it, but I apparently said that out loud. I thought I was only thinking it.

When I got back into bed, I noticed Issy looking at me with that look of, "Seriously, Jude?"

"Nah," I decided, "She didn't hear me."

She started to read, "After this the Lord appointed seventy-two others. . ."[2]

December A.D. 29, Mission of the Seventy-Two

The last few weeks have been difficult for me. We are a band of a number of people, not just the twelve, but there are about a hundred of us. That number grows and shrinks with time.

Anyway, Jesus did something he has not done in the previous two-plus years I have been with him. He empowered seventy-two others, like he had empowered us twelve.

I don't mind telling you, I was more than a little ticked off. After all, weren't we the elite ones? You might even say we were the inner circle. And me, I had constant responsibility for the money bag, which I guarded more closely than any tax collector ever would.

"If we were special," I remember thinking, "then why do we need the seventy-two? And why do we have to help manage them?"

I guess this was difficult for me because it made me feel like I wasn't so special. And Jesus then made some odd rules for them, not the least of which was, "Do not take a purse or bag or sandals."[3]

I liked this because it meant I'd hold on to everyone's money purse and figure out a way to pilfer some of it.

Fortunately, Jesus wasn't talking to me about the money bag; after all, someone had to hold it and that was my job. I did enjoy a bit of sadistic glee, watching the faces of the seventy-two, though, when He told them to not take any money along. He was saying trust the people to do what is right. Of course, that's foolish, because people never do what is right.

Nevertheless, I laughed at these seventy-two who were scared to death because they weren't going to have any money and they had to trust people in the towns to give them food.

I was surprised though by two of our group, Justus and Matthias. They had both been with us since the beginning,[4] and while everyone else was scared to death, they had an unrealistic enthusiasm. One of them said, "Yes, this is exciting, we will trust God."

Of course, in my head I'm thinking, "What fools you two are! People are untrustworthy. You should be concerned like the other seventy."

But the next few weeks, while the seventy-two were out, were not as difficult for Jesus as I would have expected. We twelve acted as district overseers going to and fro, where the seventy-two had gone, just to help them and take care of them as best we could.

Every time we returned to Jesus though, to give him our report, his attitude was very upbeat. About halfway through those few weeks He told us something which didn't make sense until the seventy-two returned. Jesus said He saw the evil one shooting down from heaven as quickly as lightning falls from the sky.[5]

But when the seventy-two returned many of them were excited. They were different than when they left. A number of them said, and then all of them agreed, "Lord, even the demons submitted to Your Name!"[6]

"Thank You for sending us out, Jesus," they said.

These men's joy was only eclipsed by Jesus' joy. He was excited for these men and their ministry results. Jesus is always, humbly upbeat, but when the seventy-two returned, He was ecstatic! I don't know what He knew that I didn't, but it was weird. That's all I can say.

Sunday, June 10th, Arlington VA

"These last few weeks have been a challenge, baby. Thank you for being my rock," Issy said when she finished reading.

She continued, "I never saw these words, that 'Jesus was full of joy.'[7] But after reading them, Jude, I realize my real attitude is not fear. I've been going to work with fear, but that's not really who I am in Christ. I am filled with joy, if for no other reason than because the Holy Spirit lives in me. But there is also the reality of the ministry I am doing each and every day. Now I understand why Jesus was filled with joy."

"Wow. What a great break through, Issy," I said to her.

"I agree, darling," she said with a great sigh of relief. Then she snorted, "Whew! That only took three and a half weeks!"

"Thank You, Lord, for the problems," she ushered up in prayer. "And the opportunity to obediently serve You in the midst of the things I dislike."

We both chuckled and I kissed her forehead. She kissed my cheek gently, and then I kissed her lips, a little more than gently. But, we *did* make it to church on time.

While at church I saw Harold. He made a beeline for me and so I braced myself, not sure what was going to happen. But the closer he got the more I realized his attitude was cheerful, as opposed to, 'I'm gonna beat you down.' I snorted at my own wit.

We shook hands and gave our 'good morning' man-hug.

"Hi, Issy," he said, and then he turned to me. "I found something that has helped me, Jude." He kept talking but immediately became more passionate. "I still don't like or understand why you work for that. . ."

I saw his wife gently touch his arm. He took a deep breath to slow down.

"I found Ephesians 5:20 which says we are to thank the Lord for everything. Actually G.W. and I were praying for you." And then he reached over and grabbed his wife's hand and G.W. smiled lovingly at him, and he corrected, "Honestly, Jude, G.W. and I were praying for me."

I looked at her and she smiled.

"Jude, I literally said to the Lord. 'Thank You for Jude working for the candidate he does.'"

He was so proud of himself that I couldn't help chuckling a bit.

Then he looked at his wife again, a bit sheepishly and said, "I started off thanking the Lord for you and then my thanking morphed into thanking Him for your candidate, too."

I just nodded and he continued, "I still think it's the absolute wrong choice, but my attitude is completely different. I now have an attitude of. . ."

He looked around as if he didn't want to be heard. "I now have an attitude of respect for your boss."

He hit me on the shoulder and he and G.W. walked out.

"Will wonders ever cease?" Issy whispered.

Same Day, Atlanta GA

Right after church I pulled Clyde aside. "I still don't have inroads into the other Religion Consultant, Clyde. Why not?"

I wanted to take his head off but his wife was there.

I was angry but being the great actress I am, I exchanged pleasantries with his wife and children, even kneeling down and playing with one of the brats.

"Clyde," I whispered, "I am reaching out regularly to the one Chief of Staff and our relationship is growing well. But what is happening with the other campaign?"

"I'm meeting with the Prayer-Guy next week. He's got the relationship which we will play off of."

'ARGHGHGHGHGH' was all my mind could think as I walked to my office and glad-handed all the people I passed on my way.

Walking up my stairs to my office I groaned in anger at all the hands I had to shake after church. I was glad all my parishioners were behind me, but they were so insensitive to my needs. "Don't those people know I am exhausted and had just given them everything I could, in my preaching? Someone once said, "Church would be great if we didn't have to deal with people." Oh, I couldn't agree more.

As I got up to my office, the groan inside me returned, but there was that masculine purr again. And I thought, "But I do like their money."

I mumbled it again, this time in a whisper, "I like their money."

And when I mumbled it again, "I like their money," and I could feel the grin on my face. I was actually a bit embarrassed.

---

[1] 2 Corinthians 10:5

[2] Luke 10:1a

[3] Luke 10:4a

[4] Acts 1:21-23

[5] Luke 10:18

[6] Luke 10:17

[7] Luke 10:21a

Chapter 32

Wednesday June 20th, Ocmulgee River Park, Macon GA

"Why are you calling me from Macon, you fool? I wanted an in-depth report from you today, here in my office."

Why do I pay this man so much?

"Clyde, did you meet with this 'Dale' guy?"

"Yes, ma'am."

"Can he do the dates I want or not?"

"No, ma'am."

"No? Did he say 'No?'"

"Yes, ma'am, but his. . ."

I cut him off. "It was a rhetorical question, Clyde. Shut up while I think."

After a few moments, I said, "Get up here so we can talk before church tonight."

Then I hung up.

Same Day, 8pm, FBI Headquarters

A special report from Homeland Security was delivered to my office late this afternoon.

OPERATION: JUDAS I.

Surveillance Report:

20, June – All Morning, Macon GA

Transcript:

> *Attached*

Summary:

> *Perps #2 & #3 met in park where lots of line of sight issues played havoc with our listening devices. Perps seemed to coordinate this with great precision.*

> *Attached transcripts are helpful, but critical details are missing.*

Distribution:

I read through all the transcripts and the report's author was correct. I had to piece together what happened, based on these disjointed transcripts and ancillary 'notes to file' which were already added.

Both men were being tailed, by two crews of three agents and two cars each, which meant, when they got to the park there would be four cars, twelve agents and the two Perps.

I shook my head and said, "They were doing it again; looking like Keystone Cops."

I could imagine the park with a few stay-at-home moms and their children, and what it must have looked like with twelve agents in four cars plus the two Perps.

I leaned back for a moment, rubbed my eyes and shook my head in disgust.

I read the transcripts wondering how quickly the surveillance was blown.

> *PERP 2: Dale, I'm glad you could meet me.*
>
> *PERP 3: Hey, I'm glad that you were able to work around my schedule, Clyde. I come out here most days now that I'm not working at the University anymore. I try to run and walk for about an hour and a half every day. Don't worry. Today is a "walk-day." I only run twice a week.*
>
> *PERP 2: I'm disappointed, Dale. I brought my running shoes and shorts. I'm up for a run.*
>
> *PERP 3: LAUGH; Well knock yourself out, Clyde. I'll wait for you back here. The older I get the more careful I am about how I exercise.*
>
> *PERP 2: No problem. I really didn't want to run anyway; LAUGH*
>
> *PERP 3: Let's walk this way.*
>
> *NOTE TO FILE: They deliberately walked towards the trees. Anticipate covert conversation/s.*
>
> *PERP 2: Dale, Pastor Mortenson wants to meet with you and she's planning a trip to Washington D.C. soon. We're wondering if we can coordinate that with you. When do you plan to return to D.C.?*
>
> *PERP 3: As a matter of fact, I will be there the week after next. And as usual I'll be there on Tuesday and Wednesday; I think that's June 26th and 27th.*

189

PERP 2: Dale, I was wondering if you can switch your trip to Thursday and Friday, you know, to accommodate the pastor?

PERP 3: I wish I could, Clyde, but there is a very important reason why I always go on Tuesday and Wednesday. You see, I. . .

UNINTELLIGIBLE

NOTE TO FILE: The two perps appeared to deliberately stand between 3 trees, so we had no line-of-sight for our scanners and directional microphones.

PERP 2: Oh, that makes perfect sense, Dale. I understand that. We will work around your dates.

NOTE TO FILE: Why did Perp #2 back off so quickly? Does Perp #3 have something over Perp #2?

SILENCE AS THEY WALKED

PERP 2: Dale, may I ask you about your leaving the University?

PERP 3: Well, you know I didn't leave, Clyde, don't you? I was fired.

PERP 2: I know, Dale, I just didn't want to say it that way. But from what I read there were some assertions of links to terrorism, weren't there?

PERP 3: LAUGH; Calling me a terrorist was accurate. My focus has always been. .
.

UNINTELLIGIBLE

PERP 2: Dale, tell me about your men's prayer meeting.

PERP 3: I'd love to. What do you want to know?

PERP 2: Well, first of all, how do you recruit men to participate and then keep coming back?

NOTE TO FILE: Check files for possible definition/s of code word "Prayer Meeting."

PERP 3: The most critical point I've learned, Clyde, about getting men to enlist is that we are relational beings, contrary to modern psychobabble. When we pray together, I tell them to get into groups, but I let them get into and then lead their own prayer groups. I have found they return for more, because of the relationships they forge.

PERP 2: I've asked around and found that you have been successful recruiting women also. How?

PERP 3: You have done your homework, haven't you, Clyde?

PERP 2: When you work where I do and for whom I do, you learn to be thorough. The women?

PERP 3: Yes, women have become an integral part of our mission. I confess I was reluctant to bring women into our group for a long time. But they do a great job and I'm proud to have them on the team. They can pray from a part of their gut men cannot. And they do spiritual warfare with an intensity and confidence I wish I had.

PERPS 2 & 3: Next 30 minutes miscellaneous discussions of nothing mission critical. See Transcripts B & C for exact details

Just to be thorough I checked the transcripts. Really, I just skimmed them. Then I went back to the pertinent documents and read the remaining transcript.

PERP 2: Dale, we are all interested in having some clout, if you will, in D.C., specifically on the Hill. How are we going to achieve it, some influence, I mean, and how can you help us there?

PERP 3: Good question, Clyde, because I want to make sure we get this absolutely, correct. Okay? If this part is handled incorrectly, every single trip I have made to the Hill will have been for nothing. And I've invested too much to see that happen.

NOTE TO FILE: Obvious agitation/excitement seen in both perps.

PERP 3: Regarding influence, control, power, authority, etc. I am very particular. I want. . .

UNINTELLIGIBLE

NOTE TO FILE: Very odd that during these critical issues our line-of-sight was impaired. The complete answers we did get are in some sort of code. Their tradecraft was brilliantly executed.

CONCLUSION:

According to Delta Airline, as of today, Dr. Dale is scheduled to be in D.C. Tuesday and Wednesday, June 26th and 27th. He is booked on DL#2638, arriving DCA 9:14 am

No flights yet for Perps #1 or #2

This subversive activity and relationship has to have been a very longtime in the making. Also, their tradecraft leads us to conclude they know they are being surveilled and are behaving as if they are "new-meets" just getting to know each other.

DISTORTION INFERENCE CONCLUSIONS:

Days of Perp #3's visits; Unknown, due to recording distortions. Why he is unswerving about those days, we do not know, but his reasoning is significant enough to cause Perps #1 & #2 to work around Perp #3

Terrorism Label; Unknown, due to recording distortions. But Perp 3 admits it fit him, even sounded like he was proud of the label

Purpose of Male & Female Recruitment: The real meanings of his words are still unknown, but both male and female are integral to operational success

Influence/Control: Unknown, due to recording distortions. We do not know the commitment made by Perp #3, but execution seems to be well underway and protected by Perp #3

I stood up looking out my window over the Mall. It was now completely dark except for the lights along the walkways.

I hated this. None of the conclusions from Homeland felt right, but what else could they be? To the best of my understanding there could be a serious breech already here or just around the corner.

NOTE TO FILE: I may have to reach out to the candidates. JJ

I sent an encrypted email to Pete:

Considering reaching out to the candidates. Do not; I repeat, DO NOT preempt me.

Jack

Same Night, Atlanta GA

"Clyde, did you get all our questions answered?" I was a little calmer today than normal. For some reason I didn't want to rip his head off.

"Yes, but let me begin with the travel plans. He can only go there June 26th and 27th."

Even that disappointment didn't bother me. And I could tell Clyde was surprised I didn't yell at him. Something had come over me and I wasn't sure what it was.

For the next hour, we walked through the questions and answers I was interested in. When we were done, I stuck out my hand, shook his, thanked him and then sent him on his way.

Okay, that I didn't like. It was too, umm. . .nice. I was just getting ready to find a reason to call him back and yell at him when a voice inside me said, "Wait. . .patience. . .that's my girl."

It wasn't the same voice which wanted me to yell at him, but it had the same feel as the masculine purring that had been coming over me more and more lately.

"Oh, yes, holy spirit. Whatever you say."

Same Night, FBI Headquarters Parking Lot

I was heading to my car when the crazy thought of asking for wisdom came into my head.

"God, my mom asks for wisdom for me all the time. Can You give that to me? Please? This Jude and Issy thing is driving me crazy and, well, I thought that since it has to do with Religious Consultants, that must be right up Your ally and You could help me, maybe, if You want to."

After a couple steps I added, "Oh, Amen, over and out."

I called my mom as I got closer to my car, "Hey, Mom. I just talked to God, I think."

"Oh, Jacky, I am so glad. Oh honey, I have been praying for you to give your life over to Christ for so long. Tell me about it, please."

"Umm, Mom, I have an important call coming in; I need to take it." And I hung up on her.

That's not what I expected from her. Then I wondered, "Is that Born-again stuff a prerequisite for talking to God?"

Chapter 33

Tuesday June 26th, Washington D.C.

I was on my way to work when I called my mom. I was behind a woman who was putting her face on while she was driving. It made me wonder when state lawmakers will expand their driving and cell phone use laws. "Hey, Mom, just checking in with you."

"Good morning, Jacky. How are you doing, Son?"

"Not bad. Good."

I heard her grunt and then she said, "Uh-huh, what's bothering you, Jacky?"

After a few quiet moments I said, "I've got a busy day today and there are a lot of religious issues on the table and Mom, I need wisdom. That's what I tried to tell you about last week."

She then said, "If it's wisdom you want, you've come to the right place, because I pray for wisdom for you all the time."

"I know you do, Mom. I know you do."

"What else, Jacky?"

"Well, from our call last week, I got the impression I can't ask for wisdom unless I've been, what's it called, 'born-again?' Isn't that what Chuck Colson called it?

Mom was silent which is unusual.

"I didn't mean to hurt your feelings last week, Son."

"I know, Mom." I was getting weepy all of a sudden. Where was that coming from?

"I love you, Son."

"I love you too, Mom."

"And Jesus loves you, too."

I didn't respond. I just said, "I need to go. Good to talk to you."

"You too, Jacky."

All throughout the day I received updates on who the Prayer-Guy was visiting. And he visited a lot. We estimated he walked about ten miles. He also never took the elevators, which must have winded our agents.

Except for lunch with Pastor Mortenson, where "she left clearly flustered," he spent the entire day visiting Congressmen and women's offices. Apparently, day two he spends on the Senate side of the Capitol.

At the end of the day I sat down with Pete's surveillance notes. After each stop he would speak into his phone and leave a brief note based on his stop, or activity, or prayer. It was actually great because we picked up on the details of each stop, without having to do any voice surveillance and run the risk of getting caught recording an elected official.

I put the file down but reread, "She left clearly frustrated," which means to Homeland that she is being ordered around by Dr. Dale.

"I don't know. It doesn't feel right." I laughed at myself thinking about these things and then decided my mom needs to pray a lot more for me.

I understood Dr. Dale's note-keeping organization. I do something similar. When you are making twenty or twenty-five stops a day, you have to record some brief notes of each visit or by the end of the day their comments and your words can be inaccurate. When I'm on the Hill meeting with these folks I do the same thing.

He basically had three different types of notes. The first is a simple "P.C." which has nothing to do with "Political Correctness." Rather, they are his Prayer Cards. We heard him say to someone in the hallway, "These men and women may be brilliant attorneys or doctors, but they're not theologians. So I leave my version of P.C. which are my prayer cards to remind them how I'm praying for them and their staff this month."

The second kind of note had to do with when he prayed with a staff person, or more than one. Listening to some of his comments after he had prayed was very interesting. This Prayer-Guy seemed to be focused on encouraging the people he prayed with. I don't think he was very creative, though. I looked it up and there are about 31,000 verses in the Bible. But he seemed to use the same one, over and over again.

I Googled the verse. It was Romans 15:13 which says, "*Now the God of hope fill you with all joy and peace in believing, that ye may abound in hope, through the power of the Holy Ghost.*" I've been told this is the version King James used back in seventeenth century England. But according to Dr. Dale's notes, people were very grateful to hear him pray for them. I guess that if something works, you stay with it. I don't know. After all, there are 31,000 verses!

The third set of notes referred to when he prayed with Congressmen and women. I made sure we did not keep a record of those notes, but I read them before they were destroyed. Many were very personal and they were all very different. Most had to do with family. Some had to do with friends and once in a while they had to do with work in Washington D.C. which I found surprising. I would have expected there to be more praying for their D.C. or district work.

It was eye-opening to read the report on him. He seemed genuine, as genuine as anyone can be, in D.C. There was one problem though, his meeting with the Atlanta Pastor.

They ate in the lunchroom under the Longworth House Office Building and there was too much noise there to use a directional mic and pick-up anything worthwhile. Pete's people think this was a deliberate maneuver to cover their conversations.

"But to what end?" I kept asking myself.

"What does he want with her? It doesn't add up."

I ate an early dinner while I finished reading the surveillance notes. My throat was feeling a little scratchy, so I had a chicken noodle soup. It's an old favorite which works for me every time.

After I finished with my soup and crackers, I made some notes:

Perp #1, Pastor, arrogant/mean/rich

Perp #2, Counterintelligence/hacker

Perp #3, Prayer Guy

Perp # 4, Religion Consultant for Candidate A

Perp # 5, Religion Consultant for Candidate B

Intersections of the Perps:

Perp #1: employs Perp #2, has lunch with Perp #3, meets boss of Perp #4 and #5

Perp #2: employed by Perp #1, meets and communicates with Perp #3, met and has periodic email contact with Perp #4

Perp #3: meets with Perp #1, meets with Perp #2, meets with Perp #3, meets with both Perps #4 and #5

Perp #4: met Perp #2, including periodic emails/texts, met with Perp #3

Perp #5: meets often with Perp #3

NOTE TO FILE: Perp #3 is the centerpiece to all of this. The question we need to figure out is what he wants with all of these folks.

I thought about this and the number of times the Prayer-Guy has met with Perp #5 made me amend my notes to include, "What do Perps #3 and #5 gain from this mission, if they are even guilty of a mission?"

While making my notes I got a call from the Safe House-3 transcriber.

"Sir, you need to hear this."

She then wired me in to a meeting in progress, in Safe House-3. It was Billy and Sammie again.

"How did you get it, Billy?"

"Well, it took longer than I expected, but when I couldn't find anything on Jack's hard drive, I had to deduce it was because his documents were in a safe, not on his computer."

"This is scary, Billy."

"I know, Sammie. I know."

"But keep going. Did you find his passwords?"

"Yes, that was pretty easy, but that was when I realized I had another problem. You see, none of his passwords got me closer to the documents I now have."

"I'm confused, Billy. If the documents were not in his computer, but in his safe, did you. . .You didn't. . ."

"Open his safe? No. I just started looking for his notes. One of the first days I was in his office, I noticed a few apps light up on his phone because I have them too."

"Which ones? Which apps, Billy?"

"There were a number, but only two were needed. He has the OneNote app and the Trello app. I simply got into those two apps, got around their firewalls and found an abbreviated version of his case notes. I think he works on a case and speaks into his phone to record notes which probably eventually make it into a report."

I heard Sammie laughing tentatively in the background and I called Grace to have her get some agents over to these two thieves and drag them in here, handcuffed. But when she came on the line, I didn't say anything to her. I just kept listening to Billy and Sammie.

"Sir?" Grace said a couple times before I hung up on her.

I had changed my mind. "Connect the dots you two. Connect the dots." I said to myself.

My Safe House-3 Transcriber was still on the phone. I told her, "Leave them alone. I don't want them touched, but bring me the raw transcript immediately after they leave."

"Yes, sir."

I called Grace back, "Grace, I'm going to be here all night, go home."

She was saying, "Yes, sir," when I hung up.

Same Evening, Safe House-3

Billy had really done it this time and we could be in big, big trouble, if we or he is ever caught.

197

I confess though, it was also kind of exciting.

Billy laid his documents out with a bulleted cover document on top. He wanted to walk me through them but I said, "Your hacker who has been getting in to snoop on Issy's computer is no longer just looking."

"Yes, I know," he said. "He's doing a combination MitM attack, gaining control of her computer, for the purpose of stuffing in more and more documents, supposedly hers. He's also continuing the SQL Injection hack to read the data he's interested in. Is that what you're seeing?"

"Yes," then I described the documents which I had found.

"Interesting," he said, "Very Interesting."

There was a long silence when he said, "Sammie, I think our window for helping Jude and Issy is rapidly closing."

I nodded my head and he continued.

"From Jack's notes I can tell that he is not sold on Jude and Issy being dirty."

"Whew," I said more loudly than I meant to.

"But he is reading Homeland's conclusions and doesn't have alternative explanations."

"We need to give them to him, Billy."

"I know, Sammie."

"What are those alternative explanations?" I pressed.

"Well, we clearly have a few of them, but these regarding Dr. Dale, the one they call the Prayer Guy, are still beyond us," he said, clearly frustrated.

I was getting frustrated too. I was concerned for two very decent people, Jude and Issy, and scared for two hackers, me and Billy.

"Sammie, we need to work, double time quick. I think that's what they say in military lingo. And, you and I have the advantage, Sammie."

"How so?"

"They are looking at all this through the lens of people who are ignorant when it comes to things of the Lord."

I must have looked a bit perplexed because Billy explained, "They aren't looking at any of these 'facts' of theirs through the lens of Christian interaction. We can."

I nodded my head slowly and asked, "So, where do we go next?" nodding to his list.

He got a big grin, a cute grin, a grin I realized I liked more and more, then he said, "This is your list. I think that if we translate these 'facts' of theirs with our knowledge as Christians, we can give Jack an alternative perspective and turn their investigation around."

"I get that," I said, a little short with him. "Again though, where do we go next?"

I could tell I had hurt his feelings a bit, but he just kept on. He turned the cover document around to me and pointed to the bottom.

"The bottom of this list has the points of entry into the Prayer Guy's data, as well as Jude and Issy's, which you already have. Based on what I showed you before, we need to look at the places on social media Dr. Dale has given us, to find out what he is all about. If Homeland is looking at these things, I don't think they are correctly discerning what they are seeing."

"I think you and I should look over everything. . ."

"Duplicating each other's work? Isn't that a little inefficient? I interrupted.

"Yes, but," he said without hesitation. "I think two eyes seeing the same documents gives us a better opportunity to analyze it more accurately, although it may take a little longer."

"But time is not an option we have, Billy," I responded.

"Correct, you're right. We'll continue to divide the work," he said.

He showed me the first item on his list. It read, "Why is Perp #3 determined to visit D.C. on Tuesday and Wednesday only?"

"Now look at this," Billy said, as he passed me over the last three calendar months from Dr. Dale, AKA the Perp dubbed, "The Prayer-Guy."

I looked at it for a few seconds and then let out a short squeal of laughter. I was embarrassed, but Billy just kept looking at me with a smile creeping onto his face too.

As I looked up my face started to flush. I was getting angry. And he could see it too. I am finding this new friend of mine already knows me well, probably better than anyone I have ever met.

He reached over his hand covered mine. It was nice and soft and I relaxed a bit.

"Sammie, it is obvious to us why Dr. Dale comes here the days he does, but don't be angry at Homeland or Jack. They wouldn't give this the same importance which you and I understand it deserves."

He was right, of course. I agreed and said so.

"You see these initials?" he asked.

I nodded.

"They need to be run down. That's your first task."

"Okay."

"Sammie, I also need you to start looking for every document Jude sends outside of the Campaign team. Where is it going, what are the contents, and can it jeopardize his employment in any way?"

"Let's get at it," I said, and we left Safe House-3.

Standing by the door to leave he said, "Sammie, you go first. I think we need to leave at different times, not just different exits."

"That makes sense," I responded, "But how did you come up with that?"

"Red 3. The latest Bruce Willis espionage action movie."

I just chuckled at him and said, "Okay."

He stuck his hand out to me to shake and I responded likewise. Looking at it I said, "When this Presidential Campaign is over, we should, umm." I hesitated. I didn't know what else to say.

He was smiling big now, and said, "We should go on a date."

"Yes," I agreed.

Same Night, FBI Headquarters

"Yes, please, put yourselves out of your misery," I agreed, listening to the end of their conversation.

"But wait until the campaign is done. I don't want Homeland to start an investigation on you two, too."

Sammie had gone when I heard a mumbling in my earpiece. It was Billy. He sounded like he was talking to himself. I turned up the volume.

"Oh, Lord," he was saying, "Your Word says that when we need wisdom, we are to ask of You, and You will give it to us generously.[1] Sammie and I really need it. And Lord, so does Jack as he directs this flawed investigation. In Your Son's Name I pray, Amen."

---

[1] James 1:5

Chapter 34

Thursday July 12th, Washington D.C.

I was in Washington D.C. to continue the process of strengthening ties with the two candidates and their CoS.

Today's visit should make the path straight and prepare the way for the anointed one,[1] who I humbly accept is me.

"Hallelujah," I shouted to myself and then smiled big.

Anthony drove me to my first appointment and I got out of my SUV-Limo with an envelope in my purse. I actually had two envelopes, one for each campaign. Today's copies of checks, again from two completely different businesses, were only two-hundred and fifty-thousand dollars each. But combined with my previous envelope it should keep their interest while I make them think I have a genuine concern for their advertising needs.

Earlier in the week, I Skyped Clyde while at my office and we talked. "Boss," he said to me with great excitement, "I think our documents are being looked at."

During the last few weeks my attitude towards him has been changing. For that matter, my attitude towards lots of people had changed. It was a little disconcerting, because on the tip of my tongue would be a sharp rebuke and something weak would sneak out of my lips.

I felt like something was preparing me from the inside out and I should just trust it.

"That's it," I said, "My sixth sense is preparing me and my attitude for dealing with the ultra-powerful people I will be connecting with and rubbing shoulders with soon."

"How exciting, praise the Lord," I thought.

Immediately my all so familiar purr began in my gut and worked its way out of my mouth.

I smiled, somewhat kindly, even courteously at Clyde on Skype. I was surprised at myself.

And it surprised him, too. "Boss, are you okay?"

I sighed deeply and said, "Yes, Clyde. Get on with your briefing."

But I didn't call him a moron, or a buffoon, or anything I normally would have. It was really weird.

I opened the file he had couriered to me and we looked at this round of documents which were in both Religion Consultants' files. We then looked at the location on the internet where they had written similar things which would irk their bosses. Of course, Clyde had written them and signed their names, including their electronic addresses, so there'd be no question as to their source.

When I needed to, I would reveal these posts' existence and confirm my worth. Then I would move in, once I knew which candidate would be elected, of course. I didn't set all this up to be a part of the losing team!

"Remember, ma'am, when you go to D.C. you are only there to begin to cast suspicion, to shine, and to look beautiful."

When he said this, he seemed to blush a bit and then hurried on.

"You are strengthening your credibility with this visit."

"I know you moron. I made the schedule and the timetable. I know what I'm doing, you idiot!'

All that went through my mind, but what came out my mouth was, "Thank you Clyde. Good reminder." And I disconnected from Skype.

Something else was weird. Last night at church, a number of people came up to me to talk and I didn't make excuses to get away from them.

"Bizarre. Very bizarre," was all I could think.

Clyde had found the employment agreement for both Religion Consultants, which were very similar. And in both of their contracts were two points we intended to now exploit.

One area is that they both agreed to not collaborate on anything religious, while under their current employment contract. And the other was like it. They could not post anything religious without the consent of the Chief of Staff.

I was ushered into the Chief of Staff's office. But before I met with the candidate and gave my next seed-offering I had decided to plunge into "Operation Judas" by throwing some suspicion onto the Religion Consultants.

Burnt coffee was brought to me, along with a stale scone, but I was charming, sitting there talking to the Chief of Staff.

"How are things going with your Religion Consultant?" I asked very innocently.

Watching the uncertain response, I thought to myself, "This is very exciting, for the suspicion wheel has already started turning."

Inside I grinned wide. It was eerie. If the smile I had inside was on my mouth, it would be wider than my entire face. It was really weird, but really pleasing, even intoxicating.

And then that low masculine purring began again. I quickly asked the Chief of Staff for a cup of water. I needed to control myself.

An aide brought in some water for me and I decided to raise the temperature of traitorous suspicion a little bit higher.

"I have thought your Religion Consultant's recent posts quiet, umm, interesting. They really "push the envelope," I think it's called."

The Chief of Staff looked surprised and then I added casually, "They sure were hard to find though." I could tell I was having an impact, which made me tingle, an odd, but satisfying sensation.

About that time, we were ushered into the candidate's office. After some small-talk and my promise to always be supportive, however I was needed, which I said while looking at the Chief of Staff, I spoke directly to the candidate. "I remain here for you. By the way, I had another conversation with your ad agency and have a copy of our decision to move forward on another group of ads."

I was brilliant. And I was sure it would go this way after lunch, when I saw the other candidate.

The only difficulty I had today was when I had lunch with that Prayer-Guy, Clyde found. I think Dr. Dale is very odd. Of course, I think he played right into my hands. I will tell Clyde to give him another donation. After all, he's a man. He'll be easy to manipulate.

However, Dr. Dale did say one interesting thing, and I am not sure if I can believe him. He said when he goes in and prays with Senators and Congressmen, or women, he doesn't care about their politics.

I don't think he was just saying it. I think he meant it. That's when I decided he is peculiar. He said his job in D.C. is merely "to bear these men and women's burdens."

"Galatians 6:2," I said.

"Yes, pastor, exactly," he responded. I could tell he was impressed.

And then he said, "I'm sure you experience the same thing when you are in a hospital praying for one who is hurting."

I just smiled at him. I didn't want to burst his bubble and tell him I don't do that. I have other pastors for that kind of stuff.

Anyway, he went on and told me of examples where after he prays, he watches these folks cast their burdens upon Him who cares for them.

"1 Peter 5:7," I said.

He just smiled and continued, "And then I watch a peace descend upon them, which clearly transcends their understanding."

He paused, looking at me, waiting for the reference.

"Philippians 4:7, of course," I said and laughed. He did too.

He seems to have a humility which cannot be real. And then, if his fake humility was not enough, he thwarted my questions when I asked him who he meets with.

"Oh, I'm sorry, ma'am. I am not able to say."

I was a little indignant and asked, "Why not? I'm a pastor too."

"Oh, I know," he said, again very humbly which I decided is a well-practiced device. And one I may try and develop.

"You see," he went on, "I have made a commitment to these folks which I fear I have to take great pains to protect."

"Of course," I said with my most magnanimous voice.

Anthony, who I had waiting at another table was now heading toward me. Lunch was coming to an end. "Thank, God," I said to myself, and just then Dr. Dale reached out his hand to mine, bowed his head and started to pray.

Well, that was nearly too much for me. I pray in church all the time, but not in public like this, around all these people I don't know! Now I knew that I definitely didn't like Dr. Dale.

I was even feeling uncomfortable inside me. Instead of the soothing purring I had come to enjoy, there was a rumbling of explosive anger.

I can't even tell you what he prayed. I was just glad to hear him getting near an "amen." The restaurant we ate is huge and is in the basement level of one of the House Office Buildings. It is wide open, but now it was feeling very claustrophobic. As I was leaving, he offered me directions to get up to the next level and then out to the proper exit door.

I laughed and told him, "Anthony is here all the time. He knows the way. But, thank you."

I just wanted to get away from Dr. Dale.

Fifteen minutes later I was ready to throttle Anthony because we still had no idea at which entrance our limo was waiting.

Finally, I made it to the next Presidential Candidate's office, which went just like the first.

By the time I left Washington D.C. I knew each Chief of Staff would be annoyed, maybe even irate at their Religion Consultant. A good day's work, I decided. The only question was, what would they do next?

From the SUV-Limo I called Clyde and told him to monitor the Chiefs of Staffs' emails. I wanted to know what steps they were taking after I left these breadcrumbs of incrimination.

I was so proud of myself.

Same Day, FBI Headquarters

Pete called me and said, "You're not going to believe this, but both CoS, for both candidates called me this afternoon, suspecting their Religion Consultants of violating their employment agreements."

"What did you say to them?" I asked.

"I said the exact same thing to both of them. I said, 'Fire them.'"

I chuckled, which Pete didn't like and said so in no uncertain terms.

Regaining my professionalism, I asked, "You didn't really say that, did you?"

"Of course, I did, Jack!"

"You fool, Pete!" I thought but didn't voice it. Instead I asked, "What was their response?"

"That's what surprised me, Jack. They both said the same thing. They said, 'I can't, my boss likes and trusts them too much.'"

"I came so close to telling each of them that these two are in our cross-hairs. . ."

"Don't you dare," I said. Maybe I screamed the words, because his response was quick and humble.

"I didn't. I won't. I'll wait. But if this goes sideways on us, Jack, I have all my documentation that you have held me back on this."

"Anything else?" I asked, ignoring his threat.

"Yeah, one thing. My cyber spooks tell me someone else is crawling through the computers of Perps #4 and #5."

I was instantly alert, but didn't want him to know, so, trying to be as nonchalant as I could, I asked, "Is it actionable or just some Junior High kid in a basement trolling?"

"They don't know yet, but it is being watched. We'll get 'em."

"Good, Pete, good," I said and hung up.

I'm sorry to say, an expletive left my mouth as soon as I hung up with Pete. I'm very careful to never do that. But I know they are seeing Billy and Sammie's tracks.

I stood up and walked to my window and looked out at the Mall. It is green and beautiful, as always, but what caught my eye was Ernie, the hotdog vender below me. I love his hotdogs, but, I'm sorry to say, my Cardiologist said, "No more," at my last checkup.

Dr. Joseph is in charge of cardiology at George Washington University Hospital. He has a great laugh and he loves to let it bellow. It comes from deep in his chest and you can always tell when he's near your exam room, even if the door is closed. Anyway, he put a halt on all my high sodium foods. So, as much as I wanted a dog from Ernie, I returned to my desk and ordered a salad.

But first I sent a short text to both Billy and Sammie.

"You're getting sloppy."

I think they'll figure it out.

I received an interesting text from my mom that evening, "Hello, Jacky. Don't want to bother, just encouraging you that I'm praying for you and perhaps I can suggest you go to church and find some nice friends away from work. Just an idea. Love you bunches, Jacky."

---

[1] Isaiah 40:3

Chapter 35

Lately Issy and I are ships, passing one another in the night. We are each putting in fourteen to sixteen-hour days. We are on calls all over the country, dealing with emails, and generally being good servants, constantly helping wherever the respective campaigns need us.

I'm not complaining. We are both committed to our jobs and our candidates, but there has been noticeably less couple-time this summer. I mentioned that to Issy last night as I was rubbing her back and stroking her long dark hair. A few years ago, she let her hair grow out and now she adds soft caramel highlights in the spring and auburn highlights in the fall. Personally, I think the colors are quite fun.

It was Sunday morning and I had just turned off my alarm.

I leaned my head close to Issy's ear to tell her how much I missed cuddling and then I heard a snore. And it wasn't a fake one. It was a real snore, from my real tired wife.

So, I let her sleep another half an hour. When she woke up, I had already gotten our coffee. Then we read, "Therefore, many of the Jews who had come to visit Mary. . ."[1]

January A.D. 30, Consequences of Raising Lazarus

This was a very troubling time for us. We had troublemakers and informants all around us. We really had no idea who we could trust.

You would think it is a good thing to raise someone from the dead. It was an amazing trick. I still don't know how Jesus did it. And the reaction of those around the tomb, their surprise, that was amazing, too. I wanted to say, "They can't be that good of actors," but they must have been.

Nevertheless, Jesus ends up on the short end of every difficult situation. Mind you, I'm not feeling bad for Him. I think He has a gift for getting into trouble. But I'd be less than honest if I didn't confess that I think He also has a gift which He could use for the good of our nation if He wanted to.

It is still astonishing to me, how many people put their trust in Him[2] because of His works. I think they are wrong. I think they should put their trust in God, not Jesus, but, my point is that He has an army of believers. If He would, He could just unite them into one blazing, glorious purpose and throw off this yoke of bondage the Romans are using to strangle us.

At any rate, later in the evening, a number of us who were in the crowd went to the Pharisees to tell them what Jesus had done.[3] I decided a long time ago it was important to make sure the Pharisees got the real happenings from an insider, namely me. These other people may see bits and pieces of what is going on, but I am able to correct any errors. I've never told Jesus I do this, but I suspect He'd be glad to know the Pharisees were getting the truth, and no exaggerations.

After I shared details and corrected people's errors, I stood in the back and listened to Caiaphas tell a strange story and an even stranger prophecy. I am not sure if I was scared of him or excited for his willingness to make a situation which was deteriorating, into a real blessing for our nation and for the scattered Children of God.[4]

On the face of it, his words were pretty harsh, but as I thought more about them while walking back to our camp, I realized Caiaphas was doing some deep thinking.

"He has a brilliant mind," I decided. Then I saw Jesus walking up to me with His three favorites. They make me sick sometimes.

"Judas," Peter called out, "What are you doing up so late?"

"Oh, you loud, arrogant, ignorant fisherman," I thought, but of course I held my tongue. Instead I simply said, "I was out praying. What a blessed day it was, seeing Jesus bring Lazarus back to life."

Peter, James and John were exhausted, but Jesus just looked intently, and yet, lovingly at me.

"Does, He know where I've been?" I wondered. "No, He can't. Because if He did, He'd have said I was lying." After all, that's what I would have done.

He laid his hand on my shoulder and looking deeply into my soul, his eyes, which tonight had such a green shine to them, said He loved me. I can't explain it. No words were conveyed, but I knew, Jesus loved Judas Iscariot.

That night we stopped moving about publicly among the Jews. Instead we camped in the desert, in a flea-bitten village named Ephraim. I hate the desert!

Sunday, July 22nd, Arlington VA

When Issy finished reading, I shook my head and said, "Can you imagine, Issy, what it must have been like in Jerusalem during all of this? Just think about how the evil one uses people. He used Mary's friends to 'tell on Jesus.' He used Caiaphas who started talking about Jesus' death long before this passage. And he used Judas Iscariot, of course."

I was still shaking my head when Issy said, "I don't think it's any different today, babe. Look at Harold's attitude toward you, which is just now changing, and it's taken months. Look at the industry we work in, we see Harolds everywhere. People whose passion leads to intolerance and then to anger and then to rage."

"And that's inside the church," I wisecracked.

We had sat there thinking for a minute when Issy went on, "What is it you always say, babe? 'These things show sataN's incredible ability to deceive.'"

"I prefer my other saying, 'Church would be great if we didn't have to deal with people.'"

We both laughed and then she picked up again, "Look at all that is going on here in the USA as forces arise to fight against the candidates, yours *and* mine."

"Yep," I said.

"And then we have to deal with various groups wanting influence," she added.

I sighed and agreed, "And some of those influencers are trying to buy influence on both sides of the aisle so they are not left out in the cold."

I was contemplating all we were talking about when I said, "Compare what we see, Issy, and you and I are in the background. Can you compare our situation to Jerusalem, a few months before Christ's death?"

"You're losing me," she said.

"The first two verses of the thirteenth chapter of Romans make it clear." I said, "God is in control, and those in office are there because God put them there. In just a few months, the person God wants in the highest office in this land will ascend. And they will have the job because God wants that person there."

"Yes," she said. "What's your point?"

I continued, "The evil one is doing everything he can to influence the voting to get what he wants. You and I see that all the time. But God is using the evil one to get what He wants in November."

"Look at how he used Caiaphas two-thousand-years-ago to do the same thing. He even allowed such pride in Caiaphas that his prophecy had more meaning than he could have ever realized."

I pointed the prophecy out to Issy, "Can't you just see Caiaphas talking about a sacrifice that will bless the whole nation? Little did he know that Christ's death would in fact be a blessing to all nations. Caiaphas got what he wanted, but not what he intended."

In fact, what happened was according to God's plan and that's what's going to happen here, at the ballot box, in a few months, babe."

Issy added, "That's a good point Jude, and that's why our Christian friends need to vote their conscience, trusting God, not their politician."

We were both silent and then Issy said, "Wow, that's a tough one to swallow."

"I know," I said, "But that is the way God works in the nations."

She then closed her eyes and prayed, "Lord, forgive me for my arrogance. I often think I have a good bead on life, but it is You who is in control. Forgive me for wanting You to do my will before I will submit to Yours."

I jumped in, "Father, I don't have to be scared of those who disagree with me. I don't have to be scared if Issy's candidate wins, because, Father, I trust You."

Issy finished our prayer, "And Lord, because You love us, we trust You, even if Jude's candidate wins. Amen."

"My surprising challenge and unusual promise are the same, namely, trusting God for the right results, even if it's different from what I believe to be right," I said.

"Interesting, Jude. Mine comes from the last verse of this passage. Jesus was a good steward of what he did for the remaining three or so months of His life. The passage says, 'Jesus no longer moved about publicly among the Jews[5]. . .' Baby," she continued, "We have got to be good stewards of every little thing we do. If people don't like what we do or stand for, let it not be because we were arrogant or prideful, sinful or stupid."

"That's why I love Ephesians 6:7 and Colossians 3:23. Everything you and I do, Issy, is to be done as if we are doing it unto the Lord, and not our candidate. This means we are to do everything with excellence. So, no one can find fault in what we do.[6]"

Issy leaned over and gave me a long slow kiss and then in her most seductive voice said. "If we don't get going we're going to be late for church."

I cannot tell you how badly I wanted to say, "Let's skip church today."

Billy's Church, Sunday Morning

I've been attending Billy's church now for a few months. I suppose this is something we'll have to tell Jack about. But truthfully, I never think about it when we are in his office.

I arrived for the morning service late and the worship music had already started. I liked that because with everyone standing, I could find Billy, sit next to him and fewer people saw us together. When I scooted beside him, he quickly squeezed my hand and then let it go.

I can't wait for the campaign to be over.

I motioned him to lean over so I could whisper, "Billy, on Friday, Jude showed me some posts which were made under his name and he asked me to help him run down their source, which I started doing yesterday. He's afraid they could compromise his job. He didn't write them but wants to find out who did."

"I know, Sammie."

"How do you know? No one knows. He even said he would not tell Issy."

"Because Issy came to me with the similar fears. Apparently, there are some posts out there with her name on them which she did not write."

I was shocked and nearly lost my balance. Billy's soft hand grabbed and held my arm but I didn't even notice. "Billy, this poor sweet couple is in a big mess and if we don't help them, it'll get worse."

"I know."

"There's another problem, Sammie. Both of our bosses, not the candidates, but the Chiefs of Staff, contacted Pete Beecham at Homeland."

I gasped and started to tear up.

After church, before we went outside, we stopped in a corner where we could talk.

"Let's meet tonight, Sammie. I have found some of our answers which can clear the Prayer-Guy."

I immediately jumped in, "I'm not worried about him, Billy."

"Shush," he responded soothingly and touched my arm so sweetly.

Am I falling in love with this guy?

He was saying, "Sammie, did you run down those initials?"

"Yes," I said. I think I was pouting. How foolish of me.

"Sammie, let's focus on these posts by Jude and Issy and clear them of any suspicion."

"How will we do that?" I asked.

"I have a couple more things to run down this afternoon, so after church tonight, we'll go to the safe house, okay? Bring those posts Jude gave you."

I sighed, "Okay."

"I know you're worried, Sammie, but I think we are very close to clearing both."

We went our separate ways and for the first time in a while I felt relieved.

Sunday Afternoon, FBI Headquarters

Pete called me, "I told you someone was trying to cover up Jude and Issy's unlawful actions. Well, we have them on tape and we know they have a safe house. They plan to meet there tonight to discuss clearing my Perps."

I sat in my Lazy-boy and didn't say a word. The Nats were leading the Atlanta Braves, in Atlanta 4-3 in the eighth inning when Pete called and ruined my afternoon.

"Are you still there?" he asked.

"Yeah, I am." I answered slowly, shaking my head. I was afraid this would happen.

After another long pause I asked, "How much do you trust me, Pete?"

"Right now, only as far as I can throw you, Jack."

I chuckled, but he didn't.

We talked for another twenty minutes, enough for me to miss the rest of the game. But eventually he agreed to my request. Reluctantly, but he agreed.

Billy's Church, Sunday Night

I wasn't late for church tonight, but I still waited in the back until people were standing and singing. Finding Billy, I made a beeline for him and this time I reached out, interlaced our fingers for the first time and squeezed his hand.

He was shocked, and embarrassed, but he smiled and held my hand for a full minute before releasing it. Very special.

We were enjoying the long moment when someone behind us said, "I don't know if I should be proud of you two kids, or embarrassed, like Billy here."

I knew that voice. We knew that voice. It was Jack Jones from the FBI. We turned to look at each other and then looked back at Jack who was standing there as if he hadn't a care in the world.

In a hushed voice, Jack said, "Homeland wanted to pick you up tonight, before you went to Safe House-3 and discussed the documents you are using to clear Jude and Issy."

Looking at Billy he said, "You've been a very naughty boy, looking for notes in my Trello and OneNote."

My eyes grew to the size of saucers, but Billy's didn't, and Jack noticed.

The worship team started another song and we remained standing. I was trembling.

Jack shook his head comprehending what I did not. "You knew it would be bugged, didn't you, Billy. You wanted me to know what you two were doing."

Billy tried really hard to hold back a grin, but he couldn't. He was proud of himself. I wasn't sure if I was too, or if I was just irritated with him.

Now Jack smiled. Then he said, "Listen kids, you have until this coming Saturday morning to put everything together. Either you have it sewn up, or the wrong people are going to jail, beginning with you two."

Everyone was clapping with the music and Jack stood back and clapped with the music also. We turned back around to the front.

I had a million questions and I didn't do a good job listening to this evening's sermon.

When we sang our closing song, I turned back to ask Jack a question, but he was gone.

As we walked out of church we agreed we'd work our tails off this week. We would be ready to show up wherever Jack wanted us to on Saturday.

"This Thursday night is Prayer night. I think I'll be here for it."

"Me too," I said.

We clasped hands as we said goodbye. Both of us were very nervous.

—————————————

[1] Luke 11:45a

[2] Luke 11:45b

[3] Luke 11:46

[4] John 11:51-52

[5] John 11:54a

[6] 2 Corinthians 6:3

Chapter 36

Saturday July 28th, Morning, FBI Headquarters

I asked Pete to be in my office before the kids arrived, so he was there at 8:45.

Pete and I had been in my office for only fifteen minutes and I couldn't handle him anymore. I asked, "Pete, why are you so hostile towards Billy and Sammie?"

"They believe lies, Jack. They judge others, they narrowly view life, and then if that weren't enough, they spread those lies to an ignorant public."

I sat there just looking at him with his unnatural rage and wondered why I never noticed it before. To me it seemed like a rage without logic. He had what seemed like 'reasons' to him, but in my judgment, they were hollow. Today would be interesting and I'd have the opportunity to see how good pimply-faced Billy and his future girlfriend really are.

Thinking about Billy and Sammie's relationship I chuckled, and Pete squawked, "Are you laughing at me, Jack?"

"Don't be silly, Pete. If I were going to laugh at you, I'd do it behind your back."

To which he laughed and said, "I'm a little agitated."

"You think?" I said and then grinned.

My old friend was doing what he accused them of doing. He was judging them.

Billy and Sammie arrived at 9:00 right on the dot, but there were a number of procedural things Pete wanted to discuss about this case, so we went over them before I let Billy and Sammie in.

Billy and I met downstairs and we took the same elevator up to Jack's office. We had to wait outside his office for nearly an hour. I was wondering if we were going to be in a big room with both teams of agents, one from the FBI and one from Homeland Security.

I don't know what I had expected. I guess I thought Billy and I would simply report our findings, to a very appreciative group of agents, answer their polite questions, and then leave.

It was not to be that simple.

I was relieved as we entered Jack's office and the occupants were only Jack and Pete Beecham, who I learned, was in charge of Homeland Security.

The only way I can describe Pete, having never met him before, is a man with a scowl-filled face which made me look to see if handcuffs were at the ready. I wondered how long Billy and I would be there before we got hauled off to a jail cell. Pete looked like he was ready for a fight.

We sat down and Jack made introductions and then he asked Billy to give them the report, "Tell us why you and Sammie believe Perps #4 and #5 are not Perps."

But before he could begin, Pete attacked them. "Let me tell you where I'm at before you even get started, Billy." And then he turned to Jack. "I have looked into this kid's background. He's no different than the Perps we are trying to put away, Jack.

Jack sat there silently as Pete disdainfully went on. "He is one of these Bible-believing fools, who in my mind are untrustworthy at best, and at worse, are probably willing to distort facts to protect those like themselves."

Jack took a deep breath and responded a lot nicer than I wanted. He said, "You may be right, Pete. But I think it's best if we let the kids speak for themselves. They can give us whatever facts they've got. And we can figure out how to interpret them. Then we can decide what actionable steps are next, okay? Are you willing to cut the kids a little bit of slack?"

"Jack," Pete said, "These two can say whatever they want to. I just wanted them to know my view of this so-called report before they begin."

Jack nodded to Billy and me to begin. And I was so proud of Billy.

"First let me say Mr. Beecham, I agree with almost everything you just said."

"Don't patronize me, Billy," Pete growled.

"I'm not, sir. I mean it. I see your attitude all over churches when they find out I have anything to do with politics. It's amazing, Mr. Beecham because they believe that they have the same right to judge me, as it sounds like you think you do. It's completely uncanny. You are doing to me what Christians do to those with whom they disagree. Even some they go to church with."

Pete sat there with his mouth open. Jack was smiling with his eyes, and I was proud of Billy, but scared to death.

Billy smiled and then said, "It's kind of ironic, isn't it?"

He paused for a beat or two and was a bit too flippant when he spoke again, "I'm sorry, did you want to talk religion?

Jack cut in immediately, moving him along, "Billy." He nodded towards Billy's papers. "Get on with your briefing."

Billy apologized and said, "Let me begin, gentlemen."

"After looking at the questions and the suspicions you have had about these five Perps, and then the conclusions you have come up with. . ."

215

"Seven Perps now, including you and Sammie," Pete said.

"Pete, calm down and give the kid some room." Jack was now getting impatient with Pete.

Billy went on without skipping a beat. "You're right, Mr. Beecham, seven of us."

"After analyzing the data your teams were looking at, I realized there was one central figure who touched all of the Perps."

"Yeah, yeah, yeah, Billy, we know this, Clyde, the Warner Robins Air Force Base Counterintelligence. . ."

"No, sir," Billy interrupted. Jack and Pete were surprised by this.

But Billy and I agreed; while the Perps were obvious, and the end result was obvious, the central player was less obvious, until we connected all the dots.

Then Billy told Jack and Pete our conclusion. "The Prayer-Guy, Dr. Dale is the one who is at the center of all of this, and he doesn't even realize it. But, once we figured out his role with all the principals, everything else fell into place, including which ones are your Perps and which ones are not."

"Jack, are you serious?" cried Pete. How long do I have to listen to this kid?"

"Pete let's see where this goes. To be honest with you, I don't know where he's going either. But I trust Billy's intuition enough to give him a few more minutes. Very few though."

Pete sat back, temporarily.

"What!?!? Only a couple of minutes," I thought. "How is Billy going to explain what we have spent three months analyzing and organizing?" I was stressing. I know Pete wanted to get up and leave and while he's at it, arrest us!

I looked at Billy and I ushered up a quick prayer. I could tell he was contemplating the same issues, and then he made me proud again.

"Do you know why Jude and Issy collaborated on that document, gentlemen?"

"So, you're admitting that they did, Billy?" Looking at Jack, Pete went on, "What more do we need?"

Billy continued confidently as if speaking only to Jack. "Of course, they did, but do you know why?"

Pete seemed to realize that he may have just stuck his foot in his mouth. Quietly he eased back in his chair but kept his arms crossed over his chest.

"Issy's boss, the Chief of Staff, Priscilla Ellsworth gave her permission to collaborate with Jude."

Out of my file I pulled an email from Priscilla to Issy relieving her of any contractual responsibilities, if she and Jude collaborated on this one, specific project.

"And Jude had to get permission from his boss too," I added and pulled out copies of that approval too. "By the way, the project was named, 'News Outlets and Religious People.'"

As soon as I was quiet, Billy plowed on.

"Would you like to know why the Prayer-Guy comes to D.C. on Tuesday and Wednesday and never varies those days?"

Billy had their attention and he nodded towards me.

Out of my file I drew six pages. They were Dr. Dale's last three months calendar, from his computer. I had two copies of everything, so I handed three pages to Jack and copies of the same three pages to Pete. On each page I had highlighted the two days each month Dr. Dale was in town.

"By the way," Billy added, too arrogantly in my opinion, "Did you know he is meeting with Warner Robins counterintelligence officers right now?"

I rolled my eyes.

Jack shook his head.

But Pete blew a head gasket, as my father would say. Pete's face got red with anger and he spewed out venom when he bellowed, "How do you know he is meeting with them?"

And in the same breath he turned to Jack and demanded, "What are you doing about this intel? Have you warned them, Jack?"

"I didn't know anything about this, Pete," replied a concerned Jack Jones.

"This is why I can't trust you, Billy. Did you even think to warn Warner Robins or were you too busy trying to figure out how to exonerate your friends?"

Pete shook his head with disgust, "You had no clue you should have warned them, did you, Billy?" And then he looked at me. "Nor did you, did you Sammie?"

Billy seemed to put on a tone of command and said, "Mr. Beecham, I completely understand your fear. Like I tried to tell you earlier, I see it in churches all the time. You're acting just like the church folk I see on Sunday."

Billy went back to his documents. I looked at Pete who seemed to not know what to say, and Jack, who was shocked by Billy's boldness. But, I kind of got the sense that Jack's shock was laced with pride for his young protégé.

"Sir, Mister Beecham," Billy went on, "There's nothing for you to be concerned about and let me explain why. Look at the calendars that Sammie just pulled out of her file and gave you."

This is a longstanding prayer meeting Dr. Dale does twice a month at his church. And why are these bigwigs from counterintelligence there? Simple, Dr. Dale is their chaplain. He visits with them weekly and has developed relationships with them, just like he has with elected officials and staffers on the Hill.

Jack and Pete were looking intently at their copies of the calendars.

"Billy," Jack asked, with interest, "What are these things marked 'CC' and then a name after the two initials. They are on his calendar every Monday, Thursday and Friday. But they are absent on Tuesday and Wednesday, the days Dr. Dale is in D.C."

Billy looked over at me and I was happy to share. "Gentlemen, I was tasked with running these initials down." I paused and then added with as little of a smile as I could. "They stand for 'Conference-Call.' The names after the 'CC' are those people who are on those weekly conference calls with him."

"What does he do on these calls? Do you know?" Pete said. I thought he was a little snarky. Then he added "And just why are you smiling, Sammie?"

"They are Prayer Conference Calls, sir." I simply said, choosing not to look him in the eye.

Jack raised his eyebrows.

Pete spoke in a subdued tone, finally, and he just said, "This guy is more serious about prayer than anyone I know."

Billy and I just sat there trying to look humble, but we were both pretty proud of ourselves.

We walked through a number of other issues and questions they both had, not the least of which were posts that appeared to be written by Jude and Issy, which they claimed were not.

"Did you compare them?" I asked.

"Why?" Pete asked, as if this was a trick question.

"Because," Billy said with a slight scowl himself, "You should have picked up that they were the same posts, simply written from a different perspective."

"One person writing two posts?" Pete asked, humbly.

"Yes, sir. We think so," I said.

After an hour and a half of this type of back and forth, Jack stood up. "It's lunch-time and I'd like us to go into my conference room, away from here, since we will be returning to this. Grace has already ordered for us."

"Our documents?" Billy questioned.

"You can leave them here. If anyone enters, Grace won't let them leave."

He chuckled, but I'm not sure why.

Saturday July 28th, Lunch, FBI Headquarters

I was very proud of Billy and Sammie. Not only had their organization of the material allowed them do some quick thinking, but Billy played hard ball with the appropriate amount of intensity. He also refrained from being disrespectful regardless of the treatment he received.

I liked this kid.

Sitting at lunch, Pete had completely settled down and being the professional he is, put the pertinent discussion aside. In fact, he was talking to both Billy and Sammie as if they were old friends.

There were some more "I's" to dot and "T's" to cross, but we would do that after lunch. I was grateful my judgment to let these two kids go where they wanted to, even my files, was vindicated.

Pete then asked a question I too was interested in. "Billy, why do you keep comparing my concerns, my legitimate concerns, and my anger, with the irrational fears of those people you call Christians?"

"Mr. Beecham," Billy started, and then was cut off.

"Just 'Pete,' Billy, you've earned the right to call me Pete."

And then he looked at me and asked, "Jack, how do they address you?"

"Sir," I responded a little harshly. But I laughed and so did everyone else.

Billy picked back up. "Mr. umm, Pete, when I hear you judge my fellow Christians, I hear you judging them just like many of them are judging their fellow Christians, whose only 'sin,' so to speak, is voting for someone they do not like"

"And sir, Pete," Billy went on, "It's embarrassing."

"Embarrassing? Why, Billy? If they are acting like idiots why is it embarrassing to you?"

"Because sir, they are a part of what we call the Body of Christ, like me and Sammie are. When they act like idiots, it is a reflection on all of us."

"Aren't you being a little harsh?" asked Jack.

"No sir, you see, we have no excuse. We have the Holy Spirit living inside of us who gives us the grace to live above our pettiness, if we want to."

"Are you talking that born-again stuff, Billy?" Pete asked with some hostility.

And then Billy did it again, he disarmed Pete. "Are you a John Fogerty and CCR fan?"

Pete looked at me and I just shrugged my shoulders. I had no idea where Billy was going.

"I am, yes," Pete responded, clearly weighing his words.

"Then you can accept that, what did you call it? That 'born-again stuff,' because in the song, 'Centerfield' Fogerty says, 'We're born again, there's new grass on the field. . .'"

"What a stretch, Billy," I said.

"I know. I was trying to be funny. I guess I wasn't," he said sheepishly but kept on talking.

"Yes, Pete," Billy continued. "I'm talking about when Christians are born-again."

Pete sincerely asked, "Well, clearly I have been wrong about a number of things thus-far in this case, but Billy, shouldn't I be allowed to have some passion, even some anger about the things I see which are wrong?"

Billy responded, "I have an old friend who is a pastor and has been for over 40 years. He often says, 'Just because you're right doesn't mean you open your mouth.'"

"Huh," Jack snickered, "You only have to be married ten minutes to begin to learn that one!"

Sammie piped in and said, "Pete, you're making the exact same mistake that you claim Christians make. But you're right about the fact that Christians do this, too."

"You lost me Sammie," said Pete. "What are you talking about?"

"Just because you're right, Pete, you are giving yourself the right to judge others. And that's not the way Jesus says we're to live, even if we are right."

She was on a roll and she kept going. "You only have to look at the political mess Jesus was in. . ."

"I didn't realize Jesus was in a political mess," interrupted Jack.

"Nor did I," added Pete.

"Yes," said Billy. "The reason Judas Iscariot was a traitor was because Jesus didn't take the political path he wanted Him to. We say, 'Judas was looking for a political Messiah.'"

"And here in the USA two-thousand years later, during our elections, we have people who claim to follow Christ (and probably do) but instead of putting their trust in Him, they are putting their trust in their political candidate. It's embarrassing."

Jack chimed in, deciding to take a turn. "You two have said that a number of times now, words to the effect that, 'the way some Christians are acting is an embarrassment' or something they should not be doing. But isn't that kind of passion the way we're wired? What's wrong with having strong opinions?"

"Nothing, as long as your passion doesn't break your fellowship with fellow believers. Too many Christian's political passion manifests itself as arrogance and then results in the breaking of fellowship with brothers and sisters in Christ. That's wrong, even if the reasoning is right."

Billy continued, "Looking into Dr. Dale's posts I found a great video he did on arrogance and politics, and he isn't talking about the arrogance of the politicians."[1]

"Of which there is plenty," scoffed Pete.

Sammie picked up, "The New Testament apostle, Paul, wrote twelve or thirteen books in the New Testament and a number of them talk about politics. He gives a clear foundational understanding for this particular issue we are discussing."

We were hanging on her words now. These two kids really knew their stuff.

"When Paul wrote the book of Romans, do you know who was controlling the nation of Rome and all its neighboring states?"

Pete and I looked at each other and shrugged our shoulders.

"It was Nero." She continued, "Did you know that Nero used to light Christians on fire and stick them on the top of poles for his night lights? The fascinating thing in my mind is that Paul never wrote about how terrible and ugly the leaders of his day were. In fact, he says they were there because God wanted those leaders there."

"Let me quote it," she said. "In the thirteenth chapter of Romans, in the first two verses, Paul writes this, 'Everyone must submit to the governing authorities, for there is no authority except from God, and those that exist are instituted by God. So then, the one who resist the authority is opposing God's command, and those who oppose it will bring judgment on themselves.'"[2]

I questioned her. "I hear that, Sammie, and I think that is a very difficult teaching, if what you are saying about Nero is true, but how does that relate to us today?"

"I don't know this for sure, guys, because I've never asked them, and they're so humble I would never embarrass them by asking. But I suspect a husband and wife team, who go to church together, and support diametrically opposed political sides are getting a lot of grief from men and women in their church, even though God has made it clear that whoever ends up in the Oval Office is there because He put them there."

"Your point?" asked Pete.

"The point is this, gentlemen," Billy was now up. "God expects us to honor and give respect to those He puts in office, because we can trust Him, God."

Billy continued, "Your unbridled judgmental attitude, Pete, has caused you to demonstrate hate and rage toward those you disagree with."

Billy smiled and told us, "There's a great story about Jesus going into a village and the people of the village rejecting Him. Instead of calling down judgement on them, like some of His disciples wanted to do,[3] He and His followers simply walked on to another village."[4]

"Men, Christians don't have an excuse for judging those around them or treating them (or anyone else for that matter) badly. God promises us the grace to live above that."

Pete got wound up in a flash and said, "How can you say that Billy, when so much has been caused by those two so-called Christians. . ."

"Clyde Smith and Pastor Mortenson, right?" interrupted Billy.

"Yes, those two hypocrites. Look at how they have acted and treated their own kind. I'm not going to feel the least bit bad about putting them behind bars."

"You shouldn't, Pete," Billy said, matching Pete's rising volume.

"I won't," he responded even louder.

"Good," Billy said, slowing the conversation, and then chuckling with that laugh which puts everyone at ease. "There are consequences to our bad choices and they will experience the governmental justice which is coming to them. And let me go further, Pete. I'm glad you're here. I'm glad you have this passion you do. I'm just glad Sammie and I were here to help you see this the right way. If you don't mind me being so bold.

I added, "Actually, Pete, I think you're making their point. There are many people, Christian and non-Christian, who willingly choose their own direction over God's. That's why you and I have a job.

Saturday July 28th, Afternoon, FBI Headquarters

We went back to my office, and Pete and I had a few more questions. But Billy and Sammie had done an excellent job and brought us a perspective which was way beyond our ability to comprehend, including the reason Pastor Mortenson had given so much money to both of these candidates.

Pete started the questions, "Why did Dr. Dale say calling him a terrorist was accurate?"

Billy responded, "I'd have to guess on that one, but I suspect it's because in a sarcastic sense, you might say he's a fanatic for fundamentalism, not Jihadist fundamentalism, but Christian fundamentalism. Dr. Dale often quotes a guy by the name of Leonard Ravenhill. He used to say, 'Our nation's problems stem from a faulty Christian fundamentalism,' which I think Dale is doing his best to correct."

I asked, "The enlisting of men and women really does have to do with just a Bible study or Prayer meeting, or something like that?"

"Yes, sir. And when he talks about wrestling, he's talking about wrestling in prayer, the way Epaphras did in Colossians 4:12."

Jack turned to Pete, "Doing prayer warfare is a term I have heard my mom use."

"Spiritual warfare," Billy corrected.

"Whatever," said Pete, slipping back into his grumpy mood.

I'm going to have to remember this quirk about him. Pete does much better when he is around food.

Sounding like his sails had just been deflated, Pete asked a question which sounded more like a statement, "So, Dale's efforts in D.C. really have no covert purpose?"

"Correct, sir. He just wants to help the elected officials and their staffers. He calls it bearing their burdens."

Pete sat back thinking, and then said, "In one of the conversations we've heard from him, he says, 'When I sit across from these elected officials, they all think I want something from them. They often give an audible sigh when they realize I don't.'"

"We're not used to people like this, Pete."

"I agree." Looking at Billy and Sammie, Pete continued. "I have a lot to thank you two for. It all makes sense now."

With a big smile, Billy simply said, "Our honor, sir, Pete, Mr. Beecham. Our honor."

"By the way," Pete asked, as if he were starting a brand-new conversation. "How did you two kids know these were the questions we had?"

After some hesitation and squirming in his seat, Billy looked at me and started to say, "Well, Pete. . ."

And then I cleared my throat loud enough to get Billy's attention, indicating for him to stop, but Pete immediately began to laugh.

An expletive went through my mind, I am embarrassed to confess.

Everyone else was quiet until Pete finished laughing and then looking at me, he said, "Billy hacked you, didn't he, Jack?"

I changed subjects, "Pete, you and I now have to reinvestigate the cyber hacking with intent, making our focus Perps #1 and #2." Pete acknowledged this, but he clearly wanted more details on Billy's hack.

When he saw there was no further info coming on that front, Pete assured Billy and Sammie that he'd get together with each Chief of Staff and assure them their Religion Consultants are squeaky clean.

I saw Billy and Sammie give a big sigh of relief. I even think Sammie might have brushed a tear from her eye.

I stood up and motioned for the two kids to get up, but before they left, Pete stood and admitted, "I would never have expected to say this," and then looking at Billy and Sammie, he said, "You know, for two young kids, you two are kind of smart."

Playfully, but with a serious edge to it, Billy said, "When you want to talk about that born-again stuff, Pete, just call me."

"Whoa, whoa, whoa," said Pete. "I'm not interested in the born-again stuff unless it's from John Fogerty."

"I'm not going to beat you over the head with it, Pete."

Billy was on a roll, so he continued. I thought it was good strategy.

"Before we go, may I make one more point about the way so-called godly men and women act, specifically with regard to their fear."

"Of course, Billy. While I didn't come to Jack's office for a Sunday School lesson, I do admit I've enjoyed the knowledge you and Sammie have on this Christian stuff."

Billy continued, but with a clearly, heavy heart. "So many of my. . ." He looked toward and included Sammie before he went on, "So many of our Christian brothers and sisters are fearful, and that fear is never more obvious than when they pray. As we were investigating Dr. Dale, we found a challenging post and video of his which shows that Christians' fear actually has them calling God a liar.[5] May I be allowed to be a little bit bold, one more time?"

I'm not sure, but I think I saw Sammie reach over and squeeze Billy's hand, as if for some moral support.

Pete completely missed it though. He was the most focused I had seen him all day with his eyes riveted on pimple-faced-Billy. "Pete, your fear this morning had you calling people liars when the truth was so near."

He added quickly, "I'm not saying that to pound on you, but just to tell you I'm concerned for you, and Sammie and I will be praying for you, if you don't mind."

And then he nodded at me and said, "And we'll be praying for you, even if you do mind."

The two kids left, and Pete and I decided on a plan of action to gather and review all of our evidence against Clyde Smith and Pastor Mortenson before we arrested them. It might keep them on the street for a few more weeks, but it'd be better to have our two cases in perfect order.

"Can you believe that kid?" Pete marveled. "He's tough as nails, for a kid. I don't think he would be fearful, even if the administration going into the presidency had the expressed desire of taking away all he and his kind hold meaningful in their lives."

I added, "To me, it makes sense that they would have the right to be fearful, but you're right, I don't think that kid or his girlfriend would be."

Pete smiled, "They're not a couple yet, though, right?"

"Correct."

"I admire their work ethic, Jack. I like them; can I have them?"

"In a word, Pete, no!"

---

[1] https://MarkMirza.com/politics-arrogance

[2] Romans 13:1-2 (HCSB)

[3] Luke 9:54

[4] Luke 9:56

[5] https://MarkMirza.com/calling-god-liar

Chapter 37

Sunday Morning July 29th, Atlanta GA

I went into church ready to speak, but something was wrong inside of me. It actually started yesterday afternoon. Over the previous few months I had gotten used to this masculine purring inside me. It was as if it were a spiritual confirmation that my desire to be an influencer in Washington D.C. was coming about.

But yesterday I experienced what I did while Dr. Dale was praying except it was stronger and longer. I can't explain it except to say, something changed. I don't know what. The purring and the inner Cheshire cat smile were gone. I called Clyde, who I had been unusually kind to and I was back to my normal self. I was able to say the things to him I wanted to. None of them pretty, of course.

Surprisingly he remained quiet and patient, as if he knew something I didn't. This paranoia made me even angrier. I could hardly control my rage. I was glad my home is on a compound with no one near me, because the yelling I did and the words I used were "unbecoming of a lady."

I had a terrible night's sleep and got up still feeling the rage and ugliness, and sick to my stomach, to boot!

When the worship music started, I was all over the auditorium. I was bouncing up and down on my toes and raising my hands. Although, now that I think about it, I couldn't raise my hands all the way up, because of bruising on my shoulders and back.

Yesterday afternoon I had fallen. Actually, I didn't fall as much as I felt thrown to the ground, which is stupid, because I was the only one in the house. At any rate, I remember falling to the ground at least three times and one of the falls was down my stairs. I decided I was lucky to have stood up with no broken bones, but I had some nasty bruising.

This morning, during the worship music I let myself go, something I encourage, but seldom do, myself. It was good to hear those in my church applauding their pastor who was "Letting the spirit lead her."

Did I hear someone say, "For a change?"

Must be my paranoia.

When it was time for me to speak, I walked up onto the stage carrying my Bible. I had an odd sensation walking up onto the dais.

Actually, I had a few interesting feelings. The first one was a sensation of heat in my hands. I had never experienced that before.

The second came when I heard my congregation gasp. I didn't understand why, until I looked at the platform and all of a sudden, in slow motion, it started to move. It was very odd. I remember thinking, "Why would my stage be moving?" And then I realized it was me. I was moving unnaturally.

Immediately I leaned over to grab the floor with my hands before I found it with my face. I feared that if my face hit first it would smudge my makeup. Then I heard Anthony, my bodyguard, running up to me. But by the time he got to me I had taken a knee and was gathering my senses.

I slowly stood and walked over to the podium. By now, my Bible was burning in my hands. It was as if I couldn't hold it, it was so hot. I said, "I suppose I need to start exercising so I can dance around our church in the future."

Everyone chuckled and then I felt the building spinning again.

I heard the congregation give another corporate gasp.

But the building wasn't spinning. I was spinning, and I was headed for the floor.

An hour later I awoke in my office. Anthony was there as was Clyde, his wife and his bratty children.

I asked, "Did I fall down?

One of Clyde's insolent kids said, "It looked like you were thrown down, pastor."

"I don't think you should be alone tonight." Clyde said.

I tried to say, there was no problem. That I was just exhausted.

But he said, "The deacons and I talked. If you don't mind, we're going to spend the night with you. Your house is big enough my kids will stay out of your way, and my wife can see to all your needs. Then tomorrow we'll see how you feel and decide what to do from there."

I was glad, but I wasn't going to admit it. Something was wrong with me, inside. I heard that rude kid say, "Yep, she looked just like my doll when I throw it on the floor."

Monday July 30th, Atlanta GA

Clyde came into my office where I was having a late breakfast. Worry was etched into his face.

"What is your problem?" I said with as much scorn as I could.

He shut the door which worried me for a moment. Was he going to do me bodily harm? But he sat in the chair next to me and said, "Ma'am, since Saturday afternoon I have seen unparalleled activity from the FBI and Homeland Security in your personal files."

"What does that mean, Clyde?"

He sat back and acted very strange. For a moment I thought he was contemplating what was best for him, rather than me.

"Talk to me, you fool." The rage I felt inside me was palpable. But he remained silent, calculating. I felt my face get flush, and then he said.

"They seem to be looking and gathering. . ."

I shouted, "Looking and gathering, what, you imbecile?"

"Information, ma'am. They are looking at travel plans, personal notes, and bank statements, both in the US and offshore. . ."

He stopped as if he had just finished calculating. And then he said calmly, "Ma'am, I think you're blown. I think they know all about you and over the weekend decided to start seriously putting together a case against you."

"This is your fault." I started to say, but stopped, because if he was right, I would need his help. I had planned for this contingency when the very first person died who was, well, within my sphere of influence.

Anyway, it was time to start schmoozing him and keeping him on my side.

"Clyde, I am prepared to make you a very rich man, if you will help me."

"Of course, ma'am. How can I serve you?"

"I need to disappear, Clyde, and disappear permanently."

"I understand."

"Just shut up and listen to me. I have been planning for this possibility. I have a house no one knows about. I will go there tonight and remain there till you have helped me with my other tasks."

"Like the church?"

"Of course not, they can take care of themselves. But Clyde, I have a fake passport and credit cards, as well as a location I'll go to. The only problem is, I will need to attend to one area that is very private, and I'll need someone I can trust. So, I'll need to you to handle it."

"Yes, ma'am. What would that be?" he asked.

I looked at him warily for a moment and then realized he was all I had to work with.

I went on, "I need all my cash and offshore accounts moved to a different account, under my new name. I can do all of it myself, except the final confirmation from my business manager which will be you. If you do this for me, I will give you a cool one million dollars, Clyde."

"Yes, ma'am," he responded and his eyes twinkled, I suspect out of greed. The fool won't know what to do with a million dollars.

Thursday Night, August 9th, Atlanta GA

I was flying to a little-known Island in the South Pacific, where my cash would sustain me for the rest of my days. I had developed a relationship with this resort a number of years ago, and paid them in advance, telling them that one day, I would just show up.

It is a decent sized island. There are a number of smaller hotels and motels and a bunch of cheap and trashy hovels, but the luxury hotel here is magnificent.

When I arrived, the manager remembered me immediately and acknowledged my new name without saying a word.

Before I had left, I ordered Clyde to get himself a throw away phone that I could reach him on when I got to my secret location, which I would never reveal to him or anyone, for that matter. The money transfers were happening according to my instructions, which I verified before I left. But now that I was here, I wanted to follow up on them.

I called Clyde and the phone rang and rang. No one picked up. "Idiot," I said into my phone, and changed into my $600 Jimmy Choo Romy 60 pumps, in black suede. I needed to have a spectacular dinner tonight.

Friday Morning, August 10th, Macon GA

I wanted to be in on this arrest and the one later in the day in Atlanta, so I flew down with my team and we met Clyde Smith entering his office at the Warner Robins Air Force Base, Counterintelligence Unit. He didn't even fight. He didn't struggle, in fact he poured out his beat-up heart so quickly I was glad we recorded his blathering while we were in the car on the way to a local jail.

Part of my team went to his home to collect his computer and anything else we needed. It is always a devastating surprise for a wife and children to find out the "love of their life" is on his way to jail. Clyde's family was now the bearer of that weight. I never let my people leave until someone comes to the home to console the wife and children. When this occurred, they headed to their business jet, on route to Dobbins Air Force Base, near Atlanta.

My plane had just been diverted from Dobbins, because the Atlanta compound, where we expected to arrest Apostle, Pastor Mortenson, was empty. She was nowhere to be found.

My team would stay there though and gather as much information as they needed to put her in jail when we found her.

Chapter 38

Thursday August 23rd, South Pacific

The manager of my lovely luxury hotel called me. I so love pampering myself.

He told me my automatic credit card charge did not go through today. The card was declined.

"No problem," I told him. I got some of the cash I had brought with me when I emptied my home safe. I then payed for the next two weeks in cash.

Where was that idiot, Clyde? I'd called him every day and the phone was never answered. I'll have to call his home which I did not want to do.

Thursday September 6th, South Pacific

I had to pay for my next two weeks in cash again. No matter, but I do need to contact that buffoon, Clyde.

I did call the international bank to have cash wired to me. The bank concierge said she was still awaiting the confirmation from the USA before she could release the funds.

"Are they there?" I asked, "The funds, I mean."

"Oh yes, ma'am. I am just awaiting the final confirmation from your business manager, Clyde Smith."

"Thank you. I'll get this done for you right away."

Some good news though, I had kept my eye on the Presidential elections in the USA, which was now only two months away and the candidate's team I preferred seemed to be making their way to the White House.

"I wonder," I thought to myself, "If I might still have an opportunity to influence them. I can do nearly anything with money."

Speaking of money, I decided to call Clyde's home. That bratty daughter answered. I could tell by her squeaky voice. And then she said, "Smith residence, Sofie speaking.

When I asked for Clyde, she said her daddy was in jail.

I immediately hung up the phone.

Saturday September 22nd, South Pacific

"Madam," the formerly gracious hotel concierge said, "Your money ran out two days ago. I must ask you to allow my staff to empty your rooms, while you wait down here, in our lobby."

I couldn't believe it. There was nothing for me to say. But I seethed and spit out the words between my gritted teeth, "Someone will pay for this. Clyde will pay for this."

I had no idea where I was going or what I was going to do. I couldn't go back to the USA, even if I got a ticket. And where could I go if I didn't have money?

Chapter 39

This Sunday marks the Sunday before we are forty days out from our Presidential campaign. It's been a long run and Issy and I are tired, but we will continue to run to the feet of Jesus, for that is where we get our daily direction, especially when we are exhausted.

I've wanted to complain a lot about the lack of cuddle-time, but I decided I would plan for us to go on Holiday as soon after the election as our winning candidate will let us go.

Harold has grown a brand-new attitude about elections since he found a 1656 Voter's Guide[1] and rewrote it for our church. I didn't have the heart to tell him I gave the same document to my candidate months ago. I don't care; he and I are back together as good buds.

I have always loved the story of Blind Bartimaeus, so I read as Issy and I drank our coffee: "Then they came to Jericho. . ."[2]

March A.D. 30, Blind Bartimaeus

What was Jesus doing? We had been keeping quiet, fairly quiet, anyway. We had done a good job staying out of sight of the Pharisees, but now, as we were leaving Old Jericho and entering into New Jericho, the crowd and the activity was growing. We were surely easy to see.

I know these crazy Pharisees, if they get the chance they'll take Jesus right now and I won't get my silver coins for turning Jesus over to them.

And the people? They're driving me crazy. They yell and scream. I quiet them down and then they yell and scream again.

As we were walking, I saw this one guy, the son of Timaeus,[3] sitting by the roadside begging. When he heard the crowds going by, he asked what was going on.[4]

I stopped and stood back, watching him closely, for I feared he'd cause trouble. He looked like he could be a real loudmouth. And I was right. As soon as he heard who was walking by, he went crazy calling out for Jesus.[5]

I was right on top of it though. I wanted us to get out of there as quickly as we could. I was hungry and if we slowed down there in Jericho our meal would be delayed all the more.

I came alongside him quickly and rebuked him as strongly as I could, telling him to be quiet.[6] But then he just started to yell all the louder.[7]

And wouldn't you know it, Jesus heard the man. He stopped and called him, ordering the loudmouth to be brought to him.[8]

"Dinner was just delayed," I thought to myself. But I also knew I had to do my part, so I leaned down to him and said, "Cheer up and get up; Jesus is calling for you.[9]

And then the most amazing thing happened. The guy threw off his cloak, jumped up and went to Jesus.[10] But, he didn't just get up slowly, like I would expect some blind guy to do. He jumped up. And then he threw off his cloak. "What a stupid thing to do," I thought. "After all, there were sure to be thieving scoundrels in this crowd." He was going to lose what was probably his only cloak.

And just when I thought I had seen it all, he ran to Jesus. Think about it! He ran to Jesus! The guy is blind! And he is running! Actually, he was not just running, he was tripping all over people to get to Jesus. If I wasn't so hungry, I would have thought it was a funny scene.

But I wanted to eat.

Sunday September 23rd, Arlington VA

I finished reading and was smiling big when Issy, tired of waiting for me to say something looked at me. "Why are you grinning?" she asked.

I was grinning at the beautiful picture in my mind of blind Bartimaeus running, but then my thoughts changed and a tear came from my eye. I wiped it away but Issy noticed and leaned into me. "Baby," I said quietly, "I don't see people running to Jesus like that anymore."

"I never thought about it like that, Jude. But you're right; they run to our respective candidates like that, but not to Jesus."

Two Weeks Later

The next couple of weeks were insanely busy, but the part I reveled in, was Harold. He and I had come a long way over the past few months and when he showed me his outline for the voters' guide, which he had been tweaking, I was very proud of him. He even headed the booklet with a quote from the 1656 pastor, William Gurnall, which I know had to rankle him. . . "I will not endeavor to tell you for whom you should vote."

His outline was:

1) Why We Vote

   a) We Steward for God

b) We Speak for God

c) We Stand for God

2) Who Should Get Your Vote

   a) First, Look for the Fear of God in Those you Choose

   b) Second, Look for Wisdom and Proper Gifts

   c) Third, Enquire Whether They are Christians

   d) Fourth, Look for Courage and Resoluteness

   e) Fifth, Find Purposeful Focus on the Nation's Public Affairs

   f) Sixth, Choose Those Who Have Healing Spirits

   g) Seventh, Look for a Desire to Serve

   h) Finally, Find Those Faithful to Ministers and the Ministry of the Gospel

3) What Occurs After We Vote

   a) We Pray for God's Chosen Leader

   b) We Pray Without Sin Being an Obstruction to our Prayer Life

   c) We Do Not Worry, For God is in Control

A few months earlier, Harold had seemed to me like Judas, betraying me for the politics he preferred. I would never tell Harold this, but when I saw this wonderful work he put together, I confess I thought of the New Testament passage which says, "When Judas, who had betrayed Him, saw that Jesus was condemned, he was seized with remorse. . ."[11]

Harold was remorseful and our relationship was blossoming, full and strong. Our schedules finally allowed us to attend a small group meeting and the question of our relationship challenges came up. I think he handled it brilliantly.

Issy and I sat there and listened as Harold said, "If you think I'm less passionate about my politics, you're crazy." To which his wife G.W. shook her head and said, "Amen."

Harold smiled and then looked at me and said, "And I don't expect my friend to be less passionate either. But when our passion for our politics puts even the slightest wedge in our relationship, the passion is wrong, even though one of us might be right." He paused ever so slightly and then added, "Of course I'm the one who's right."

We all laughed and then he said, "This election is important, and I think they get more and more important with each subsequent election. Just like Issy and Jude work hard for their candidate, I don't see anything wrong in us working hard for our candidate, if we believe God is calling us to do so. Just do not make the same mistake I made. I let my politics be more important than unity in Christ."

"Why did you do that, Harold?" someone asked.

There was a long silence, broken by a humbled man saying, "I refused to trust God to do what He wants to do, the raising up and putting down of a nation's leaders."[12]

After another long pause he spoke with a cracking voice, "If God loves me, I can trust Him."

"Do you have anything to add," Harold asked me.

"Just one thing," and I stood up, turning to everyone in the room. "You all heard Harold say he will still like me after November 7th, right?"

Issy shook her head and Harold and I hugged, but it wasn't a typical man-hug. We stayed clenched for a while.

When everyone started to clap, we unclenched.

"Love you, man." I told him.

"Love you too, Jude."

---

[1] The actual full sermon, from 1656, rewritten into modern English is in the appendix of this book and is available at https://MarkMirza.com/Politics

[2] Mark 10:46a

[3] Mark 10:46m

[4] Luke 18:35b-36

[5] Mark 10:47

[6] Luke 18:39a

[7] Matthew 20:31b

[8] Luke 18:40

[9] Mark 10:49b

[10] Mark 10:50

[11] Matthew 27:3a

[12] Psalm 75:7, Daniel 2:21

Chapter 40

March A.D. 30, The Weekend Jesus was Crucified

I had been standing on the outskirts of Jerusalem, but close enough to watch everything Jesus was going through. Whatever had been inside me and driving me was now gone. I don't know why, or how, or even what it was, but it was gone. And, when I looked at what was being done to this man I had lived with for three years, I was seized with remorse and returned the thirty pieces of silver.[1]

I don't remember everything the Pharisees said. I seem to recall they laughed at me. The only thing I know for sure is that I ran out of their presence and then I kept running until I could run no more.

With every step I recounted the previous three years. Jesus had loved me and I had betrayed Him. I remembered my excitement, my hope, my disillusionment, and then my sin, my greed, and now my end.

So Judas threw the money into the temple and left. Then he went away and hanged himself.[2]

Wednesday October 10ᵗʰ, FBI Headquarters

"Mom, I'm in a meeting, but I took your call because I know why you are calling."

"Happy Birthday, Jacky. I love you and I miss you."

I rolled my eyes at the phone, but only in jest, for my visitors knew what was going on. They could hear her voice through my phone. My visitors chuckled and then I said, "Mom, I have to go, but I think you should be the first to know, well, outside of those in my office, that this is my birthday for another reason, too."

I heard her suck in a deep breath and I had tears in my eyes. "Where in the world did they come from?" I wondered. But my visitors just smiled, knowingly and lovingly.

"Mom, I've given my life over to Christ."

When I heard my mom start to cry, my tears began to flow too. I don't know for sure but I think I even felt my chest heaving.

We remained on the phone for a few minutes before I let her go and I told her I'd come see her this weekend and tell her all about it.

My guests were all smiles and had glistening eyes too. I looked down at their coupled hands and said, "Only do that in my office until after the election."

Billy and Sammie just smiled.

They had come by with a mini birthday cake.

Billy said, "Getting into your files gave me a lot of information about you, and your birthdate was one of them."

Sammie picked it up from there and said, "We decided to come and celebrate your birthday with you, Jack, and tell you about another birthday you could have."

I'm glad they did.

October 23rd and 24th, Washington D.C.

Issy and I decided to have dinner with Dr. Dale. We met him at the Capitol South Metro Station. He insisted we eat at his new favorite Mexican Restaurant, the Tortilla Coast. Issy shook her head in displeasure, which Dale noticed and quickly tried to unwind from, asking for a restaurant she preferred.

I reassured him it was okay and then I whispered in Issy's ear, "We'll have to take our clothes off downstairs, because of the Fajita "perfume," baby."

She just looked at me, then at the ceiling and shook her head. I grinned and led them half a block down First Street to the restaurant at First and D.

At dinner we learned he had made his final trip to the Hill before all of these elected officials went back to their districts and their election campaigns. "It's funny," he said, "Few of them asked for prayer that they would win and a number of them are in tough races."

"How did you pray for them?" asked Issy.

"Romans 13:1 and 2, Issy. I just said, 'Lord we trust you to put into office whom you desire, and we will honor your choice, but we do ask that it be,' and I would insert the name of who I was with."

"Submit to the governing authorities," I said, and then continued, "Because God has instituted them, meaning if I resist them, I am opposing God."

"Tough passage to live out, Jude," said Dale.

"Which is why our identity needs to be in Christ, and not our politics," added Issy.

"Yeah," I said a little warily. "One of us will be ticked off on November 6th or 7th, depending upon the results, Baby."

"But not at each other, right?" asked Dale.

"No," we agreed, "Not at each other."

As we were leaving the restaurant, Dale said, "You know, I don't understand why the Fajita aroma has to stick to your clothes so much. I really don't like that."

Issy started to agree with him and I cut her off, "I never used to either." She remained silent, smiled and reached over and pinched me.

November 7th, The New President is Announced

Another Presidential election was over. Who knows what allegations will creep up over the next few days? All I know is, it's over, and I think our hands are squeaky clean, praise the Lord.

I called Pete. "Yeah, Jack, what's up?"

"Do you remember those two kids talking about that Born-Again stuff?"

"Yeah, why?" Pete responded.

"Well, I'd like to tell you what happened to me, recently."

There was a long silence on the phone and then Pete let out a long sigh. There was his "tell" and I knew we would talk about Jesus.

That night I was having dinner with Pete at the Tortilla Coast Mexican Restaurant when Billy and Sammie came in, smiling and publicly holding hands. I pointed them out to Pete who turned around to see them.

They didn't see us. In fact, they didn't see anything but themselves.

It was cute to see.

I got ready to say as much when Pete said, "Jack, these two have been falling in love for the last six months. This must be their first date and they come here?"

I just laughed and shrugged my shoulders.

"I told you I couldn't trust him, Jack." Pete laughed and then added, "Do you think they care that their clothes are going to smell?"

We both snickered and went back to our discussion of Christ.

11,000 Miles Away

I'm still in the south pacific, but my days are running together. I have no idea if the Presidential election was yesterday or the day before. I've seen the results, but just barely.

I don't have a television in my embarrassing little hovel. When I head in to work, I either slow down at the restaurant under my shanty or at the guard house; those are the only two places near me that have T.V.

I've had to sell all my things. I've never lived like this before. My black suede pumps are grey with dust and will not last long if I remain a chambermaid.

But somehow, I'll get out of here. Somehow, I'll find that idiot Clyde and make him suffer for all I've had to go through these last few weeks. This was all his fault.

"He's such a moron."

I walked up the stairs to the employee entrance. We have small lockers for our clothes. As I got to the top step I tripped and a heel came off my now tacky $600 Jimmy Choo. . .

"Oh, brother!" I fumed.

"Broken shoes and stinky clothes! I'm tired of everything I wear smelling like that blasted restaurant!"

---

[1] Matthew 27:3b

[2] Matthew 27:5

Appendix: The 1656 Voter Guide

The 1656 Sermon by William Gurnall may be read below. It was rewritten by the author, from the Olde English so today's readers can understand it. The author left a few items as they were written to maintain the spirit of the 1656 English tongue. The reader will see them throughout.

The sermon includes two sections. The first half is Gurnall applying chapter one of Isaiah to his very divided nation, England. One may find the comparison to be eerily like the USA of today.

In the second half of the sermon, he tells his congregation, "I will not tell you who to vote for…" However, he brilliantly points out the Scriptural principals for voting.

Believe me, they are brilliantly done.

You can get the entire 1656 document, FREE and in .PDF format here: www.MarkMirza.com/Politics

Part 1: The Sermon Application

> *"Then I will restore your judges as at the first, And your counselors as at the beginning;"*

Isaiah 1:26a (NASB)

Introduction

If we consider the great wickedness of the people to whom this holy Prophet, Isaiah, was sent, we may wonder why God caused a rare Jewel to hang so long on such a disobedient ear, as theirs. After all, God lent His Prophet for so long, to a people that made him and his message un-welcome.

And again, if we consider how long heaven indulged the Jews; this incomparable mercy of Isaiah in their midst; and calculate the long race of his Prophetic course, we have to acknowledge, though he found them so bad, he left them no better.

These people did not relent, not under sixty years or more of this holy man's preaching. They were wicked enough in Uzziah's and Jotham's reign, when he first ascended the state of Prophecy, but by Manasses' time, (in which he died, and that by a violent and bloody death, being sawn asunder) they were still wicked.

Jerusalem had become a sea, covered with idolatry, oppression, and the work of sin, which might have been expected anywhere else, rather than among a people so divinely taught. But weeds grow nowhere so rank, as in fat soil; we may know enough of this wretched people, if we read this chapter [Isaiah 1], which like a true glass, will give us the feature of that people, as it looked in the Prophet's time. I wish with all my soul, that we did not see our own Nation's countenance in their face.

Our Nation Likened to Isaiah's

A Sermon-Proof People

First, they were Sermon-Proof. They had "listened-away" their hearing ear. It is a sad deafness, and rarely cured, which comes from hearing sermons and are no longer moved by them.

How far they were gone in this we may guess by the Prophets strange Apostrophe, ver. 2. Hear O Heavens, and give ear O earth, for the Lord hath spoken, I have nourished and brought up children, and they have rebelled against Me. Take the words however you will, they speak of a people past counsel, and instruction.

Surely, he must have believed he was speaking, as it were, to inanimate creatures. That Preacher surely thinks his people bad indeed, who directs his speech to the seats they sit on, and the pillars they lean against, Hear, O you seats, and hearken O you pillars. He reproached their obstinacy.

An Affliction-Proof People

Second, as they were Sermon-Proofed, so also they were Affliction-Proof. So mad on their lusts were they, that rather than not have them, they would swim through their own blood to them. Heavy judgements were on them, but no medicine wrought kindly on them. God was weary of sin, but they were not weary of sinning.

Therefore, we find Isaiah making his moan as a Physician does who has run through the whole Art of medicine to do his Patient good but finds him growing worse under his hand. He, therefore at last speaks of giving up on them, in verse 5. Why should ye be stricken any more, the whole head is sick, and the whole heart is faint?

Basically, he was saying, "If affliction would do you good, you have had enough of that; I have beaten you till I have not left you one sound part, from head to heal, and yet you will run after your lusts, while your blood runs after your heels."

A Religiously Hypocritical People

Third, in a word, they were Impudent in their Hypocrisies. At the very same time they acted out all their abominations, they kept up a gaudy Pageant of Religion. They spared no cost in the multitude of their sacrifices, but appeared great Zealots in the Temple, which the Prophet, in verse 11. protests against, as the worst part of all their wickedness. Indeed, spiritual wickedness carries in it the very spirits of wickedness.

And all this is not charged upon some petty party, or a faction in the Nation, but the indictment is laid against the whole Nation, verse 3. Israel doth not know, verse 4. Ah sinful Nation. Oh, that the whole head and heart were as sick of sin, as they were of suffering.

It is sad when all the entire household is down with sickness together, or those that are well, are not well enough to look after the sick. There were indeed some gracious ones in that degenerate age, but so few, that their Religion, like a pint of wine in a ton of water, could hardly be tasted amidst such a multitude of ungodly ones.

A Diseased Nation

In the diseases of the body, when a general illness has invaded the whole family (as in a fever or the like,) there is commonly someone, whose disorder has affected all the rest. A wise Physician, then, bestows his chief skill to find this out, so as to make the cure most conducive to the entire household.

So here, the sad ailment which the Jewish Nation lay under, in regard to both sin and misery, is observed by the Prophet in a great measure, to have proceeded from one principal rank, and order of people among them, and that was their Rulers and Magistrates, their leaders of the land. verses 22 & 23. Thy silver is become dross, thy wine mixed with water, thy Princes are rebellious.

Therefore, the Lord levels His threatenings directly at them, in a specific manner, in verse 24. Therefore, saith the Lord, Ah, I will ease Me of Mine [deliver Myself from] adversaries. As they had the greatest hand in the sin, so they should have the deepest draught in the judgement. No sins lie heavier on God's stomach, and make him more heart-sick, then theirs who stand in high and public place of Rule and Government.

Certainly, the few godly would be discouraged at the calamities coming against them, for they knew it would be a sad day for the whole Land, when God should make such an overturning of the land's leadership. The storm of God's vengeance seldom falls so upon Princes and Rulers, but that the people are not taken in the shower and share with them in their sufferings.

A Godly Few

So, to fortify the hearts of those few godly ones, He opens His design of mercy [His future plans] which He had towards them, even in the captivity which would be coming upon them, verse 25. I will turn my hand upon thee, and purely purge away thy dross, and take away all thy Tin. Here He compares their captivity to a furnace, themselves to silver, the ungodly among them, especially the leaders of the land (Magistrates) to dross and tin, and Himself to the Refiner.

He makes clear, His design is not to consume them, but purge them from this dross that brought the nation to this low point. And when He had done this (once the wicked generation were worn out) then He would provide better for them; faithful Magistrates and leaders in place of the ungodly ones, He intends to remove, verse 26. And I will restore thy Judges as at the first

These words were as a lump of sugar after a bitter draught, given to this poor people, to take away that unpleasing future, which the threatening of a captivity might leave on their thoughts and imaginations.

Here observe God's love and tender care over the godly in evil times. When His wrath is at its greatest height against the wicked, even then His thoughts of mercy are full at work in His heart for His people. He is carving a mercy for them out of the same Providence, in which He deals out vengeance to the ungodly.

The Promise

God can blow both hot and cold, wrath and mercy to His enemies in the same breath. Yea, He does not merely content Himself with this promise of love to His people, but He also makes them acquainted with it [aware of it].

And while they could not be immediately put in possession of the promise, He shared it, to enable them to more comfortably wait, and expect the eventual performance of it, His promise.

No such sweet companion goes with the Saints to a prison, as a Promise. The bed of affliction by itself is hard, and to prevent their tossing and tumbling in it, through anguish of their present sorrow, He lays this soft pillow of the Promise under their head; I will refine.

Look closely at the Promise. We see three points:

1. The Person promising is God, I will restore

2. The mercy promised is Governmental, Judges as at the first, and Counselors as at the beginning.

3. The timing of the fulfilled promise is sobering.

When and how the promise will be performed is wrapped up in the word, And; which stands in the front of the Text, pointing to the preceding words, They indeed tell us when and how God will do this for them. I will turn My hand upon thee, and purely purge away thy dross, and take away thy sin. Then follows the Promise in the Text, which comes in as a consequence of the great National calamity to come upon them, namely, the Babylonian captivity. So that though the birth would be joyous, yet before this Promise could be delivered, many a sad pain and bitter sorrow would precede.

The people of God usually have their hardest labors in their greatest mercies. So, Churches and Nations have their greatest Reformations, raised out of their greatest Confusions [disarray]. Indeed, as a vessel of silver, (to which God compares Judah) that is cleaned of much dross, and very battered and cracked, can never be refined and made fashionable, without melting and new casting.

So, God lets them know, they had grown so corrupt, they needed a hot and long-lasting fire to burn up their dross, so their Nation might be cast into a new mold, so new, the very form of Government was to be changed.

Branch 1, Who is Promising

God Owns the Responsibility

First, of the Person promising, I will restore; Observe, how in promising to give Judges and Counselors, He owns this prerogative and claims it as His Ordinance, under His authority, whom, God Himself sets up. Then He speaks of a time of more Reformation than ordinary. In that time He will restore. Here is Divinity stamped upon the face of what is indeed called, an Ordinance of man in 1 Peter 2:13.

This is not man's invention: for all Powers are of God, but it is discharged by men, and intended for man's good. This concept is so distasteful to the ungodly world, because it lays their lusts in chains, and so torments them before their time, that if God had not been in this bush (so often on fire) it would have been consumed before this.

There has been much tugging to pluck this plant [of government] up, but being of God's planting, it stands too sure for man's hand to root up. So natural is it to the principles and notions of man's mind that Governments are found, where no Scripture is found to teach it.

Thanking God for Government

Let us bless God for a Government, even though it is not the best. Where there is Governmental Leadership, some may be oppressed and wronged under it, but none can be righted where there is no Government at all. If might be right, then right will be wrong, and better poor people should sit under a scratching bramble, than to have no hedge at all to shelter them from wind and weather, including storms of popular fury.

The Persians had a custom, that when their Prince died, five days of misrule were indulged the people, in which they might do what they would without control, the thinking was they might be brought in love the more with the Person and Government of their succeeding Prince. It is a sad way I confess, but a sure one, to know the happiness of a Government, by experiencing the confusion of an Anarchy.

What shall we think of those who would befriend governmental leadership we disagree with? This is no new issue. We find it in the indictment of those seducers, Jude 8. That they despised Dominion [authority], and spoke evil of Dignity. It was not the persons who so much displeased them, as the office itself; and it would have been well for the churches of Christ, if this error had died with the first Broachers of it.

Deception in the Church

Contemporary Author's Note: Gurnall now argues against those wanting NOTHING to do with the Magistracy. But we in the 21st Century have done the same by doing the opposite. We have put our trust in princes, causing us to worship some and loath others. Read this next section with this "equally-ungodly-attitude" in mind.

Some Anabaptists of late times have declared themselves heirs to a spirit of confusion and disorder. Among other positions of this Sect in Transylvania, published in 1568, I find this one, openly vouched by them, that it is a mark of Antichrist to have in their Church Kings, Princes, and the sword of the Magistrate, which Christ (say they) can no way allow in his Church; I wish the sea, which runs between that land and ours, had been able to keep this error from setting foot on English ground.

Is Magistracy such an uncircumcised thing, that it must be shut out of the pale of the Church? Is it an office fitted and formed for Heathens, and not Christians? Truly, then I would choose to live among Heathens rather than Christians.

If you think that way, how can you read the Scriptures and not blush? Were the Saints at Rome Heathens or Christians? And does the Apostle say these things to them? Does he tell people to disregard the Magistrates? No, He is the Minister of God to them for good; and Paul tells them they must be subject, (though then the Magistrate was no friend to the Church) and that not only for wrath sake, to save one's skin from man's wrath, but for conscience's sake, to save their souls from God, Romans 13:4, 5.

This blasphemous view of Magistracy is a brat, reared by man, but not upon the Scripture. No, it is a misshapen brat conceived in the womb of ignorance and begotten by pride. It will appear so by the two principles, which are the very seed, by which this error is formed.

- Invented Liberty. They have found a liberty which they claim Christ has given them, saying, subjection under Magistracy is inconsistent with following Christ. But look what their strong imagination has found in the Scriptures, namely, a pretext which was never written. And yet, it is their strong desire, so they back it. They back a liberty which is a strange liberty for it leads to licentiousness and ends in bondage. True liberty is to choose good, and reject evil, which this Magistracy is erected to defend you in doing, Romans 13:3. Rulers are not a terror to good works.

- Imagined Perfection. A perfection that they dream of, which lifts them up so high, that now they need not the Ministry of the Magistracy to keep them within bounds. The Magistrate is an avenger (they say) to execute wrath to them who do evil, but Saints, who are led by the Spirit, do not do evil.

Well, suppose them to be as holy as they think they are, do they not live among those who are wicked? And do they not need the Magistrates help, so they may be defended in the exercise of holiness? The Saints do not find the world so kind, that they should dismiss their guards, before they get safely to Heaven.

Further, what horrible pride is it, to pretend to such a conduct of the Spirit, as to be privileged from sin? I trust the Apostles, which we know were of as high a form in the Spirit as any who think this way. And they were willing to be branded as loud liars, if they should pretend to have a perfection as stated above. If we say we have no sin, we deceive ourselves, and the truth is not in us, 1 John 1:8.

But the churches of Christ have had too much experience with many of those who believe they are above our Magistracy, to think of them as great Saints; No, no, it is not their perfection that lifts them up above Magistracy, but their lusts that make them not able to bear the Magistrates power. Those Scholars who at first burn their master's rod, have most need of it.

I am sure this sort of men has shown, that they have need of Magistracy as much as others. And some of them, those at Munster in Germany convinced the world, (for all their loud cries against Magistracy) that they liked the Magistrates seat well enough, once they could get themselves in it.

If God intends mercy for England [and the USA], then this Anti-Magistratical spirit shall not prevail; If we are too good to live under Magistrates, God's Vicegerents, we are too bad to live under God's own care and Government.

The Hebrews have a Proverb, we had best make haste from that place where the King is not feared, as if some heavy judgement is on its way to that place where Magistrates are despised. I am sure that those fanatic spirits in Germany quickly found vengeance from God, a vengeance from God they did not expect.

God's Expectation Upon Us

Since Magistracy is an Order of God's erecting, a word then is needed to you into whose lap the lot of voting, is, this day, your calling. Do not decline your responsibility for neither fear nor ease. God has given you a Commission, which is this opportunity to vote, and you need not fear to act. You are under-Officers, and would be considered as Cowards, if you dare not follow, when God leads. Go in this thy might (said God to Gideon) have not I sent thee? Judges 6:14. God's Word was His Warrant [His written order], and God's Warrant was His Protection, unto us.

When Frederick, Duke of Saxony had read Luther's book, he put out in Vindication of the divine Authority of Magistracy against those sects contrary to the Magistracy. He then lifted up his hands to heaven, and blessed God, that he lived to see the place of Magistracy, wherein he stood, so clearly proved from Scriptural evidence, to be a place where he might, with a good conscience act, so as to please God therein.

The Magistrate's office we see is honorable, because it is of God, yet sometimes it goes a begging [falls short of honor]. But worse, it is a certain sign of calamitous times, when good and worthy Patriots refuse to appear on the stage of Government. For, Kings, Palaces, and Senate-houses do not usually stand long empty and your participation, or not, determines who will occupy the magisterial position.

Too often, when political times are evil and troubled, we hear potential politicians say, as in that deplored time of Judah's declining-state, in Isaiah 3:7. I will not be a healer, make me not a Ruler of the people.

Consider this, if the Physician will not take the Patient in hand, it is to be feared, the physician thinks the disease too far gone, and his reputation will be in peril if the patient succumbs under his hand.

Indeed, State Physicians, can hardly escape blame, if they do not seek the cure. The multitude judges the Pilot good or bad, based upon whether the voyage he makes is gainful or losing to the Owners.

But I hope you have learned not to judge yourselves by other's thoughts. No man is made miserable by what others think of him. If you be not willing to give up your own name [reputation] to be sacrificed by the multitude, there is little hope of being a saviour to your Country.

Christ could not have saved man, if He preferred to save His reputation among men. He was willing to do them good, though He was thought and spoken ill of by them for His pains. Do your duty and leave the issue to God.

I confess, that it is a blustering time, but sometimes Mariners find fair weather at sea, even though they launch out in a storm. God has the wind in his fist that sends you to sea, and if a storm meets you in your work, Christ can soon be with you in it, and save you from it.

God is not more seen in sea tempests, than He is in land-storms, confusions, I mean, of course, with States and Nations. He that stills the noise of the seas also stills the tumult of the people, Psalm 65:7.

Well, whatever comes of it, it will be more honorable and safe for you (when called to vote, or run for office) to be found in Parliament, endeavoring to heal the bleeding wounds of the Nation, though it may cost you your good reputation, than saving your own skins at home.

Is it not sad, that a poor woman in travail should die for want of help, because it is midnight when she calls, and her neighbors are loath to break their rests, or come out in the cold to save her life? England [and indeed the USA] is now in travail and call you to her labor. Take heed that the ghost of your ruined Nation does not haunt you to your graves, for your act of denying her your help.

I confess, it is likely to get worse in our nation, because of some unhappy disappointments in former Assemblies. But it is the same with England [as well as the USA], as it is with a woman who has often called her maids just when her pains have gone away. But who knows that now the full time is not come for a birth? Better to go twenty times, when called needlessly than have your place be found empty once, when the work indeed needed to be done.

God, by this Promise (Isaiah 1:26) of giving Judges as at the first, and Counselors as at the beginning, owns this order and state of Magistracy. So, He lays claim to the discarding of persons that bear office, I will restore. This implies, that He had a hand in taking away those holy Governors which ruled them in the first and better times. He did this because of their sins; and He ordered [caused to be voted-in] worse Magistrates in their places, which He did as a plague upon their sins.

And now He will fill the Magistrate's Seats again, but this time with faithful Judges and Counselors like their first ones.

Magistrates, Good or Bad

Doctrines. Not only the office of Magistracy is of God's erecting, but the people who are the Magistracy, (whether good or bad) are of God's appointing.

When the Magistrate's place is to be filled, everyone lifts up a head for his own faction [party]. And while I wish there were not too much of this, too many come who are motivated to serve a party, or some particular person, rather than God and their Country.

Well, plot what you can, Heaven will carry it from you all. You, with all the bussle [scurrying] and pudder [turmoil] that is made, are but the fly upon the wheel, it is the wheel of Providence, not you, that determines the issue of this day's voting.

Matches are made in heaven between Magistrates and people.

- When they voted for Christ to die, and Barabbas to live, they only did what God had given their hands to do. Choose well or ill, you cannot deny God His calling voice.

- When the ten tribes made a rent [an exit] from the house of David, it is said in Hosea 8:4. They have set up Kings, and not by me; they have made Princes, and I knew it not; that is, they did not ask God's permission. Yet God tells them, He gave them these very Kings and Princes, Hosea 13:11.

In both cases above, God's secret Providence ordered the matter. While the people pleased their own lust, they fulfilled Gods counsel of wrath. Meaning, by their own wicked choice, God plagued them for their sins.

Application

Are Magistrates, whether they be good or bad, sent by God? See how to make a good choice this day when you vote. That good choice is done by plying hard [pleading hard] the throne of grace. If we have faithful Magistrates, they must be of God's sending, and will restore, and no Key is like prayer to open God's heart. God rules the world by the lusts of His enemies, and by the prayers of His Saints;

By disappointing the one, and stirring up the other, He accomplishes His own ends in the affairs of the world. The Egyptian's policies, and Israel's prayers, helped bring on the ruin of the one and the deliverance of the other. When Israel groaned under the bondage of Pharaoh, the Lord heard their cry, and saved them by the hand of Moses. It was worth their groaning to get such a change, a Moses who carried them tenderly on his shoulder, compared to a Pharaoh who cruelly rode on their backs.

Prayer moves the great wheel of the Clock, that sets all the rest going. Persuade [Trust] God, and He will persuade man.

- Jacob was afraid of Esau, and made God his friend, and God made Esau his [Jacob's] friend.

- He who would give Saul another spirit, and so altered the property [character] of the man, that before he was aware, Saul, then Paul, rightly prophesied with the Prophets.

This God can alter those purposes which men had in their hearts when they came forth this day to vote and make them Vote for those they had little thought on [considered]. He can make profane ones cast their votes into the lap of those that are godly. In fact, I truly wonder how a faithful, godly Parliamentarian could even be chosen in England [or even the USA], when we see the current heap [unrighteous crowds] who will likely carry the vote, this day.

It has been a custom in former times, for letters to come thick from Court, when Parliaments were to be chosen, to Towns and Hamlets and Cities, which almost had the effect of a Mandamus [ordering you how to vote, much like our political television ads today].

To be sure, God can send into the bosoms of voters His secret messages, which shall awe their consciences, Genesis 31:29. It is in the power of my hand (said Laban to Jacob,) to do you hurt, but the God of your fathers spake unto me yesternight, saying, Take heed. Poor Laban! He thought Jacob's life was in his power. When the reality is, God had tied his hands behind him, and sealed up his mouth, so he could not speak a word but what God formed for him to say.

Has not God already met some of you, who are on your way to vote? Has He not over-powered your hearts against your former thoughts? If He has not met with you, as you come, so He should bind up your hand from voting for an unworthy person, you may expect to meet Him as you go home, or, perhaps, upon a sadder-errand. Better Cain had met God before he gave the bloody blow, to have stayed his hand from striking it, then afterward to meet Him with that dismal Question, O what have you done?

O it will pierce thy heart like a Dagger, when God shall ask you on another day, "What have you done in giving your vote for such as will help to ruin, not to heal the land? You are the Murderer of your Country, and its blood I will require at your hands."

Branch 2, The Mercy Promised

The mercy promised: Judges as at the first, and Counselors as at the beginning.

Three Questions may here be propounded:

- Why are Judges and Counselors here promised, and not Kings and Princes?

- Why is the Promise doubled to include both Judges and Counselors?

- And why, Judges as at the first?

Why Judges and Counselors and not Kings and Princes

Because this Promise had a particular respect to a time, when their Government was not to be Monarchical [as it had been], that is, after their return from captivity, when this Promise took place in the times of Nehemiah, Ezra, Zerubbabel, and other faithful Judges, who after them ruled the Jewish State.

Observe, I pray, that it does not matter so much what kind of Government a people live under, as what kind of Governors they have. Let the Government be what it will. The Jews saw happy days under Kingly Government, when the Kings were gracious and wise. Likewise, they experienced happiness under Judges and Counselors, (such as Moses, Joshua, Zerubbabel,) though with less worldly splendor. And they saw miserable days, under both Kings and Judges. The sword of Government cuts, as the hand is that holds it.

Why is the Promise for both Judges and Counselors

I answer, because by this Synecdoche [comparison] the writer includes the entirety of Magistracy. Two things comprise, or complete [make-up] a Government.

- Wisdom to make wholesome Laws, and advice for the good of the People; and

- Faithfulness with courage to execute these Laws.

First, there are Counselors to advise and form Laws. And second, there are Judges to inform and execute these Laws. Counselors without Judges are as a head without a hand; Judges without Counselors, are as a hand without a head.

Why Judges As At the First

I answer, to imply their present degeneracy when compared to when they were first formed into a Commonwealth by Moses, or even afterwards, into a Kingdom led by David. And notice, we see, that the best constituted Governments are prone in time to degenerate. The nearer the Spring, the clearer the water: the farther the stream runs from its first source, the muddier it is and troubled. And indeed, as it is true of States, so it is true of Churches, purest at first planting, like Apples, faire and sound when first plucked from the tree, but in time specked and rotten.

The world we live in is muggish [as overwhelming as extreme humidity] and rancid. And truly, the best things soon decay in it. Hence, it is God who brings revolutions upon Nations and Churches.

Note that one change causes another. First, they change in purity, and then they grow corrupt. Then God changes their peace and prosperity, sometimes even their very form.

But we shall not go down that rabbit trail. Instead we will take up one Conclusion, which arises from the Subject matter of the Promise in general.

Why Faithful Magistrates are a blessing to a Nation.

I will restore Judges as at the first. None of God's gifts are, gift-less gifts. It is worth having what God thinks is worth promising. When He gives a people faithful Governors, He gives them a mercy that is not of the least magnitude.

Observe on what design God makes this Promise. This speaks to a choice mercy; which is meant to calm their thoughts in light of this expectation of their captivity which would soon be upon them. This also served to make them the more willing to leave their own land, on the account of when they return, they should gain, by all their sufferings, Judges as at the first.

To God, this would be a satisfactory result for their coming losses and troubles. And yet, they understood it is as if He were asking them some great thing, like agreeing to have an arm cut off, or endure some great torment. God gives this Promise, to make them patiently bear the calamities which their long captivity will bring with it, and therefore it is not torment, but rather, a great mercy.

Observe how this is promised, not as a single mercy, but as a mercy that has many others in the womb. It is a mercy representative of all the good He had in His thoughts to bestow upon them.

He shows the Jews, as the choice of his large heart, to best assure them of His love towards them. I will restore Judges as at the first, which is as if He had said, I will restore all manner of blessings into your bosom; Remember, as Magistrates are, so we may expect things will go in a Nation.

There is no one place where we may stand at greater advantage to see what God intends for a people (good or evil) than by observing what Rulers and Governors, His Providence orders out to them.

Without both Religion and Righteousness, Nations are but forests of wild beasts, where the stronger devour the weaker. As the Magistrate is, so are these lifted up or cast down. No sooner here in the text is Religion and Righteousness set down in the Choice of Government, than we find the influence of it among the people, I will restore thy Judges as at the first, then follows, Afterward you shalt be called a City of Righteousness, a faithful City.

The City learns to write [expresses itself], after the manner which the Court sets for her. The Septuagint renders Psalm 24:7. Lift up your heads, O ye gates, to read, Lift up the Gates, O ye Princes. The Gate leads the way to the City, and the Magistrate has the command of the Gate, as he opens or shuts the Gate, so is Religion entertained or shut out of a Nation, meaning the public Profession of it.

Therefore, the open idolatry of a Nation is laid by God Himself at the Magistrate's door, Micah, 1:5. For the transgressions of Jacob is all this, and for the sins of the House of Israel. Now mark the next words, What is the transgression of Jacob? is it not Samaria? and what are the high places of Judah? are they not Jerusalem? That is, what is the Spring [cause] of all this idolatry, and the other abominations of these two Kingdoms? Is it not their two chief Cities, and the Prince's Courts which are kept there?

Read Scripture's Stories, and you shall find that Religion flourished and faded among the Jews, as their Magistrates were good or bad.

- When Moses by death let fall his leading staff, and there was a godly Joshua to take it up, it yet went well with Religion.

- When Joshua went off the stage, and there were those faithful Elders left, who shared with him in the Government to hold the helm, Religion was safe.

- But when they were gathered to their fathers, and none were left to come into their place [replace them], then all went to wreck in Church and State, as we find in Judges 2:11. Then the children of Israel did evil in the sight of the Lord, and served Balaam.

It goes well or ill with a people, as the Magistrates are. Outward peace and prosperity fares, and opens or shuts, based on the Magistrates. The Queen of Sheba without a Spirit of Prophecy, was able to see happy days coming on the Jews from the piety and wisdom she observed in their Prince, 2 Chronicles 9:8. Because thy God loved Israel to establish them forever, therefore made He thee King over them to do Judgement and Justice.

So the wickedness of the Kings of the ten Tribes, after their rent [exit] from the house of David, is by the Spirit of God interpreted, to proceed from His displeasure and purposes of wrath, that He had taken up against them, to break and ruin them, Hosea 13.11. I gave thee a King in Mine anger and took him away in My wrath. This is spoken (if you observe the place) not of Saul, but of the ten Tribes after their rent from Judah; and not of a particular person, but of the whole succession of Kings from Jeroboam to the last, which resulted in their captivity.

God gave them, because of His wrath, such leaders as were fit instruments to be a plague to them, and execute God's wrath upon them. And when He took any of them away, it was to make room for a worse one, till by degrees the Nation (as a morsel prepared for a foreign enemy) dropped into the Assyrians mouth, and was devoured by them.

The whole Series of the Jewish Chronicle will confirm that when God intended mercy for them, He gave them faithful Magistrates; when He intended wrath and judgement He opened the door for it, by taking those faithful Magistrates out of the way. Josiah came to the throne in an ill time and found it deep in arrears [indebtedness] to God.

By God's execution, on account of the abominations of former times, and the current people [nation], not much amended [improved]. They were kept by His royal Sanction, rather than by their own inclination, for it is said, that He gave them the ability to stand to the Covenant.

This implies, that they would soon have fallen to idolatry, and their own ways, had not He, Himself shorn them up [held them up] by His authority. Yet Josiah's zeal for God and Religion, doing as much as he could, reprieved them, and was their Bail to keep them out of prison, as long as he was above ground; but no sooner had his head laid in the dust, and his wicked children came to the throne, then God called for the nation's debt, and He would wait no longer.

Are faithful Magistrates such a choice blessing? Then in the fear of God, be serious, and consider the weight of the work of voting, about which from all quarters of this Country you will meet this day. God forbid, that I should think that any of you came with so wicked a mind, as to do this Nation, the place of your Nativity, mischief. Yet, let me tell you, that if you do plan to spite this nation, rather than to bring peace and happiness, I know no better way for you to do that than by choosing unfaithful Counselors.

Part 2: The Voting Instructions

When David meant to curse God's enemy, to his credit, he wished that God would set a wicked man over himself, Psalm 109:6, as one who would not hesitate to oppress him, and tyrannically lord it over him. Even God puts evil leadership among his dreadful curses, Leviticus 26:17. I will set my face against you, and those that hate you shall reign over you.

I shall now lay three Arguments before you, to persuade you to a conscientious care in your business of voting.

Why We Vote

We Steward for God

Consider that there are great things which you will trust them with, whom you choose to sit in the great Senate of the Nation.

- You trust them with your purse, and I am sure most of you consider that important. You should know him well, to

255

whom you will give the Key of your chest, where your money lies.

- You trust them with your liberties and lives, and those your purses have paid soundly for.

- You trust them with your Religion, without which the others are not worth the taking up.

- In one word, you trust them with all that is dear to you as English men [as Americans], as Christians.

You put that power into their hands, which if they are not the more faithful, may turn like a cannon upon your own breasts, and so you would, most truly, become guilty of your own miseries. And let me tell you, those sorrows have a peculiar bitterness in them above all other, which are not imposed on us, but chosen by us.

Better an enemy should come in and turn us by force of armies, out of possession of these, than we send those who shall Vote us out of them [all that is dear to us]. We shall receive little pity when it is seen that the rod with which we are whipped was of our own gathering [our own voting].

The inward guilt will add a further stinging to our sorrows and deprive us of comforts which, had we done our duty we would have experienced, rather than a great calamity which could now befall us.

He who is an accessory to the burning down of his house, by the negligence of a drunken person, whom he trusted to watch and keep it, has more reason to be troubled, than he who has it consumed by a fire from heaven, or some other Providence.

O voters, men and women, there are matters other than these, which you must also consider and contemplate. For example

- If you were to choose a Nurse for your child, you would look for one of a healthful constitution and good disposition. You are now to choose Nurses for your Nation, so Magistrates are called in Scripture, Nursing Fathers and Mothers; You are to choose these in a time of this Nation's languishing [deteriorating], under God, to recover the consumptive state of this great body [nation].

- If you were to choose a Shield, should it be one that would let the arrow come through it, to pierce you to the heart?

Magistrates are the Shields of the earth. You value the life of the Nation little, who will put a Shield into its hand you have not well tried; David threw away Armor, though it were a King's, because he had not tried it.

- If you were to choose a Shepherd, or a Herdsman, just anyone would not serve your turn. Pharaoh a King thought it not beneath his care, to get workers for so unimportant a business, Genesis 47:6. If you knowest any man, of activity amongst thy brethren, make them rulers over my cattle. As you vote today, you are to choose such, as are not to go before beasts, but to lead in and out the Lord's people and flock.

We Speak for God

Consider that your voices and votes are not your own, to bestow them where you list, to gratify this friend, or that party. No, if you do, you give away what is not your own.

- What Jehoshaphat said to his Judges, I may with a little alteration apply to you who are Electors this day, 2 Chronicles 19:6. Take heed what you do, for ye choose not for man, but for the Lord, who is with you in the choice. He is with you to observe who you give your hand for, and why you give it. When Bishop Latimer heard a pen going behind the hanging, as he was upon examination before the Queens council, it made him more watchful of what he said. And shall not God's pen, that walks behind the Tent, where you vote, make you conscientious? It is God we are accountable to in this matter of voting. He is the Supreme Lord of Nations; all Magistrates are His under-Officers, and hold their place because of Him, and are to do faithful service for Him.

- Moses was faithful as a servant, Hebrews 3:5. Now, of what dangerous consequence is it for a people, to put one into an office, who is a Traitor to his Prince? This you do, when you vote for an unfaithful person. Magistrates are said to be taken into God's throne, 2 Chronicles 9:8. Now, do you dare set God's enemy on God's throne? What is this, but to set up a Standard against God, and declare to the world you would shake off [reject] His Government.

This day the temper [character] of this Nation will be discovered. No way that I know of is like this, to feel how a nation's heart pulses, or beats. And for my own part, as this solemn National act shall appear, I cannot look upon [voting] any other way than as our owning or disowning God, to be our God, to rule over us. And if the Nation votes God to be their God, by a godly choice, I shall not bury my hopes for our future happiness.

God comes in mercy many times before He is sent for. But He departs when they give Him leave to go, when they drive Him away. Oh, how unhappy are you, O England [O USA], if you may still have access to your God, but choose to drive Him away.

We Stand for God

Consider the solemn Obligation that lies upon us, by a National Covenant, (famous through the Christian world, and we, infamous for the breach of it) to promote, and procure with our utmost endeavors the Reformation of the Land. [In general, to stand for and support Christian ideals]

If you give your voice for an unworthy person to sit in Parliament, whom your conscience, (if you will listen to it,) will tell you that he or she:

- Is not, nor never will be, a person to help this work.

- Is, in fact, an enemy to Christian Ideals.

- Or, fears them more than desires them.

If you have gotten mastery of your conscience, and still choose to do this bold act, of voting for them, let me tell you what you do; you come this day to declare in the face of all the Country, yea, before God, men, and Angels, that you are a forsworn wretch.

And if you get this brand upon your forehead once, [unwilling to stand for Christian ideals] go where you will, you drag a chain after you that will bind you over to the fearful expectation of God's wrath. And that fear (for vengeance will come sooner or later) will take hold of you. Now tell me, would it not be better to have been asleep in your bed, or sick in your bed, or dead in your grave, than to have come here to do so unhappy a day's work?

Oh, think when you go this day to give your vote. See the Covenant of promoting Reformation in the land, spread before you. Dare you venture, to blot out this covenant by a wicked and unworthy choice at the ballot box?

Suppose you should put yourself under an oath of friendship, to promote the good and the welfare of another, (as Jonathan to David) and suppose this friend, to whom you are thus engaged, falls sick, and you have been asked to bring a Physician. But instead, image that you fetch a murderer to poison him, or an imposter who by his ignorance killed him, (which would of course, be the same).

Oh, how would your oath rot upon your conscience? This you do, only you do it to a Nation, not merely a private person.

Therefore, before you vote, spend one more thought on the matter [think one more time about whom you will vote for]. Consider, that you stand at the greatest opportunity of paying your vows, by performing your Covenant to vote this day. Perhaps it may be the most important opportunity you may have in all of your life.

Before the next Parliament comes about, you may be summoned into another world, to give an account of how you bestowed your voice; or if you are still alive, you may see a poor Nation helped to its ruin by your hand, by your vote.

Consider this, the greatest hopes our enemies have is to ruin us by our own Councils. Time was when the plot was to blow up our Parliaments, now they labor to blow us up by our Parliaments; to make our Parliaments blow us up by their destructive Councils. A Nation cannot die a worse death, than to be ruined by their "saviors."

Who Should Get Your Vote

Question. You may ask, Who is fit for our votes?

Answer: It is a hard Question. Who is fit for such a place, among such a people, and at such a time. I hope you have been asking yourselves, and others, wiser than this Preacher, the same question before you arrived here. It would be impudent for me to undertake a direct answer. Yet I shall not be too bold, if I lay a few lines of Scripture together, which will make up an excellent Portrait of a Parliamentarian, though, I fear, your choices this day may not be as beautiful as you would like.

The face is seldom as fair as the picture. I am sure you will find it impossible to meet with any among the sons of men, whose graces are so orient and unsullied, as to answer the Magistrates face, as it is drawn by the Holy Spirit's curious pencil in the Word. And therefore, your responsibility is to come as near the pattern, as the imperfections of the best among you will permit.

You may see on a piece of clay, that has been pressed with a curious cut seal, its true stamp, though so ragged, as will tell you, it is a clay seal and not a gold seal. So, there are some among us on whom you may find some of those Magistratical endowments and graces that are engraved by the Spirit of God on the seal of the Word. But as you see their imperfections, it will tell you that they are printed upon frail flesh and blood.

FIRST. Look for the Fear of God in those you choose

This is written with so large a character in Scripture upon the Magistrates forehead, and is so principal a letter in his Name, that it cannot be well spelled without. In Exodus 18:21. Moses bids them provide such men as fear God. And by stamping Authority upon a wicked man, you present the beautiful face of God to the world in, as it were, a broken glass.

Some Kings have commanded, that none should carve his Portraiture in any lesser a metal than gold. And would it not be a pity that God's Image should be stamped upon a person of base metal? Every ungodly man is no better than base metal, no matter how much their names swell in riches and honors of the world's style.

Antiochus was called a vile person, Daniel 11:21. The poorest Saint he persecuted was a Star, and he was as vile as dirt, even while he stamped them under his foot of pride.

He who willingly puts a wicked man in place, would, if he could, pull a righteous God out of place.

We need to look for the fear of God in those we choose to be in Government. If for no other reason than that they are so far above the fear of man. If they have not the fear of God to keep them right no wonder if they miscarry [go amiss] in their decisions.

- When Joseph tried to persuade his brothers to honestly deal with him, notice what pawn he gives them, Genesis 42:18 This do, for I fear God. Indeed, his power was so great, that if the fear of God had not been the law of his conscience, and he had them at such advantage, he might have revenged himself upon them for their unkindness, yea, for their cruelty to him.

- The Governors that went before Nehemiah, wanted to do cruelty to him, whereas good Nehemiah himself, had no other cord but this to tie his hands, Nehemiah 5:15. But so did not I, because of the fear of the Lord.

SECOND. Look for Wisdom and proper Gifts

The work to which you choose them, should be work to which they are adept, Exodus 18:21. Provide out of all the people able men, such as fear God. NOTE:

All who fear God are not able men. Every godly man does not carry a Counselors head on his shoulders.

There are some who are so holy, that in regard of their Prayers and the Power of godliness in their lives may be said to be "saviors." And I am sure the Nation would have drowned, had they not helped to hold its chin above water by their praying.

But if they were called to Parliament-work, they might, because of their lack of wisdom and a governing spirit, be in danger of proving destroyers of it. Is it not a pity, that they who do such service to the public in their private capacities should be called from praying for the nation, to ruining it?

Every good Christian could not make a good Minister. The Apostle speaks of a special gift, besides grace in common with others, that belongs to them, they must be apt to teach. So, a Senator must be apt to advise and counsel. Without this all is insufficient, because he lacks that which would enable him to reach the end of his place.

A knife, though it had as a sheath of gold, and a haft of diamond, if it has no edge, is not a good knife. It may be good to sell and make money off, but not to cut.

Look therefore for people of wisdom. You will not ask for a suit or a shoe to be made, merely because the person before you is an honest godly man? No! You desire something of the trade in the man, or else you may be uneasy. But you will say, if they are honest, then honest men will do no hurt. And I would answer you, "Not willingly."

In a dangerous disease, that medicine which does no good, does hurt, because what might have been given, could have done good. The ills of the Nation at this time are many, and they are complicated, it will require skills as unique as ever sat within those walls to find a remedy. And I am of this judgement, if we must die, let it be under the hand of the ablest Physicians, for therein we shall be least accessory to our own ruin.

THIRD. Enquire whether they are Christians

Are they Christians? Are they found in the faith, for this is doubly important.

The care of keeping a Religion pure in a Nation, is part of the Christian Magistrate's charge, and not the least part. The Kings of Israel were commanded to keep the Book of the Law by them that they might learn to fear the Lord, and keep all the words of this Law, Deuteronomy 17:18. which was not meant only personally (that was to be the endeavor of every private Israelite) but as a Ruler to see the Law of God kept, and the true Religion there commanded, preserved in their Kingdom.

Hence, we find those Kings sharply reproved [criticized], who either set up, or connived on behalf of idolatry in their reign. And those commended, who removed the Monuments of idolatry, and restored the Worship of God to its purity.

Thus, we find of Hezekiah, the most famous Reformer of them all. A large testimony is given by God to him, for his zeal to restore the nation. That he cleaved to the Lord, and kept His Commandments, which the Lord commanded Moses. And truly, if it were the Magistrates work then, it continues to be so now. Unless, of course, if we can find where Christ minimized their power in matters of Religion, which He has not done.

There is no danger, said that Reverend Author, to allow the Magistrate now as much power, as God then approved of. Well, is Religion the Magistrate's care? Then for the Lord's sake, and Religion's sake, do not choose such as are corrupt and rotten in their principles, unless you have a mind to spread the infection presently over the whole Land. The plague of this spiritual leprosy is spreading too fast already in the body of the Nations [around us]. God keep it from among our Rulers, if it takes the head once, we may then pronounce the whole Land unclean.

Consider for a moment at what door our ruin is likely to come in upon us. Truly, it is easier to foretell this, then it is to shut it [fix it]. They say of the Hectic Fever, at first it is easily cured, but hardly known; afterward easily known, then hardly cured. The evils which now threaten us most, might with more facility have been at first prevented, could they have been as easily known. But now, they have a strength, which, though they are easily known, they are hard to cure.

Many of those errors, which at first appeared as innocent things, grow now more formidable. Indeed, it is observed that when diseases, such as Pox, Purples and Malignant Fevers, abound, it is a sign that the plague is not far off. Their malignity is soon heightened to a Pestilence.

FOURTH. Look for Courage and Resoluteness

There are some who may be blown like glasses, into any shape, with the flattering or threatening breath of others. Not all men and women are born to rule. It is well if they will follow, but never expect that they will lead on in a time of danger.

A coward cannot be a good Christian; much less a good Magistrate. Such a one will be won with a nut, and lost with an apple. Solomon's throne of ivory was supported by Lions. Innocence and integrity cannot be preserved in Magistracy without courage.

It was base fear which made Pilate cruel to Christ, to save his sorry stake which he had in Caesars hand. The man had no mind to shed innocent blood, therefore he sought how he might release him, but when he heard the Jews cry out, If you let this man go, you are not Caesar's friend, the very wind of this bullet killed that man's heart, and made him steer a totally contrary course, John 19:12-13. When Pilate therefore heard that, he brought Jesus forth and sat in the judgment seat, and basely proceeded to an unrighteous sentence against his conscience.

Magistrates are great blessings, if they dare do their conscience. Choose those who will dare to be righteous, I just wish we were wise enough to distinguish between a humble boldness in a good cause, and a proud stoutness in any cause, be it right or wrong.

The courage, which is of the right metal, is like steel, it will bend, and stand bent. Some, however, will, if they are once challenged, bend and bow into partiality.

FIFTH. *Find Purposeful Focus on the Nation's Public Affairs*

It is said of Job, he put on Righteousness, and it clothed him. He could as easily have forgotten to put on his cloths in a morning and therefore do his work as an unrighteous Magistrate. It would be a sad thing if we should vote-in one, who when they are chosen, should sleep out their time in the Country, or socialize their time away in the City, not caring whether the Nation sinks or swims.

Non-residence is as bad in a Magistrate, as in a Minister, they are God's Ministers, as well as Preachers are. So says Paul, Romans 13:6. For they are Gods Ministers attending continually upon this very thing. Where should the tradesman be but in his shop? And where should a Parliamentarian be, but where his or her work lies, in the houses of congress.

They are not worthy of honor, who are weary of the labor, which goes with the Office. The faithful Magistrate is said to bear the burden of the people; Exodus 18:22. Away then those who will shift all the burden off themselves onto other's shoulders. And who will hear themselves applauded at the ballot box but will not likely carry the burden of their Country's affaires. Neither in their head, nor heart, have they ears to hear the cry of the oppressed, when they come to them for relief.

SIXTH. *Choose those who have Healing spirits*

They should make it their study, to make up the breaches that are among us, and not make them wider. Though the war is over, and swords are put up, yet the minds of men have not come to their right temper; the fever is hardly quenched in men's spirits, which must be, before all is well. As long as embers are kept burning in the bosom, there is danger of breaking out into a flame.

Suppose a man is shot with a bullet, he may be cured of his wound, yet die of a fever his wound put him into. If you can find any who have more compassion towards this divided Nation than others, those are the people fit for such a time as this.

He is the surgeon, who has not only a Lyon's heart, but a Lady's hand, to dress the wounds of the Nation gently. We are like a person who has lain in bed so long, and grown so weak, that the same strong medicine which might have cured him at first, would now kill him out of hand.

SEVENTH. *Look for a Desire to Serve*

I do not desire you to vote based upon this single characteristic alone but take it into consideration with the rest. To choose merely for estate, is too much like the Israelites folly, who set up a golden calf in Moses' place.

So, do not let anyone, receive any prejudice from you because they are enameled with riches, and dwell in a great house.

It is noted as a sign of a declining State, when the money, and coin of a Nation become worthless. Often it is seen in the metal being less pure, or less weighty. Additionally, for gold, and silver, there is substituted brass, lead, or leather. This too has sometimes been seen.

The Spirit of God compares Magistrates to one of the purest of metals, silver. And surely, it shows that a people are going down the hill of honor, when the places of Magistracy that used to be filled with the chief heads of the Country, come to be despicable folks of lowest character.

Thanks be to God, there are a few good folks to be found, who are able to do God, and their Country, service.

FINALLY. *Find those Faithful to Ministers and the Ministry of the Gospel*

I confess, I was under a temptation to have drowned this in silence, knowing with what disadvantage [stumbling block, for you may find me self-serving] I shall speak on this subject. Many will think me but selfish in this, and only too kind to my own Tribe; but to know that, you must be content to wait for the great day, when the world shall know, why I speak for, and others against the Ministry. I am not therefore afraid or ashamed to press this again.

Look for leaders who will be faithful friends to the Ministry. It hath been resolved long since in the evil one's mind, that the surest and speediest way to cheat England [and the USA] of her Religion, and Gospel, is to divide the people from their Ministers. That still holds true in ungodly men's minds.

The enemies of the gospel by their rigorous endeavor, peruse this one thing, hence there are so many bitter invectives printed against the faithful Ministers of Christ, their Persons, and Office. There are railing Rabshekahs [who distort the minister's words] sent about the Land, to throw dirt upon the Minister's face, and to turn the hearts of the children from their spiritual Fathers, by making them out to be base and filthy to their hearers. And have they not prevailed? Look at how many thousands [millions] in the Land are made Proselytes to the agenda focused [on removing ministers from a position of influence in their congregant's lives].

Can you think him worthy of the Magistrate's seat, who would not allow you a Minister in the Pulpit? Oh, my brethren, know the Ministry has the same Authority to show for their calling as the Magistrate has. The same God, who gave Moses, gave Aaron. It is said that He led his people by the hands of Moses and Aaron. The same hand that planted one Olive-tree, on the one side of the bowl, Zerubbabel the Magistrate, planted Joshua, the Minister, on the other, and both were given to drop their oil, to feed the same lamp of God's Church.

The great blessings have been given by a concurrence of both, as we see in Reformations of the Jewish Church under several Kings. I have heard that when Queen Elizabeth, coming into our County of Suffolk, observed that the Leaders of the County, who came out to meet her, had every one their Minister by their side, she said, "Now I have learned why my County of Suffolk is so well governed, it is because the Magistrates and Ministers go together." Indeed, they are the two legs on which a Church and State stand. He that would saw off the one, cannot mean well to the other.

An Anti-ministerial spirit is an Anti-magistratical spirit. The Pulpit guards the throne. Take that away, and you give the Magistrate's enemy's room to fetch a full blow at them. The Duke of Somerset in King Edward VI days, by consenting to his brother's death, made way for his own, by the same axe and hand.

What Occurs After We Vote

I have no more counsel for you, as to the transaction of this day, namely voting. But my dear friends, do not think that you have done all your duty to God and your afflicted Country by simply voting. But labor to crown the work of this day with the following things.

Prayer

Follow those you shall choose with your prayers. Our Lord Jesus, when He sent His disciples to sea, went into a mountain to pray for them. He knew a storm was coming toward them, and they would need His help; Truly, you send these leaders, whoever they shall be, to sea.

And God grant it may not be a winter-voyage.

Oh, help them to as much strength as you can for their work, and there is no strength gotten like that which is gotten from Heaven.

Indeed, the whole success of that great Assembly must begin there. The Lord has made both the hearing ear and the seeing eye, Proverbs 20:12. Neither of these can be spared if this Parliament is to end well. They must have a seeing eye, to see what counsel and advice is both wholesome and seasonable. And the people must have a hearing ear, to submit to the Laws there concluded.

Obstruction

Take heed that you do not obstruct your prayers for them. Not for them, nor for their counsels, or for you or for the poor Nation by you having unconfessed sin. Go home, repent, and reform, and that in earnest, or else all your praying will be a waste.

If your sins get between your prayers and God, he cannot hear your prayers.

If you do not reform and deal with unconfessed sin, lay no fault on the Parliament, though no good comes of their meeting. A careless Patient disgraces a good Physician.

Samuel's counsel to Israel shall be mine to you with the change of a word; Fear the Lord, and serve Him in truth with all your heart, for consider how great things He hath done for you, but if you continue still to do wickedly, you shall be consumed, you and your Parliament.

Worry

In doing your duty, do not torment yourselves with worry. God has eased us of this burden, had we but faith to take His kindness, who bids us cast our burden upon the Lord. Why should we go sweating under that load, which God is willing to take off our shoulders?

We should sow and plough and pray. And God will never charge it upon us, if a happy harvest does not crown our labors.

In the Parable of the man fallen among thieves and wounded, the Host was not commanded by Christ to undertake to cure him, but to take care of him. Leave the curing of the Nation's wounds to God.

You will be a happy people if you are found to have taken so much care of your poor Nation, as to discharge the duty of your place, namely, today's voting, which you owe to God and your Nation.

FINIS.